We hope you enjoy this book. Please return or renew it by the due date.

You can renew it at www.norfolk.gov.uk/libraries or by using our free library app.

Otherwise you can phone 0344 800 8020 - please have your library card and PIN ready.

You can sign up for email reminders too.

02-01-18

D1390319

Patricia Cornwell

Black Notice

sphere

SPHERE

First published in the United States in 1999 by G.P. Putnam's Sons
First published in Great Britain in 1999 by Little, Brown and Company
Paperback edition published in 2000 by Warner Books
This reissue published in 2010 by Sphere

5 7 9 10 8 6

A CIP catalogue record for this book
is available from the British Library.

ISBN 978-0-7515-4483-1

Typeset in Garamond 3 by Palimpsest Book Production Limited,
Falkirk, Stirlingshire
Printed and bound in Great Britain by
Clays Ltd, St Ives plc

Papers used by Sphere are from well-managed forests
and other responsible sources.

MIX
Paper from
responsible sources
FSC® C104740

Sphere
An imprint of
Little, Brown Book Group
Carmelite House
50 Victoria Embankment
London EC4Y 0DZ

An Hachette UK Company
www.hachette.co.uk

www.littlebrown.co.uk

To Nina Salter

Water and Words

And the third angel poured out his vial upon the rivers and fountains of waters; and they became blood.

Revelation 16:4

BW

December 6, 1996
Epworth Heights
Luddington, Michigan

My Dearest Kay,

I am sitting on the porch, staring out at Lake Michigan as a sharp wind reminds me I need to cut my hair. I am remembering when we were here last, both of us abandoning who and what we are for one precious moment in the history of our time, I need you to listen to me.

You are reading this because I am dead. When I decided to write it, I asked Senator Lord to deliver it to you in person in the early part of December, a year after my death. I know how hard Christmas has always been for you, and now it must be unbearable. Loving you was when my life began. Now that it has ended, your gift to me is to go on.

Of course you haven't dealt with a damn thing, Kay. You have sped like hell to crime scenes and done more autopsies than ever. You have been consumed by court and running the institute, with lecturing, worrying about Lucy, getting irritated with Marino, eluding your neighbors and fearing the night. You haven't taken a vacation or a sick day, no matter how much you've needed it.

ix

It's time to stop dodging your pain and let me comfort you. Hold my hand in your mind and remember the many times we talked about death, never accepting that any disease or accident or act of violence has the power of absolute annihilation because our bodies are just the suites we wear. And we are so much more than that.

Kay, I want you to believe I am somehow aware of you as you read this, somehow looking after you, and that everything's going to be all right. I ask you to do one thing for me to celebrate a life we've had that I know will never end. Call Marino and Lucy. Invite them over for dinner tonight. Cook one of your famous meals for them and save a place for me.

I love you forever, Kay,
Benton

1

The late morning blazed with blue skies and the colors of fall, but none of it was for me. Sunlight and beauty were for other people now, my life stark and without song. I stared out the window at a neighbor raking leaves and felt helpless, broken and gone.

Benton's words resurrected every awful image I had repressed. I saw beams of light picking out heat-shattered bones in soggy trash and water. Shock rocked me again when confusing shapes turned into a scorched head with no features and clumps of sooty silver hair.

I was sitting at my kitchen table sipping hot tea that Senator Frank Lord had brewed for me. I was exhausted and lightheaded from storms of nausea that had sent me fleeing to the bathroom twice. I was humiliated, because beyond all things I feared losing control, and I just had.

"I need to rake the leaves again," I inanely said to my old friend. "December sixth and it's like October. Look out there, Frank. The acorns are big. Have you noticed? Supposedly that means a hard winter, but it doesn't even look like we're

1

going to have winter. I can't remember if you have acorns in Washington."

"We do," he said. "If you can find a tree or two."

"Are they big? The acorns, I mean."

"I'll be sure to look, Kay."

I covered my face with my hands and sobbed. He got up from the table and came around to my chair. Senator Lord and I had grown up in Miami and had gone to school in the same archdiocese, although I had attended St. Brendan's High School only one year and long after he was there. Yet that somewhat removed crossing of paths was a sign of what would come.

When he was the district attorney, I was working for the Dade County Medical Examiner's Office and often testified in his cases. When he was elected a United States senator and then appointed the chairman of the judiciary committee, I was the chief medical examiner of Virginia and he began calling on me to lend my voice in his fight against crime.

I was stunned when he called me yesterday to say he was coming to see me and had something important to deliver. I barely slept all night. I was devastated when he walked into my kitchen and slipped the simple white envelope out of a pocket of his suit.

As I sat with him now, it made perfect sense that Benton would have trusted him this much. He knew Senator Lord cared deeply for me and would never let me down. How typical of Benton to have a plan that would be executed perfectly, even though he wasn't around to see it through. How typical of him to predict my behavior after his death and for every word of it to be true.

"Kay," Senator Lord said, standing over me as I wept in my chair, "I know how hard this must be and wish I could

2

make it all go away. I think one of the hardest things I've ever done was promise Benton I would do this. I never wanted to believe this day would come, but it has and I'm here for you."

He fell silent, then added, "No one's ever asked me to do anything like this before, and I've been asked a lot of things."

"He wasn't like other people," I quietly replied as I willed myself to calm down. "You know that, Frank. Thank God you do."

Senator Lord was a striking man who bore himself with the dignity of his office. He had thick gray hair and intense blue eyes, was tall and lean and dressed, as was typical, in a conservative dark suit accented by a bold, bright tie, cuff links, pocket watch and stickpin. I got up from my chair and took a deep, shaky breath. I snatched several tissues from a box and wiped my face and nose.

"You were very kind to come here," I said to him.

"What else can I do for you?" he replied with a sad smile.

"You've done it all by being here. I can't imagine the trouble you've gone to. Your schedule and all."

"I must admit I flew in from Florida, and by the way, I checked on Lucy and she's doing great things down there," he said.

Lucy, my niece, was an agent for the Bureau of Alcohol, Tobacco and Firearms, or ATF. Recently, she had been reassigned to the Miami field office, and I hadn't seen her for months.

"Does she know about the letter?" I asked Senator Lord.

"No," he answered, looking out the window at a perfect day. "I think that's your call to make. And she's feeling rather neglected by you, I might add."

3

"By me?" I said, surprised. "She's the one who can't be reached. At least I'm not undercover chasing gun traffickers and other persons of such fine character. She can't even talk to me unless she's at headquarters or on a pay phone."

"You're not easy to find, either. You've been elsewhere in your spirit since Benton died. Missing in action, and I don't even think you realize it," he said. "I know. I've tried to reach out to you, too, haven't I?"

Tears flooded my eyes again.

"And if I get hold of you, what do you tell me? *Everything's fine. Just busy.* Not to mention, you haven't come to see me once. Now and then in the old days, you even brought me some of your special soups. You haven't been taking care of those who love you. You haven't been taking care of yourself."

He had covertly glanced up at the clock several times now. I got up from my chair.

"Are you heading back to Florida?" I asked in an unsteady voice.

"Afraid not. Washington," he said. "I'm on *Face the Nation* again. More of the same. I'm so disgusted by it all, Kay."

"I wish I could do something to help you," I said to him.

"It's dirty out there, Kay. If certain people knew I was here alone in your house with you, they'd start some vicious rumor about me. I'm sure of it."

"I wish you hadn't come here, then."

"Nothing would have stopped me. And I shouldn't be railing on about Washington. You have enough to deal with."

"I'll vouch for your sterling character anytime," I said.

"It wouldn't do any good, if it came to that."

I walked him through the impeccable house I had designed, past fine furniture and art and the antique medical instruments I collected, and over bright rugs and hardwood floors. Everything was precisely to my taste but not at all the same as it had been when Benton was here. I paid no more attention to my home than I did to myself these days. I had become a heartless custodian of my life, and it was evident everywhere I looked.

Senator Lord noticed my briefcase open on the great room couch, and case files, mail and memos spilled over the glass coffee table, and legal pads on the floor. Cushions were askew, an ashtray dirty because I'd started smoking again. He didn't lecture me.

"Kay, do you understand I've got to have limited contact with you after this?" Senator Lord said. "Because of what I just alluded to."

"God, look at this place," I blurted out in disgust. "I just can't seem to keep up anymore."

"There've been rumors," he cautiously went on. "I won't go into them. There have been veiled threats." Anger heated his voice. "Just because we're friends."

"I used to be so neat." I gave a heartbroken laugh. "Benton and I were always squabbling about my house, my shit. My perfectly appointed, perfectly arranged shit." My voice rose as grief and fury flared up higher than before. "If he rearranged or put something in the wrong drawer . . . That's what happens when you hit middle age and have lived alone and had everything your own goddamn way."

"Kay, are you listening to me? I don't want you to feel I don't care if I don't call you very much, if I don't invite you up for lunch or to get your advice about some bill I'm trying to pass."

"Right now I can't even remember when Tony and I got divorced," I bitterly said. "What? Nineteen eighty-three?

He left. So what? I didn't need him or anyone else who followed. I could make my world the way I wanted it, and I did. My career, my possessions, my investments. And look."

I stood still in the foyer and swept my hand over my beautiful stone house and all that was in it.

"So what? So fucking what?" I looked Senator Lord in the eye. "Benton could dump garbage in the middle of this fucking house! He could tear the goddamn place down! I just wish none of it had ever mattered, Frank." I wiped away furious tears. "I wish I could do it over and never criticize him once about anything. I just want him here. Oh, God, I want him here. Every morning I wake up not remembering, and then it hits again and I can barely get out of bed."

Tears ran down my face. It seemed every nerve in my body had gone haywire.

"You made Benton very happy," Senator Lord said gently and with feeling. "You meant everything to him. He told me how good you were to him, how much you understood the hardships of his life, the awful things he had to see when he was working those atrocious cases for the FBI. Deep down, I know you know that."

I took a deep breath and leaned against the door.

"And I know he would want you to be happy now, to have a better life. If you don't, then the end result of loving Benton Wesley will prove damaging and wrong, something that ruined your life. Ultimately, a mistake. Does that make sense?"

"Yes," I said. "Of course. I know exactly what he would want right now. I know what I want. I don't want it like this. This is almost more than I can bear. At times I've thought

6

I would snap, just fall apart and end up on a ward some-where. Or maybe in my own damn morgue."

"Well, you won't." He took my hand in both of his. "If there's anything I know about you, it's that you will prevail against all odds. You always have, and this stretch of your journey happens to be the hardest, but there's a better road ahead. I promise, Kay."

I hugged him hard.

"Thank you," I whispered. "Thank you for doing this, for not leaving it in some file somewhere, not remembering, not bothering."

"Now, you'll call me if you need me?" he pretty much ordered, as I opened the front door. "But you'll keep in mind what I said and promise you won't feel ignored."

"I understand."

"I'm always there if you need me. Don't forget that. My office always knows where I am."

I watched the black Lincoln drive off, then went into my great room and built a fire, although it wasn't cold enough to need one. I was desperate for something warm and alive to fill the emptiness left by Senator Lord's leaving. I read Benton's letter again and again and heard his voice in my mind.

I envisioned him with sleeves rolled up, veins prominent in strong forearms, his firm, elegant hands holding the silver Mont Blanc fountain pen I had given him for no special reason other than that it was precise and pure like him. Tears would not stop, and I held up the page with his engraved initials so his writing would not smear.

His penmanship and the way he expressed himself had always been deliberate and spare, and I found his words a comfort and a torment as I obsessively studied them, dissecting, excavating for one more hint of meaning or tone. At intervals, I almost believed he was cryptically telling me his death wasn't real, was part of an intrigue, a plan, something orchestrated by the FBI, the CIA, God only knew. Then the truth returned, bringing its hollow chill to my heart. Benton had been tortured and murdered. DNA, dental charts, personal effects had verified that the unrecognizable remains were his.

I tried to imagine how I would honor his request tonight and didn't see how I could. It was ludicrous to think of Lucy's flying to Richmond, Virginia, for dinner. I picked up the phone and tried to reach her anyway, because that was what Benton had asked me to do. She called me back on her portable phone about fifteen minutes later.

"The office said you're looking for me. What's going on?" she said cheerfully.

"It's hard to explain," I began. "I wish I didn't always have to go through your field office to get to you."

"Me, too."

"And I know I can't say much . . ." I started to get upset again.

"What's wrong?" She cut in.

"Benton wrote a letter . . ."

"We'll talk another time." She interrupted again, and I understood, or at least I assumed I did. Cell phones were not secure.

"Turn in right there," Lucy said to someone. "I'm sorry," she got back to me. "We're making a pit stop at Los Bobos to get a shot of colada."

"A what?"

"High-test caffeine and sugar in a shot glass."

"Well, it's something he wanted me to read now, on this day. He wanted you . . . Never mind. It all seems so silly."

I fought to sound as if I were held together just fine.

"Gotta go," Lucy said to me.

"Maybe you can call later?"

"Will do," she said in her same irritating tone.

"Who are you with?" I prolonged the conversation because I needed her voice, and I didn't want to hang up with the echo of her sudden coolness in my ear.

"My psycho partner," she said.

"Tell her hi."

"She says hi," Lucy said to her partner, Jo, who was Drug Enforcement Agency, or DEA.

They worked together on a High Intensity Drug Trafficking Area, or HIDTA, squad that had been relentlessly working a series of very vicious home invasions. Jo and Lucy's relationship was a partnership in another way, too, but they were very discreet. I wasn't sure AFT or DEA even knew.

"Later," Lucy said to me, and the line went dead.

2

Richmond police captain Pete Marino and I had known each other for so long it sometimes seemed we were inside each other's heads. So it really came as no great surprise when he called me before I had a chance to track him down.

"You sound really stopped up," he said to me. "You got a cold?"

"No," I said. "I'm glad you called because I was getting ready to call you."

"Oh, yeah?"

I could tell he was smoking in either his truck or police car. Both had two-way radios and scanners that this moment were making a lot of noise.

"Where are you?" I asked him.

"Cruising around, listening to the scanner," he said, as if he had the top down and was having a wonderful day. "Counting the hours till retirement. Ain't life grand? Nothing missin' but the bluebird of happiness."

His sarcasm could have shred paper.

"What in the world's wrong with you?" I said.

"I'm assuming you know about the ripe one they just found

at the Port of Richmond," he replied. "People puking all over the place, is what I hear. Just glad it ain't my fucking problem."

My mind wouldn't work. I didn't know what he was talking about. Call-waiting was clicking. I switched the cordless phone to the other ear as I walked into my study and pulled out a chair at the desk.

"What ripe one?" I asked him. "Marino, hold on," I said as call-waiting tried again. "Let me see who this is. Don't go away." I tapped the hang-up button.

"Scarpetta," I said.

"It's Jack," my deputy chief, Jack Fielding, said. "They've found a body inside a cargo container at the Port of Richmond. Badly decomposed."

"That's what Marino was just telling me," I said.

"You sound like you've got the flu. I think I'm getting it, too. And Chuck's coming in late because he's not feeling so great. Or so he says."

"Did this container just come off a ship?" I interrupted him.

"The *Sirius*, as in the star. Definitely a weird situation. How do you want me to handle it?"

I began scribbling notes on a call sheet, my handwriting more illegible than usual, my central nervous system as crashed as a bad hard drive.

"I'll go," I said without pause even as Benton's words pulsed in my mind.

I was off and running again. Maybe even faster this time.

"You don't need to do that, Dr. Scarpetta," Fielding said as if he were suddenly in charge. "I'll go down there. You're supposed to be taking the day off."

"Who do I contact when I get there?" I asked. I didn't want him to start in again.

Fielding had been begging me for months to take a break,

11

to go somewhere for a week or two or even consider a sabbatical. I was tired of people watching me with worried eyes. I was angered by the intimation that Benton's death was affecting my performance at work, that I had begun isolating myself from my staff and others and looked exhausted and distracted.

"Detective Anderson notified us. She's at the scene," Fielding was saying.

"Who?"

"Must be new. Really, Dr. Scarpetta, I'll handle it. Why don't you take a break? Stay home."

I realized I still had Marino on hold. I switched back to tell him I'd call as soon as I got off the line with my office. He'd already hung up.

"Tell me how to get there," I said to my deputy chief.

"I guess you're not going to accept my pro bono advice."

"If I'm coming from my house, Downtown Expressway, and then what?" I said.

He gave me directions. I got off the phone and hurried to my bedroom, Benton's letter in hand. I couldn't think of a place to keep it. I couldn't just leave it in a drawer or file cabinet. God forbid I should lose it or the housekeeper should discover it, and I didn't want it in a place where I might run across it unawares and be undone again. Thoughts spun wildly, my heart racing, adrenaline screaming through my blood as I stared at the stiff, creamy envelope, at "Kay' written in Benton's modest, careful hand.

I finally focused on the small fireproof safe bolted to the floor in my closet. I frantically tried to remember where I had written down the combination.

"I'm losing my goddamn mind," I exclaimed out loud.

The combination was where I always kept it, between pages 670 and 671 of the seventh edition of *Hunter's Tropical*

Medicine. I locked the letter in the safe and walked into the bathroom and repeatedly splashed cold water on my face. I called Rose, my secretary, and instructed her to arrange for a removal service to meet me at the Port of Richmond in about an hour and a half.

"Let them know the body's in very sorry shape," I emphasized.

"How are you going to get there?" Rose asked. "I'd tell you to stop here first and get the Suburban, but Chuck's taken it in for an oil change."

"I thought he was sick."

"He showed up fifteen minutes ago and left with the Suburban."

"Okay, I'll have to use my own car. Rose, I'm going to need the Luma-Lite and a hundred-foot extension cord. Have someone meet me in the parking lot with them. I'll call when I'm close."

"You need to know that Jean's in a bit of an uproar."

"What's the problem?" I asked, surprised.

Jean Adams was the office administrator and she rarely showed emotion, much less got upset.

"Apparently all the coffee money disappeared. You know this isn't the first time . . ."

"Damn!" I said. "Where was it kept?"

"Locked up in Jean's desk drawer, like always. Doesn't look like the lock was pried open or anything, but she went into the drawer this morning, no money. A hundred and eleven dollars and thirty-five cents."

"This has got to stop," I said.

"I don't know if you're aware of the latest," Rose went on. "Lunches have started disappearing from the break room. Last week Cleta accidentally left her portable phone on her desk overnight and the next morning it was gone. Same thing happened to Dr. Riley. He left a nice pen in the pocket of his lab coat. Next morning, no pen."

"The crew that cleans up after hours?"

"Maybe," Rose said. "But I will tell you, Dr. Scarpetta—and I'm not trying to accuse anyone—I'm afraid it might be an inside job."

"You're right. We shouldn't accuse anyone. Is there any good news today?"

"Not so far," Rose matter-of-factly replied.

Rose had worked for me since I had been appointed chief medical examiner, which meant she had been running my life for most of my career. She had the remarkable ability to know virtually everything going on around her without getting caught up in it herself. My secretary remained untainted, and although the staff was somewhat afraid of her, she was the first one they ran to when there was a problem.

"Now you take care of yourself, Dr. Scarpetta," she went on. "You sound awful. Why don't you let Jack go to the scene and you stay in for once?"

"I'll just take my car," I said as a wave of grief rolled over me and sounded in my voice.

Rose caught it and rode it out in silence. I could hear her shuffling through papers on her desk. I knew she wanted to somehow comfort me, but I had never allowed that.

"Well, make sure you change before you get back in it," she finally said.

"Change what?"

"Your clothes. Before you get back into your car," she said as if I'd never dealt with a decomposed body before.

"Thank you, Rose," I said.

I set the burglar alarm and locked the house, turning on the light in the garage, where I opened a spacious locker built of cedar, with vents along the top and bottom. Inside were hiking boots, waders, heavy leather gloves and a Barbour coat with its special waterproofing that reminded me of wax.

Out here I kept socks, long underwear, jumpsuits and other gear that would never see the inside of my house. Their end of tour landed them in the industrial-size stainless steel sink and washer and dryer not meant for my normal clothes.

I tossed a jumpsuit, a pair of black leather Reeboks and an Office of Chief Medical Examiner, or OCME, baseball cap inside the trunk. I checked my large Halliburton aluminum scene case to make sure I had plenty of latex gloves, heavy-duty trash bags, disposable sheets, camera and film. I set out with a heavy heart as Benton's words drifted through my mind again. I tried to block out his voice, his eyes and smile and the feel of his skin. I wanted to forget him and more than anything, I didn't.

I turned on the radio as I followed the Downtown Expressway to I-95, the Richmond skyline sparkling in the sun.

I was slowing at the Lombardy Toll Plaza when my car phone rang. It was Marino.

"Thought I'd let you know I'm going to drop by," he said.

A horn blared when I changed lanes and almost clipped a silver Toyota in my blind spot. The driver swooped around me, yelling obscenities I couldn't hear.

"Go to hell," I angrily said in his wake.

"What?" Marino said loudly in my ear.

"Some goddamn idiot driver."

"Oh, good. You ever heard of road rage, Doc?"

"Yes, and I've come down with it."

I took the Ninth Street exit, heading to my office, and let Rose know I was two minutes away. When I pulled into the parking lot, Fielding was waiting with the hard case and extension cord.

"I don't guess the Suburban's back yet," I said.

"Nope," he replied, loading the equipment in my trunk. "Gonna be something when you show up in this thing. I can just see all those dockworkers staring at this good-looking blond woman in a black Mercedes. Maybe you should borrow my car."

My bodybuilding deputy chief had just finalized a divorce and celebrated by trading in his Mustang for a red Corvette.

"Actually, that's a good idea," I dryly said. "If you don't mind. As long as it's a V-eight."

"Yeah, yeah. I hear ya. Call me if you need me. You know the way, right?"

"I do."

His directions led me south, and I was almost to Petersburg when I turned off and drove past the back of the Philip Morris manufacturing plant and over railroad tracks. The narrow road led me through a vacant land of weeds and woods that ended abruptly at a security checkpoint. I felt as if I were crossing the border into an unfriendly country. Beyond was a train yard and hundreds of boxcar-size orange containers stacked three and four high. A guard who took his job very seriously stepped outside his booth. I rolled down my window.

"May I help you, ma'am?" he asked in a flat military tone.

"I'm Dr. Kay Scarpetta," I replied.

"And who are you here to see?"

"I'm here because there's been a death," I explained. "I'm the medical examiner."

I showed him my credentials. He took them from me and studied them carefully. I had a feeling he didn't know what a medical examiner was and wasn't about to ask.

"So you're the chief," he said, handing the worn black wallet back to me. "The chief of what?"

"I'm the chief medical examiner of Virginia," I replied. "The police are waiting for me."

He stepped back inside his booth and got on the phone as my impatience grew. It seemed every time I needed to enter a secured area, I went through this. I used to assume my being a woman was the reason, and in earlier days this was probably true—at least some of the time. Now I believed the threats of terrorism, crime and lawsuits were the explanation. The guard wrote down a description of my car and the plate number. He handed me a clipboard so I could sign in and gave me a visitor's pass, which I didn't clip on.

"See that pine tree down there?" he said, pointing.

"I see quite a few pine trees."

"The little bent one. Take a left at it and just head on towards the water, ma'am," he said. "Have a nice day."

I moved on, passing huge tires parked here and there and

several red brick buildings with signs out front to identify the U.S. Customs Service and Federal Marine Terminal. The port itself was rows of huge warehouses with orange containers lined up at loading docks like animals feeding from troughs. Moored off the wharf in the James River were two container ships, the *Euroclip* and the *Sirius*, each almost twice as long as a football field. Cranes hundreds of feet high were poised above open hatches the size of swimming pools.

Yellow crime-scene tape anchored by traffic cones circled a container that was mounted on a chassis. No one was nearby. In fact, I saw no sign of police except for an unmarked blue Caprice at the edge of the dock apron, the driver, apparently, behind the wheel talking through the window to a man in a white shirt and a tie. Work had stopped. Stevedores in hard hats and reflective vests looked bored as they drank sodas or bottled water or smoked.

I dialed my office and got Fielding on the phone.

"When were we notified about this body?" I asked him.

"Hold on. Let me check the sheet." Paper rustled. "At exactly ten fifty-three."

"And when was it found?"

"Uh, Anderson didn't seem to know that."

"How the hell could she not know something like that?"

"Like I said, I think she's new."

"Fielding, there's not a cop in sight except for her, or at least I guess that's her. What exactly did she say to you when she called in the case?"

"DOA, decomposed, asked for you to come to the scene."

"She specifically requested me?" I asked.

"Well, hell. You're always everybody's first choice. That's nothing new. But she said Marino told her to get you to the scene."

"Marino?" I asked, surprised. "He told *her* to tell *me* to respond?"

"Yeah, I thought it was a little ballsy of him."

I remembered Marino's telling me he would *drop by* the scene, and I got angrier. He gets some rookie to basically give me an order, and then if Marino can fit it in, he might swing by and see how we're doing?

"Fielding, when's the last time you talked to him?" I asked.

"Weeks. Pissy mood, too."

"Not half as pissy as mine's going to be if and when he finally decides to show up," I promised.

Dockworkers watched me climb out of my car and pop open the trunk. I retrieved my scene case, jumpsuit and shoes, and felt eyes crawl all over me as I walked toward the unmarked car and got more annoyed with each labored step, the heavy case bumping against my leg.

The man in the shirt and tie looked hot and unhappy as he shielded his eyes to gaze up at two television news helicopters slowly circling the port at about four hundred feet.

"Darn reporters," he muttered, turning his eyes to me.

"I'm looking for whoever's in charge of this crime scene," I said.

"That would be me," came a female voice from inside the Caprice.

I bent over and peered through the window at the young woman sitting behind the wheel. She was darkly tanned, her brown hair cut short and slicked back, her nose and jaw strong. Her eyes were hard, and she was dressed in relaxed-leg faded jeans, lace-up black leather boots and white T-shirt. She wore her gun on her hip, her badge on a ball chain tucked into her collar. Air-conditioning was blasting, light rock on the radio surfing over the cop talk on the scanner.

"Detective Anderson, I presume," I said.

"Rene Anderson. The one and only. And you must be the doc I've heard so much about," she said with the arrogance I associated with most people who didn't know what the hell they were doing.

"I'm Joe Shaw, the port director," the man introduced himself to me. "You must be who the security guys just called me about."

He was about my age, with blond hair, bright blue eyes and skin lined from years of too much sun. I could tell by the look on his face that he detested Anderson and everything about this day.

"Might you have anything helpful to pass along to me before I get started?" I said to Anderson over loud blowing air and rotating helicopter blades. "For example, why there are no police securing the scene?"

"Don't need 'em," Anderson said, pushing open her door with her knee. "It's not like just anybody can drive right on back here, as you found out when you tried."

I set the aluminum case on the ground. Anderson came around to my side of the car. I was surprised by how small she was.

"Not much I can tell you," she said to me. "What you see is what we got. A container with a real stinker inside."

"No, there's a lot more you can tell me, Detective Anderson," I said. "How was the body discovered and at what time? Have you seen it? Has anybody gotten near it? Has the scene been contaminated in any way? And the answer to the last one had better be *no*, or I'm holding you responsible."

She laughed. I began pulling the jumpsuit over my clothes.

"Nobody's even gotten close," she told me. "No volunteers for that one."

"You don't have to go inside the thing to know what's there," Shaw added.

I changed into the black Reeboks and put on the baseball cap. Anderson was staring at my Mercedes.

"Maybe I should go work for the state," she said.

I looked her up and down.

"I suggest you cover up if you're going in there," I said to her.

"I gotta make a couple calls," she said, walking off.

"I don't mean to tell people how to do their jobs," Shaw said to me. "But what the hell's going on here? We got a dead body right over there and the cops send in a little shit like that?"

His jaw muscles were clenching, his face bright red and dripping sweat.

"You know, you don't make a dime in this business unless things are moving," he went on. "And not a darn thing's moved for more than two and a half hours."

He was working so hard not to swear around me.

"Not that I'm not sorry about someone being dead," he went on. "But I sure would like you folks to do your business and leave." He scowled up at the sky again. "And that includes the media."

"Mr. Shaw, what was being shipped inside the container?" I asked him.

"German camera equipment. You should know the seal on the container's latch wasn't broken. So it appears the cargo wasn't tampered with."

"Did the foreign shipper affix the seal?"

"That's right."

"Meaning the body, alive or dead, most likely was inside the container before it was sealed?" I said.

"That's what it looks like. The number matches the one on the entry filed by the customs broker, nothing the least out of the ordinary. In fact, this cargo's already been released by Customs. Was five days ago," Shaw told me. "Which is why it was loaded straight on a chassis. Then we got a whiff and no way that container was going anywhere."

I looked around, taking in the entire scene at once. A light breeze clinked heavy chains against cranes that had been offloading steel beams from the *Euroclip*, three hatches at a time, when all activity stopped. Forklifts and flatbed trucks had been abandoned. Dockworkers and crew had nothing to do and kept their eyes on us from the tarmac.

Some looked on from the bows of their ships and through the windows of deckhouses. Heat rose from oil-stained asphalt scattered with wooden frames, spacers and skids, and a CSX train clanked and scraped through a crossing beyond the warehouses. The smell of creosote was strong but could not mask the stench of rotting human flesh that drifted like smoke on the air.

"Where did the ship set sail from?" I asked Shaw as I noticed a marked car parking next to my Mercedes.

"Antwerp, Belgium, two weeks ago," he replied as he looked at the *Sirius* and the *Euroclip*. "Foreign flag vessels like all the rest we get. The only American flags we see anymore are if someone raises one as a courtesy," he added with a trace of disappointment.

A man on the *Euroclip* was standing by the starboard side, looking back at us with binoculars. I thought it strange he was dressed in long sleeves and long pants, as warm as it was.

Shaw squinted. "Darn, this sun is bright."

"What about stowaways?" I asked. "Although I can't

imagine anyone choosing to hide inside a locked container for two weeks on high seas."

"Never had one that I know of. Besides, we're not the first port of call. Chester, Pennsylvania, is. Most of our ships go from Antwerp to Chester to here, and then straight back to Antwerp. A stowaway's most likely going to bail out in Chester instead of waiting till he gets to Richmond.

"We're a niche port, Dr. Scarpetta," Shaw went on.

I watched in disbelief as Pete Marino climbed out of the cruiser that had just parked next to my car.

"Last year, maybe a hundred and twenty oceangoing ships and barges called in the port," Shaw was saying.

Marino had been a detective as long as I'd known him. I had never seen him in uniform.

"If it were me and I was trying to jump ship or was an illegal alien, I think I'd want to end up in some really big port like Miami or L.A. where I could get lost in the shuffle."

Anderson walked up to us, chewing gum.

"Point is, we don't break the seal and open them up unless we suspect something illegal, drugs, undeclared cargo," Shaw continued. "Every now and then we preselect a ship for a full shakedown search to keep people honest."

"Glad I don't have to dress like that anymore," Anderson remarked as Marino headed toward us, his demeanor cocky and pugilistic, the way he always acted when he was insecure and in an especially foul mood.

"Why's he in uniform?" I asked her.

"He got reassigned."

"Clearly."

"There's been a lot of changes in the department since Deputy Chief Bray got here," Anderson said as if she were proud of the fact.

I couldn't imagine why anyone would throw someone so valuable back into uniform. I wondered how long ago this had happened. I was hurt Marino hadn't let me know, and I was ashamed I hadn't found out anyway. It had been weeks, maybe a month, since I had called just to check on him. I couldn't remember the last time I'd invited him to drop by my office for coffee or to come to my house for dinner.

"What's going on?" he gruffly said as a greeting.

He didn't give Anderson a glance.

"I'm Joe Shaw. How you doing?"

"Like shit," Marino sourly replied. "Anderson, you decide to work this one all by yourself? Or is it just the other cops don't want nothing to do with you?"

She glared at him. She took the gum out of her mouth and tossed it as if he had ruined the flavor.

"You forget to invite anyone to this little party of yours?" he went on. "Jesus!" He was furious. "Never in my mother-fucking life!"

Marino was strangled by a short-sleeved white shirt buttoned up to the collar and a clip-on tie. His big belly was in a shoving match with dark blue uniform pants and a stiff leather duty belt fully loaded with his Sig-Sauer nine-millimeter pistol, handcuffs, extra clips, pepper spray and all the rest. His face was flushed. He was dripping sweat, a pair of Oakley sunglasses blacking out his eyes.

"You and I have to talk," I said to him.

I tried to pull him off to the side, but he wouldn't budge. He tapped a Marlboro out of the pack he always had on him somewhere.

"You like my new outfit?" he sardonically said to me. "Deputy Chief Bray thought I needed new clothes."

"Marino, you're not needed here," Anderson said to him.

"In fact, I don't think you want anyone to know you even thought about coming here."

"It's *captain* to you." He blew out his words on gusts of cigarette smoke. "You might want to watch your smart-ass mouth because I outrank you, babe."

Shaw watched the rude exchange without a word.

"I don't believe we call female officers *babe* anymore," Anderson said.

"I've got a body to look at," I said.

"We've got to go through the warehouse to get there," Shaw told me.

"Let's go," I said.

He walked Marino and me to a warehouse door that faced the river. Inside was a huge, dimly lit, airless space that was sweet with the smell of tobacco. Thousands of bales of it were wrapped in burlap and stacked on wooden pallets, and there were tons of magfilled sand and orifet that I believed were used in processing steel, and machine parts bound for Trinidad, according to what was stamped on crates.

Several bays down, the container had been backed up to a loading dock. The closer we got to it, the stronger the odor. We stopped at the crime-scene tape draped across the container's open door. The stench was thick and hot, as if every molecule of oxygen had been replaced by it, and I willed my senses to have no opinion. Flies had begun to gather, their ominous noise reminding me of the high-pitched buzzing of a remote-control toy plane.

"Were there flies when the container was first opened?" I asked Shaw.

"Not like this," he said.

"How close did you get?" I asked as Marino and Anderson caught up with us.

25

"Close enough," Shaw said.

"No one went inside it?" I wanted to make sure.

"I can guarantee you that, ma'am." The stench was getting to him.

Marino seemed unfazed. He shook out another cigarette and mumbled around it as he fired the lighter.

"So, Anderson," he said. "I don't guess it could be live-stock, you know, since you didn't look. Hell, maybe a big dog that accidentally got locked up in there. Sure would be a shame to drag the doc here and get the media all in a lather and then find out it's just some poor ol' wharf dog rotted in there."

He and I both knew there was no dog or pig or horse or any other animal in there. I opened my scene case while Marino and Anderson went on carping at each other. I dropped my car key inside and pulled on several layers of gloves and a surgical mask. I fitted my thirty-five-millimeter Nikon with a flash and a twenty-eight-millimeter lens. I loaded four-hundred-speed film so the photographs wouldn't be too grainy, and slipped sterile booties over my shoes.

"It's just like when we get bad smells coming from a closed-up house in the middle of July. We look through the window. Break in if we have to. Make sure what's in there's human before we call the M.E.," Marino continued to instruct his new protégé.

I ducked under the tape and stepped inside the dark container, relieved to find it was only half full of neatly stacked white cartons, leaving plenty of room to move around. I followed the beam of my flashlight deeper, sweeping it from side to side.

Near the back, it illuminated a bottom row of cartons soaked with the reddish purge fluid that leaks from the nose and mouth of a decomposing body. My light followed shoes

26

and lower legs, and a bloated, bearded face jumped out of the dark. Bulging milky eyes stared, the tongue so swollen it protruded from the mouth as if the dead man were mocking me. My covered shoes made sticky sounds wherever I stepped.

The body was fully clothed and propped up in the corner, the container's metal walls bracing it from two sides. Legs were straight out, hands in the lap beneath a carton that apparently had fallen. I moved it out of the way and checked for defense injuries, or for abrasions and broken nails that might suggest he had tried to claw his way out. I saw no blood on his clothes, no sign of obvious injuries or that a struggle had taken place. I looked for food or water, for any provisions or holes made through the container's sides for ventilation, and found nothing.

I made my way between every row of boxes, squatting to shine oblique light on the metal floor, looking for shoe prints. Of course, they were everywhere. I moved an inch at a time, my knees about to give out. I found an empty plastic wastepaper basket. Then I found two silvery coins. I bent close to them. One was a deutsche mark. I didn't recognize the other one and touched nothing.

Marino seemed a mile away, standing in the container's opening.

"My car key's in my case," I called out to him through the surgical mask.

"Yeah?" he said, peering inside.

"Could you go get the Luma-Lite? I need the fiber-optic attachment and the extension cord. Maybe Mr. Shaw can help you find somewhere to plug it in. Has to be a grounded receptacle, one-fifteen VAC."

"I love it when you talk dirty," he said.

27

4

The Luma-Lite is an alternate light source with a high-intensity arc tube that emits fifteen watts of light energy at 450 nanometers with a twenty-nanometer bandwidth. It can detect body fluids as well as expose drugs, fingerprints, trace evidence and unexpected surprises not evident to the naked eye.

Shaw found a receptacle inside the warehouse, and I slipped disposable plastic covers on the Luma-Lite's aluminum feet to make sure nothing from a previous scene would be transferred to this one. The alternate light source looked very much like a home projector, and I set it inside the container on top of a carton and ran the fan for a minute before turning on the power switch.

While I waited for the lamp to reach its maximum output, Marino appeared with the amber-tinted glasses needed to protect our eyes from the strong energy light. Flies were getting thicker. They drunkenly knocked against us and droned loudly in our ears.

"Goddamn, I hate those things!" Marino complained, swatting wildly.

I noticed he didn't have on a jumpsuit, only shoe covers and gloves.

"You going to drive home in a closed car like that?" I asked.

"I got another uniform in the trunk. In case something gets spilled on me or whatever."

"In case *you* spill something on you or whatever," I said, looking at my watch. "We got one more minute."

"Notice how Anderson's conveniently disappeared? I knew she would the minute I heard about this one. I just didn't figure on nobody else being here. Shit, something really weird's going on."

"How in the world did she become a homicide detective?"

"She kisses Bray's ass. I hear she even runs errands for her, takes her brand-new fancy-schmansy black Crown Vic to the car wash, probably sharpens her pencils and shines her shoes."

"We're ready," I said.

I began scanning with a 450-nanometer filter that was capable of detecting a large variety of residues and stains. Through our tinted glasses, the inside of the container became an impenetrably black outer space scattered with shapes that fluoresced white and yellow in different shades and intensities wherever I pointed the lens. The projected blue light exposed hairs on the floor and fibers everywhere, just as I would expect in a high-traffic area used to store cargo handled by many people. White cardboard cartons glowed a soft white, like the moon.

I moved the Luma-Lite deeper inside the container. Purge fluid didn't fluoresce, and the body was a dejected dark shape sitting in the corner.

"If he died naturally," Marino said, "then why's he sitting up like that with his hands in his lap like he's in church or something?"

29

"If he died of suffocation, dehydration, exposure, he could have died sitting up."

"It sure looks wacko to me."

"I'm just saying it's possible. It's getting tight in here. Can you hand me the fiber optics, please?"

He bumped into cartons as he made his way in my direction.

"You might want to take off your glasses until you get here," I suggested, because one couldn't see anything through them except the high-energy light, which wasn't in Marino's line of sight at the moment.

"No friggin' way," he said. "I hear all it takes is one quick look. And zap. Cataracts, cancer, the whole nine yards."

"Not to mention turning to stone."

"Huh?"

"Marino! Careful!"

He bumped into me and I wasn't sure what happened after that, but suddenly cartons were caving in and he almost knocked me over as he fell.

"Marino?" I was disoriented and frightened. "Marino!"

I cut the power on the Luma-Lite and took off my glasses so I could see.

"Goddamn fucking son of a bitch!" he yelled as if he'd been bitten by a snake.

He was flat on his back on the floor, shoving and kicking boxes out of the way. The plastic bucket sailed through the air. I got down next to him.

"Stay still," I firmly told him. "Don't go thrashing around until we're sure you're all right."

"Oh God! Oh shit! I got this shit all over me!" he yelled in a panic.

"Are you hurting anywhere?"

30

"Oh, Jesus, I'm gonna puke. Oh Jesus, oh Jesus."

He rushed to his feet and knocked boxes out of the way as he stumbled toward the container's opening. I heard him vomit. He groaned and vomited again.

"That should make you feel better," I said.

He ripped open his white shirt, gagging and heaving as he struggled out of its sleeves. He stripped down to his undershirt, balled up what was left of his uniform shirt and hurled it out the door.

"What if he's got AIDS?" Marino's voice sounded like a bell at midnight.

"You're not going to get AIDS from this guy," I said.

"Oh, fuck!" He gagged some more.

"I can finish up in here, Marino," I said.

"Just give me a minute."

"Why don't you go on and find a shower."

"You can't tell anyone about this," he said, and I knew he was thinking about Anderson. "You know, I bet you could get a really good deal on some uh this camera shit."

"I bet you could."

"Wonder what they're gonna do with it."

"Has the removal service come yet?" I asked him.

He raised his portable radio to his lips.

"Christ!" He spat and gagged some more.

He vigorously wiped the radio on the front of his pants and coughed and conjured up spittle from the bottom of his throat and let it fly.

"Unit nine," he said on the air, holding the radio a good twelve inches from his face.

"Unit nine."

The dispatcher was a woman. I detected warmth in her voice and was surprised. Dispatchers and 911 operators almost always remained calm and showed no emotion, no matter the emergency.

"Ten-five Rene Anderson," Marino was saying. "Don't know her unit number. Tell her if she doesn't mind, we sure would like removal service guys to show up down here."

"Unit nine. You know the name of the service?"

"Hey, Doc," Marino stopped transmitting and raised his voice to me. "What's the name of the service?"

"Capital Transport."

He passed that along, adding, "Radio, if she's a ten-two, ten-ten, or ten-seven or if we should ten-twenty-two, get back to me."

A storm of cops keyed their mikes, their way of laughing and cheering him on.

"Ten-four, unit nine," the dispatcher said.

"What did you just say that got you such an ovation? I know ten-seven is out of service, but I didn't get the rest of it."

"Told her to let me know if Anderson was a *weak signal* or *negative*, or had *time to get around to it.* Or if we should fucking *disregard her.*"

"No wonder she likes you so much."

"She's a piece of shit."

"By chance do you know what happened to the fiber-optic cable?" I asked him.

"I had it in my hand," he replied.

I found it where he had fallen and knocked over cartons.

"What if he's got AIDS?" He started in on that again.

"If you're determined to worry about something, try gram-negative bacterias. Or gram-positive bacterias. Clostridia. Strep. If you have an open wound, which you don't as best I know."

32

I attached one end of the cable to the wand, the other to the assembly, tightening thumbscrews. He wasn't listening.

"No way anybody's saying that about me! That I'm a goddamn fairy! I'll eat my gun, don't think I won't."

"You're not going to get AIDS, Marino," I repeated myself.

I turned on the source lamp again. It would have to run at least four minutes before I could turn on the power.

"I picked a hangnail yesterday and it bled! That's an open wound!"

"You have on gloves, don't you?"

"If I get some bad disease, I'm going to kill that fucking little lazy snitch."

I assumed he meant Anderson.

"Bray's gonna get hers, too. I'll find a way!"

"Marino, be quiet," I said.

"How would you like it if it was you?"

"I can't tell you how many times it's been me. What do you think I do every day?"

"You sure as hell don't slop around in dead juice!"

"*Dead juice?*"

"We don't know a thing about this guy. What if they got some weird diseases in Belgium that we can't treat here?"

"Marino, be quiet," I said again.

"No!"

"Marino . . ."

"I got a right to be upset!"

"All right then, leave." My patience had walked off. "You're interfering with my concentration. You're interfering with everything. Go take a shower and throw back a few shots of bourbon."

The Luma-Lite was ready and I put on the protective glasses. Marino was quiet.

"I'm not leaving," he finally said.

I gripped the fiber-optics wand like a soldering iron. The intense pulsing blue light was as thin as pencil lead, and I began scanning very small areas.

"Anything?" he asked.

"Not so far."

His sticky booties moved closer as I worked slowly, inch by inch, into places that could not be reached by the broad scan. I leaned the body forward to probe behind the back and head, then between the legs. I checked the palms of his hands. The Luma-Lite could detect body fluids such as urine, semen, sweat and saliva, and of course, blood. But again, nothing fluoresced. My back and neck ached.

"I'm voting for him being dead before he ended up in here," Marino said.

"We'll know a lot more when we get him downtown."

I straightened up and the rapid-fire light caught the corner of a carton Marino had displaced when he'd fallen. The tail of what looked like the letter Y blazed neon green in the dark.

"Marino," I said. "Look at this."

Letter by letter I illuminated words that were French and written by hand. They were about four inches high and an odd boxy shape, as if a mechanical arm had formed them in square strokes. It took me a moment to make out what they said.

"*Bon voyage, le loup-garou*," I read.

Marino was leaning over me, his breath in my hair. "What the hell's a *loup-garou*?"

"I don't know."

I examined the carton carefully. The top of it was soggy, the bottom of it dry.

"Fingerprints? You see any on the box?" Marino asked.

34

"I'm sure there're prints all over the place in here," I replied. "But no, none are popping out."

"You think whoever wrote this wanted someone to find it?"

"Possibly. In some kind of permanent ink that fluoresces. We'll let fingerprints do their thing. The box goes to the lab, and we need to sweep up some of the hair on the floor for DNA, if it's ever needed. Then do photographs and we're out of here."

"May as well get the coins while I'm at it," he said.

"May as well," I said, staring toward the container's opening.

Someone was looking in. He was backlit by bright sunlight and a blue sky and I could not make out who it was.

"Where are the crime-scene techs?" I asked Marino.

"Got no idea."

"Goddamn it!" I said.

"Tell me about it," Marino said.

"We had two homicides last week and things weren't like this."

"You didn't go to the scenes, either, so you don't know what they were like," he said, and he was right.

"Someone from my office did. I would know if there was a problem . . ."

"Not if the problem wasn't obvious, you wouldn't," he told me. "And the problem sure as hell wasn't obvious because this is Anderson's first case. Now it's obvious."

"What?"

"Brand spanking new detective. Hell, maybe she stashed this body in here herself so she'd have something to do."

"She says you told her to call me."

"Right. Like I can't bother, so I dis you, and then you get pissed off at me. She's a fucking liar," he said.

35

An hour later we were done. We walked out of the foul-smelling dark, returning to the warehouse. Anderson stood in the open bay next to ours, talking to a man I recognized as Deputy Chief Al Carson, head of investigations. I realized it was he whom I had seen at the mouth of the container earlier. I moved past her without a word and greeted him as I looked out to see if the removal service had shown up yet. I was relieved to see two men in jumpsuits standing by their dark blue van. They were talking to Shaw.

"How are you, Al?" I said to Deputy Chief Carson.

He'd been around as long as I had. He was a gentle, quiet man who had grown up on a farm.

"Hangin' in, Doc," he said. "Looks like we got a mess on our hands."

"Looks like it," I agreed.

"I was out and thought I'd drop by to make sure everything's all right."

Carson didn't just "drop by" scenes. He was uptight and looked depressed. Most important, he paid no more attention to Anderson than the rest of us did.

"We've got it covered," Anderson outrageously broke rank and answered Deputy Chief Carson. "I've been talking to the port director . . ."

Her voice trailed off when she saw Marino. Or maybe she smelled him first.

"Hey, Pete," Carson said, cheering up. "What you know, old boy? They got some new dress code in the uniform division I don't know about?"

"Detective Anderson," I said to her as she got as far away from Marino as she could. "I need to know who's working this case. And where are the crime-scene techs? And why did the removal service take so long to get here?"

"Yeah. This is how we do undercover work, boss. We take our uniforms off," Marino was saying loudly.

Carson guffawed.

"And why, Detective Anderson, weren't you in there collecting evidence and helping in any way possible?" I continued grilling her.

"I don't answer to you," she said with a shrug.

"Let me tell you something," I said in a tone that got her attention. "I'm exactly who you answer to when there's a dead body."

". . . bet Bray had to go undercover a lot, too. Before rising to the top. Types like her, they gotta be on top," Marino said with a wink.

The light blinked out in Carson's eyes. He looked depressed again. He looked tired, as if life had pushed him as far as he could go.

"Al?" Marino got serious. "What the fuck's going on? How come nobody showed up at this little party?"

A gleaming black Crown Victoria was driving toward the parking lot.

"Well, I've got to head on," Carson abruptly said, his face etched with his mind elsewhere. "Let's hook up at the F.O.P. It's your turn to buy the beer. Remember when Louisville beat Charlotte and you lost the bet, old boy?"

Then Carson was gone without acknowledging Anderson in any way, because it was clear he had no power over her.

"Hey, Anderson?" Marino said, pounding her back.

She gasped, clamping her hand over her nose and mouth.

"How you like working for Carson? Pretty nice guy, huh?" he said.

She backed away and he stayed with her. Even I was rather appalled by Marino and his stinking uniform pants, filthy gloves and booties. His undershirt would never be white again, and there were big holes where seams had succumbed to his big belly. He got so close to Anderson, I thought he might kiss her.

"You stink!" She tried to get away from him.

"Funny how that happens in a job like this."

"Get away from me!"

But he wouldn't. She darted this way and that, and with each step he blocked her like a mountain until she was pressed against super-sacks of injectable carbon bound for the West Indies.

"Just what the fuck do you think you're doing?" his words grabbed her by the collar. "We get some rotting body in a cargo container in a fucking international shipping port where half the people don't speak fucking English and you decide you're gonna handle things all by yourself?"

Gravel popped outside in the parking lot, the black Crown Victoria driving fast.

"Miss Junior Detective gets her first case. And may as well have the chief medical examiner show up, along with a few helicopter news crews?"

"I'm turning you in to internal affairs," Anderson yelled at him. "I'm taking out a warrant on you!"

"For what? Stinking?"

"You're dead!"

"No. What's dead is that guy in there." Marino pointed at the container. "What's dead is your ass if you ever have to testify about this case in court."

"Marino, come on," I said as the Crown Victoria brazenly drove onto the restricted dock.

"Hey!" Shaw was running after it, waving his arms. "You can't park there!"

"You're nothing but a used-up, washed-up, redneck loser," Anderson said to Marino as she trotted off.

Marino yanked off gloves inside out and freed himself of his blue plasticized paper booties by stepping down on the heel of each with the opposite toe. He picked up his soiled white uniform shirt by the clip-on tie, which didn't stay attached, so he stomped them as if they were a fire to put out. I quietly collected them and dropped them and mine into a red biological hazard bag.

"Are you quite finished?" I asked him.

"Ain't even begun," Marino said, staring out as the driver's door of the Crown Victoria opened and a uniformed male officer climbed out.

Anderson rounded the side of the warehouse and walked quickly toward the car. Shaw was hurrying, too, dockworkers looking on as a striking woman in uniform and sparkling brass climbed out of the back of the car. She looked around as the world looked back. Someone whistled. Someone else did. Then the dock sounded like referees protesting every foul imaginable.

"Let me guess," I said to Marino. "Bray."

5

The air was filled with the static of greedy flies, their volume turned up high by warm weather and time. The removal service attendants had carried the stretcher into the warehouse and were waiting for me.

"Whooo," one of the attendants said, shaking his head, a bad expression on his face. "Lordy, lordy."

"I know, I know," I said as I pulled on clean gloves and booties. "I'll go in first. This won't take long. I promise."

"Fine by me, you want to go first."

I went back inside the container and they came after me, choosing their steps carefully, stretcher held tight at their waists like a sedan chair. Their breathing was labored behind their surgical masks. Both were old and overweight and should not have been lifting heavy bodies anymore.

"Get it by the lower legs and feet," I directed. "Real careful, because the skin's going to slip and come off. Let's get him by his clothing as best we can."

They set down the stretcher and bent over the dead man's feet.

"Lordy," one of them muttered again.

I hooked my arms under the armpits. They took hold of the ankles.

"Okay. Let's lift together on the count of three," I said. "One, two, three."

The men struggled to maintain their balance. They huffed and backed up. The body was limp because rigor mortis had come and left, and we centered it onto the stretcher and wrapped it in the sheet. I zipped up the body bag and the attendants carried their client away. They would drive him to the morgue, and there I would do all I could to make him talk to me.

"Damn!" I heard one of them say. "They don't pay me enough for this."

"Tell me."

I followed them out of the warehouse into sunlight that was dazzling and air that was clean. Marino was still in his filthy undershirt, talking to Anderson and Bray on the dock. I gathered from the way he was gesturing that the presence of Bray had restrained him somewhat. Her eyes landed on me as I got close. She did not introduce herself, so I went first without offering my hand.

"I'm Dr. Scarpetta," I said to her.

She returned my greeting with vague regard, as if she had not a clue as to who I was or why I was there.

"I think it would be a good idea for the two of us to talk," I added.

"Who did you say you are?" Bray asked.

"Oh, for Chrissake!" Marino erupted. "She knows damn well who you are."

"Captain." Bray's tone had the effect of a riding whip cracking.

Marino got quiet. Anderson did, too.

"I'm the chief medical examiner," I told Bray what she already knew. "Kay Scarpetta."

Marino rolled his eyes. Anderson's expression puckered with resentment and jealousy when Bray motioned for me to step away from them. We moved to the edge of the dock, where the *Sirius* towered above us and barely stirred in the ruffled muddy-blue current.

"I'm so sorry I didn't recognize your name at first," she began.

I didn't say a word.

"That's very ungracious of me," she went on.

I remained silent.

"I should have gotten around to meeting you before now. I've been so busy. So here we are. And it's a good thing, really. Perfect timing, you might say"—she smiled—"that we should meet like this."

Diane Bray was a haughty beauty with black hair and perfect features. Her figure was stunning. Dockworkers could not take their eyes off her.

"You see," she went on in her same cool tone, "I have this little problem. I supervise Captain Marino, yet he seems to think he works for you."

"Nonsense." I finally spoke.

She sighed.

"You have just robbed the city of the most experienced, decent homicide detective it's ever known, Chief Bray," I told her. "And I should know."

"I'm sure you should."

"Just what is it you're trying to accomplish?" I asked.

"It's time for young blood, for detectives who don't mind turning on a computer, using e-mail. Are you aware that Marino doesn't even know how to use word processing? Still hammers on a typewriter with two fingers?"

I couldn't believe she was saying this to me.

"Not to mention the very small problem that he's unteachable and insubordinate, his behavior a disgrace to the department," she went on.

Anderson had walked off, leaving Marino alone by the car, leaning against it, smoking. His arms and shoulders were thick and hairy, and his trousers, belted under his gut, were about to fall off. I knew he was humiliated because he refused to look our way.

"Why are there no crime-scene techs here?" I asked Bray.

One dockworker elbowed another and cupped his hands under his chest, fondling air as if it were Bray's big breasts.

"Why are you here?" I then asked her.

"Because I was alerted that Marino was," she replied. "He's been warned. I wanted to find out for myself if he was so blatantly disregarding my orders."

"He's here because someone had to be."

"He's here because he chose to be." She fixed her eyes on me. "And because you chose to be. That's really why, now isn't it, Dr. Scarpetta? Marino's your own personal detective. Has been for years."

Her eyes bored into places even I couldn't see, and she seemed to wind her way through sacred parts of me and sense the meaning of my many walls. She took in my face and my body and I wasn't sure if she was comparing what I had to hers, or if she was assessing something she might decide she wanted.

"Leave him alone," I told her. "You're trying to kill his spirit. That's what this is all about. Because you can't control him."

"No one has ever been able to control him," she replied. "That's why he was given to me."

"*Given* to you?"

"Detective Anderson is new blood. God knows, this department needs new blood."

"Detective Anderson is unskilled, unschooled and a coward," I replied.

"Certainly with your continents of experience, you can tolerate someone new and do a little mentoring, Kay?"

"There's no cure for someone who doesn't care."

"I suspect you've been listening to Marino. According to him, no one is skilled, schooled or cares enough to do what he does."

I'd had it with her. I adjusted my position to take full advantage of the shift in the wind. I stepped closer to her because I was going to rub her nose in a little dose of reality.

"Don't you ever do this to me again, Chief Bray," I said. "Don't you ever call me or anyone in my office to a scene and then saddle us with some fuckup who can't be bothered collecting evidence. And don't call me *Kay*."

She stepped away from my stinking presence, but not before I caught her flinch.

"We'll do lunch sometime," she said, dismissing me as she summoned her driver.

"Simmons? What time is my next appointment?" she asked, staring up at the ship and clearly enjoying all the attention.

She had a seductive way of massaging her lower lumbar spine or wedging her hands in the back pockets of her uniform pants, shoulders thrown back, or absently smoothing her tie over the steep slope of her chest.

Simmons was handsome and had a fine body, and when he slipped out a folded sheet of paper, it shook as he looked at it. She moved closer to him, and he cleared his throat.

"Two-fifteen, Chief," he said.

"Let me see." She leaned closer, brushing against his arm,

taking her time as she looked at her itinerary and complained, "Oh, God! Not that school board idiot again!"

Officer Simmons shifted his position, and a bead of sweat rolled down his temple. He looked terrified.

"Call him and cancel," Bray said.

"Yes, Chief."

"Well, I don't know. Maybe I should just reschedule."

She took the itinerary from him, brushing against him again like a languid cat, and I was startled by the rage that flashed across Anderson's face. Marino caught up with me on my way to my car.

"You see the way she flaunts herself around?" he asked.

"It wasn't lost on me."

"Don't think that ain't a topic of conversation. I'm telling you, that bitch is poison."

"What's her story?"

Marino shrugged. "Never been married, no one's good enough. Screws around with powerful, married types, supposedly. She's all about power, Doc. The rumor is that she wants to be the next Secretary of Public Safety so every cop in the Commonwealth will have to kiss her pretty ass."

"It will never happen."

"Don't be so sure. I hear she's got friends in high places, Virginia connections, which is one of the reasons we got stuck with her. She's got a plan, no doubt about that. Snakes like her always got a plan."

I opened the trunk, exhausted and depressed as the earlier trauma of the day returned to me so hard it seemed to slam me against the car.

"You aren't gonna do him tonight, are you?" Marino asked.

"No way," I muttered. "It wouldn't be fair to him."

Marino gave me a questioning look. I felt him watching

me as I stripped off my jumpsuit and shoes and double-bagged them.

"Marino, give me one of your cigarettes, please."

"I can't believe you're doing that again."

"There're about fifty million tons of tobacco in that warehouse. The smell put me in the mood."

"That ain't what I was smelling."

"Tell me what's going on," I said as he held out his lighter.

"You just saw what's going on. I'm sure she explained it."

"Yes, she did. And I don't understand it. She's in charge of the uniformed division, not investigations. She says no one can control you, so she's elected to take care of the problem herself. Why? When she got here, you weren't even in her division. Why should you matter to her?"

"Maybe she thinks I'm cute."

"That must be it," I said.

He exhaled smoke as if he were putting out birthday candles, and looked down at his T-shirt as if he had forgotten it was there. His big, thick hands were still dusted with talc from the surgical gloves, and he at first looked lonely and defeated, then turned cynical and indifferent again.

"You know," he said, "I could retire if I wanted to and draw about forty grand a year pension."

"Come over for dinner, Marino."

"Add that to what I could get doing some security consulting or whatever, and I could live pretty good. Wouldn't have to shovel this shit no more day after day with all these little maggots crawling out from everywhere thinking they know it all."

"I've been asked to invite you."

"By who?" he asked suspiciously.

"You'll find out when you get there."

"What the hell does that mean?" he asked, scowling.

"For God's sake, go take a shower and put on something that won't clear out the city. Then come over. Around six-thirty."

"Well, in case you haven't noticed, Doc, I'm working. Three-to-eleven shift this week. Eleven-to-seven shift week after next. I'm the new hot-shit watch commander for the entire friggin' city, and the only hours they need a friggin' watch commander is when all the other commanders ain't on duty, which is evening shift and midnight shift and weekends, meaning the only dinner I'm gonna get the rest of my life is in my car."

"You've got a radio," I told him. "I live in the city, so it's not out of your jurisdiction. Come over, and if you get called out, you get called out."

I got inside my car and started the engine.

"I don't know," he said.

"I was asked to . . ." I started to say as tears threatened again. "I was about to call you when you called me."

"Huh? This isn't making any sense. Who asked you? What? Is Lucy in town?"

He seemed pleased she would think of him, if that's what my hospitality was all about.

"I wish she were. See you at six-thirty?"

He hesitated some more, swatting flies and smelling awful.

"Marino, I really need you to come over," I told him, clearing my throat. "It's very important to me. It's personal and very important."

It was so hard to say that to him. I didn't think I'd ever told him I needed him in a personal way. I couldn't remember the last time I'd said words like this to anyone but Benton.

"I mean it," I added.

Marino crushed the cigarette beneath his foot until it was

47

a tobacco smear and pulverized paper. He lit up again, eyes wandering around.

"You know, Doc, I really got to quit these things. And Wild Turkey. I've been going through that stuff like buttered popcorn. Depends on what you're cooking," he said.

6

Marino headed off to find a shower somewhere and I felt lighter of spirit, as if a terrible spasm had gone into remission for a while. When I pulled into my driveway, I collected the bag of scene clothes out of the trunk and began the same disinfectant ritual I had gone through most of my working life.

Inside the garage, I tore open the garbage bags and dropped them and the shoes into a sink of scalding water, detergent and bleach. I tossed the jumpsuit into the washing machine, stirred the shoes and bags around with a long wooden spoon and rinsed them. I enclosed the disinfected bags in two clean bags that went into a Supercan, and I parked my soaked shoes on a shelf to dry.

Everything I had on from jeans to lingerie went into the washing machine, too. More detergent and bleach, and I hurried naked through my house and into the shower, where I scrubbed hard with Phisoderm, not an inch spared, not the inside of my ears and nose, or under my nails, fingers and toes, and I brushed my teeth in there.

I sat on a ledge and let water pound the back of my neck

and head and remembered Benton's fingers kneading my tendons and muscles. *Untangling* them was what he always said. Missing him was a phantom pain. I could feel what I remembered as if I were feeling it now, and I wondered what it would take for me to live where I was instead of back then. Grief held on. It would not let go of loss, because to do that was to accept it. I told that to grieving families and friends all the time.

I dressed in khakis, loafers and a blue-striped shirt, and played Mozart on the CD player. I watered plants and pinched off dead leaves. I polished or rearranged whatever needed it, and tucked reminders of work out of sight. I called my mother in Miami because I knew Monday was bingo night and she wouldn't be home and I could just leave a message. I did not turn on the news because I didn't want to be reminded of what I had just worked so hard to wash away.

I poured a double Scotch, walked into my study and turned on a light. I scanned shelves crowded with medical and science books, and astronomy texts, and Britannica encyclopedias, and all sorts of aids to gardening, flora and fauna, insects, rocks and minerals, and even tools. I found a French dictionary and carried it over to my desk. A *loup* was a wolf, but I had no luck with *garou*. I tried to think my way out of this problem and seized upon a simple plan.

La Petite France was one of the city's finest restaurants, and although it was closed Monday nights, I knew the chef and his wife very well. I called them at home. He answered the phone and was as warm as always.

"You don't come see us anymore," he said. "We say this too often."

"I haven't been out much," I replied.

"You work too much, Miss Kay."

50

"I need a translation," I said. "And I also need you to keep this between us. Not a word to anyone."

"But of course."

"What is a *loup-garou*?"

"Miss Kay, you must be dreaming bad things!" he exclaimed, amused. "I'm so glad it's not a full moon! *Le loup-garou* is a werewolf!"

The doorbell rang.

"In France, hundreds of years ago, if you were believed to be a *loup-garou* you were hanged. There were many reports of them, you see."

I looked at the clock. It was six-fifteen. Marino was early and I was unprepared.

"Thank you," I told my friend the chef. "I'll come see you soon, I promise."

The doorbell sounded again.

"Coming," I said to Marino through the intercom.

I turned off the alarm and let him in. His uniform was clean, his hair was neatly combed and he had splashed on too much aftershave.

"You look a little better than when I saw you last," I commented as we headed toward the kitchen.

"Looks like you cleaned up this joint," he said as we passed through the great room.

"It's about time," I said.

We walked into the kitchen and he sat in his usual spot at the table by the window. He watched me with curious eyes as I got garlic and fast-acting yeast out of the refrigerator.

"So what are we having? Can I smoke in here?"

"No."

"You do."

"It's my house."

"How 'bout if I open the window and blow it out."

"Depends on which way the wind is blowing."

"We could get the ceiling fan going and see if that helps. I smell garlic."

"I thought we'd have pizza on the grill."

I pushed aside cans and jars in the pantry, looking for crushed tomatoes and high-gluten flour.

"The coins we found are English and German," he told me. "Two pounds and one deutsche mark. But this is where it starts getting real interesting. I hung around the port a little longer than you did, showering and whatever. And by the way, they sure as hell didn't waste any time hauling cartons out of that container and cleaning up. You watch, they'll sell that camera shit like nothing happened to it."

I mixed half a package of yeast, warm water and honey in a bowl and stirred, then I reached for the flour.

"I'm hungry as hell."

His portable radio was upright on the table, blurting ten codes and unit numbers. He yanked off his tie and unbuckled his duty belt with all its gear. I began kneading dough.

"My lower back's killing me, Doc," he complained. "You got any idea what it's like wearing twenty pounds of shit around your waist?"

His mood seemed considerably improved as he watched me work, sprinkling flour and shaping dough on the butcher's-block.

"A *loup-garou* is a werewolf," I told him.

"Huh?"

"As in a wolf man."

"Shit, I fucking hate those things."

"I wasn't aware you'd ever met one."

"You remember seeing Lon Chaney with all that fur

52

growing on his face when the moon came out? Scared the hell out of me. Rocky used to watch *Shock Theater*, remember that?"

Rocky was Marino's only child, a son I'd never met. I placed the dough in a bowl and covered it with a warm, wet cloth.

"Do you ever hear from him?" I cautiously asked. "What about at Christmas? Will you see him then?"

Marino nervously tapped an ash.

"Do you even know where he lives?" I asked.

"Yeah," he said. "Oh, hell, yeah."

"You act as if you don't like him at all," I said.

"Maybe I don't."

I scanned the wine rack for a nice bottle of red. Marino sucked smoke and exhaled loudly. He had nothing more to say about Rocky than he ever had.

"One of these days you're going to talk to me about him," I said as I poured crushed tomatoes in a pot.

"You know as much about him as you need to," he said.

"You love him, Marino."

"I'm telling you, I don't love him. I wish he'd never been born. I wish I'd never met him."

He stared out the window at my backyard fading into night. This moment I didn't seem to know Marino at all. He was a stranger in my kitchen, this man in uniform who had a son I'd never met and knew nothing about. Marino wouldn't look me in the eye or thank me when I set a cup of coffee on his place mat.

"How about peanuts or something?" I asked.

"Naw," he said. "I been thinking about going on a diet."

"Thinking about it won't help much. It's been proven in studies."

"You gonna wear garlic around your neck or something when you post our dead werewolf? You know, you get bit by one, you turn into one. Sort of like AIDS."

"It's nothing like AIDS, and I wish you'd get off this AIDS thing."

"You think he wrote that on the box himself?"

"We can't assume that box and what was written on it are connected with him, Marino."

"*Have a nice trip, werewolf.* Yeah, you find that written on camera boxes all the time. Especially when they're near dead bodies."

"Let's get back to Bray and your new fashion statement," I said. "Start from the beginning. What did you do to make her such a fan?"

"It started about two weeks after she got here. Remember that auto-erotic hanging?"

"Yes."

"She shows up and just walks right into the middle of everything and starts telling people what to do, like she's the detective. She starts looking through the porno magazines the guy was having fun with when he strung himself up in his leather mask. She starts asking his wife questions."

"Whoa," I said.

"So I tell her to leave, that she's in the way and screwing up everything, and the next day she calls me into her office. I figure she's going to be tear-ass about what happened, but she doesn't say a word. Instead, she asks what I think of the detective division."

He took a gulp of coffee and stirred in two more teaspoons of sugar.

"Thing is, I could tell that really wasn't what she was interested in," he went on. "I knew she wanted something.

She wasn't in charge of investigations, so why the hell was she asking me about the detective division?"

I poured myself a glass of wine.

"Then what did she want?" I asked.

"She wanted to talk about you. She started asking me a thousand questions about you, said she knew we had been 'partners in crime,' as she put it, for a long time."

I checked the dough, then the sauce.

"She was asking me background stuff. What the cops thought of you."

"And what did you say?"

"I told her you was a doctor-lawyer-Indian chief with an IQ bigger than my paycheck, that the cops was all in love with you, including the women. And let's see, what else?"

"That was probably quite enough."

"She asked about Benton and what happened to him and how much it had affected your work."

Anger heated me up.

"She started quizzing me about Lucy. About why she left the FBI and if the way she swings is the reason."

"This woman's fast sealing her fate with me," I warned.

"I told her Lucy left the Bureau because NASA asked her to become an astronaut," Marino kept going. "But when she got into the space program, she decided she liked flying helicopters better and signed on as a pilot for ATF. Bray wanted me to tell her next time Lucy was in town, to arrange for the two of them to meet because Bray might want to recruit her. I said that was sort of like asking Billie Jean King to be a ball girl. End of story? I didn't tell Bray shit except I ain't your social secretary. One week later, my ass was back in uniform."

I reached for my pack and felt like a junkie. We shared

an ashtray, smoking in my house, silent and frustrated. I was trying not to feel hateful.

"I think she's jealous as hell of you, plain and simple, Doc," Marino finally said. "She's the big shot moving here from D.C., and all she hears about is the great Dr. Scarpetta. And I think she got a cheap thrill out of busting up the two of us. Gave the bitch a little power rush."

He smashed the cigarette butt in the ashtray and ground it out.

"This is the first time you and me haven't worked together since you moved here," he said as the doorbell rang for a second time this night.

"Who the hell's that?" he said. "You invite someone else and not tell me?"

I got up and looked into the video screen of the Aiphone on the kitchen wall. I stared, incredulous, at the images picked up by the front-door camera.

"I'm dreaming," I said.

7

Lucy and Jo seemed apparitions, physical presences that could not be flesh and blood. Both of them had been riding the streets of Miami barely eight hours ago. Now they were in my arms.

"I don't know what to say," I said at least five times as they dropped duffel bags on the floor.

"What the hell's going on?" Marino boomed, intercepting us in the great room. "What do you think you're doing here?" he demanded of Lucy, as if she had done something wrong.

He had never been able to show affection in a normal way. The gruffer and more sarcastic he got, the happier he was to see my niece.

"They fire your ass down there already?" he asked.

"What's this, trick or treat?" Lucy said just as loudly, tugging a sleeve of his uniform shirt. "You trying to make us finally believe you're a real cop?"

"Marino," I said as we went into the kitchen, "I don't think you've met Jo Sanders."

"Nope," he said.

"You've heard me talk about her."

He gave Jo a blank look. She was an athletically built strawberry blond with dark blue eyes, and I could tell he thought she was pretty.

"He knows exactly who you are," I said to Jo. "He's not being rude. He's just being him."

"You work?" Marino asked her, fishing his smoldering cigarette out of the ashtray and drawing one last puff.

"Only when I have no choice," Jo answered.

"Doing what?"

"A little rappelling out of Black Hawks. Drug busts. Nothing special."

"Don't tell me you and Lucy are in the same field division down there in South America."

"She's DEA," Lucy told him.

"No shit?" Marino said to Jo. "You seem kind of puny for DEA."

"They're into quotas," Jo said.

He opened the refrigerator and shoved things around until he found a Red Stripe beer. He twisted off the cap and started chugging.

"Drinks are on the house," he called out.

"Marino," I said. "What are you doing? You're on duty."

"Not anymore. Here, let me show you."

He set the bottle down hard on the table and dialed a number.

"Mann, what'cha know," he said into the phone. "Yeah, yeah. Listen, I ain't joking. I'm feeling like shit. You think you could cover for me tonight? I'll owe ya."

Marino winked at us. He hung up, hit the speaker button on the phone and dialed again. His call was answered on the first ring.

"Bray," the deputy chief of administration, Diane Bray, announced in my kitchen for all to hear.

"Deputy Chief Bray, it's Marino," he said in the voice of someone dying of a terrible scourge. "Really sorry to bug you at home."

He was answered with silence, having instantly and deliberately irritated his direct supervisor by addressing her as "Deputy Chief." According to protocol, deputy chiefs were always addressed as "Chief," while the chief himself was called "Colonel." Calling her at home didn't win him any points, either.

"What is it?" Bray tersely asked.

"I feel like hell," Marino rasped. "Throwing up, fever, the whole nine yards. I gotta mark off sick and go to bed."

"You certainly weren't sick when I saw you a few hours ago."

"It happened real sudden. I sure hope I didn't catch some bacteria thing . . ."

I quickly dashed out *Strep* and *Clostridia* on a notepad.

". . . you know, like strep or clos-ter-ida out there at the scene. One doctor I called warned me about that, because of getting in such close proximity to that dead body and all . . ."

"When does your shift end?" she interrupted him.

"Eleven."

Lucy, Jo and I were red-faced, strangled by laughter we were fighting to hold in.

"It's not likely I can find someone to be watch commander this late in the shift," Bray coldly replied.

"I already got hold of Lieutenant Mann in third precinct. He's nice enough to work the rest of tour for me," Marino let her know as his health failed precipitously.

"You should have notified me earlier!" Bray snapped.

"I kept hoping I could hang in there, Deputy Chief Bray."

"Go home. I want to see you in my office tomorrow."

"If I'm well enough, I'll drop by, I sure will, Deputy Chief Bray. You take care, now. Sure hope you don't get whatever I got."

She hung up.

"What a sweetheart," Marino said as laughter leapt out.

"God, no wonder," Jo said when she could finally talk again. "I hear she's pretty much hated."

"How'd you hear that?" Marino frowned. "They talk about her in Miami?"

"I'm from here. On Old Mill, right off Three Chopt, not too far from the University of Richmond."

"Your dad teach there?" Marino asked.

"He's a Baptist minister."

"Oh. That must be fun."

"Yeah," Lucy chimed in, "kind of bizarre to think she grew up around here and we never met until Miami. So, what are you going to do about Bray?"

"Nothing," he said, draining the bottle of beer and going into the refrigerator for another one.

"Well, I sure as hell would do something," she said with huge confidence.

"You know, you think shit like that when you're young," he remarked. "Truth, justice and the American way. Wait till you're my age."

"I'll never be your age."

"Lucy told me you're a detective," Jo started talking to Marino. "So why are you dressed like that?"

"Story time," Marino said. "You want to sit on my knee?"

"Let me guess. You pissed somebody off. Probably her."

60

"DEA teach you to make deductions like that, or are you just unusually smart for someone almost grown up?"

I sliced mushrooms, green peppers and onions, and pinched off pieces of whole-milk mozzarella while Lucy watched. Finally, she made me look her in the eye.

"Right after you called this morning, Senator Lord did," she quietly told me. "It about shocked the entire field office, I might add."

"I bet it did."

"He told me to get on a plane immediately and come here . . ."

"If only you minded me so well." I was getting shaky inside again.

"That you needed me."

"I can't tell you how glad I am . . ." My voice caught as I tumbled back down into that frigid, dark space.

"Why didn't you tell me you needed me?"

"I didn't want to interfere. You're so involved down there. You didn't seem to want to talk."

"All you had to say was, *I need you.*"

"You were on a cell phone."

"I want to see the letter," she said.

8

I laid the knife on the cutting board and wiped my hands on a towel. I gave Lucy my eyes and she saw the pain and fear in them.

"I want to read it alone with you," she said.

I nodded and we went back to my bedroom and I got the letter out of the safe. We sat on the edge of my bed and I noticed the Sig-Sauer 232 pistol tucked in an Uncle Mike's Sidekick ankle holster peeking out of the cuff of her right pants leg. I couldn't help but smile as I thought about what Benton would say. Of course he would shake his head. Of course he would go into some phony-baloney psychologizing that would leave us weak with laughter.

But his humor was not without its point. I was aware of the more somber, foreboding side of what I was seeing right now. Lucy had always been an ardent worshiper of self-defense. But since Benton's murder, she had become an extremist.

"We're in the house," I said to her. "Why don't you give your ankle a rest?"

"Only way to get used to wearing one of these things is

to wear it a lot," she replied. "Especially stainless steel. It's so much heavier."

"Then why wear stainless steel?"

"I like it better. And down there with all that humidity and salt water."

"Lucy, how much longer are you going to be doing this undercover thing?" I blurted out.

"Aunt Kay." She met my eyes and put her hand on my arm. "Let's don't start that again."

"It's just . . ."

"I know. It's just that you don't want one of these letters from me someday."

Her hands were steady as she held the creamy sheet of paper.

"Don't say that," I said with dread.

"And I don't ever want one from you," she added.

Benton's words were just as powerful and alive as they had been this morning when Senator Lord had brought them to me, and I heard Benton's voice again. I saw his face and the love in his eyes. Lucy read very slowly. When she was done, she could not speak for a moment.

Then she said, "Don't you ever send me one of these. I don't ever want one of these."

Her voice shook with pain and anger.

"What's the point? So you can just upset someone all over again?" she said, getting up from the bed.

"Lucy, you know his point." I wiped away tears and hugged her. "Deep down, you know."

I carried the letter into the kitchen and Marino and Jo read it, too. His reaction was to stare out the window at the night, his big hands listless in his lap. Hers was to get up and hover in the room, not sure where to go.

"I really think I should go." She repeated herself and we overruled her. "He wanted the three of you here. I don't think I should be."

"He would have wanted you here had he known you," I said.

"Nobody leaves." Marino said it like a cop drawing down on a room full of suspects. "We're all in this together. Goddamn."

He got up from the table and rubbed his face in his hands.

"I sort of wish he hadn't done that." He looked at me. "Would you do that to me, Doc? 'Cause if you got any ideas, I'm telling you right now to forget it. I don't want no words from the crypt after you're gone."

"Let's put this pizza on," I said.

We went out on the patio and I worked the dough off a cookie sheet and placed it on the grill. I spread sauce and sprinkled the meats, vegetables and cheese on top of it. Marino, Lucy and Jo sat in iron rocking chairs because I would not let them help me. They tried to keep a conversation going but no one had the heart for it. I drizzled olive oil over the pizza, careful not to make the coals flare up.

"I don't think he brought you together just so you could be depressed," Jo finally said.

"I'm not depressed," Marino said.

"Yes, you are," Lucy countered.

"About what, wiseass?"

"Everything."

"At least I'm not afraid to say I miss him."

Lucy stared at him in disbelief. Their sparring had just drawn blood.

"I can't believe you just said that," she told him.

"Believe it. He's the only goddamn father you ever had, and I've never heard you say you miss him. Why? 'Cause you still think it's your fault, right?"

"What's wrong with you?"

"Well, guess what, Agent Lucy Farinelli." Marino wouldn't stop. "It ain't your fault. It's fucking Carrie Grethen's fault, and no matter how many times you blow the bitch out of the sky, she'll never be dead enough for you. That's the way it works when you hate someone that bad."

"And you don't hate her?" Lucy pushed back.

"Hell." Marino swilled what was left of his beer. "I hate her worse than you do."

"I don't think it was Benton's plan for us to sit around here talking about how much we hate her or anybody," I said.

"Then how do you handle it, Dr. Scarpetta?" Jo asked me.

"I wish you would call me Kay." I had told her this many times. "I carry on. That's all I can do."

The words sounded banal, even to me. Jo leaned into the light of the grill and looked at me as if I held the answers to every question she had ever asked in life.

"How do you go on?" she asked. "How do people go on? All these bad things we deal with every day, yet we're on the other side of it. It's not happening to us. After we shut the door, we don't have to keep looking at that stain on the floor where someone's wife was raped and stabbed to death, someone's husband's brains blown out. We lull ourselves into believing that we work cases and won't ever become cases. But you know better."

She paused, still leaning into the light of the grill, and shadows from the fire played on a face that looked far too young and pure to belong to someone so full of such questions.

"How do you go on?" she asked again.

"The human spirit is very resilient." I didn't know what else to say.

"Well, I'm afraid," Jo said. "I think all the time about what I would do if something happened to Lucy."

"Nothing's going to happen to me," Lucy said.

She got up and kissed Jo on the top of the head. She put her arms around her, and if this clear signal about the nature of their relationship was news to Marino, he didn't show it or seem to care. He had known Lucy since she was ten, and in some measure, his influence on her had a lot to do with her going into law enforcement. He had taught her to shoot. He had let her drive the streets with him and even put her behind the wheel of one of his sacred trucks.

When he first realized she didn't fall in love with men, he had been the consummate bigot, probably because he feared his influence had fallen short of what, by his standard, mattered most. He may even have wondered if he were somehow to blame. That was many years ago. I couldn't remember the last time he'd made a narrow-minded comment about her sexual orientation.

"But you work around death every day," Jo gently persisted. "Aren't you reminded . . . of what happened, when you see it happen to someone else? I don't mean to, well, I just don't want to be so afraid of death."

"I don't have a magic formula," I said, getting up. "Except you learn not to think too much."

The pizza was bubbling and I worked a big spatula under it.

"That smells good," Marino said with a worried look. "You think it's gonna be enough?"

I made a second, then a third one, and I built a fire and we sat before it with the lights out in the great room. Marino stuck with beer. Lucy, Jo and I sipped a white burgundy that was crisp and clean.

"Maybe you should find somebody," Lucy said, the light and shadow of flames dancing on her face.

"Shit!" Marino erupted. "What is this all of a sudden? *The Dating Game?* Maybe if she wants to tell you personal stuff like that, she will. You shouldn't be asking. It ain't nice."

"Life isn't nice," Lucy said. "And why should you care if she plays *The Dating Game?*"

Jo silently stared into the fire. I was getting fed up. I was beginning to wonder if I might have been better off staying alone tonight. Even Benton hadn't always been right.

"Remember when Doris left you?" Lucy went on. "What if people hadn't asked you about it? What if no one had cared what you did next or if you were holding yourself together? You sure wouldn't have volunteered anything. Same goes for the idiots you've gone out with since. Every time one of them didn't work out, your friends had to jump in again and pry things out of you."

Marino set the empty beer bottle on the hearth so hard I thought he might break the slate.

"Maybe you ought to think about growing up one of these days," he said. "You gonna wait until you're thirty before you stop being such a goddamn, stuck-up brat? I'm getting another beer."

He stalked out of the room.

"And let me tell you another thing," Marino threw back

at her, "just because you fly helicopters and program computers and bodybuild and do all the other friggin' shit you do doesn't mean you're better than me!"

"I've never said I was better than you!" Lucy yelled after him.

"The hell you haven't!" His voice carried from the kitchen.

"The difference between you and me is I do what I want in life," she called out. "I don't accept limitations."

"You're so full of shit, Agent Asshole."

"Ah, now we're getting to the root of the matter," Lucy said as he reappeared, gulping beer. "I'm a federal agent fighting big bad crime on big bad streets of the world. And you're in uniform riding around baby-sitting cops at all hours of the night."

"And you like guns because you wish you had a dick!"

"So I can be what? A tripod?"

"That's it," I exclaimed. "Enough! The two of you ought to be ashamed of yourselves. Doing this . . . of all times . . ."

My voice splintered and tears stung my eyes. I was determined I wouldn't lose control again, and I was horrified that I no longer seemed able to help it. I looked away from them. Silence was heavy, the fire popping. Marino got up and opened the screen. He stirred embers with the poker and tossed on another log.

"I hate Christmas," Lucy said.

9

The next morning, Lucy and Jo had an early flight and I could not bear the emptiness that would return with the shutting door. So I went out with them, briefcase in hand. I knew this day was going to be awful.

"I wish you didn't have to go," I said. "But I guess Miami might not survive another day if you stayed here with me."

"Miami's probably not going to survive anyway," Lucy said. "But that's what we get paid to do—fight wars already lost. Sort of like Richmond, when you think about it. God, I feel like shit."

Both of them were in scruffy jeans and wrinkled shirts and had done nothing more than push gel through their hair. All of us were exhausted and hung over as we stood in my driveway. Carriage lanterns and streetlights had gone out as the sky turned dusky blue. We could not see each other well, just our shapes and shining eyes and foggy breath. It was cold. Frost on our cars looked like lace.

"Except the One-Sixty-Fivers aren't going to survive," Lucy talked big. "And I'm looking forward to that."

"The who?" I asked.

"The gun-trafficking assholes we're after. Remember, I told you we call them that because their ammo of choice is one-sixty-five-grain Speer Gold Dot. Real high end, hot stuff. That and all sorts of goodies—AR-fifteens, two-twenty-three-caliber rifles, fully automatic Russian and Chinese shit—coming in from maggot-promise land. Brazil, Venezuela, Colombia, Puerto Rico.

"Point is, some of this is being smuggled piecemeal by container ships that have no idea," she went on. "Take the port in L.A. It unloads one cargo container every one and a half minutes. No way anybody can search all that."

"Oh, that's right." My head was throbbing.

"We're real flattered to get the assignment," Jo added dryly. "A couple of months ago, the body of some guy from Panama eventually linked to this cartel turned up in a South Florida canal. When they did the autopsy, they found his tongue in his stomach because his compatriots cut it off and made him eat it."

"I'm not sure I want to hear all this," I said as the poison seeped into my mind again.

"I'm Terry," Lucy let me know. "She's Brandy." She smiled at Jo. "U of M girls who didn't quite graduate, but hey, who needs to because during our hardworking semesters of being dopers and getting laid, we learned some pretty good addresses for home invasions. We've developed a nice social relationship with a couple One-Sixty-Fivers who do home invasions for guns, cash, drugs. We're setting up a guy on Fisher Island right now who's got enough guns to open his own damn gun store and enough coke to make it look like it's fucking snowing."

I couldn't stand to hear her talk this way.

"Of course, the victim's undercover, too," Lucy went on

70

as big, dark crows began making rude noises and lights went on across the street.

I noticed candles in windows and wreaths on doors. I had given virtually no thought to Christmas and it would be here in less than three weeks. Lucy dug her wallet out of her back pocket and showed me her driver's license. The photograph was her, but nothing else was.

"Terry Jennifer Davis," she read to me. "White female, twenty-four years old, five-six, one hundred and twenty-one pounds. It's really strange to be someone else. You ought to see my setup down there, Aunt Kay. I got this cool little house in South Beach and drive a Benz V-twelve sports car confiscated in a drug raid in São Paulo. Sort of silver, smoky. And you ought to see my Glock. A collector's model. Forty-caliber, stainless steel slide, small. Talk about sweet."

The poison was beginning to suffocate me. It cast a purple hue behind my eyes and made my hands and feet go numb.

"Lucy, how 'bout we cut the show and tell," Jo said, sensing how all this was affecting me. "It's like you're watching her do an autopsy. Maybe more than you want to know, right?"

"She's let me watch," Lucy bragged on. "I've seen maybe half a dozen."

Jo was getting annoyed, now.

"Police academy demos." My niece shrugged. "No axe murders."

I was rocked by her insensitivity. It was as if she were talking about restaurants.

"Usually people who died of natural causes or suicide. Families donate the bodies to the anatomical division."

Her words drifted around me like noxious gas.

"So it doesn't bother them if Uncle Tim or Cousin Beth is autopsied in front of a bunch of cops. Most of the families can't afford a burial anyway, and might in fact get paid something for body donations, isn't that right, Aunt Kay?"

"No, they don't, and bodies donated by families to science are not used for demo autopsies," I said, appalled. "What in God's name is wrong with you?" I lashed out at her.

Bare trees were spidery against the overcast dawn, and two Cadillacs drove past. I felt people staring at us.

"I hope you don't plan on making this tough act a habit." I dashed my cold words in her face. "Because it sounds stupid enough when ignorant, lobotomized people do it. And for the record, Lucy, I have let you watch three autopsies, and although police academy demos may not have been axe murders, the cases were human beings. Someone loved those three dead people you saw. Those three dead people had feelings. In love, happy, sad. They ate dinner, drove to work, went on vacations."

"I didn't mean . . ." Lucy started to say.

"You can be sure when those three poor people were alive they never thought they'd end up in a morgue with twenty rookies and some kid like you staring at their naked, opened-up bodies," I went on. "Would you want them to hear what you just said?"

Lucy's eyes brightened with tears. She swallowed hard and looked away.

"I'm sorry, Aunt Kay," she quietly replied.

"Because it's always been my belief you ought to imagine the dead listening when you speak. Maybe they hear those sophomoric jokes and asides. For sure, *we* hear them. What does it do to you when you hear yourself say them or hear someone else say them?"

"Aunt Kay . . ."

"I'll tell you what it does to you," I said with simmering fury. "You end up just like this."

I threw my hand out as if introducing the world to her, as she looked on, stunned.

"You end up doing just what I'm doing right now," I said. "Standing on a driveway as the sun comes up. Imagining someone you love in a fucking morgue. Imagine people making fun of him, joking, making comments about the size of his penis or how much he stinks. Maybe they banged him around a little too hard on the table. Maybe halfway into the goddamn job they threw a towel over his empty chest cavity and went to lunch. And maybe cops wandering in and out on other cases made comments about *crispy critters* or being *burned by a snitch* or *FBI flambé.*"

Lucy and Jo were staring at me in astonishment.

"Don't think I haven't heard it all," I said, unlocking my car door and yanking it open. "A life passing through indifferent hands and cold air and water. Everything so cold, cold, cold. Even if he had died in bed, it's all so cold in the end. So don't you talk to me about autopsies."

I slid behind the wheel.

"Don't you ever wave an attitude around me, Lucy." I couldn't seem to stop.

My voice seemed to be coming from another room. It even occurred to me that I was losing my mind. Wasn't this what happened when people went insane? They stood outside themselves and watched themselves do things that really weren't them, like killing someone or walking off a window ledge.

"These things ring your head like a bell forever," I said. "Slamming their ugly clapper against the sides of your skull. It isn't true that words will never hurt you. Because yours just hurt the hell out of me," I said to my niece. "Go back to Miami."

Lucy was paralyzed as I jammed my car into drive and sped off, a back tire bumping over the granite border. I caught her and Jo in my rearview mirror. They were saying something to each other, and then getting inside their rental car. My hands shook so badly I couldn't light a cigarette until I was stopped in traffic.

I didn't let Lucy and Jo catch up with me. I turned off on the Ninth Street exit and imagined them flying by toward I-64, heading to the airport, back to their lives of undercover crime.

"Goddamn you," I muttered to my niece.

My heart slammed against me, as if trying to break free.

"Goddamn you, Lucy." I wept.

10

The new building where I worked was the eye of a fierce storm of development I never could have imagined when I moved into it in the seventies. I remembered feeling rather betrayed when I charged in from Miami just as Richmond's businesses decided to charge out to neighboring counties and malls. People stopped shopping and dining downtown, especially at night.

The city's historic character turned victim to neglect and crime until the mid-nineties, when Virginia Commonwealth University began to reclaim and revitalize what had been relegated to ruin. It seemed that handsome buildings began springing up almost overnight, all of similar brick and glass design. My office and morgue shared space with the labs and the recently established Virginia Institute of Forensic Science and Medicine, which was the first training academy of its type in the country, if not the world.

I even had a choice parking space near the lobby door, where I sat in my car this moment gathering my belongings and my spinning thoughts. I had childishly turned off my car phone so Lucy couldn't get hold of me after I'd sped off. I turned it on now, hoping it would ring. I stared at it. The last time I had acted like this was after Benton and I had our worst fight and I ordered him to leave my house and never come back. I unplugged my phones, only to plug them back in an hour later and panic when he didn't call.

I looked at my watch. Lucy would be boarding her flight in less than an hour. I considered calling USAir and having her paged. I was shocked and humiliated by the way I had behaved. I felt powerless because I couldn't apologize to some-one named Terry Davis who didn't have an Aunt Kay or an accessible phone number and lived somewhere in South Beach.

I looked pretty rough when I walked into the glass-block and terrazzo lobby. Jake, who worked the security desk, noticed right away.

"Good morning, Dr. Scarpetta," he said with his usual nervous eyes and hands. "You don't look like you're feeling so hot."

"Good morning, Jake," I replied. "How are you?"

"Same-o, same-o. Except the weather's supposed to start turning real fast and get nasty, and I could do without that."

He was clicking a pen open and shut.

"Can't seem to get rid of this pain in my back, Dr. Scarpetta. It's right between my shoulder blades."

He rolled his shoulders and neck.

"Sort of pinches like something's caught back there. Happened after I was lifting weights the other day. What do you think I should do? Or do I need to write you?"

I thought he was trying to be funny, but he wasn't smiling.

"Moist heat. Lay off the weights for a while," I said.

"Hey, thanks. How much you charge?"

"You can't afford me, Jake."

76

He grinned. I swiped my computer card over the electronic lock on the door outside my office door and the lock clicked free. I could hear my clerks, Cleta and Polly, talking and typing. The phones were already ringing and it wasn't even seven-thirty yet.

". . . It's really, really bad."

"You think people from other countries smell different when they decompose?"

"Come on, Polly. How stupid is that?"

They were tucked inside their gray cubicles, sifting through autopsy photographs and entering data into computers, cursors jumping field to field.

"Better get some coffee while you can," Cleta greeted me with a judgmental look on her face.

"If that ain't the truth." Polly smacked the return key.

"I heard," I said.

"Well, I'm keeping my mouth shut," said Polly, who couldn't if she tried.

Cleta made a zipping motion across her lips without missing a keystroke.

"Where is everyone?"

"In the morgue," Cleta told me. "We've got eight cases today."

"You've lost a lot of weight, Cleta," I said, collecting death certificates from my inner-office mailbox.

"Twelve and a half pounds," she exclaimed as she dealt gory photographs like playing cards, arranging them by case numbers. "Thank you for noticing. I'm glad somebody 'round here does."

"Damn," I said, glancing at the death certificate on top of my stack. "You think we might ever convince Dr. Carmichael that 'cardiac arrest' is not a cause of death?

77

Everyone's heart stops when he dies. The question is *why* did it stop. Well, that one gets amended."

I flipped through more certificates as I followed the long teal- and plum-carpeted hallway to my corner office. Rose worked in an open space with plenty of windows, and it wasn't possible to reach my door without entering her airspace. She was standing before an open filing cabinet drawer, fingers impatiently fluttering through labeled tabs.

"How are you?" she asked around a pen clamped in her mouth. "Marino's looking for you."

"Rose, we need to get Dr. Carmichael on the line."

"Again?"

"'Fraid so."

"He needs to retire."

My secretary had been saying this for years. She pushed the drawer shut and pulled open another one.

"Why is Marino looking for me? Did he call me from home?"

She took the pen out of her mouth.

"He's here. Or was. Dr Scarpetta, do you remember that letter you got last month from that hateful woman?"

"Which hateful woman?" I asked, looking up and down the hallway for Marino and seeing no sign of him.

"The one in prison for murdering her husband right after she took out a million-dollar life insurance policy on him."

"Oh, that one," I said.

I slipped off my suit jacket as I walked into my office and set my briefcase on the floor.

"Why is Marino looking for me?" I asked again.

Rose didn't answer. I had noticed she was getting hard of hearing, and every reminder of her encroaching frailties frightened me. I put the death certificates on top of a stack of about a hundred others I hadn't gotten around to reviewing yet and draped my suit jacket over my chair.

"Point is," Rose loudly said, "she's since sent you another letter. This time accusing you of racketeering."

I retrieved my lab coat from the back of the door.

"She claims you conspired with the insurance company and changed her husband's manner of death from accident to homicide so they wouldn't have to pay out the money. And for this you got quite a large kickback, which is—according to her—how you can afford your Mercedes and expensive suits."

I threw my lab coat over my shoulders and pushed my arms through the sleeves.

"You know, I can't keep up with the crazies anymore, Dr. Scarpetta. Some of them really frighten me, and I think the Internet is making all of it worse."

Rose peeked around the doorway.

"You aren't listening to a word I'm saying," she said.

"I get suits on sale," I replied. "And you blame everything on the Internet."

I probably wouldn't bother shopping for clothes at all if Rose didn't force me out the door every now and then when stores were clearing out last season's styles. I hated shopping, unless it was for good wine or food. I hated crowds. I hated malls. Rose hated the Internet and believed the world would end one day because of it. I'd had to force her to use e-mail.

"If Lucy calls, will you make sure I get it no matter where I am?" I said as Marino walked into Rose's office. "And try her field office, too. You can patch her through."

The thought of Lucy knotted my stomach. I'd lost my temper and hurled words at her I didn't mean. Rose glanced at me. Somehow she knew.

"Captain," she said to Marino, "you look mighty spiffy this morning."

Marino grunted. Glass rattled as he opened a jar of lemon drops on her desk and helped himself.

"What do you want me to do with this crazy lady's letter?" Rose peered through the open doorway at me, reading glasses perched on her nose as she dug through another drawer.

"I think it's time we forward the lady's file—if you ever find it—to the A.G.'s office," I said. "In case she sues. Which will probably be next. Good morning, Marino."

"You still talking about that nutcake I locked up?" he asked, sucking candy.

"That's right," I remembered. "That nutcake was one of your cases."

"So I guess I'll get sued, too."

"Probably," I muttered as I stood at my desk, shuffling through yesterday's telephone messages. "Why does everybody call when I'm not here?"

"I'm kinda getting into being sued," Marino said. "Makes me feel special."

"I just can't get used to you in uniform, Captain Marino," Rose said. "Should I salute?"

"Don't turn me on, Rose."

"I thought your shift didn't start until three," I said.

"Nice thing about me being sued is the city's gotta pay. Ha. Ha. Screw 'em."

"We'll see how *Ha Ha* it is when you end up paying one of these days and lose your truck and aboveground swimming pool. Or all those Christmas decorations and extra fuse boxes, God forbid," Rose told him as I opened and shut my desk drawers.

"Has anybody seen my pens?" I asked. "I don't have a

80

single goddamn pen. Rose? Those Pilot rolling ball pens. I had at least a box of them on Friday. I know I did because I bought them myself last time I was at Ukrops. And I don't believe it. My Waterman's missing, too!"

"Don't say I didn't warn you about leaving anything valuable around here," Rose told me.

"I gotta smoke," Marino said to me. "I've had it with these damn smoke-free buildings. All these dead people in your joint and the state's worried about smoking. What about all those formalin fumes? A few good whiffs of that will drop a horse."

"Damn!" I shoved one drawer shut and yanked open another. "And guess what else? No Advil, no BC powders and no Sudafed. Now I'm really getting angry."

"Coffee money, Cleta's portable phone, lunches, and now your pens and aspirin. I've gotten to where I take my pocket-book everywhere I go. The office's started calling whoever it is 'The Body Snatcher,'" Rose angrily said. "Which I don't think is funny in the least."

Marino walked over and put his arm around her.

"Sweetheart, you can't blame a guy for wanting to snatch your body," he sweetly said in her ear. "I've been wanting to ever since I first laid eyes on you way back when I had to teach the doc everything she knows."

Rose demurely pecked his cheek and leaned her head against his shoulder. She looked defeated and suddenly very old.

"I'm tired, Captain," Rose muttered.

"Me too, sweetheart. Me, too."

I looked at my watch.

"Rose, please tell everyone staff conference's going to be a few minutes late. Marino, let's talk."

The smoking room was a corner in the bay where there were two chairs, a Coke machine and a dirty, dented ashcan that Marino and I put between us. Both of us lit up, and I felt the same old bite of shame.

"Why are you here?" I asked. "Didn't you cause enough problems for yourself yesterday?"

"I was thinking about what Lucy said last night," Marino said. "About my current situation, you know. How it's like I'm hitting the bricks, out of service, finished, Doc. I can't take it, if you want to know the truth. I'm a detective. I've been one almost all my life. I can't do this uniform shit. I can't work for assholes like Diane 'Donkey' Bray."

"That's why you took the field investigation exam last year," I reminded him. "You don't have to stay with the police department, Marino. Not with *any* police department. You've got more than enough years in to retire. You can make your own rules."

"No offense, Doc, but I don't want to work for you, either," he said. "Not part-time or on a case basis or whatever."

The state had given me two slots for field investigators, and I had not filled either one of them yet.

"The point is, you have options," I replied, touched by hurt I would not show.

He was silent. Benton walked into my mind and I saw his feelings in his eyes, and then he was gone. I felt the cooling shadow of Rose and feared the loss of Lucy. I thought of getting old and people vanishing from my life.

"Don't quit on me, Marino," I told him.

He didn't answer me right away, and when he did, his eyes blazed.

"Fuck 'em all, Doc," he said. "No one's telling me what to do. If I want to work a case, I'll goddamn work it."

He tapped an ash and seemed very pleased with himself.

"I don't want you fired or demoted," I said.

"They can't demote me no lower than I am," he said with another lightning bolt of anger. "They can't make me less than a captain, and there's no assignment worse than I got. And let 'em fire me. But guess what? They won't. And you want to know why? Because I could go to Henrico, Chesterfield, Hanover, you name it. You don't know how many times I've been asked to take over investigations in other departments."

I remembered the cigarette in my hand.

"A few of 'em have even wanted me to be chief." He hobbled further along his Pollyanna path.

"Don't fool yourself," I said as menthol made its hit. "Oh, God, I can't believe I'm doing this again."

"I'm not trying to fool anyone," he said, and I could feel his depression moving in like a low-pressure front. "It's like I'm on the wrong planet. I don't know the Brays and Andersons of the world. Who are these women?"

"Power gluttons."

"You're powerful. You're a hell of a lot more powerful than them or anybody I ever met, including most men, and you aren't like that."

"I don't feel very powerful these days. I couldn't even control my temper this morning on my own driveway in front of my niece and her girlfriend and probably a few neighbors." I blew out smoke. "And I feel sick about it."

Marino leaned forward in his chair. "You and me are the only two people who give a flying fuck about that rotting body in there."

He jerked his thumb toward the door leading into the morgue.

"I bet Anderson don't even show up this morning," he

went on. "One thing's for damn sure, she ain't gonna hang around watching you post him."

The look on his face sent my heart out of rhythm. Marino was desperate. What he had done all his life was really all he had left, except for an ex-wife and an estranged son named Rocky. Marino was trapped in an abused body that most assuredly was going to pay him back one of these days. He had no money and awful taste in women. He was politically incorrect, slovenly and foul-mouthed.

"Well, you're right about one thing," I said. "You shouldn't be in uniform. In fact, you're rather much a disgrace to the department. What's that on your shirt anyway? Mustard again? Your tie's too short. Let me see your socks."

I bent over and peeked under the cuffs of his uniform pants.

"They don't match. One black, one navy," I said.

"Don't let me get you into trouble, Doc."

"I'm already in trouble, Marino," I said.

11

One of the more heartless aspects of my work was that unknown remains became "The Torso" or "The Trunk Lady" or "The Superman Man." They were appellations that robbed the person of his identity and all he'd been or done on earth as surely as his death had.

I considered it a painful personal defeat when I could not bring about the identification of someone who came under my care. I packed bones in bankers' boxes and stored them in the skeleton closet, in hopes they might tell me who they were someday. I kept intact bodies or their parts in freezers for months and years, and would not give them up to a pauper's grave until there was no more hope or space. We didn't have room enough to keep anyone forever.

This morning's case had been christened "The Container Man." He was in very grim shape, and I hoped I would not have to hold him long. When decomposition was this advanced, even refrigeration couldn't stop it.

"Sometimes I don't know how you stand it," Marino grumbled.

We were in the changing room next to the morgue, and

no locked door or concrete wall could completely block the smell.

"You don't have to be here," I reminded him.

"I wouldn't miss it for the world."

We suited up in double gowns, gloves, sleeve protectors, shoe covers, surgical caps and masks with shields. We didn't have air packs because I didn't believe in them, and I'd better never catch one of my doctors sneaking Vicks up his nose, although cops did it all the time. If a medical examiner can't handle the unpleasantries of the job, he should do something else.

More to the point, odors are important. They have their own story to tell. A sweet smell might point at ethchlorvynol, while chloral hydrate smells like pears. Both might make me wonder about an overdose of hypnotics, while a hint of garlic might point at arsenic. Phenols and nitrobenzene bring to mind ether and shoe polish respectively, and ethylene glycol smells exactly like antifreeze because that's exactly what it is. Isolating potentially significant smells from the awful stench of dirty bodies and rotting flesh is rather much like archaeology. You focus on what you are there to find and not on the miserable conditions around it.

The decomposed room, as we called it, was a miniature version of the autopsy suite. It had its own cooler and ventilation system and a single table I could roll up and attach to a big sink. Everything, including cabinets and doors, was stainless steel. Walls and the floors were coated with a non-absorbent acrylic that could withstand the most brutal washes with disinfectants and bleach. Automatic doors were opened by steel buttons that were big enough to push with elbows instead of hands.

When the doors slid shut behind Marino and me, I was

startled to find Anderson leaning against a countertop, the
gurney bearing the pouched body parked in the middle of
the floor. The body is evidence. I never left an investigator
alone with an unexamined body, certainly not since the badly
botched O. J. Simpson trial, when it became the vogue for
everyone except the defendant to be impeached in court.

"What are you doing here and where's Chuck?" I asked
Anderson.

Chuck Ruffin was my morgue supervisor and should have
been here some time ago inspecting surgical instruments,
labeling test tubes and making sure I had all of the necessary
paperwork.

"He let me in and went off somewhere."

"He let you in here and just left you? How long ago was
that?"

"Maybe twenty minutes ago," Anderson replied.

Her eyes were warily on Marino.

"Do I detect a little Vicks up the nose?" Marino sweetly
inquired.

The petroleum jelly shone on Anderson's upper lip.

"See that industrial-size deodorizer up there?" Marino
nodded his head to the special ventilation system in the
ceiling. "Guess what, Anderson? It ain't gonna do a goddamn
bit of good when this bag's unzipped."

"I'm not planning on staying," she replied.

That was obvious. She hadn't even put on a pair of surgical
gloves.

"You shouldn't be in here at all without protective wear,"
I said to her.

"I just wanted to let you know I'll be out talking to
witnesses and want you to page me when you have information on what happened to him," she said.

"What witnesses? Bray sending you over to Belgium?" Marino asked, his breath fogging up his shield.

I didn't believe for a minute that she had come into this unpleasant place to tell me anything. Anderson had shown up with some agenda other than this case. I looked at the dark red body pouch to see if it might have been disturbed in any way, as cool fingers of paranoia touched my brain. I glanced up at the clock on the wall. It was almost nine.

"Call me," Anderson said to me as if it were an order.

The doors sucked shut in her wake. I picked up the intercom phone and buzzed Rose.

"Where the hell's Chuck?" I asked.

"God only knows," Rose said, making no attempt to hide the disdain she felt for the young man:

"Please find him and tell him to get here *now*," I said. "He's making me crazy. And make a note of this phone call, as usual. Document everything."

"I always do."

"I'm going to fire him one of these days," I said to Marino when I hung up. "As soon as I get enough on him. He's lazy and completely irresponsible, and he didn't used to be."

"He's *more* lazy and irresponsible than he used to be," Marino replied. "That guy ain't connecting the dots right, Doc. He's up to something, and just so you know, he's been trying to get on with the police department."

"Good," I said. "You guys can have him."

"One of these wannabes who jacks off over uniforms, guns and flashing lights," he said as I began to unzip the pouch.

Marino's voice was losing its bluster. He was doing his best to be stoical.

"You all right?" I asked.

"Oh, yeah."

The stench slammed into us like a storm front.

"Shit!" he complained as I opened the sheets shrouding the body. "Goddamn-fucking-son-of-a-bitch!"

There were times when a body was in such horrific shape it became a surreal miasma of unnatural colors and textures and odors that could distort and disorient and drop someone to the floor. Marino fled to the counter, getting as far away from the gurney as he could, and it was all I could do not to laugh.

He looked perfectly ridiculous in surgical garb. When he wore shoe covers he tended to skate across the floor, and because the cap couldn't get much of a purchase on his balding head, it tended to pucker up like a cupcake paper. I gave him another fifteen minutes before he snatched it off as he always did.

"He can't help the condition he's in," I reminded Marino. He was busy stuffing a Vicks inhaler up each nostril.

"Now that's a little hypocritical," I commented as the doors slid open again and Chuck Ruffin walked in with X rays.

"It's not a good idea to escort someone in here and just disappear," I let Ruffin know with far more reserve than I felt. "Especially a rookie detective."

"I didn't know she was a rookie," Ruffin replied.

"Whad'd you think she was?" Marino said. "She's never been down here before and looks about thirteen."

"Damn sure is flat-chested. Not the way I like 'em, let me tell you." Ruffin's words swaggered. "Lesbo alert! RWIRR-RWIRR-RWIRR!" He imitated a siren, flashing his hands like emergency lights.

"We don't leave unauthorized people alone with unexamined bodies. That includes cops. Experienced or not." I wanted to fire him on the spot.

"I know." He tried to be cute. "O. J. and the planted leather glove again."

Ruffin was a tall, slender young man with sleepy brown eyes and undisciplined blond hair that seemed to grow in many different directions, giving him a tousled, just-out-of-bed look that women seemed to find irresistible. He could not charm me and no longer tried.

"What time did Detective Anderson show up this morning?" I asked him.

His answer was to go around flipping on light boxes. They glowed blankly along the upper walls.

"Sorry I'm late. I was on the phone. My wife's sick," he went on.

He had used his wife as an excuse so many times by now that she was chronically ill or a hypochondriac, had Munchausen syndrome, or was almost dead.

"I guess Rene decided not to stay . . ." he said, referring to Anderson.

"*Rene?*" Marino interrupted him. "Didn't know the two of you was close."

Ruffin began slipping films out of their big manila envelopes.

"Chuck, what time did Anderson get here?" I tried again.

"To be exact?" He thought for a moment. "I guess she got here about quarter after."

"After eight," I said.

"Yup."

"And you let her in the morgue when you knew everybody would be in staff meeting?" I said as he slapped films on the light boxes. "When you knew the morgue would be deserted. Paperwork, personal effects and bodies all over the place."

90

"She'd never seen all of it, so I gave her the quick tour . . ." He talked on. "Plus, I was here. Trying to catch up on counting pills."

He referred to the endless supply of prescription drugs that came in with most of our cases. Ruffin had the tedious chore of counting pills and disposing of them down the sink.

"Wow, look at that," he said.

X rays of different angles of the skull showed metal sutures in the left side of the jaw. They were as vivid as the stitches in a baseball.

"The Container Man's got a busted jaw," Ruffin said. "That right there's enough to I.D. him, isn't it, Dr Scarpetta?"

"If we can ever get hold of his old films," I replied.

"That's always the big *if*," Ruffin said, and he was doing all he could to distract me because he knew he was in trouble.

I scanned the radio-opaque shadows and shapes of sinus and bone and saw no other fractures, no deformities or oddities. However, when I cleaned off the teeth, there was an accessory cusp of the Carabelli. All molars have four cusps, or protrusions. This one had had five.

"What's a Carabelli?" Marino wanted to know.

"Some person. I don't know who." I pointed out the tooth in question. "Upper maxilla. Lingual and mesial or towards the tongue and forward."

"I guess that's good," Marino said. "Not that I have a friggin' clue what you just said."

"An unusual feature," I said. "Not to mention his sinus configuration, fractured jaw. We got enough to I.D. him about half a dozen times if we find something premortem for comparison."

"We say that all the time, Doc," Marino reminded me.

"Hell, you've had people in here with glass eyes, artificial legs, plates in their heads, signet rings, braces on their teeth, you name it, and we still never figure out who the hell they are because they're never reported missing. Or maybe they were and the case got lost in space. Or else we couldn't find a single damn X ray or medical record."

"Dental restorations here and here," I said, pointing to several metal fillings that showed up brilliant white on the opaque shapes of two molars. "Looks like he had pretty good dental care. Fingernails neatly trimmed. Let's get him on the table. We need to move along. He's only getting worse."

12

Eyes bulged froglike, and the scalp and beard were sloughing off with the outer layer of darkening skin. His head lolled and he leaked what little fluid was left in him as I grabbed him around the knees and Ruffin got him under the arms. We struggled to lift him onto the portable table as Marino steadied the gurney.

"The whole point of these new tables," I gasped, "is so we don't have to do this!"

Not all removal services and funeral homes had caught on yet. They still clattered in with their stretchers and transferred the body to whatever old gurney they found instead of one of the new autopsy tables that we could roll right up to the sink. So far, my efforts to save our backs hadn't amounted to much.

"Yo, Chuckie-boy," Marino said. "I hear you want to sign on with us."

"Who says?" Ruffin was clearly startled and instantly on the defensive.

The body thudded on stainless steel.

"That's the word on the street," Marino said.

Ruffin didn't reply as he hosed off the gurney. He mopped it dry with a towel, then covered it and a countertop with clean sheets while I took photographs.

"Well, let me just tell you," Marino said, "it ain't all it's cut out to be."

"Chuck," I said. "We need some more Polaroid film."

"Coming up."

"Reality's always a little different," Marino went on in his condescending tone. "It's driving around all night with nothing going on, bored out of your friggin' mind. It's being spat at, cussed, unappreciated, driving piece-of-shit cars while little assholes play politics and kiss ass and get nice offices and play golf with the brass."

Air blew, water drummed and flowed. I sketched the metal sutures and accessory cusp and wished the heaviness inside me would lift. Despite all I knew about how the body worked, I didn't understand—not really—how grief could begin in the brain and spread through the body like a systemic infection, eroding and throbbing, inflaming and numbing, and ultimately destroying careers and families, or in some sad cases, a person's physical life.

"Nice threads," Ruffin was saying. "Ar-man-i. Never seen it up close before."

"His crocodile shoes and belt alone probably cost a thousand dollars," I said.

"No shit?" Marino commented. "That's probably what killed him. His wife buys it for his birthday, he finds out what it cost and has a heart attack. You care if I light up in here, Doc?"

"Yes, I do. What about the temperature in Antwerp when the ship left? Did you ask Shaw about that?"

"Low of forty-nine, high of sixty-eight," Marino answered.

"Same weird warm weather everybody else's been having. May as well spend Christmas with Lucy in Miami if the weather stays like this. Either that or put up a palm tree in my living room."

The mention of Lucy's name squeezed my heart with a hard, cold hand. She had always been difficult and complicated. Very few people knew her, even if they thought they did. Crouched behind her bunker of intelligence, overachievement and risk-taking was a furious, wounded child who went after dragons the rest of us feared. She was terrified of abandonment, imagined or not. Lucy always did the rejecting first.

"You ever notice how most people don't seem to be dressed very nice when they die," Chuck said. "Wonder why that is."

"Look, I'll put on clean gloves and stand in the corner," Marino said. "I need a cigarette bad."

"Except last spring when those kids got killed on their way home from the prom," Chuck went on. "The guy's in this blue tux and comes in with the flower in his lapel."

The waistband of the jeans was wrinkled inside the belt.

"Pants are too big in the waist," I said, sketching it on a form. "Maybe by a size or two. He may have been heavier at some point."

"Hard to tell what the hell size he was," Marino said. "Right now he's got a gut bigger than mine."

"He's full of gas," I said.

"Too bad that's not your excuse." Ruffin was getting bolder.

"Sixty-eight inches and weighs one hundred pounds, meaning, when you consider fluid loss, he was probably one-forty, one-fifty in life," I calculated. "An average-sized man who, as I just said, may have been heavier at some earlier point, based on his clothing. He's got weird hair on his clothes. Six, seven inches long, very pale yellow."

I turned the jeans' left pocket inside out and found more hair and a sterling silver cigar clipper and lighter. I set them on a clean sheet of white paper, careful not to ruin potential fingerprints. In the right pocket were two five-franc coins, an English pound and a lot of folded foreign cash that I was not familiar with.

"No wallet, no passport, no jewelry," I said.

"Definitely looks like robbery," Marino said. "Except for the stuff in his pockets. That doesn't make much sense. You'd think if he was robbed, the person would've taken that, too."

"Chuck, have you called Dr. Boatwright yet?" I asked.

He was one of the odontologists, or forensic dentists, we routinely borrowed from the Medical College of Virginia.

"Just gonna do that."

He peeled off his gloves and went to the phone. I heard him opening drawers and cabinets.

"You seen the phone sheet?" he asked.

"You're the one who's supposed to keep up with things like that," I said testily.

"I'll be right back." Ruffin couldn't wait to disappear somewhere yet one more time.

He trotted off, and Marino followed him with his eyes.

"Dumb as a bag of hammers," he said.

"I don't know what to do about him," I commented. "Because he really isn't dumb, Marino. That's part of the problem."

"You tried asking him what the shit's going on? Like is he having memory lapses, attention disorder or something? Maybe he hit his head on something or's been playing with himself too much."

"I haven't asked him those things specifically."

"Don't forget last month when he lost a bullet down the sink, Doc. Then he acted like it was your fault, which was the bullshit of all time. I mean, I was standing right there."

I was struggling with the dead man's wet, slimy jeans, trying to work them down his hips and thighs.

"You want to give me a hand?" I asked.

We carefully pulled the jeans over the knees and feet. We pulled off black briefs, socks and the T-shirt, and I placed them on the sheet-covered gurney. I examined them carefully for tears or holes or any obvious trace evidence. I noted that the back of the trousers, especially the seat of them, was much dirtier than the front. The backs of the shoes were scuffed.

"Jeans, black briefs and T-shirt are Armani and Versace. The briefs are inside out," I continued taking inventory. "Shoes, belt, socks are Armani. See the dirt and scuffing?" I pointed them out. "Could be consistent with him being dragged from behind, if someone had him under the arms."

"That's what I'm thinking," Marino said.

Some fifteen minutes later, the doors slid open and Ruffin walked in, a phone sheet in hand. He taped it up on a cabinet door.

"I miss anything?" he cheerfully asked.

"We'll take a look at the clothes with the Luma-Lite, then let them dry and trace can do their thing with them," I instructed Ruffin in an unfriendly tone. "Let his other personal effects air-dry, then bag them."

He yanked on gloves.

"Ten-four," he said with an edge.

"Looks like you're already studying to get into the academy." Marino picked on him some more. "Good for you, kid."

13

I lost myself in what I was doing, my mind pulled into a body that was completely autolyzed and putrefied and hardly recognizable as human.

Death had rendered this man defenseless, and bacteria had escaped from the gastrointestinal tract, invading as it pleased, fomenting, fermenting, and filling every space with gas. Bacteria broke down cell walls and turned the blood in veins and arteries a greenish-black, making the entire circulatory system visible through the discolored skin like rivers and tributaries on a map.

Areas of the body that had been covered by clothing were in much better shape than the head and hands.

"God, how would you like to run into him when you're skinny-dipping at night?" Ruffin said, looking at the dead man.

"He can't help it," I said.

"And guess what, Chuckie-boy?" Marino said. "After you die someday, you're gonna look ugly as hell, too."

"Do we know exactly where the container was in the ship's hold?" I asked Marino.

"A couple rows down."

"What about weather conditions during the two weeks it was out at sea?"

"Mostly mild, averaging around sixty with a high of seventy. Merry El Niño. People are doing Christmas shopping in their friggin' shorts."

"So you're thinking maybe this guy died on board and someone stuck him inside the container?" Ruffin asked.

"No, that ain't what I'm thinking, Chuckie-boy."

"The name's Chuck."

"Depends on who's talking to you. So here's the daily double, Chuckie-boy. If you got tons of containers stacked like sardines in a hold, tell me how you sneak a dead body into one," Marino said. "No way you could even open the door. Plus the seal was intact."

I pulled a surgical lamp close and collected fibers and debris, using forceps and a lens, or, in some instances, swabs.

"Chuck, we need to check on how much formalin we've got," I said. "It was low the other day. Or have you already taken care of that?"

"Not yet."

"Don't inhale too many fumes," Marino said. "You can see what it does to all those brains you haul over to MCV."

Formalin was a diluted formaldehyde, a highly reactive chemical used to preserve or "fix" surgical sections or organs, or in anatomical donations, entire bodies. It killed tissue. It was extremely corrosive to respiratory passages, skin and eyes.

"I'll go check out the formalin," Ruffin said.

"Not now you won't," I said. "Not until we're done here."

He pulled off the cap of a permanent marker.

"How about buzzing Cleta to see if Anderson left," I said. "I don't want her wandering around somewhere."

"I'll do it," Marino said.

"I gotta admit, it still blows my mind a little to see chicks chasing after killers." Ruffin directed this at Marino. "Back when you got started, they probably did nothing but check parking meters."

Marino went to the phone.

"Take off your gloves," I called after him, because he always forgot, no matter how many *Clean Hands* signs I posted.

I moved the lens slowly and stopped. The knees looked abraded and dirty, as if he had been kneeling on a rough, dirty surface without his pants on. I checked his elbows. They looked dirty and abraded, too, but it was hard to tell with certainty because his skin was in such bad shape. I dipped a cotton swab in sterile water as Marino hung up the phone. I heard him tear open another pair of gloves.

"Anderson ain't here," he said. "Cleta said she left about a half hour ago."

"So what do you think about women lifting weights?" Ruffin asked Marino. "You see the muscles in Anderson's arms?"

I used a six-inch ruler as a scale and started taking photographs with a thirty-five-millimeter camera and a macro lens. I found more dirty areas on the underside of the arms, and I swabbed them.

"I'm wondering if it was a full moon when the ship left Antwerp," Marino said to me.

"I guess if you want to live in a man's world you gotta be as strong as one," Ruffin went on.

Running water was relentless and steel clanged against steel and overhead lights allowed no shadows.

"Well, it will be a new moon tonight," I said. "Belgium's

in the eastern hemisphere, but the lunar cycle would be the same there."

"So it could have been a full moon," Marino said.

I knew where he was going with this and my silence told him to stay away from the subject of werewolves.

"So what happened, Marino? The two of you arm-wrestle over your job?" Ruffin asked, cutting the twine around a bale of towels.

Marino's eyes were double barrels pointed at him.

"And I guess we know who won since she's the detective now and you're back in uniform," Ruffin said, smirking.

"You talking to me?"

"You heard me." Ruffin slid open a glass cabinet door.

"You know, it must be I'm getting old." Marino snatched off his surgical cap and slammed it into the trash. "My hearing ain't what it used to be. But if I'm not mistaken, I believe you just pissed me off."

"What do you think of those iron women on TV? What about women wrestlers?" Ruffin kept going.

"Shut the fuck up," Marino told him.

"You're single, Marino. Would you go out with a woman like that?"

Ruffin had always resented Marino, and now he had a chance to do something about it, or so he thought, because Ruffin's egocentric world turned on a very weak axis. In his dim way of seeing things, Marino was down and wounded. It was a good time to kick him around.

"Question is, would a woman like that go out with you?" Ruffin didn't have sense enough to run out of the room. "Or would *any* woman go out with you?"

Marino walked up to him. He got so close to Ruffin, they were face shield to face shield.

"I got a few little words of advice for you, asshole," Marino said, fogging up the plastic protecting his dangerous face. "Zip those sissy lips of yours before they kiss my fist. And put that tiny dick back in its holster before you hurt yourself with it."

Chuck's face turned scarlet, all this going on while the doors slid open and Neils Vander walked in carrying ink, a roller and ten print cards.

"Straighten up, and I mean now," I ordered Marino and Ruffin. "Or I'm throwing both of you out of here."

"Good morning," Vander said, as if it were.

"His skin's slipping badly," I told him.

"Just makes it easier."

Vander was the section chief of the fingerprints and impression lab, and wasn't bothered by much. It wasn't uncommon for him to shoo maggots away while he finger-printed decomposed bodies, and he didn't flinch in burn cases when it was necessary to cut off the victim's fingers and carry them upstairs in a jar.

I had known him since the beginning of my time here, and he never seemed to get any older or change at all. He was still bald, tall and gangly and always lost in oversized lab coats that swirled and flapped around him as he hurried up and down halls.

Vander put on a pair of latex gloves and lightly held the dead man's hands, studying them, turning them this way and that.

"Easiest thing's gonna be to slide off the skin," he decided.

When a body was as decomposed as this one, the hand's top layer of skin slips off like a glove and, in fact, is called a glove. Vander worked fast, sliding off the gloves intact from each hand and working his own latex-sheathed hands inside them. Wearing the dead man's hands, in a sense, he inked each finger and rolled it onto a ten-print card. He removed the skin gloves and left them neatly on a surgical tray, then popped off his latex ones, before heading back upstairs.

"Chuck, put those in formalin," I said. "We'll want to save them."

He was sullen, screwing the lid off a plastic quart jar.

"Let's turn him," I said.

Marino helped us flip the body facedown. I found more dirt, mostly on the buttocks, and got swabs of that, too. I saw no injuries, only an area over the right upper back that seemed darker than the skin around it. I looked at it through a lens, staring, blanking out my thought process as I always did when looking for pattern injuries, bite marks or other elusive evidence. It was like scuba diving in water with almost no visibility. All I could make out were shades and shapes and wait until I bumped into something.

"Do you see this, Marino? Or is it just my imagination?" I asked.

He sniffed more Vicks vapors up his nose and leaned against the table. He looked and looked.

"Maybe," he said. "I don't know."

I wiped off the skin with a wet towel, and the outer layer, or epidermis, slipped right off. The flesh beneath, or dermis, looked like soggy brown corrugated paper stained with dark ink.

"A tattoo." I was pretty sure. "The ink penetrated to the dermis, but I can't make out anything. Just a big splotch."

"Like one of those purple birthmarks some people have," Marino offered.

I leaned closer with the lens and adjusted a surgical lamp to its best advantage. Ruffin was obsessively polishing a stainless steel countertop and pouting.

"Let's try UV," I decided.

The multiband ultraviolet lamp was very simple to use and looked rather much like the handheld scanners in airports. We dimmed the lights and I tried longwave UV first, holding the lamp close to the area I was interested in. Nothing fluoresced, but a hint of purple seemed to feather out in a pattern, and I wondered if this might mean we were picking up white ink. Under UV light, anything white, such as the sheet on the nearby gurney, will radiate like snow in moonlight and possibly pick up a blush of violet from the lamp. I slid the selector down and tried shortwave next. I could see no difference between the two.

"Lights," I said.

Ruffin turned them up.

"I would think tattoo ink would light up like neon," Marino said.

"Fluorescent inks do," I replied. "But since high concentrations of iodine and mercury aren't so great for your health, they're not used anymore."

It was past noon when I finally began the autopsy, making the Y incision and removing the breastplate of ribs. I found pretty much what I expected. The organs were soft and friable. They virtually fell apart at the touch and I had to be very careful when weighing and sectioning them. I couldn't tell much about the coronary arteries except that they were not occluded. There was no blood left, only the putrefied fluid called oily effusate that I collected from the pleural cavity. The brain was liquefied.

"Samples of the brain and the effusate go to tox for a STAT alcohol," I said to Ruffin as I worked.

Urine and bile had seeped through the cells of their hollow organs and were gone, and there was nothing left of the stomach. But when I reflected back flesh from the skull, I thought I had my answer. He had staining of the petrous ridge of the temporal bones and mastoid air cells, bilaterally.

Although I couldn't diagnose anything with certainty until all toxicology results were back, I was fairly certain this man had drowned.

"What?" Marino was staring at me.

"See the staining here?" I pointed it out. "Tremendous hemorrhaging, probably while he struggled as he was drowning."

The phone rang and Ruffin trotted over to answer it.

"When's the last time you dealt with Interpol?" I asked Marino.

"Five, maybe six years ago, when that fugitive from Greece ended up over here and got in a fight in a bar off Hull Street."

"There certainly are international connections in this one. And if he's missing in France, England, Belgium or God knows where, if he's some sort of international fugitive, we're never going to know it here in Richmond unless Interpol can link him with someone in their computer system."

"You ever talked to them?" he asked me.

"No. That's for you guys to do."

"You ought to hear all these cops hoping they get a case that involves Interpol, but if you ask 'em what Interpol is, they ain't got a clue," Marino said. "You want to know the truth, I got no interest in dealing with Interpol. They scare me like the CIA. I don't even want people like that knowing I exist."

"That's ridiculous. You know what Interpol means, Marino?"

"Yeah. Secret Squirrels."

"It's a contraction of *international police.* The point is to get police in member countries to work together, talk to each other. Sort of what you wish people in your department would do."

"Then they must not have a Bray working for them."

I was watching Ruffin on the phone. Whomever he was talking to, he was trying to keep it private.

"Telecommunication, a restricted worldwide law enforcement web . . . You know, I don't know how much more I can stand this. He not only counters me, he flaunts it," I muttered, staring at Ruffin as he hung up.

Marino glared at him.

"Interpol circulates color-coded notices for wanted and missing people, warnings, inquiries," I went on in a distracted way as Ruffin stuffed a towel in the back pocket of his scrubs and got a pill counter out of a cabinet.

He sat on a stool in front of a steel sink, his back to me. He opened a brown paper bag marked with a case number and pulled out three bottles of Advil and two bottles of prescription drugs.

"An unidentified body is a black notice," I said. "Usually suspected fugitives with international ties. Chuck, why are you doing that in here?"

"Like I told you, I'm behind on it. Never seen so many damn pills come in with bodies, Dr Scarpetta. I can't keep up anymore. And I get up to sixty or seventy or something, and the phone rings and I lose count and have to start all over again."

"Yeah, Chuckie-boy," Marino said. "I can see why you'd lose count real easy."

Ruffin started whistling.

"What are you so happy about all of a sudden?" Marino

irritably asked, as Ruffin used tweezers to fill rows with pills on the little blue plastic tray.

"We're going to need to get fingerprints, dental charts, anything we can," I said to Marino as I removed a section of deep muscle from the thigh for DNA. "Anything we can get needs to be sent to them," I added.

"Them?" Marino asked.

I was getting exasperated.

"Interpol," I said tersely.

The phone rang again.

"Hey, Marino, can you get that? I'm counting."

"Tough shit," he said to Ruffin.

"Are you listening to me?" I looked up at Marino.

"Yeah," he said. "The state liaison's at State Police Criminal Investigation, used to be some guy who was a first sergeant and I remember asking him if he wanted to have a beer sometime at the F.O.P., or go grab a bite at Chetti's with some of the guys. You know, just being friendly, and he never even changed his tone of voice. I'm pretty sure I was being taped."

I worked on a section of vertebral bone that I would clean with sulfuric acid and have trace check it for microscopic organisms called diatoms that were found in water all over the world.

"Wish I could remember his name," Marino was saying. "So he took all the info, contacted D.C., and D.C. contacted Lyon, where all the secret squirrels are. I hear they got this real spooky-looking building on a hidden road, sort of like Batman and his cave. Electrified fences, razor wire and gates and guards carrying machine guns, the whole nine yards."

"You've watched too much James Bond," I said.

"Not since Sean Connery quit. Movies suck these days, and nothing's good on TV anymore. I don't even know why I bother."

"Maybe you ought to consider reading a book now and then."

"Dr. Scarpetta?" Chuck said, hanging up. "That was Dr Cooper. The STAT alcohol's oh-point-oh-eight in the effusate, and zip-o in the brain."

The 0.08 didn't mean much, since the brain didn't show an alcohol level, too. Perhaps the man was drinking before he died, or maybe what we had was postmortem-generated alcohol caused by bacteria. There were no other fluids for comparison, no urine or blood or fluid of the eye known as vitreous, which was too bad. If 0.08 was a true level, it might, at the very least, show that this man would have been somewhat impaired and therefore more vulnerable.

"How are you going to sign him out?" Marino asked.

"Acute seasickness." Ruffin popped a towel at a fly.

"You know, you're really beginning to get on my nerves," Marino warned him.

"Cause of death undetermined," I said. "Manner, homicide. This isn't some poor dockworker who accidentally got locked inside a container. Chuck, I need a surgical pan. Leave it right here on the counter, and before the day is out, you and I need to talk."

His eyes darted away from me like minnows. I pulled off my gloves and called Rose.

"Would you mind going into archives and finding one of my old cork cutting boards?" I asked her.

OSHA had decided that all cutting boards had to be Teflon-coated because porous ones were susceptible to contamination. That was appropriate if one worked around live patients or was making bread. I complied, but it didn't mean I threw anything away.

"I also need wig pins," I went on. "There should be a little plastic box of them in the right top drawer of my desk. Unless someone stole those, too."

"Not a problem," Rose said.

"I think the boards are on a bottom shelf in the back of storage, next to the boxes of old medical examiner handbooks."

"Anything else?"

"I don't guess Lucy's called," I said.

"Not yet. If she does, I'll find you."

I thought for a minute. It was past one o'clock. She was off the plane by now and could have called. Depression and fear rolled over me again.

"Send flowers to her office," I said. "With a note that says, 'Thanks for the visit, love, Aunt Kay.'"

Silence.

"Are you still there?" I asked my secretary.

"You sure that's what you want to say?" she asked.

I hesitated.

"Tell her I love her and I'm sorry," I said.

14

Ordinarily, I would have used a permanent marker to outline the area of skin I needed to excise from a dead body, but in this case, no marker was going to show up on skin in such bad condition.

I did the best I could with a six-inch plastic ruler, measuring from the right base of the neck to the shoulder, and down to the bottom of the shoulder blade and back up.

"Eight and a half by seven by two by four," I dictated to Ruffin.

Skin is elastic. Once it is excised, it will contract, and it was important when I pinned it to the corkboard that I stretched it back to its original dimensions or any images that might be tattooed on the skin would be distorted.

Marino had left, and my staff was busy in their offices or the autopsy suite. Every now and then the closed-circuit TV showed a car pulling into the bay to bring a body or take one away. Ruffin and I were alone behind the closed steel doors of the decomposed room. I was going to hold him to a conversation.

"If you'd like to go with the police department," I said, "fine."

Glass clacked as he placed clean blood tubes in a rack.

"But if you're going to stay here, Chuck, you're going to have to be present, accountable and respectful."

I retrieved a scalpel and a pair of forceps from the surgical table, and glanced at him. He seemed to be expecting what I said and had already thought about how he was going to reply.

"I may not be perfect, but I'm accountable," he said.

"Not these days. I need more clamps."

"There's a lot going on," he said as he retrieved them from a tray and set them within my reach. "In my personal life, I mean. The wife, the house we bought. You wouldn't believe all the problems with it."

"I'm sorry for your difficulties, but I have an entire state system to run. I frankly don't have time for excuses. If you don't carry your load, we have big problems. Don't make me walk into the morgue and find you haven't set up first. Don't make me look for you one more time."

"We already have big problems," he said as if this were the shot he'd been waiting to fire.

I began the incision.

"You just don't know it," he added.

"Then why don't you tell me what these big problems are, Chuck?" I said. I reflected back the dead man's skin, down to the subcutaneous layer. Ruffin watched me clamp cut edges together to keep the skin taut. I stopped what I was doing and looked across the table at him.

"Go on," I said. "Tell me."

"I don't think it's my place to tell you," Ruffin said, and I saw something in his eyes that unnerved me. "Look, Dr. Scarpetta. I know I haven't been Johnny-on-the spot. I know I've slipped off to go to job interviews and maybe just

111

haven't been accountable like I should be. And I don't get along with Marino. I admit all of it. But I'll tell you what everyone else won't if you promise not to punish me for it."

"I don't punish people for being honest," I said, angry that he would even suggest such a thing.

He shrugged, and I caught a glint of self-satisfaction because he had rattled me and he knew it.

"I don't punish, period," I said. "I simply expect people to do what's right, and if they don't, they punish themselves. If you don't last in this job, it's your fault."

"Maybe I used the wrong word," he replied, moving back to the counter and leaning against it, arms crossed. "I don't express myself as good as you do, that's for sure. I just don't want you to get upset with me for shooting straight with you. Okay?"

I didn't answer him.

"Well, everybody's sorry about what happened last year," he began his opening argument. "No one can imagine how you've dealt with it. Really. I mean, if someone did that to my wife, I don't know what I would do, especially if it was something like what happened to Special Agent Wesley."

Ruffin had always referred to Benton as "special agent," which I'd always thought was rather silly. If anyone had been unpretentious, if not embarrassed by the title, it was Benton. But as I pondered Marino's derisive remarks about Ruffin's infatuation with law enforcement, I gained more understanding. My wispy, weak morgue supervisor had probably been in awe of a veteran FBI agent, especially one who was a psychological profiler, and it occurred to me that Ruffin's good behavior in those earlier days might have had more to do with Benton than me.

"It affected all of us, too," Ruffin was saying. "He used to come down here, you know, and order deli trays, pizza, joke around with us and shoot the breeze. A big, important guy like him not having any kind of attitude. It blew my mind."

The pieces of Ruffin's past slipped into place, too. His father had died in an automobile accident when Ruffin was a child. He had been raised by his mother, a formidable, intelligent woman who taught school. His wife was very strong, too, and now he worked for me. I always found it fascinating that so many people returned to the scenes of their childhood crimes, repeatedly seeking out the same villain, which in this case was a female authority figure like me.

"Everybody's been treating you like we're walking on eggshells," Ruffin kept on making his case. "So no one's said anything when you don't pay attention, and all kinds of things are going on that you don't have a clue about."

"Like what?" I asked as I carefully turned a corner with the scalpel.

"Well, for one thing, we got a damn thief in the building," he retorted. "And I'm betting it's someone on our staff. It's been going on for weeks and you haven't done a thing about it."

"I didn't know about it until recently."

"Proving my point."

"That's ridiculous. Rose doesn't withhold information from me," I said.

"People treat her with kid gloves, too. Face it, Dr Scarpetta. To the office, she's your snitch. People don't confide in her."

I willed myself to concentrate as his words stung my feelings and my pride. I continued reflecting back tissue, careful not to buttonhole it or cut through it. Ruffin waited for my reaction. I met his eyes.

"I don't have a snitch," I said. "I don't need one. Every member of my staff has always known he can come into my office and discuss anything with me."

His silence seemed a gloating indictment. He continued his defiant, smug pose, enjoying this immensely. I rested my wrists on the steel table.

"I don't think it's going to be necessary to plead my case to anyone, Chuck," I said. "I think you're the only one on my staff who has a problem with me. Of course, I can understand why you might feel at odds with a woman boss when it appears that all of the power figures in your life have been women."

The gleam in his eyes blinked out at the touch of his switch. Then anger hardened his face. I resumed reflecting back slippery, fragile tissue.

"But I appreciate your expressing your thoughts," I said in a cool, calm way.

"It's not just my thoughts," he replied, rudely. "Fact is, everyone thinks you're on your way out."

"I'm glad you seem to know what everybody thinks," I replied without showing the fury I felt.

"It's not hard. I'm not the only one who's noticed how you don't do things the way you used to. And you know you don't. You've got to admit that."

"Tell me what I should admit."

He seemed to have a list all ready.

"Out-of-character things. Like working yourself into the ground and going to scenes you don't need to, so you're tired all the time and don't notice what's going on in the office. And then upset people call and you don't take time to talk to them like you used to."

"What upset people?" My self-control was about to snap.

"I always talk to families, to anyone who asks, as long as the individual has a right to the information."

"Maybe you should check with Dr. Fielding and ask him how many of your calls he's taken, how many families of your cases he's dealt with, how much he's covered up for you. And then your thing on the Internet. That's what's really gone too far. It's sort of the last straw."

I was baffled.

"What *thing* on the Internet?" I demanded.

"Your chats or whatever it is you do. To be honest, since I don't have a home computer and don't use AOL or anything, I haven't seen it for myself."

Bizarre, angry thoughts flew through my mind like a thousand starlings and overshadowed every perception I'd ever had about my life. A myriad of ugly, dark thoughts clung to my reason and dug in with their claws.

"I didn't mean to make you feel bad," Chuck said. "And I hope you know I understand how everything could get like this. After what you've been through."

I didn't want to hear another goddamn word about what I'd been through.

"Thank you for your understanding, Chuck," I said, my eyes piercing his until he looked away.

"We've got that case coming in from Powhatan, and it should have been here by now, if you want me to check on it," he said, anxious to leave the room.

"Do that, and then get this body back in the fridge."

"Sure thing," he said.

The doors shut behind him, returning silence to the room. I reflected back the last of the tissue and placed it on the cutting board as frigid paranoia and self-doubt seeped under the heavy door of my self-confidence. I began anchoring the tissue with hatpins, stretching it and measuring and stretching. I set the corkboard inside the surgical pan and covered it with a green cloth and placed it inside the refrigerator.

I showered and changed in the locker room, and cleared my thoughts of phobias and indignation. I took a long enough break to drink a cup of coffee; it was so old, the bottom of the pot was black. I started a new coffee fund by giving my office administrator twenty dollars.

"Jean, have you been reading these chat sessions that I'm supposedly having on the Internet?" I asked her.

She shook her head but looked uncomfortable. I tried Cleta and Polly next and asked the same question.

Blood rose to Cleta's cheeks, and with eyes cast down she said, "Sometimes."

"Polly?" I asked.

She stopped typing and also blushed.

"Not all the time," she replied.

I nodded.

"It's not me," I told them. "Someone is impersonating me. I wish I'd known about it before now."

Both of my clerks looked confused. I wasn't sure they believed me.

"I can certainly understand why you didn't want to say anything to me when you became aware of these so-called chat sessions," I went on. "I probably wouldn't have either if the roles were reversed. But I need your help. If you have any ideas about who might be doing this, will you tell me?"

They looked relieved.

"That's awful," Cleta said with feeling. "Whoever's doing that ought to go to jail."

"I'm sorry I didn't say anything," Polly contritely added.

"I don't have any idea about who would do something like that."

"I mean it sort of sounds like you when you read it. That's the problem," Cleta added.

"Sort of sounds like me?" I said, frowning.

"You know, it gives advice about accident prevention, security, how to deal with grief and all sorts of medical things."

"You're saying it sounds like a doctor is writing it, or someone trained in health care?" I asked as my incredulity grew.

"Well, whoever it is seems to know what he's talking about," Cleta replied. "But it's more conversational. Not like reading an autopsy report or anything like that."

"I don't think it sounds much like her," Polly said. "Now that I think about it."

I noticed a case file on her desk that was open to color computer-generated autopsy photographs of a man whose shotgun-blasted head looked like a gory eggcup. I recognized him as the murder victim whose wife had been writing me from prison, accusing me of everything from incompetence to racketeering.

"What's this?" I asked her.

"Apparently, the *Times-Dispatch* and the A.G.'s office have heard from that crazy woman, and Ira Herbert called here a little while ago, asking about it," she told me.

Herbert was the police reporter for the local newspaper. If he was calling, that probably meant I was being sued.

"And then Harriet Cummins called Rose to get a copy of his records," Cleta explained. "It appears his psycho wife's latest story is he put the shotgun in his mouth and pulled the trigger with his toe."

"The poor man was wearing army boots," I replied. "He couldn't possibly have pulled the trigger with his toe, and he was shot at close range in the back of the head."

"I don't know what it is with people anymore," Polly said with a sigh. "All they do is lie and cheat, and if they get locked up, they just sit around and stir up trouble and file lawsuits. It makes me sick."

"Me, too," Cleta agreed.

"Do you know where Dr. Fielding is?" I asked both of them.

"I saw him wandering around a little while ago," Polly said.

I found him in the medical library thumbing through *Nutrition in Exercise and Sport.* He smiled when he saw me, but looked tired and a little out of sorts.

"Not eating enough carbos," he said, tapping a page with his index finger. "I keep telling myself if I don't get fifty-five to seventy percent of my diet in carbos, I get glycogen depletion. I haven't had much energy lately . . ."

"Jack." My tone cut him off. "I need you to be as honest as you've ever been with me."

I shut the library door. I told him what Ruffin had said, and a glint of painful recognition showed in my deputy chief's face. He pulled out a chair and sat down at a table. He closed his book. I sat next to him and we turned our chairs facing each other.

"Something's been going around about Secretary Wagner getting rid of you," he said. "I think it's bullshit and I'm sorry you even heard about it. Chuck's an idiot."

Sinclair Wagner was the Secretary of Health and Human Services, and only he or the governor could appoint or fire the chief medical examiner.

"When did you start hearing these rumors?" I asked.

"Recently. Weeks ago."

"Fired for what reason?" I quizzed him.

"Supposedly, you two aren't getting along."

"That's ridiculous!"

"Or he's not happy with you or something, and consequently, the governor isn't, either."

"Jack, please be more specific."

He hesitated and shifted uncomfortably in his chair. He looked guilty, as if my problems were somehow his fault.

"Okay, to lay it all out, Dr. Scarpetta," he said, "the word is that you've embarrassed Wagner with this chat stuff you're doing on the Internet."

I leaned closer to him and put my hand on his arm.

"It's not me doing it," I promised him. "It's someone impersonating me."

He gave me a puzzled look.

"You're kidding," he said.

"Oh, no. There's nothing funny about any of this."

"Jesus Christ," he said with disgust. "Sometimes I think the Internet's the worst thing that's ever happened to us."

"Jack, why didn't you just ask me about it? If you thought I was doing something as inappropriate . . . well, have I somehow managed to estrange everybody in this office so nobody feels he can tell me anything anymore?"

"It's not that," he said. "It's not a reflection of people not caring or feeling estranged. If anything, we care so much I guess we got overprotective."

"Protecting me from what?" I wanted to know.

"Everyone should be allowed to grieve and even sit it out on the bench for a while," he quietly replied. "No one's expected you to function on all cylinders. I sure as hell wouldn't be. Christ, I barely made it through my divorce."

"I'm not sitting it out on the bench, Jack. And I'm functioning on all cylinders. My private, personal grief is just that."

He looked at me for a long moment, holding my gaze and not buying what I'd just said.

"I wish it were that easy," he said.

"I never said it was easy. Getting up some mornings is the hardest thing I've ever done. But I can't let my own problems interfere with what I'm doing here, and I don't."

"Frankly, I haven't known what to do, and I feel really bad about it," he confessed. "I haven't known how to handle his death, either. I know how much you loved him. Over and over it's gone through my mind to take you out to dinner or ask if there's anything I can fix or do around your house. But I've had my own problems, too, as you know. And I guess I didn't feel there was anything I could offer you except carrying as much of the load here as I can."

"Have you been covering calls for me? When families have needed to get me on the phone?" I was out with it.

"It's not been a problem," he said. "It's the least I can do."

"Good God," I said, bending my head and running my fingers through my hair. "I don't believe this."

"I was just doing . . ."

"Jack," I interrupted him, "I've been here every day except when I'm in court. Why would any of my calls be deflected to you? This is something I know nothing about."

Now it was Fielding's turn to look confused.

"Don't you realize how despicable it would be for me to refuse to talk to bewildered, grieving people?" I went on. "For me not to answer their questions or even seem to care?"

"I just thought . . ."

"This is crazy!" I exclaimed, and my stomach was a tight fist. "If I were like that, I wouldn't deserve to do this work. If I ever become like that, I should quit! Of all people, how could I not care about another person's loss? How could I not feel and understand and do everything I could to answer the questions, lessen the pain and fight to send the bastard who did it to the fucking electric chair?"

I was near tears. My voice shook.

"Or lethal injection. Shit, I think we should go back to hanging assholes in the public square," I declared.

Fielding glanced toward the shut door as if he were afraid someone might hear me. I took a deep breath and steadied myself.

"How many times has this happened?" I asked him. "How many times have you taken my calls?"

"A lot lately," he reluctantly told me.

"How many is a lot?"

"Probably almost every other case you've done in the last couple months."

"That can't be right," I retorted.

He was silent, and as I thought about it, doubts crowded my mind again. Families hadn't seemed to be calling me as much as they used to, but I hadn't paid much attention because there was never a pattern, never a way to predict. Some relatives wanted every detail. Others called to vent their rage. Some people went into denial and wanted to know nothing.

"Then I can assume there have been complaints about me," I said. "Grieving, upset people thinking I'm arrogant and cold-blooded. And I don't blame them."

"Some have complained."

I could tell by his face that there had been more than just a few complaints. I had no doubt that letters had been written to the governor, too.

"Who's been rolling these calls over to you?" I asked matter-of-factly and quietly because I was afraid I might roar like a tornado down the hall and swear at everyone once I left this room.

"Dr. Scarpetta, it didn't seem unusual that you wouldn't want to talk about some things to traumatized people right now," he tried to make me understand. "Some painful things that might remind you . . . it made sense to me. Most of these people just want a voice, a doctor, and if I've not been around, either Jill or Bennett has," he said, referring to two of my resident doctors. "I guess the only big problem is when none of us has been available and somehow Dan or Amy have ended up with the calls."

Dan Chong and Amy Forbes were rotating medical students here to learn and observe. Never in a million years should they have been put in a position to talk to families.

"Oh, no," I said, closing my eyes at the nightmarish thought.

"Mainly after hours. That damn answering service," he said.

"Who's been rolling the telephone calls over to you?" I asked him again, this time more firmly.

He sighed. Fielding looked as grim and as worried as he'd ever been.

"Tell me," I insisted.

"Rose," he said.

15

Rose was buttoning her coat and wrapping a long silk scarf around her neck when I walked into her office a few minutes before six o'clock. She had been working late as usual. Sometimes I had to make her go home at the end of the day, and although that had impressed and touched me in the past, now it made me uneasy.

"I'll walk you to your car," I offered.

"Oh," she said. "Well, you certainly don't have to do that."

Her face got tight, her fingers suddenly fumbling with kid leather gloves. She knew I had something on my mind she didn't want to hear, and I suspected she knew exactly what it was. We said little to each other as we followed the hallway to the front office, our feet quiet on the carpet, the awkwardness between us palpable.

My heart was heavy. I wasn't sure if I was angry or crushed, and I began to wonder all sorts of things. What else had Rose kept from me and how long had it been going on? Was her fierce loyalty a possessiveness I hadn't recognized? Did she feel I belonged to her?

"I don't guess Lucy ever called," I said as we emerged into the empty marble lobby.

"No," Rose replied. "I tried her office several times, too."

"She got the flowers?"

"Oh, yes."

The night guard waved at us.

"It's cold out there! Where's your coat?" he said to me.

"I'll be all right," I answered him with a smile, and then to Rose I said, "We know that Lucy actually saw them?"

She looked confused.

"The flowers," I said. "Do we know if Lucy saw them?"

"Oh, yes," my secretary said again. "Her supervisor said she came in and saw them, read the card and everybody was teasing her, asking who'd sent them."

"I don't guess you know if she took them home with her."

Rose glanced over at me as we went out of the building into the dark, empty parking lot. She looked old and sad, and I didn't know if her eyes were tearing up because of me or the cold, sharp air.

"I don't know," she answered me.

"My scattered troops," I muttered.

She turned her collar up to her ears and tucked in her chin.

"It has come to this," I said. "When Carrie Grethen murdered Benton, she took out all the rest of us, too. Didn't she, Rose?"

"Of course it's had its horrendous effect. I've not known what I can do for you, but I've tried."

She glanced over at me as we walked, hunched against the cold.

"I've tried as hard as I can and still do," she went on.

"Everybody scattered," I muttered. "Lucy's angry with me, and when she gets that way, she always does the same thing. She shuts me out. Marino's not a detective anymore. And now I find out that you've been rolling my telephone calls over to Jack without asking me, Rose. Distraught families haven't been allowed to get through to me. Why would you do such a thing?"

We had reached her blue Honda Accord. Keys jingled as she dug for them in her big pocketbook.

"Isn't that funny," she said. "I was afraid you were going to ask me about your schedule. You're teaching at the Institute more than ever, and as I worked on next month's calendar, I realized you are terribly overcommitted. I should have picked up on it earlier and prevented it."

"That's the least of my worries at the moment," I replied, and I tried not to sound upset. "Why did you do this to me?" I said, and I wasn't talking about my commitments. "You shielded me from phone calls? You hurt me as a person and a professional."

Rose unlocked the door and started the engine, turning on the heat to warm up the car for her lonely ride home.

"I'm doing what you instructed me to do, Dr. Scarpetta," she finally answered me, her breath smoking out.

"I *never* instructed you to do such a thing, nor would I *ever*," I said, not believing what I was hearing. "And you know that. You know how I feel about being accessible to families."

Of course she knew. I had gotten rid of two forensic pathologists in the last five years because they had been so unavailable and indifferent to the grieving left behind.

"It wasn't with my blessing," Rose said, sounding like her mothering self again.

"When did I supposedly say this to you?"

"You didn't say it. You e-mailed it. This was back in late August."

"I never e-mailed such a thing to you," I told her. "Did you save it?"

"No," she said with regret. "I generally don't save e-mail. I have no reason to. I'm sorry I have to use it at all."

"What did this e-mail message allegedly from me say?"

"*I need you to redirect as many calls from families as you can. It's too hard for me right now. I know you understand.* Or words to that effect."

"And you didn't question this?" I said in disbelief.

She turned the heat down.

"Of course I did," she replied. "I e-mailed you right back and asked you about it. I voiced my concerns, and you replied that I was just to do it and not discuss it anymore."

"I never got an e-mail like that from you," I told her.

"I don't know what to say," she replied, fastening her shoulder harness. "Except is it possible you just don't remember? I forget e-mails all the time. I'll say I didn't say something and then find out I did."

"No. It isn't possible."

"Then it would seem to me someone is pretending to be you."

"*Is?* Have there been more?"

"Not many," she replied. "Just one here and there, warm ones thanking me for being so supportive. And let's see . . . ?"

She searched her memory. Lights in the parking lot made her car look dark green instead of blue. Her face was in shadows and I could not read her eyes. She tapped her gloved fingers on the steering wheel while I stood looking down at her. I was freezing.

"I know what it was," she suddenly said. "Secretary Wagner wanted you to meet with him and you told me to let him know you couldn't at that time."

"What?" I exclaimed.

"This was early last week," she added.

"E-mail again?"

"Sometimes it's the only way to get hold of people these days. His assistant e-mailed me and I e-mailed you—you were in court somewhere. Then you e-mailed me back that evening, I guess from home."

"This is crazy," I said, my mind running after possibilities and catching nothing.

Everyone in my office had my e-mail address. But no one except me should have my password, and obviously, no one could sign on as me without it. Rose was thinking the same thing.

"I don't know how this could happen," she said, then exclaimed, "Wait a minute. Ruth sets up AOL on each person's computer."

Ruth Wilson was my computer analyst.

"Of course. And she had to have my password in order to do that," I carried out the thought. "But Rose, she would never do anything like this."

"Never in a million years." Rose agreed. "But she must have the passwords written down somewhere. She couldn't possibly remember all of them."

"One would think so."

"Why don't you get inside the car before you die of exposure," she said.

"You go on home and get some rest," I replied. "I'm going to do the same thing."

"Of course you won't," she chided me. "You'll go right back into your office and try to figure everything out."

She was right. I walked back to the building as she drove off, and I wondered how I could be so foolish as to have gone out the door without a coat. I was stiff and numb. The night guard shook his head.

"Dr. Scarpetta, you need to dress warmer than that!"

"You're absolutely right," I said.

I passed the magnetic key over the lock and the first set of glass doors clicked free, then I unlocked the one to my wing of the building. It was absolutely silent inside, and when I turned into Ruth's office, I stood for a moment, just looking around at upright microcomputers and printers, and a map on a screen that showed if the connections to our other offices were trouble-free.

The floor behind her desk was a thick hank of cables, and printouts of software programming that made no sense to me were stacked all over the place. I scanned crammed bookshelves. I walked over to filing cabinets and tried to open a drawer. Every one of them was locked.

Good for you, Ruth, I thought.

I returned to my office and tried her home number.

"Hello?" she answered.

She sounded harried. There was a baby screaming in the background, and her husband was saying something about a frying pan.

"I'm sorry to bother you at home," I said.

"Dr. Scarpetta." She was very surprised. "You're not bothering me. Frank, can you take her in the other room?"

"I've got just one quick question," I said. "Is there a place you keep all our AOL passwords?"

"Is there a problem?" she quickly replied.

"It appears someone knows my password and is signing on to AOL as me." I didn't mince words. "I want to know how someone could possibly have gotten hold of my password. Is there any way?"

"Oh, no," she said, dismayed. "Are you sure?"

"Yes."

"Obviously, you haven't told anybody what it is," she suggested.

I thought hard for a moment. Not even Lucy knew my password. Nor would she care.

"Other than you," I said to Ruth, "I can't imagine who."

"You know I wouldn't give it to anyone!"

"I believe that," I replied, and I did.

For one thing, Ruth would never jeopardize her job that way.

"I keep everyone's addresses and passwords in a computer file that no one can access," she said.

"What about a hard copy?"

"In a file in a filing cabinet, which I keep locked."

"At all times?"

She hesitated, then said, "Well, not *all* the time. Certainly after hours, but they're unlocked much of the day, unless I'm in and out a lot. But I'm in my office most of the time. Really, it's only when I get coffee and eat lunch in the break room."

"What's the file's name?" I asked as paranoia towered like storm clouds.

"*E-mail*," she replied, knowing how I was going to feel about that. "Dr. Scarpetta, I've got thousands of files filled with programming codes and updates, patches, bugs, new things coming out, you name it. If I don't label them fairly precisely, I can never find anything."

"I understand," I said. "I have the same problem."

"I can change your password first thing in the morning."

"That's a good idea. And Ruth, let's not put it anywhere that anyone can find it this time. Not in that file, okay?"

"I hope I'm not in trouble," she uneasily said as her baby continued to scream.

"You aren't, but someone is," I told her. "And maybe you can help me figure out who that is."

It didn't take much intuition on my part to immediately think of Ruffin. He was clever. It was obvious he didn't like me. Ruth routinely kept her door shut so she could concentrate. I didn't suppose it would have been hard for Ruffin to slip inside her office and shut the door while she was in the break room.

"This conversation is absolutely confidential," I said to Ruth. "You can't even tell friends or family."

"You have my word on that."

"What's Chuck's password?"

"R-O-O-S-T-R. I remember because it irritated me when he wanted it assigned to him. As if he's the rooster in the henhouse," she said. "His address, as you probably know, is C-H-U-K-O-C-M-E, as in Chuck, Office of the Chief Medical Examiner."

"And what if I were signed on and someone else tried at the same time?" I then asked.

"The person trying would be kicked off and told someone was already signed on. There would be an error message and an alert. Now the reverse isn't true. If, let's say, the bad guy's already signed on and you try, although you get the error message, he isn't alerted at all."

"So someone could try to do it while I'm already logged on, and I'm not going to know it."

"Exactly."

"Does Chuck have a home computer?"

"He asked me one time what to get that was affordable, and I told him to try a consignment shop. I gave him the name of one."

"The name?"

"Disk Thrift. It's owned by a friend of mine."

"Any way you could call this person at home and find out if Chuck bought anything from them?"

"I can try."

"I'll be at the office for a while," I said.

I brought up the menu on my computer and looked at the icon for AOL. I logged on without a problem, meaning no one else had done so first. I was tempted to sign on as Ruffin to see who he might be corresponding with and if it might tell me more about what he was up to, but I was afraid. I was chilled by the thought of breaking into someone's mailbox.

I paged Marino, and when I got him on the phone, I explained the situation to him and asked his opinion about what I should do.

"Hell," he said without pause. "I'd do it. I always told you I didn't trust that little shit. And you know what else, Doc? How do you know he hadn't gone into your mail and deleted things, or even sent things to people other than Rose?"

"You're right," I said, infuriated by the idea. "I'll let you know what I find."

Ruth called back minutes later and sounded excited.

"He bought a computer and printer last month," she reported. "For about six hundred dollars. And the computer came with a modem."

"And we have AOL software here."

"Tons of it. If he didn't buy his own, he certainly could have gotten his hands on it."

"We may have a very serious situation on our hands. It's vital you don't say a word," I reminded her again.

"I've never liked Chuck."

"And you can't say that to people either," I said.

131

I hung up and put my coat on and felt bad about Rose. I was certain she was upset. It wouldn't have surprised me if she had cried all the way home. She was stoical and rarely conveyed how she felt, and I knew if she thought she had hurt me, she would be undone. I went out to my car. I wanted to make her feel better and I needed her help. Chuck's e-mail would have to wait.

Rose had gotten weary of running a house and had moved into an apartment in the near West End, off Grove Avenue, several blocks from a café called Du Jour, where I now and then ate Sunday brunch. Rose lived in an old three-story dark red brick building shaded by big oaks. It was a relatively safe area of town, but I always scanned my surroundings before I got out of my car. As I parked next to Rose's Honda, I noticed what looked like a dark-colored Taurus several cars away.

Someone was sitting inside it, engine and lights off. I knew that most unmarked Richmond police cars were Tauruses these days, and I wondered if there was a reason a cop might be waiting out here in the dark, cold air. It was also possible the person was waiting for someone to come down to go somewhere, but again, one generally didn't do that with headlights and engine off.

I felt I was being watched and got my seven-shot Smith & Wesson revolver out of my satchel and slipped it into my coat pocket. I followed the sidewalk and caught the car's tag number on the front bumper. I committed it to memory. I felt eyes on my back.

The only way to get to Rose's third-floor apartment was to take stairs illuminated wanly by a single light overhead at each landing. I was anxious. I paused every few steps to see if anyone might be coming up behind me. No one was. Rose had hung a fresh Christmas wreath on her door, and its fragrance stirred powerful feelings inside me. I could hear Handel's music playing inside. I dug into my satchel, pulled out a pen and writing pad and jotted the tag number on it. Then I rang the bell.

"Goodness!" Rose exclaimed. "What brings you here? Do come in. What a nice surprise."

"Did you look through the peephole before you opened the door?" I quizzed her. "At least you could ask who it is."

She laughed. She was always teasing me about my security worries, which were extreme in the minds of most people because they did not live my life.

"Did you come here to test me?" she teased me once more.

"Maybe I should start doing that."

Rose's furniture was warm and perfectly polished, and although I would not call her taste formal, it was very proper and exactly arranged. Floors were the beautiful hardwood one didn't find anymore, and small Oriental rugs were spots of color on them. A gas fire was burning, and electric candles glowed in windows overlooking a grassy area where people used their Hibachis and charcoal grills in warmer weather.

Rose sat in a wing chair and I settled on the couch. I had been to her apartment only twice before, and it seemed so sad and strange to see no sign of her beloved animals. The last two of her adopted greyhounds had gone to her daughter, and her cat had died. All she had left was an aquarium with a modest number of guppies, goldfish and mollies constantly moving around, because pets were not allowed in the building.

"I know you miss your dogs," I said, not mentioning the cat, because cats and I didn't get along. "One of these days I'm going to get a greyhound. My problem is I would want to save all of them."

I remembered hers. The poor dogs would not let you stroke their ears because they had been yanked by trainers, one of the many cruelties they suffered at dog tracks. Rose's eyes got bright with tears, and she turned her face from me and rubbed her knees.

"This cold is hard on my joints," she commented, clearing her throat. "They were getting so old. It's just as well Laurel has them now. I couldn't bear another thing dying on me. I wish you would get one. If every nice person would just get one."

The dogs were put to death by the hundreds every year when they could no longer perform up to speed. I shifted on the couch. There was so much in life that angered me.

"Can I get you hot ginseng tea that dear Simon gets for me?" She mentioned the hairstylist she adored. "Maybe something a little stronger? I've been meaning to stop and pick up shortbread cookies."

"I can't stay long," I said. "But I just wanted to drop by and make certain you're all right."

"Why, of course," she replied as if there were no reason in the world she wouldn't be.

I paused, and Rose looked at me, waiting for me to explain why I really had dropped by.

"I talked to Ruth," I began. "We're following a couple of leads and have our suspicions . . ."

"Which I'm sure lead right to Chuck," she announced, nodding her head. "I've always thought he's a bad apple. And he avoids me like the plague because he knows I see right through him. It will be a cold day in hell before the likes of him will charm me."

"No one could charm you," I said. Handel's *Messiah* began, and intense sadness tucked itself into my heart.

Her eyes searched my face. She knew how hard last Christmas had been for me. I had spent it in Miami, where I could avoid it as much as I could. But it wasn't possible for me to get away from music and lights, not even if I fled to Cuba.

"What are you going to do this year?" she asked.

"Maybe go out west," I replied. "If it would snow here, that would be easier, but I can't stand gray skies. Rain and ice storms, Richmond weather. You know, when I first moved here, we always got at least one or two good snows every winter."

I envisioned snow piled on tree branches and blowing against my windshield, the world whited out as I drove to work even though all state offices were closed. Snow and tropical sunshine were antidepressants for me.

"It was very nice of you to check on me," my secretary said, getting up from the deep-blue wing chair. "You've always worried too much about me, though."

She went into the kitchen and I heard her digging around in the freezer. When she returned to the living room, she handed me a Tupperware container with something frozen inside it.

"My vegetable soup," she said. "Just what you need tonight."

"You can't know how much," I told her with heartfelt appreciation. "I'll go home and warm it up now."

"Now, what will you do about Chuck?" she asked with a very serious expression on her face.

I hesitated. I didn't want to ask her this.

"Rose, he says you're my office snitch."

"Well, I am."

"I need you to be," I went on. "I'd like you to do what-ever it takes to find out what he's up to."

"What the little son of a bitch is up to is sabotage," said Rose, who almost never swore.

"We've got to get the evidence," I said. "You know how the state is. It's harder to fire somebody than walk on water. But he's not going to win."

135

She didn't respond right away. Then she said, "To start with, we mustn't underestimate him. He's not as smart as he thinks he is, but he's clever. And he has too much time to think and move about unnoticed. What's unfortunate is he knows your patterns better than anyone, better even than me, because I don't help you in the morgue—for which I'm grateful. And that's your center stage. That's where he could really ruin you."

She was right, although I couldn't bear to admit the power he had. He could swap labels or toe tags or contaminate something. He could leak lies to reporters who would forever protect his identity. I could scarcely imagine the breadth of what he could do.

"By the way," I said, getting up from the couch, "I'm fairly sure he has a computer at home, so he lied about that."

She walked me to the door, and I remembered the car parked near mine.

"Do you know anybody in the building who drives a dark Taurus?" I asked.

She frowned, perplexed. "Well, they're rather much all over the place. But no, I can't think of anyone around me who drives one."

"Possibly there's a police officer who lives in your building and might drive such a car home now and then?"

"I know nothing about it if there is. Don't get too carried away by all those little goblins that will rise up in your head if you let them. I have a firm belief about not giving a life to things, you know. The old bit about a self-fulfilled prophecy."

"Well, it's probably nothing, but I just had an odd feeling when I saw this person sitting inside a dark car, engine off, lights off," I said. "I got the tag number."

"Good for you." Rose patted my back. "Why am I not surprised?"

16

My shoes seemed loud on the stairs as I left Rose's apartment, and I was conscious of my handgun when I went out the door into the cold night. The car was gone. I looked around for it as I approached mine.

The parking lot was not well lit. Bare trees made slight sounds that turned ominous in my mind, and shadows seemed to hide fearful things. I quickly locked my doors, looking around some more, and called Marino's pager as I drove off. He called back right away because, of course, he was in uniform on the street without a damn thing to do.

"Can you run a tag?" I said right off when he answered.

"Lay it on me."

I recited it to him.

"I'm just leaving Rose's apartment," I said, "and I have a weird feeling about this car parked out there."

Marino almost always took my weird feelings seriously. I was not one to have them often without justification. I was a lawyer and a physician. If anything, I was more inclined to stay inside my clinical, fact-only lawyer's mind and was not given to overreactions and emotional projections.

"There are other things," I went on.

"You want me to drop by?"

"I sure would."

He was waiting in my driveway when I got there, and he awkwardly climbed out of his car because his duty belt got in his way and the shoulder harness he never wore tended to snag him somewhere.

"Goddamn it!" he said, yanking his belt free. "I don't know how much more I can stand this." He kicked the door shut. "Piece-of-shit car."

"How'd you get here first if it's such a piece-of-shit car?" I asked.

"I was closer than you. My back's killing me."

He continued to complain as we went up the steps and I unlocked the front door. I was startled by silence. The alarm light was green.

"Now that ain't good," Marino said.

"I know I set it this morning," I said.

"The housekeeper come?" he asked, looking, listening.

"She always sets it," I said. "I've never known her to forget, not once in the two years she's worked for me."

"You stay here," he said.

"I most certainly will not," I replied, because the last thing I wanted was to wait here alone, and it was never a good idea for two armed people to be nervous and on guard in different areas of the same space.

I reset the alarm and followed him from room to room, watching him open every closet and look behind every shower curtain, drapery and door. We searched both floors and nothing was the least bit amiss until we went back downstairs, where I noticed the runner in the hallway. Half of it was vacuumed, while the other wasn't, and in the guest bath right off it, Marie, my housekeeper, had neglected to replace soiled hand towels with fresh ones.

"She's not absentminded like that," I said. "She and her husband are supporting young children on very little and she works harder than anyone I know."

"I hope nobody calls me out," Marino complained. "You got any coffee in this joint?"

I made a strong pot with the Pilon espresso that Lucy sent me from Miami, and the bright red and yellow bag made me feel hurt again. Marino and I carried our cups into my office. I logged onto AOL using Ruffin's address and password and was extremely relieved when I didn't get bumped off.

"Coast is clear," I announced.

Marino pulled up a chair and looked over my shoulder. Ruffin had mail.

There were eight messages, and I didn't recognize who any of them were from.

"What happens if you open them?" Marino wanted to know.

"They'll still be in the box as long as you save them as new," I replied.

"I mean, can he tell you opened them?"

"No. But the sender can. The sender can check the status of the mail he sent and see what time it was opened."

"Huh," Marino said with a shrug in his voice. "So what? How many people are gonna check what friggin' time their mail was opened?"

I didn't answer him as I began to go into Chuck's mail. Maybe I should have felt frightened by what I was doing, but I was too angry. Four of the e-mails were from his wife, who had many instructions for him about domestic matters that made Marino laugh.

"She's got his balls in a box on top of the fireplace," he gleefully said.

The address of the fifth message was MAYFLR, who simply said, "Need to talk."

"That's interesting," I commented to Marino. "Let's check out mail he might have sent to whoever this *Mayflower* is."

I went into the mail-sent menu and discovered Chuck had been sending e-mail to this person almost daily for the past two weeks. I quickly scanned through the notes, Marino looking on, and it became obvious in no time that my morgue supervisor was having rendezvous with this person, possibly an affair.

"I wonder who the hell she is?" Marino said. "That'd be a nice little bit of leverage to hold over the son of a bitch."

"Not going to be easy to find out," I said.

I quickly signed off, feeling as if I were escaping from a house I'd just burglarized.

"Let's try Chatplanet," I said.

The only reason I was familiar with chat rooms was that on occasion colleagues of mine from around the world used them to meet and ask for help in particularly difficult cases or share information that we might find useful. I signed on and downloaded the program and selected a box that made it possible for me to be in the chat room without anybody's seeing me.

I scanned the list of chat rooms and clicked on one called *Dear Chief Kay*. Dr. Kay herself was in the midst of moderating a chat session with sixty-three people.

"Oh, shit. Give me a cigarette, Marino," I tensely said.

He shook one out of the pack and pulled up a chair, sitting next to me while we eavesdropped.

<PIPEMAN> DEAR CHIEF KAY, IS IT TRUE ELVIS DIED ON THE TOILET AND THAT MANY PEOPLE DIE ON THE TOILET? I'M A PLUMBER, SO YOU CAN SEE WHY I'M WONDERING. THANKS, INTERESTED IN ILLINOIS

<DEAR CHIEF KAY> DEAR INTERESTED IN ILLINOIS, YES, I'M SORRY TO SAY THAT ELVIS DID DIE ON THE TOILET AND THAT THIS ISN'T UNCOMMON BECAUSE PEOPLE STRAIN AND STRAIN AND THEIR HEART CAN'T TAKE IT. ELVIS'S MANY YEARS OF BAD EATING AND PILLS, I'M SORRY TO SAY, FINALLY CAUGHT UP WITH HIM, AND HE DIED OF CARDIAC ARREST IN HIS LUXURIOUS BATHROOM IN GRACELAND. AND THIS SHOULD BE A LESSON TO ALL OF US.

<MEDSTU> DEAR CHIEF KAY, WHY DID YOU DECIDE YOU'D RATHER WORK WITH DEAD PATIENTS INSTEAD OF LIVING ONES? MORBID IN MONTANA

<DEAR CHIEF KAY> DEAR MORBID IN MONTANA, I DON'T HAVE MUCH OF A BEDSIDE MANNER AND DON'T HAVE TO WORRY HOW MY PATIENT IS FEELING. I FOUND OUT DURING MY MEDICAL SCHOOL DAYS THAT LIVING PATIENTS ARE A PAIN IN THE ASS.

"Holy motherfucking shit," Marino said.

I was incensed and there was nothing I could do about it.

"You know," Marino said with indignation, "I wish people would leave Elvis alone. I'm tired of hearing about him dying on the toilet."

"Be quiet, Marino," I said. "Please. I'm trying to think."

The session went on and on, all of it awful. I was tempted to butt into the conversations to tell everyone Dear Chief Kay wasn't me.

"Any way to find out who Dear Chief Kay really is?" Marino asked.

"If this person is the moderator of the chat room, the answer's no. He or she can know who everybody else is but not the other way around."

<Julie W> Dear Chief Kay, since you know everything there is about anatomy, does that make you more aware of pleasure points, if you know what I mean? My boyfriend seems bored in bed and sometimes he even falls asleep in the middle of it! Wanna Be Sexy
<Dear Chief Kay> Dear Wanna Be Sexy, is he on any kind of medications that might make him sleepy? If not, sexy lingerie's not a bad idea. Women don't do enough anymore to make their men feel important and in charge.

"That's it!" I announced. "I'm going to kill him . . . or her . . . whoever the hell this Chief Kay is!"

I jumped out of my chair, so frustrated I didn't know what to do.

"You don't fuck with my credibility!"

Fists clenched, I practically racewalked to the great room, where I suddenly stopped and looked around as if I were in some place that I'd never been before.

"Two can play this game," I said as I returned to my study.

"But how can two play when you don't even know who Chief Kay number two is?" Marino asked.

"Maybe I can't do anything about that goddamn chat room, but there's always e-mail."

"What kind of e-mail?" Marino warily asked.

"Two can play this game. Just wait and see. Now. How about we check on our suspicious car."

Marino slipped his portable radio off his belt and switched to the service channel.

"What'd you say it was again?" he asked.

"RGG-7112," I recited it from memory.

"Virginia tags?"

"Sorry," I replied. "I didn't get that good of a look."

"Well, we'll start there."

He relayed the tag number to the Virginia Criminal Information Network, or VCIN, and asked for a 10-29. By now it was after ten o'clock.

"Any way you could make me a sandwich or something before I leave?" Marino asked. "I'm about to die of hunger. VCIN's been a little slow tonight. I hate that."

He requested bacon, lettuce and tomato with Russian dressing and thick slices of onion, and I cooked the bacon well in the microwave instead of frying it.

"Ah gee, Doc, why'd you have to do that?" he said, holding up a crispy, non-greasy strip of bacon. "It ain't good unless it's chewy and got some flavor left that wasn't soaked up in all those paper towels."

"It will have plenty of flavor," I said. "And the rest is up to you. I'm not going to be blamed for clogging up your arteries any worse than they probably already are."

Marino toasted rye bread and slathered it with butter and Russian dressing he conjured up from Miracle Whip, ketchup and chopped butter pickles. He topped this with lettuce, tomato liberally dashed with salt and thick slices of raw sweet onion.

He made two of these healthy creations and wrapped them in aluminum foil as the radio got back to him. The car was not a Ford Taurus, but a 1998 Ford Contour. It was dark blue and registered to Avis Leasing Corporation.

"That's kinda interesting," Marino said. "Usually in Richmond all rental cars begin with an R, and you have to request a plate that doesn't. They started doing that so it wasn't so obvious to carjackers that someone was from out of town."

There were no outstanding warrants and the car wasn't listed as stolen.

17

At eight o'clock the next morning, Wednesday, I squeezed into a metered space. Across the street, the eighteenth-century capitol of the Commonwealth was pristine behind wrought iron and fountains in the fog.

Dr. Wagner, other cabinet members and the attorney general worked in the Ninth Street Executive Office Building, and security had gotten so extreme that I'd begun to feel like a criminal when I came here. Just inside the door was a table, where a capitol police officer checked my satchel.

"If you find anything in there," I said, "let me know, because I can't."

The smiling officer looked very familiar, a short, fleshy man I guessed to be in his mid-thirties. He had thinning brown hair and the face of one who had been boyishly cute before advancing years and added weight had begun to have their way with him.

I held out my credentials and he barely gave them a glance.

"Don't need those," he cheerfully said. "You remember me?

I had to respond to your building a couple times when you used to be over there."

He pointed in the direction of my old building on Fourteenth Street, which was only five short blocks east.

"Rick Hodges," he said. "That time they had the uranium scare. 'Member that?"

"How could I not?" I said. "Not one of our finer moments."

"And me and Wingo used to hang out sometimes. During lunch I'd come down when nothing much was going on."

A shadow crossed his face. Wingo was the best, most sensitive morgue supervisor I'd ever had. Several years ago he died of smallpox. I squeezed Hodges's shoulder.

"I still miss him," I said. "You have no idea how much."

He looked around and leaned closer to me.

"You keep up with his family any?" he asked in a low voice.

"From time to time."

He knew from the way I said it that his family didn't want to talk about their gay son, nor did they want me calling. Certainly, they didn't want Hodges or any of Wingo's friends calling, either. Hodges nodded, pain dimming his eyes. He tried to smile it away.

"That boy sure was crazy about you, Doc," he said to me. "I've been wanting to tell you that for a long time."

"That means a lot," I said to him with feeling. "Thank you, Rick."

I passed through the scanner without incident, and he handed me my satchel.

"Don't stay away so long," he said.

"I won't," I said, meeting his young, blue eyes. "It makes me feel safer having you around."

"You know where you're going?"

"Think so," I said.

"Well, just remember the elevator has a mind of its own."

I took worn, granite steps to the sixth floor, where Sinclair Wagner's office overlooked Capitol Square. On this dark, rainy morning, I could barely see the statue of George Washington astride his horse. The temperature had plummeted twenty degrees during the night, and rain was small and hard like shotgun pellets.

The waiting area of the Secretary of Health and Human Services was handsomely arranged with graceful colonial furniture and flags that were not Dr. Wagner's style. His office was cramped and cluttered. It bespoke a man who worked extremely hard and understated his power.

Dr. Wagner was born and raised in Charleston, South Carolina, where his first name, Sinclair, was pronounced *Sinkler*. He was a psychiatrist with a law degree, and oversaw person-service agencies such as mental health, substance abuse, social services and Medicare. He had been on the faculty of the Medical College of Virginia, or MCV, before his appointment to a cabinet-level position, and I'd always respected him enormously and knew he respected me, too.

"Kay." He rolled back his chair and got up from his desk. "How are you?"

He motioned for me to sit on the couch, and he closed the door and returned to the barrier of his desk, which was not a good sign.

"I'm pleased with how everything's going at the Institute, aren't you?" he asked.

"Very much so," I replied. "Daunting, but better than I ever hoped."

He picked up his pipe and pouch of tobacco from an ashtray.

"I've been wondering what's been going on with you," he said. "You seem to have vanished off the face of the earth."

"I don't know why you'd say that," I answered him. "I'm doing as many cases as always, if not more."

"Oh, yes. Of course, I keep up with you through the news."

He began tamping tobacco into the pipe. There was no smoking of any sort in the building and Wagner tended to suck on a cold pipe when he was ill at ease. He knew I hadn't come here to talk about the Institute or tell him how busy I'd been.

"I certainly know how busy you are," he went on, "since you don't even have time to see me."

"I just found out today, Sinclair, that you tried to see me last week," I replied.

He held my gaze, sucking on the pipe. Dr. Wagner was in his sixties but looked older than that, as if bearing the painful secrets of patients for so many years had finally begun to erode him. He had kind eyes, and it was greatly to his advantage that people tended to forget he also had the shrewdness of a lawyer.

"If you didn't get my message that I wanted to see you, Kay," he said, "then it would seem to me you have a staffing problem."

His slow, low tone nudged words along, always taking the long way around a thought.

"I do, but not of the sort you might imagine."

"I'm listening."

"Someone's been getting into my e-mail," I flatly replied. "Apparently this person got into the file where our passwords are kept and got hold of mine."

"So much for security . . ."

I held up my hand to stop him.

"Sinclair, security's not the problem. I'm being hurt from within my own ranks. It's clear to me that someone—or perhaps more than one person—is trying to cause me trouble. Perhaps even get me fired. Your secretary e-mailed mine to let her know you wanted to see me. My secretary passed this along to me, and I allegedly replied that I was *too busy* to see you at that time."

I could tell Dr. Wagner found this confusing, if not ridiculous.

"There are other things," I went on, getting increasingly uncomfortable with the sound of my own voice spinning what seemed such a fantastic web. "E-mails asking calls to be rolled over to my deputy chief, and worst of all, this so-called chat room I'm doing on the Internet."

"I know about that," he grimly said. "And you're telling me that whoever is doing this Dear Dr. Kay stuff is the same person using your password?"

"It's definitely someone using my password and posing as me."

He was silent, sucking his pipe.

"I'm very suspicious that my morgue supervisor is connected with all this," I added.

"Why?"

"Erratic behavior, hostility, disappearing acts. He's disgruntled and up to something. I could go on."

Silence.

"When I can prove his involvement," I said, "I'll take care of the problem."

Dr. Wagner returned the pipe to the ashtray. He got up from his desk and came around to where I was sitting. He settled into a side chair. He leaned forward and looked intensely at me.

"I've known you for a long time, Kay," he said in a kind but no-nonsense voice. "I'm well aware of your reputation. You're a tribute to the Commonwealth. You've also been through a horrendous tragedy, and it wasn't that long ago."

"Are you trying to play the role of psychiatrist with me, Sinclair?" I wasn't joking.

"You aren't a machine."

"Nor am I given to wild thinking. What I'm telling you is real. Every brick of the case I'm building. There are just a lot of insidious activities going on, and while it may be true I've been more distracted than usual, what I'm telling you has nothing to do with that."

"How can you be so sure, Kay, if you've been distracted, as you put it? Most people wouldn't even have returned to work for a while—if ever—after what you've suffered. When *did* you go back to work?"

"Sinclair, we all have our ways of coping."

"Let me answer my own question for you," he went on. "*Ten days*. And not a very happy environment to return to, I might add. Tragedy, death."

I didn't say anything as I fought for composure. I had been in a dark cave and scarcely remembered scattering Benton's ashes out to sea in Hilton Head, the place he loved most. I scarcely remembered clearing out his condo there, then attacking his drawers and closets at my house. At a maniacal speed, I removed everything right then that would have had to go eventually.

Had it not been for Dr. Anna Zimmer, I couldn't have survived. She was an older woman, a psychiatrist who had been my friend for years. I had no idea what she did with Benton's fine suits and ties and polished leather shoes and colognes. I didn't want to know what happened to his

BMW. Most of all, I couldn't bear to know what had been done with the linens that had been in our bathroom and on our bed.

Anna had been wise enough to keep all belongings that mattered. She didn't touch his books or jewelry. She left his certificates and commendations hanging on the walls of his study, where nobody would see them, because he was so modest. She wouldn't let me remove the photographs arranged everywhere because she said it was important for me to live with them.

"You must live with the memory," she told me repeatedly in her heavy German accent. "It is still present, Kay. You cannot run away from it. Don't try."

"On a scale of ten, how depressed are you, Kay?" Dr. Wagner's voice sounded somewhere in the background.

I was still hurt and unable to accept that Lucy had never shown up once during all of this. Benton left me his condo in his will, and Lucy was furious with me for selling it, although she knew as well as I did that neither of us could ever pass through its rooms again. When I tried to give her his much-loved, scarred, scuffed bomber jacket he had worn in college, she said she didn't want it, that she would give it to someone else. I knew she never did. I knew she hid it somewhere.

"There's no shame in admitting it. I think it's hard for you to admit you're human," Dr. Wagner's voice surfaced.

My eyes cleared.

"Have you thought of going on an antidepressant?" Dr. Wagner asked me. "Something mild like Wellbutrin."

I paused before I said anything.

"In the first place, Sinclair," I said, "situational depression is normal. I don't need a pill to magically take away my grief. I may be stoical. I may find it difficult to show my emotions around others, to show my deepest feelings, and yes, it's easier for me to fight and get angry and overachieve than to feel pain. But I'm not wrapped tight in denial. I've got sense enough to know that grief has to run its course. And this isn't easy when those you trust begin to chip away at what little you have left in your life."

"You just switched from first person to second person," he pointed out. "I'm just wondering if you're aware . . . ."

"Don't dissect me, Sinclair."

"Kay, let me paint for you the portrait of tragedy, of violence, that those untouched by it never see," he said. "It has a life of its own. It continues its rampage, although with more stealth and with less visible wounds as time moves on."

"I see the portrait of tragedy every day," I said.

"What about when you look in the mirror?" he asked.

"Sinclair, it's terrible enough to suffer loss, but to compound that with everyone looking askance at you and doubting your abilities to function anymore is to be kicked and degraded while you're supposedly down."

He held my gaze. I had just switched to second person again, to that safer place, and I saw it in his eyes.

"Cruelty thrives on what it perceives as weakness," I went on.

I knew what evil was. I could smell it and recognize its features when it was in my midst.

"Someone seized what happened to me as the long-awaited-for opportunity to destroy me," I concluded.

"And you don't think this is perhaps a little paranoid?" he finally spoke.

"No."

"Why would someone do that, besides being petty and jealous?" he inquired.

"Power. To steal my fire."

"An interesting analogy," he said. "Tell me what you mean by that."

"I use my power for good," I explained. "And whoever is trying to hurt me wants to appropriate my power for his own selfish use, and you don't want power in the hands of people like that."

"I agree," he thoughtfully said.

His phone buzzed. He got up and answered it.

"Not now," he said over the line. "I know. He's just going to have to wait."

He returned to his chair and blew out a long breath, took his glasses off and set them on the coffee table.

"I think the best thing to do is send out a press release informing people that someone is impersonating you on the Internet, to do what we can to clear this up as much as possible," he said. "We'll put an end to it, even if it requires a court order."

"That would make me very happy," I said.

He got up and I did, too.

"Thank you, Sinclair. Thank God I have a shield like you."

"We'll just hope the new secretary will be the same," he remarked as if I knew what he was talking about.

"What new secretary?" I asked as anxiety hummed again, this time more loudly.

A strange expression passed over his face. Then he looked angry.

"I've sent you several memos marked private and confidential. Goddamn it! Now this is going too far."

"I've gotten nothing from you," I said.

He pressed his lips together, his cheeks turning red. It was one thing to tamper with e-mail; it was another to intercept the secretary's sealed, classified memorandums. Not even Rose opened anything like that.

"Apparently the Governor's Crime Commission's gotten stuck on the notion that we should transfer your office out of Health and into Public Safety," he told me.

"For God's sake, Sinclair," I exclaimed.

"I know, I know." He raised his hand to quiet me.

This same ignorant proposal had come up shortly after I'd been hired. The police and forensic labs were under Public Safety, meaning, among other things, that if my office fell under Public Safety, too, there would be no checks and balances anymore. The police department, in essence, would have a say-so in how I worked my cases.

"I've written position papers on this before," I told Dr. Wagner. "Years ago, I fought it off by preaching to prosecutors and police chiefs. I even went to the defense attorneys' bar. We can't let this happen."

Dr. Wagner said nothing.

"Why now?" I persisted. "Why has this just come up now? The issue's been dormant for more than ten years."

"I think Representative Connors is pushing it because some of the higher-ups in law enforcement are pushing him," he said. "Who the hell knows."

I did, and as I drove toward my office, I got energized. I thrived on unanswered questions, on excavating for what wasn't plain to see, on getting to the truth. What detractors like Chuck Ruffin and Diane Bray had not factored into their machinations was that they'd served to wake me up.

A scenario was materializing in my mind. It was very simple. Someone wanted me shot out of the air so my office would be vulnerable to a takeover by Public Safety. I had heard rumblings that the current secretary, whom I liked very much, was retiring. Wouldn't it be a coincidence if Bray just happened to take his place.

When I reached my office, I smiled at Rose and bid her a cheery good morning.

"Aren't we in a good mood today!" she said, enormously pleased.

"It's your vegetable soup," I commented. "I have it to look forward to. Where's Chuck?"

Just his name gave Rose a sour look.

"Off delivering several brains to MCV," she replied.

Now and then when cases were neurologically suspicious and complicated, I would fix the brain in formalin and have it delivered to the neuropathology lab for special studies.

"Let me know when he comes back," I told her. "We need to set up the Luma-Lite in the decomposed room."

She placed her elbow on her desk, chin in her hand and shook her head, eyes on me.

"I hate to be the one who tells you this," she said.

"Oh God, now what? Just when I thought it might be a good day."

"The Institute's doing a mock crime scene and it appears their Luma-Lite is in for repairs."

"Don't tell me."

"Well, all I know is someone called here and Chuck took our Luma-Lite to them before he left for MCV."

"Then I'll just go get it back."

"It's at an outdoor mock scene some ten miles away."

"Who gave Chuck the authority to lend it to anyone?" I asked.

"Just be glad it isn't stolen like half of everything else around here," she said.

"I guess I'll just have to go upstairs and do the examination in Vander's lab," I said.

I walked into my office and sat down at my desk. I took my glasses off and massaged the bridge of my nose. I decided the time had come to set up a rendezvous between Bray and Chuck. I signed on to Ruffin's address and e-mailed a note to Bray.

Chief Bray,

*Have some information **you must know**. Please meet me at Beverly Hills Shopping Center at 5:30. Park on back row near Buckhead's. We can talk in your car so nobody sees us. If you can't meet me, page me. Otherwise I'll see you then.*

Chuck

Then I sent him a text message page, purportedly from Bray, inviting him to the meeting.

"Done," I said, yielding to self-congratulation just as the phone rang.

"Yo," Marino said. "Your personal investigator here. What'cha doing after work?"

"More work. Remember I said two can play this game? You're taking me to Buckhead's. We wouldn't want to miss a little rendezvous between two people near and dear to our hearts, would we? So I thought it might be nice if you took me out to dinner and we just happened to run into them," I said.

18

Marino met me in the parking lot as planned and we got in his monster Dodge Ram Quad Cab pickup truck because I didn't want to take the chance that Bray might recognize my Mercedes. It was dark and frigid out but the rain had stopped. I was riding so high I could almost look transfer truckers in the eye.

We followed Patterson Avenue toward Parham Road, a major thoroughfare in the city where people ate out and shopped and swarmed inside Regency Mall.

"I gotta warn you there ain't always a pot of gold at the end of the rainbow," he said, throwing a cigarette butt out the window. "One or both of them might decide not to show. Hell, they may be on to us for all I know. But, gotta give it a shot, right?"

The Beverly Hills Shopping Center was a small strip of salons and a Ben Franklin Crafts & Frames store. The location was not at all where one might expect to find the city's finest chophouse.

"Don't see no sign of them," Marino said as we scanned. "But we're a few minutes early."

He parked some distance away from the restaurant, between two cars in front of Ben Franklin, and cut the engine. I opened my door.

"Just where do you think you're going?" he protested.

"Inside the restaurant."

"What if they roll up any minute and see you?"

"I have every right to be here."

"What if she's in there at the bar?" he worried. "What are you going to say to her?"

"I'll offer to buy her a drink and then come out and get you."

"Christ, Doc." Marino was getting increasingly adamant. "I thought the whole point of this is to burn her."

"Relax and let me do the talking."

"Relax? I want to break the bitch's neck," he said.

"We have to be smart. We walk out from behind a bunker and start firing, we might just get hit first."

"You telling me you ain't going to tell her to her face you know what she's done? The e-mail to Chuck and everything?"

He was incredulous and furious and kept repeating himself.

"Then what the hell are we doing here?" he went on.

"Marino," I tried to calm him down. "You know better than this. You're an experienced detective, and that's what you have to be with her. She's formidable. I'm going to tell you right now you'll never muscle this woman into a corner."

He was silent.

"Keep a lookout from your truck while I check the inside of the restaurant. If you spot her before I do, send me a ten-four on my pager and call the restaurant asking for me, just in case I don't get the page for some reason," I said.

He angrily lit a cigarette as I opened my door.

"It ain't fucking fair," he said. "We know fucking well what she's doing. I still say we confront her and show her she ain't as smart as she thinks."

"You, of all people, know about building cases," I reiterated. I was getting worried that he wouldn't be able to control himself.

"We saw what she sent Chuck."

"Lower your voice," I said. "We can't prove she sent that e-mail anymore than I can prove I *didn't* send e-mail that's being attributed to me. I can't even prove I didn't write that dreadful column, for that matter."

"Maybe I should just become a soldier of fortune."

He blasted smoke into the rearview mirror, scanning.

"Page or call me?" I asked as I climbed out.

"What if you don't get the message in time?"

"Then run her over with your truck," I impatiently replied, pushing the door shut.

I looked around as I walked toward the restaurant and saw no sign of Bray. I had no idea what her personal car was but suspected she wouldn't show up in it, anyway. I pulled open the heavy wooden door of Buckhead's and was greeted by carefree voices and ice clinking in glasses as the bartender made drinks with a flourish. A mounted buck's head explained the restaurant's name. Lights were low, the paneling dark, and crates and racks of wine were stacked almost to the ceiling.

"Well, good evening." The hostess at the podium smiled in a surprised way. "We've missed you, but I certainly know from the news that you've been a little busy. What can I help you with?"

"A reservation in the name of Bray?" I inquired. "I'm not sure of the time."

She scanned the big reservation book, running a pencil down names and times. Then she tried again. She looked embarrassed. After all, it was impossible to stroll into a good restaurant unannounced even on a weeknight.

"I'm afraid not," she quietly told me.

"Hmmm. Maybe it's in my name?" I tried again.

She tried again, too.

"Gosh, I'm so sorry, Dr. Scarpetta. And we're full tonight because we have a group taking up the entire front room."

It was twenty of six now. Tables were covered with red-checked cloths, small lamps burning on them, and the room was completely empty because civilized people rarely dined before seven.

"I was going to have a drink with a friend." I continued my act. "I suppose we could eat early if you could fit us? Maybe around six?"

"That's no problem at all," she said, brightening up.

"Then put me down," I replied as my worries intensified.

What if Bray realized Chuck's car wasn't in the lot and became suspicious?

"Then six it is . . ."

I was acutely aware of the pager on my belt and listening for a phone to ring.

"Perfect," I said to the hostess.

This scenario curdled my sensibilities. It was my nature, my training and my professional practice to always tell the truth, in no way to slip into the behavior of the wily, low-life trial lawyer I could have been had I given myself up to manipulation, evasion and the gray areas of the law.

The hostess penciled my name in the book as my pager vibrated like a big insect. I read the 10-4 on the display and hurried back through the bar. I had no choice but to

160

open the front door because the windows were opaque and I could not see through them. I spotted the dark Crown Victoria.

Marino didn't do anything right away. My anxiety grew as Bray parked and turned her headlights off. I felt sure she wouldn't wait for Chuck very long and could already imagine her annoyance. Little nobodies like him didn't dare to keep Deputy Chief Diane Bray waiting.

"Is there something I can do for you?" the bartender asked me as he dried off a glass.

I continued to peer through the barely open door, wondering what Marino was going to do next.

"I'm expecting someone who isn't sure exactly where you're located," I said.

"Just tell 'em we're next to Michelle's Face Works," he said as Marino got out of his truck.

I met him in the parking lot and we walked with purpose toward Bray's car. She didn't notice us because she was talking on her portable phone and writing something down. When Marino tapped on her window, she turned to us, startled. Then her face turned hard. She said something else on her portable and ended her call. The window hummed down.

"Deputy Chief Bray? Thought that was you," Marino said as if they were old friends.

He bent down and peered inside her car. Bray was clearly off balance and one could almost see her calculating thoughts regrouping in her head as she pretended there was nothing unusual about our running into her here.

"Good evening," I politely said. "What a pleasant coincidence."

"Kay, what a surprise," she said in a flat voice. "How are you? So you've discovered Richmond's little secret."

"By now, I know most of Richmond's little secrets," I said with irony. "There are many of them if you know where to look."

"I stay away from red meat as much as possible." Bray switched conversational lanes. "But their fish is very good."

"That's like going to a whorehouse and playing solitaire," Marino remarked.

Bray ignored him and tried to stare me down with no success. I'd learned from many years of warring with bad employees, dishonest defense attorneys and ruthless politicians that if I stared between a person's eyes, he didn't know I wasn't, in fact, staring into his eyes, and I could keep up the intimidation all day.

"I'm eating dinner here," she said as if she were distracted and in a hurry.

"We'll wait until your guest shows up," Marino said. "Sure don't want you sitting alone out here in the dark or being bothered inside. Truth is, Deputy Chief Bray, you shouldn't be roaming around without security, as recognizable as you've gotten to be since you moved here. You've kind of gotten to be a celebrity, you know."

"I'm not meeting anyone," she said, irritation honing her tone.

"We've never had a woman so high up in the department, especially one so attractive and so loved by the media." Marino wouldn't shut up.

She collected her pocketbook and mail off the seat, her cold anger palpable.

"Now if you'll please excuse me?" She said it as an order.

"It's not going to be easy to get a table tonight," I let her know as she opened her door. "Unless you have a reservation," I added, implying I knew damn well she didn't.

Bray's poise and self-confidence slipped just enough to unmask the evil coiling within. Her eyes struck at me, then revealed nothing as she climbed out of the car and Marino blocked her way. She couldn't get past him without ducking around him and brushing against him, and her enormous ego would never allow that.

She was almost pinned against the door of her shiny new car. It didn't escape my notice that she was dressed in corduroys, running shoes, and a Richmond Police Department jacket. Vain woman that she was, she would never show up in a fine restaurant dressed like that.

"Excuse me," she said loudly to Marino.

"Oh gee, I'm sorry," he gushed, stepping to one side.

I chose my next words carefully. I could not directly accuse her, but I intended to make sure she knew she'd gotten away with nothing and if she persisted in her ambushes, she would lose and she would pay.

"You're an investigator," I thoughtfully said to her. "Maybe you can tell me your opinion on how someone might have gotten hold of my password and e-mailed messages, impersonating me. And then someone—most likely the same person—started an asinine, lobotomized chat room on the Internet called *Dear Dr. Kay*."

"How awful. I'm sorry, I can't help you. Computers are not my specialty," she said with a smile.

Her eyes were dark holes, her teeth flashing like steel blades in the glow of sodium lights.

"All I can suggest is you look at the people closest to you, perhaps someone disgruntled, a friend you've fallen out with," she continued her act. "I really have no idea, but I would expect it's someone with a link to you. I've heard your niece is an expert in computers. Maybe she could help you."

163

Her mention of Lucy infuriated me.

"I've been wanting to talk to her," Bray said as a by-the-way. "You know, we're implementing COMPSTAT and need a computer expert."

COMPSTAT, or computer-driven statistics, was a new model of enlightened, technologically advanced policing devised by the New York Police Department. Computer experts would be needed for it, but to suggest a project like that for someone with Lucy's skills and experience was an insult.

"You might pass this along to her when you talk next," Bray added.

Marino's rage was boiling like water in a pot.

"We really should sit down sometime, Kay, and let me tell you about some of my experiences in Washington," she said as if I had never worked anywhere but in a small town. "You can't even begin to know the things people will try to bring you down. Especially women against the women, sabotage in the workplace. I've seen the best topple."

"I'm sure you have," I said.

She locked her car door and said, "Just so you know, you don't need a reservation to sit at the bar. That's where I usually eat anyway. They're famous for their steak fromage, but I recommend you try the lobster, Kay. And you, Captain Marino, would love their onion rings. I hear they're to die for."

We watched her walk off.

"Fucking bitch," Marino said.

"Let's get out of here," I said.

"Yeah, last thing I want to do is eat anywhere near poison like that. I ain't even hungry."

"That won't last."

164

We climbed into his truck and I sank beneath a heavy depression that held me down like tar. I wanted to find some victory, some ray of optimism in what had just transpired, but I couldn't. I felt defeated. Worse, I felt foolish.

"Want a cigarette?" Marino asked inside the dark cab as he punched in the lighter.

"Why not," I muttered. "I'm going to stop again pretty soon."

He handed one to me and lit his. He gave me the lighter. He kept glancing over at me, knowing how I felt.

"I still think it was a good thing we did," he said. "I bet she's in that restaurant belting down whiskeys because we got her good."

"We didn't get her good," I replied, squinting at the lights of cars passing by. "With her, I'm afraid the only silver bullet is prevention. We have to guard against further damage by not only anticipating but also following up on everything we do."

I opened the window several inches, cold air touching my hair. I blew out smoke.

"No-show Chuck," I commented.

"Oh, he showed up. You just didn't see him because he saw us first and hightailed it out of there."

"You sure?"

"I saw his piece-of-shit Miata turning into the road leading to the shopping center, and then about halfway to the parking lot it suddenly did a U-turn and got the hell out of Dodge. And this was at the exact time Bray said something else on her portable after she saw us outside her car."

"Chuck's a direct conduit from me to her," I said. "She may as well have a key to my office."

"Hell, maybe she does," he said. "But, Doc, you just leave Chuckie-boy to me."

"Now, that scares me," I said. "Please don't go doing something reckless, Marino. He does work for me, after all. I don't need any other problems."

"My point exactly. You don't need any more problems."

He dropped me off at the office and waited until I got into my car. I followed him out of the parking lot, and he went his way and I went mine.

19

The tiny moon-eyes from the dead man's skin glowed in my mind. They looked out from that deep, off-limits place where I stored my fears, which were many and of a kind not felt by anyone else I knew. Wind shook bare trees and clouds streamed like banners across the sky as a cold front rushed in.

I had heard on the news the temperature might dip into the twenties that night, which seemed impossible after weeks that felt like fall. It seemed everything was out of balance and abnormal in my life. Lucy wasn't Lucy so I couldn't call her and she wasn't speaking to me. Marino was working a homicide even though he wasn't a detective anymore, and Benton was gone, and everywhere I looked for him I found an empty frame. I still waited for his car to drive up, for the phone to ring, for the sound of his voice, because it was too soon for my heart to accept what my brain knew.

I turned off the Downtown Expressway onto Cary Street, and as I drove past a shopping center and the Venice Restaurant, I became aware of a car behind me. It was driving very slowly and too far away for me to tell anything about the person behind the wheel. Instinct told me to slow down, and when I did, so did the car. I turned right on Cary Street, and the car stayed with me. When I took a left into Windsor Farms, there it was, maintaining the same safe distance.

I didn't want to get any deeper into this neighborhood because the roads were winding and narrow and dark. There were many cul-de-sacs. I took a right on Dover and dialed Marino's number as the car turned right, too, and my fear grew.

"Marino," I said out loud to nobody there. "Be home, Marino."

I ended the call and tried again.

"Marino! Goddamn it, be home!" I said to the hands-free phone in the dashboard as Marino's clunky cordless phone inside his house rang and rang.

He probably had it parked by the TV, as usual. Half the time he couldn't find it because he didn't return it to its base. Maybe he wasn't home yet.

"What?" his loud voice surprised me.

"It's me."

"Goddamn-motherfucking-son-of-a-bitch. If I hit my knee on that goddamn table one more time . . . !"

"Marino, listen to me!"

"Once more and it's out in the yard and I'm gonna smash the shit out of it with a hammer! Right in the fucking kneecap! I can't see the fucking thing 'cause it's glass and guess who said it would look so nice there?"

"Calm down," I exclaimed, watching the car in my mirror.

"I've had three beers and I'm hungry and tired as hell. What?" he asked.

"There's someone following me."

I turned right on Windsor Way, heading back to Cary Street.

I drove at a normal speed. I did nothing out of the ordinary except not head for my house.

"What do you mean, someone's following you?" Marino asked.

"What the hell do you think I mean?" I said as my anxiety heated up more.

"Then head this way right now," he said. "Get out of that dark neighborhood of yours."

"I am."

"Can you see a plate number or anything?"

"No. He's too far behind me. It seems he's deliberately staying far enough behind me so I can't read the tag or see his face."

I got back on the expressway, heading to the Powhite Parkway, and the person tailing me apparently gave up and turned off somewhere. Lights of moving cars and trucks and the iridescent paint on signs were confusing, and my heart was beating hard. The half-moon slipped in and out of clouds like a button, and gusts of wind rushed the side of the car like linebackers.

I dialed my answering service at home. I had three hangups and a fourth message that was a slap in the face.

"Chief Bray here," it began. "So nice to run into you at Buckhead's. I have a few policy and procedural issues to discuss with you. Managing crime scenes and evidence, and so on. I've been meaning to discuss them with you, Kay."

The sound of my first name coming out of her mouth infuriated me.

"Maybe we can have lunch in the next few days," her recorded voice went on. "A nice private lunch at the Commonwealth Club?"

My home phone number was unlisted and I was very

careful who I gave it to, but it was no riddle how she'd gotten it. My staff, including Ruffin, had to be able to reach me at home.

"In case you haven't heard," Bray's message went on, "Al Carson resigned today. You remember him, I'm sure? Deputy chief of investigations. A real shame. Major Inman will be acting deputy chief."

I slowed at a toll booth and tossed a token into the bin. I moved on and a beat-up Toyota full of teenaged boys stared boldly at me as they passed. One of them mouthed *mother-fucker* for no apparent reason.

I concentrated on the road as I thought about what Wagner had said. Someone was pressuring Representative Connors to push legislation that would transfer my office out of Health and Human Services and into Public Safety, where the police department would have more control over me.

Women could not join the prestigious Commonwealth Club, where half of the major business deals and politics affecting Virginia were made by male power brokers with old family names. Rumor had it that these men, many of whom I knew, congregated around the indoor swimming pool, most of them naked. They bartered and pontificated in the locker room, a forum where women weren't allowed.

Since Bray couldn't walk through the door of that ivy-draped eighteenth-century club unless she was the guest of a member, my suspicions about her ultimate ambition were virtually confirmed. Bray was lobbying members of the General Assembly and powerful businessmen. She wanted to be the Secretary of Public Safety and have my office transferred to that secretariat. Then she could fire me herself.

I reached Midlothian Turnpike and could see Marino's house long before I got near it. His gaudy, outrageous

Christmas decorations, including some three hundred thousand lights, glowed above the horizon like an amusement park. All one had to do was follow the steady traffic heading that way, because Marino's house had risen to number one on Richmond's annual Christmas Tacky Tour. People couldn't resist coming to see what was truly an amazing sight.

Lights of every color were sprinkled in trees like neon candy. Santas, snowmen, trains and toy soldiers glowed in the yard, and gingerbread cookies held hands. Candy canes brightly stood sentry along his sidewalk, and lights spelled out *Seasons Greetings* and *Think Snow* on the roof. In a part of the yard where scarcely a flower grew and grass was patchy brown all year long, Marino had planted happy electric gardens. There was the North Pole, where Mr. and Mrs.. Claus seemed to be discussing plans, and nearby choir-boys sang while flamingos perched on the chimney and ice skaters twirled around a spruce.

A white limousine crept past, followed by a church van, as I hurried up his front steps, feeling irradiated and trapped in a spotlight.

"Every time I see this, it confirms you've lost your mind," I said when Marino came to the door and I quickly ducked away from curious eyes. "Last year was bad enough."

"I'm up to three fuse boxes," he proudly announced.

He was in jeans and socks and a red flannel shirt with the tail hanging out.

"Least I can come home and something makes me happy," he said. "Pizza's on the way. I got bourbon if you want some."

"What pizza?"

"One I ordered. Everything on it. My treat. Papa John's don't even need my address anymore. They just follow the lights."

"What about hot decaffeinated tea," I said, quite certain he would have no such thing.

"You got to be kidding," he replied.

I looked around as we walked through the living room into his small kitchen. Of course, he had decorated the inside of his house, too. The tree was up and flickering by the fireplace. Presents, almost all of them fake, were piled high, and every window was framed by strands of red chili pepper lights.

"Bray called me," I said, filling the teakettle with water. "Someone gave her my home number."

"Guess who." He yanked open the refrigerator door, his good mood retreating fast.

"And I think I might know why that happened."

I set the kettle on the stove and turned on the burner. Lights flickered.

"Deputy Chief Carson resigned today. Or supposedly resigned," I said.

Marino popped open a beer. If he was aware of this news, he didn't show it.

"Did you know he quit?" I asked.

"I don't know nothing anymore."

"Apparently Major Inman is the acting deputy chief . . ."

"Oh, of course, of course," Marino loudly said. "And you know why? Because there're two majors, one in uniform, the other in investigations, so of course Bray sends her boy from uniform in there to take over investigations."

He'd finished the beer in what seemed three gulps. He violently crushed the can and threw it into the trash. He missed, and the can clattered across the floor.

"You got any idea what that means?" he said. "Well, let me tell you. It means Bray's now running uniform *and* investigations, meaning she's running the entire fucking department and probably controlling the entire budget, too. And the chief's her biggest fan because she makes him look good. Tell me how this woman comes in and not even three months later can do all that?"

"Clearly she's got connections. Probably did before she took this job. And I don't mean just to the chief."

"Well, to who then?"

"Marino, it could be anyone. It doesn't matter at this point. It's too late for it to matter. Now we have to contend with her, not the chief. Her, not the person who might have pulled strings."

He popped open another beer, angrily pacing the kitchen.

"Now I know why Carson showed up at the scene," he said. "He knew this was coming. He knows how bad this shit stinks and maybe he was trying to warn us in his own way, or just signing off. His career's over. The end. Last crime scene. Last everything."

"He's such a good man," I said. "Goddamn it, Marino. There's got to be something we can do."

His phone rang, startling me. The sound of cars on the street out front was a steady rumble of engines. Marino's continuous tinny Christmas music was playing "Jingle Bells" again.

"Bray wants to talk to me about so-called changes she's instigating," I told him.

"Oh, I'm sure she does," he said, his stocking feet padding across linoleum. "And I guess you're just supposed to drop everything when she suddenly wants to have you for lunch, which is what she's gonna do, have you between rye with lots of mustard."

He grabbed the phone.

"What?" he yelled at the poor person on the other end.

"Uh huh, uh huh. Yeah," Marino said, listening.

I rummaged in cabinets and found one smashed box of Lipton tea bags.

"I'm here. Why the hell don't you talk to me?" Marino indignantly said into the phone.

He listened, pacing about.

"Now that's a good one," he said. "Hold on a minute. Let me just ask her."

He put his hand over the receiver and asked in a hushed voice, "Are you *sure* you're Dr. Scarpetta?"

He got back to the person on the phone. "She says she was last time she checked," and he irritably shoved the receiver my way.

"Yes?" I asked.

"Dr. Scarpetta?" an unfamiliar voice said.

"Here."

"I'm Ted Francisco, ATF field office in Miami."

I froze as if someone were pointing a gun at me.

"Lucy told me Captain Marino might know where you are if we couldn't reach you at home. Can you speak to her?"

"Of course," I said, alarmed.

"Aunt Kay?" Her voice came over the line.

"Lucy! What is it?" I said. "Are you all right?"

"I don't know if you heard what happened down here . . ."

"I haven't heard anything," I quickly said as Marino stopped what he was doing and stared at me.

"Our takedown. It didn't go right, too much to go into, but it went really, really bad. I had to kill two of them. Jo got shot."

"Oh, dear God," I said. "Please tell me she's all right."

"I don't know," she said with a steadiness that was

completely abnormal. "They have her in Jackson Memorial under some other name and I can't call her. They've got me in isolation because they're afraid the others will try to find us. Retribution. The cartel. All I know is she was bleeding from her head and leg, unconscious when the ambulance got her."

Lucy registered no emotion at all. She sounded like one of the robots or artificial intelligence computers she had programmed at earlier times in her career.

"I'll get . . ." I started to say when Agent Francisco suddenly was back on the line.

"I know you're going to hear about this on the news, Dr. Scarpetta, and I wanted to make sure you knew. Especially that Lucy's not hurt."

"Maybe not physically," I said.

"I want to tell you exactly what will happen next."

"What will happen next," I interrupted him, "is I'm flying down there immediately. I'll get a private plane if I have to."

"I'd like to ask you not to do that," he said. "Let me explain. This is a very, very vicious group, and Lucy and Jo know far too much about them, about who some of them are and how they do business. Within hours of the shooting, we sent a Miami-Dade bomb squad to Lucy and Jo's respective undercover residences and our bomb dog detected pipe bombs wired under each of their cars."

I pulled a chair out from Marino's kitchen table and sat down. I felt weak all over. My vision was blurred.

"Are you there?" he said.

"Yes, yes."

"What's happening right now, Dr. Scarpetta, is Miami-Dade is working the cases, just as you might expect, and normally, we'd have a shooting review team on its way in addition to peer support guys—agents who have been involved in critical incidents and are trained to work with other agents going through things like this. But because of the threat level, we're sending Lucy north, to D.C., to wherever she's safe."

"Thank you for taking such good care of her. God bless you," I said in a voice that didn't sound like me.

"Look, I know how you feel," Agent Francisco said. "I promise you I do. I was at Waco."

"Thank you," I said again. "What will DEA do with Jo?"

"Transfer her to another hospital a million miles away from here as soon as we can."

"What about MCV?" I asked.

"I'm not familiar . . ."

"Her family lives in Richmond, as you may know, but more to the point, MCV is excellent and I'm on the faculty," I said. "If you get her here, I'll personally make sure she's well taken care of."

He hesitated, then said, "Thank you. I will take that under advisement and discuss it with her supervisor."

When he hung up, I stood staring at the phone.

"What?" Marino asked.

"The takedown went haywire. Lucy shot two people to death . . ."

"Was it a good shooting?" he cut me off.

"No shooting is good!"

"Goddamn it, Doc, you know what I mean. Was it justified? Don't tell me she fucking shot two agents by accident!"

"No, of course not. Jo was shot. I'm not sure of her condition."

"Fuck!" he exclaimed, pounding his fist so hard on the

kitchen counter, dishes rattled in the drain board. "Lucy just had to go slug it out with somebody, didn't she? They shouldn't have even had her in a takedown like this! I coulda told them that! She's just been waiting to shoot the shit out of someone, to go in like a damn cowboy with pistols blazing to pay back everyone she hates in life . . . !"

"Marino, stop it."

"You saw what she was like at your house the other night," he railed on. "She's been a damn psycho ever since Benton got killed. There's no payback that's enough, not even shooting that damn helicopter out of the air and chumming the water with Carrie Grethen's and Newton Joyce's pieces and parts."

"That's enough," I said, exhausted. "Please, Marino. This isn't helping anything. Lucy's a professional, and you know that. ATF would never have given her an assignment like this if she weren't. They know her story very well and evaluated and counseled her extensively after what happened to Benton and all the rest of it. In fact, how she handled that entire nightmare only gave them more respect for her as both an agent and a human being."

He was silent as he opened a bottle of Jack Daniel's.

Then he said, "Well, you and I know she ain't handling it so well."

"Lucy has always been able to compartmentalize."

"Yeah, and how healthy is that?"

"I guess we should ask each other that."

"But I'm telling you right now, this time she ain't gonna handle it well, Doc," he said, splashing bourbon into a glass and dropping in several ice cubes. "She killed two people in the line of duty barely a year ago, and now she's just done it again. Most guys go their entire careers and don't even take a shot at somebody. That's why I'm trying to make you understand it's gonna be viewed differently this time. The big guys in Washington are gonna consider that maybe they got a gunslinger on their hands, someone who's a problem."

He handed the drink to me.

"I've known cops, agents like that," he said. "They always have justifiable reasons for judicial homicide, but if you look hard at it, you begin to get the drift that they subconsciously set things up to go bad. They thrive on it."

"Lucy's not like that."

"Yeah, she's only been pissed off since the day she was born. And by the way, you ain't going anywhere tonight. You're staying here with me and Father Christmas."

He poured himself a bourbon, too, and we went into his shabby, crowded living room with its crooked lampshades, its dusty, bent Venetian blinds and the sharp-cornered glass coffee table he blamed on me. He dropped into his recliner chair, which was so old he had repaired splits in the brown Naugahyde with duct tape. I remembered the first time I walked into his house. After recovering from the dismay, I realized he was proud of how thoroughly he wore every-thing out, except for his truck, aboveground pool, and now his Christmas decorations.

He caught me staring dismally at his chair as I curled up in a corner of the green corduroy couch I tended to choose. It might have been missing its wale wherever bodies came in touch with it, but it was cozy.

"One day I'll get a new one of these," he said, pushing down the lever on the side of the chair and sliding the footrest out.

He wiggled his stocking feet as if his toes were cramped, and flicked on the TV. I was surprised when he changed the channel to twenty-one, the Arts & Entertainment network.

"I didn't know you watched *Biography*," I said.

"Oh yeah. And the real-life cops shows they usually got on. This may sound like I been sniffing glue, but does it strike you how everything in the world's gone to hell ever since Bray came to town?"

"I'm sure it would strike you that way, after what she's been doing to you."

"Huh. And she's not been doing the same thing to you?" he challenged, sipping his drink. "I'm not the only person in this room she's trying to ruin."

"I don't think she has the power to cause everything else going on in life," I replied.

"Let me just run through the list for you, Doc, and make sure to remember we're talking about a three-month period, okay? She arrives in Richmond. I get thrown back in uniform. You suddenly have a thief in your office. You have a snitch who breaks into your e-mail and turns you into Dear Abby.

"Then this dead guy shows up in a container and Interpol's suddenly in the picture, and now Lucy kills two people, which is convenient for Bray, by the way. Don't forget, she's been all hot and bothered about getting Lucy to sign on with Richmond, and if ATF throws Lucy back like a fish, she's gonna need a job. And oh yeah, now someone's following you."

I watched a young, gorgeous Liberace playing the piano and singing while a voice-over of a friend talked about what a kind, generous man the musician had been.

"You're not listening to me," Marino raised his voice again.

"I'm listening."

He heaved himself up again with an exasperated huff and padded into the kitchen.

"Have we heard anything from Interpol?" I called out as

he made a lot of noise tearing open paper and rummaging through the silverware drawer.

"Nothing worth passing on."

The microwave hummed.

"It would be nice if you'd pass it on anyway," I said, annoyed.

Stage lights caught Liberace blowing kisses to his audience and his sequins flashed like an intense red and gold fireworks display. Marino walked back into the living room with a bowl of ruffled potato chips and a container of some sort of dip.

"The guy at State Police got a computer message back from them within an hour. They just requested more info, that's all."

"That tells us a lot," I said, disappointed. "That probably means they didn't get a hit on anything significant. The old fracture of the jaw, the unusual accessory cusp of the Carabelli, not to mention fingerprints. None of it matched up with anybody wanted or missing."

"Yeah. It's a pisser," he said, his mouth full as he held out the bowl to me.

"No, thanks."

"It's really good. What you do is soften the cream cheese in the microwave first and put in jalapeños. It's a lot better for you than onion dip."

"I'm sure."

"You know, I always liked him." He pointed a greasy finger at the TV. "I don't care if he was queer. You gotta admit he had style. If people are gonna pay all that money for records and concert tickets, by God they ought to get people who don't look and act like some schmoe on the street.

180

"Let me tell you," Marino said with his mouth full, "shootings are a bitch. You get investigated as if you made an attempt on the damn president, and then there's all the counseling and everybody worrying about your mental health so much it makes you crazy."

He threw back bourbon and crunched more chips.

"She's gonna get some time on the bricks," he went on, using cop jargon for involuntary time off. "And Miami detectives are gonna work it like they always work homicides. Got to. And everything will have the hell reviewed out of it."

He looked over at me, wiping his hands on his jeans.

"I know this won't make you feel good, but maybe you're the last person she wants to see right now," he said.

20

There was a rule in our building that any evidence, even something as innocuous as a ten-print card, had to be transported on the service elevator. This was located at the end of a hallway where two cleaning ladies were this minute pushing their carts as I headed to Neils Vander's lab.

"Good morning, Merle. And Beatrice, how are you?" I smiled at them.

Their eyes landed on the towel-covered surgical pan and the paper sheets covering the gurney I was pushing. They had been around long enough to know that whenever I carried something bagged or pushed something covered, it was nothing they wanted to know about.

"Uh-oh," Merle said.

"Uh-oh is right," Beatrice chimed in.

I pushed the elevator button.

"You going anyplace special for Christmas, Dr. Scarpetta?"

They could tell by the look on my face that Christmas was a topic I didn't particularly care to talk about.

"You're probably too busy for Christmas," Merle quickly said.

Both women got uncomfortable for the same reason everybody else did when they were reminded of what had happened to Benton.

"I know this time of year gets real busy," Merle awkwardly changed the subject. "All those people drinking on the road. More suicides and people getting mad at each other."

Christmas would be here in about two weeks. Fielding was on call that day. I couldn't count how many Christmases I had worn a pager.

"People burning up in fires, too."

"When bad things happen this time of year," I said to them as the elevator doors opened, "we feel them more. That's a lot of it."

"Maybe that's it."

"I don't know 'bout that, remember that electrical fire . . . ?"

The doors shut and I headed up to the second floor, which had been designed to accommodate tours for citizens and politicians and anyone else interested in our work. All labs were behind big expanses of plate glass, and at first this had seemed odd and uncomfortable to scientists used to working in secret behind cinder block walls. By now, nobody cared. Examiners tested trigger pulls and worked with bloodstains, fingerprints and fibers without paying much attention to who was on the other side of the glass, which at this moment included me pushing my gurney past.

Neils Vander's world was a large space of countertops, with all sorts of unusual technical instruments and jury-rigged contraptions scattered all over the place. Against one wall were wooden cabinets with glass doors, and these Vander had turned into glue chambers, using clothesline and clothespins to hold up objects exposed to the Super Glue fumes generated by a hot plate.

In the past, scientists and police had had very little success in lifting prints from nonporous objects such as plastic bags, electrical tape and leather. Then, quite by accident, it was discovered that the fumes from Super Glue adhere to ridge detail, much as traditional dusting powder does, and out pops a white latent print. In a corner was another glue chamber called a Cyvac II that could accommodate larger objects such as a shotgun or rifle or car bumper, or theoretically even an entire body.

Humidity chambers raised prints off porous items, such as paper or wood, that had been treated with ninhydrin, although Vander sometimes resorted to the quick method of using a household steam iron, and once or twice had scorched the evidence, or so I'd heard. Scattered about were Nederman lights equipped with vacuums to suck up fumes and residues from drug baggies.

Other rooms in Vander's domain housed the Automatic Fingerprints Identification System known as AFIS, and darkrooms for digital audio and video enhancement. He oversaw the photo lab, where more than a hundred and fifty rolls of processed film came off the speedmaster every day. It took me a while to locate Vander, but I finally caught him in the impression lab, where pizza boxes ingenious cops used to transport plaster casts of tire tracks and footwear prints were neatly stacked in corners, and a door someone had tried to kick in was leaning against a wall.

Vander was seated before a computer, comparing footwear impressions on a split screen. I left the gurney outside the door.

"You're nice to do this," I said.

His pale blue eyes always seemed to be elsewhere, and as

usual, his lab coat was stained purple from ninhydrin and a felt-tip pen had bled through one of his pockets.

"This is a real good one," he said, tapping the video screen as he got out of his chair. "Guy buys new shoes and you know how slippery they are if the bottoms are leather? So he gets a knife and slashes them, you know, roughs them up because he's getting married and doesn't want to slip coming down the aisle."

I followed him out of the lab, not really in the mood for anecdotes.

"Well, he gets burglarized. Shoes, bunch of other clothes and stuff, gone. Two days later a woman in his neighborhood is raped. Police find these weird shoeprints at the scene. In fact, there'd been quite a lot of burglaries in that area."

We entered the alternate light source lab.

"Turns out it was this kid. Thirteen." Vander was shaking his head as he flipped on the lights. "I just don't know about kids anymore. When I was thirteen, the worst thing I ever did was shoot a bird with a BB gun."

He mounted the Luma-Lite on a tripod.

"That's pretty bad in my book," I told him.

While I laid out the clothes on white paper under the chemical hood, he plugged in the Luma-Lite and its fans began to whir. A minute later he started the source lamp, rotating the intensity knob to full power. He set a pair of protective glasses near me and placed a blue 450 nanometer optical filter over the output lens. We put on our glasses and turned out the lights. The Luma-Lite cast a blue glow across the floor. Vander's shadow moved as he did, and nearby jars of dye lit up Brilliant Yellow and Blitz Green and Redwop. Their dust was a constellation of neon stars scattered throughout the room.

"You know, we've got these idiots at police departments these days who are getting their own Luma-Lites and processing their own scenes," Vander's voice sounded in the dark. "So they dust with Redwop and put the print on a black background, so I have to photograph it with the Luma-Lite on and reverse the damn print to white."

He started with the plastic wastepaper basket found inside the container and was instantly rewarded with the faint ridges of fingerprint smudges, which he dusted with Redwop, its electric red dust drifting through the dark.

"Good way to start," I said. "Keep it up, Neils."

Vander moved the tripod closer to the dead man's black jeans and the inside-out right pocket began to glow a dull rouge. I poked the material with my gloved finger and found smears of iridescent orange.

"Don't believe I've ever gotten a red like that before," Vander mused.

We spent an hour going over all of the clothing, including shoes and belt, and nothing else fluoresced.

"Definitely two different things there," Vander said as I turned on the lights. "Two different things fluorescing naturally. No dye stains involved except the one I used on the bucket."

I picked up the phone and called the morgue. Fielding answered.

"I need everything that was in the pockets of our unidentified man. It should be air-drying on a tray."

"That would be some foreign money, a cigar clipper and a lighter."

"Yes."

Lights off again and we finished scanning the exterior of all the clothing, finding more of the odd pale hair.

"Is that coming off his head?" Vander asked as my forceps entered the cool, blue light, gently grabbing hairs and placing them inside an envelope.

"His head hair is dark and coarse," I replied. "So no, this hair can't be his."

"Looks like cat hair. One of these long haired types that I don't allow in the house anymore. Angora? Himalayan?"

"Rare. Not too many people have either one," I said.

"My wife loves cats," Vander went on. "She had this one named Creamsicle. Damn thing would look for my clothes and lie on them, and when I'd find them to get dressed, damn if they didn't look just like this."

"I guess it could be cat hair," I supposed.

"Too fine for dog hair, don't you think?"

"Not if it's something like a Skye terrier. Long, straight silky hair."

"Pale yellow?"

"They can be tawny," I said. "Maybe the undercoat? I don't know."

"Maybe the guy's a breeder or works with one," Vander suggested. "Aren't there longhair rabbits, too?"

"Knock, knock," Fielding's voice sounded as he opened the door.

He walked in, tray in hand, and we turned on the lights.

"There are angora rabbits," I said. "The ones the sweaters are made from."

"You look like you've been working out," Vander said to Fielding.

"You mean I haven't looked that way before?" Fielding asked.

Vander looked puzzled as if he'd never noticed that Fielding was a body-sculpting fanatic.

"We've picked up on some sort of residue in one of the pockets," I told Fielding. "It's the same pocket the money was in."

Fielding removed the towel that covered the tray.

"I recognize the pounds and deutsche marks," he said. "But not those two coppery things."

"I think they're Belgian francs," I said.

"And I got no clue what this cash is."

It had been lined up bill by bill to dry.

"It looks like it's got some sort of temple on it and what? What's a dirham? Arabic?"

"I'll get Rose to check."

"Why would somebody have four different kinds of money on him?" Fielding asked.

"If he was in and out of a lot of countries in a short period of time," I ventured a guess. "That's all I can think of. Let's get the residues analyzed ASAP."

We put on our protective glasses and Vander turned out the lights. The same dull rouge and brilliant orange fluoresced on several of the bills. We scanned all of them on both sides, finding flecks and smudges here and there, and then the ridge detail of a latent fingerprint. It was barely visible on the upper left corner of a hundred-dirham bill.

"We must be living right," Fielding said.

"Hot dog," Vander chortled. "Two for two! I'm going to hop on this right away. Get one of my buddies at Secret Service to run 'em through MORPHO, PRINTRAK, NEC-AFIS, WIN, whatever—every database out there, all forty-fifty million prints."

Nothing excited Vander more than finding a loop or whorl he could hurl through cyberspace to hog-tie a criminal.

"Is the FBI's national database up and running yet?" Fielding asked.

"Secret Service already has every damn print the FBI does, but as usual, the Bureau has to re-create the wheel. Spending all this money to create their own database, and using different vendors so everything is incompatible with everybody else. I've got a dinner to go to tonight."

He focused the Luma-Lite on the foul, dark flesh pinned to the cutting board, and instantly two specks fluoresced bright yellow. They were not much bigger than a nailhead, and were parallel and symmetrical and could not be rubbed off.

"I'm pretty sure it's a tattoo," I said.

"Yeah," Vander agreed. "Don't know what else it could be. Nothing else is doing anything."

The flesh from the dead man's back was murky and muddy in the cool, blue light.

"But see how dark this is in here?" Vander's gloved finger outlined an area about the size of my hand.

"I wonder what the hell that is," Fielding said.

"I just don't know why it's so dark," Vander mused.

"Maybe the tattoo's black or brown," I suggested.

"Well, we'll give Phil a whirl at it," Vander said. "What time's it getting to be? You know, I wish Edith hadn't said we'd do this dinner tonight. I gotta go. Dr. Scarpetta, you're on your own. Damn, damn. I hate it when Edith wants to *celebrate* something."

"Ah, come on, big guy," Fielding said. "You know what a party animal you are."

"I don't drink much anymore. I feel it."

"You're supposed to feel it, Neils," I said.

Phil Lapointe was not in a good mood when I walked

189

into the image enhancement lab, which looked more like a production studio than a place where scientists worked with pixels and contrasts in all shades of light and dark to put a face on evil. Lapointe was one of our first Institute graduates, and he was skilled and determined but had not yet learned to move on when a case absolutely wouldn't.

"Damn," he said, raking his fingers through thick red hair and squinting as he leaned into a twenty-four-inch screen.

"I hate to do this to you," I said.

He impatiently tapped keys, rolling another shade of gray down a freeze-frame from a convenience store videotape. The figure in dark glasses and hairnet cap was not made much clearer, but the store clerk was certainly vivid as blood sprayed in a fine mist from his head.

"I tweak it and it's almost there, and then it's not," Lapointe wearily complained with a sigh. "I see this damn thing in my sleep."

"Unbelievable," I said, staring. "Look how relaxed he is. It's like all of it is an afterthought, no big deal. A what-the-hell, may-as-well."

"Yeah, that much I've got." Lapointe stretched his back. "Just wasted the guy for no reason. That's what I don't get."

"I give you a few more years and you'll get it," I said.

"I don't want to become cynical, if that's what you're saying."

"It's not getting cynical. It's about finally figuring out there don't have to be reasons," I told him.

He stared at the computer screen, lost in the last picture that had ever captured Pyle Gant alive. I had performed his autopsy.

"Let's see what we've got here," Lapointe said, removing the towel from the surgical pan.

190

Gant was twenty-three with a two-month-old baby and working overtime to pay for his wife's birthday necklace on layaway.

"This must be from The Container Man. You're thinking a tattoo?"

Gant lost control of his bladder before he was shot.

"Dr. Scarpetta?"

I knew this because the back of his jeans and the seat of the chair behind the counter were soaked with urine. When I looked out the window, two cops were restraining his hysterical wife in the parking lot.

"Dr. Scarpetta?"

She was screaming and slapping. She still had braces on her teeth.

"Thirty-one dollars and twelve cents," I muttered.

Lapointe saved the file and closed it.

"What was?" he asked me.

"That's what was in the cash register," I replied.

Lapointe rolled his chair around, opening drawers and getting out different-colored filters and rummaging for gloves. The phone rang and he answered it.

"Hold on." He held the receiver out to me. "It's for you."

It was Rose.

"I got hold of someone in the foreign currency department of Crestar," she said. "The money you asked me about is Moroccan. To date, there are nine-point-three dirham to the dollar. So two thousand dirham would be about two hundred and fifteen dollars."

"Thank you, Rose . . ."

"And there's one other thing you might find interesting," she went on. "It's forbidden for Moroccan money to be brought in or taken out of the country."

"I have a feeling this guy was into a lot of things that are forbidden," I said. "Can you try Agent Francisco again?"

"Certainly."

My understanding of ATF protocols was fast turning into the fear that Lucy had rejected me. I desperately wanted to see her. I wanted to do whatever I had to do to make that happen. I hung up and lifted the cork cutting board out of the pan, and Lapointe looked at it under a strong light.

"I'm not feeling real optimistic about this," he let me know.

"Well, don't start seeing this one in your sleep, too," I told him. "I'm not hopeful, either. All we can do is try."

What was left of the epidermis was as greenish-black as a quarry or a swamp, and the flesh underneath was getting darker and dryer like curing meat. We centered the corkboard under a high-resolution camera that was connected to the video screen.

"Nope," Lapointe said. "Too much reflection."

He tried oblique light and then switched to black and white. He fitted various filters over the camera lens. Blue was no good, nor was yellow, but when he tried red, the iridescent specks peeked out at us again. Lapointe enlarged them. They were perfectly round. I thought of full moons, of a werewolf with evil yellow eyes.

"I'm not going to be able to get this any better live. I'll just grab it," Lapointe said, disappointed.

He captured the image onto his hard drive and began to process it, the software making it possible for us to see some two hundred shades of gray that we couldn't detect with the unaided eye.

Lapointe worked the keyboard and mouse, going in and out of windows, and using contrast, brightness, and enlarging, shrinking and adjusting. He eliminated background noise, or *trash*, as he called it, and we began to see hair pores, and then the stippling made by a tattoo needle. Out of the murk emerged black wavy lines that became fur or feathers. A black line sprouting daisy petals became a claw.

"What do you think?" I asked Lapointe.

"I think this is the best we're going to get," he impatiently said.

"We know anybody who's an expert in tattoos?"

"Why don't you start with your histologist," he said.

21

I found George Gara in his lab, retrieving his bagged lunch from a refrigerator posted with a sign that read *No Food*. Inside were stains such as silver nitrate and mucicarmine, in addition to Schiff reagents, none of which was compatible with anything edible.

"That's not such a great idea," I said.

"I'm sorry," he stuttered, setting the bag on the counter and shutting the refrigerator door.

"We have a fridge in the break room, George," I said. "You're more than welcome to use it."

He didn't respond, and I realized that he was so painfully shy he probably didn't go into the break room for a reason. My heart ached for him. I couldn't imagine the shame he must have felt when he was growing up and couldn't talk without stuttering. Maybe that explained the tattoos slowly taking over his body like kudzu. Maybe they made him feel special and manly. I pulled out a chair and sat down.

"George, can I ask you about your tattoos?" I asked.

He blushed.

"I'm fascinated by them and need some help with a problem."

"Sure," he said with uncertainty.

"Do you have someone you go to? A real expert? Someone very experienced in tattooing?"

"Yes, ma'am," he replied. "I wouldn't go to just anyone."

"You get your tattoos locally? Because I need to find a place where I can ask some questions and not run into bad characters, if you know what I mean."

"Pit," he immediately said. "As in pit bull, but Pit's his real name. John Pit. He's a really good guy. You want me to call him for you?" he asked, stuttering badly.

"I would be grateful if you would," I said.

Gara pulled a small address book out of his back pocket and looked up a number. When he got Pit on the line, he explained who I was, and apparently Pit was very agreeable.

"Here." Gara handed me the phone. "I'll let you explain the rest of it."

That took several efforts. Pit was home and just waking up.

"So you think you might have some luck?" I asked.

"I've seen pretty much all the flash out there," he replied.

"I'm sorry. I don't know what that is."

"Flash's the stencils, I guess you could call them. You know, the design people pick out. Every inch of wall space I got is covered with flash. That's why I'm thinking you might want to come here instead of me coming to your office. We might see something that gives us a clue. But I will tell you I'm not open Wednesdays or Thursdays. And payday weekend just about killed me. I'm still recovering. But I'll open up for you, since this must be important. You bringing in whoever's got this tattoo?"

He still didn't quite get it.

"No, I'm bringing the tattoo," I said. "But not the person who goes with it."

"Wait a minute," he said. "Okay, okay, now I'm hearing you. So you cut it off the dead guy."

"Can you handle that?"

"Oh, hell, yeah. I can handle anything."

"What time?"

"How 'bout as soon as you can get here?"

I hung up and was startled to see Ruffin in the doorway watching me. I had a feeling he'd been there for a while, listening to my conversation, since my back was to him as I'd taken notes. His face was tired, his eyes red, as if he'd been up half the night drinking.

"You don't look well, Chuck," I said without much sympathy.

"I was wondering if I could go home," he said. "I think I'm coming down with something."

"I'm so sorry to hear that. There's a new, very contagious strain going around, thought to be carried by the Internet. It's called the *six-thirty bug*," I said. "People dash home from work and log onto their home computers. If they have a home computer."

Ruffin's face turned white.

"That's pretty funny," Gara said. "But I don't get the six-thirty part of it."

"The time half the world signs onto AOL," I replied. "Of course, Chuck, you can go home. Get some rest. I'll walk you out. We need to stop in the decomposed room first and get the tattoo."

I had removed it from the corkboard and placed it inside a jar of formalin.

"They say it is going to be a really weird winter," Ruffin

196

began to prattle. "I was listening to the radio this morning while I was driving in to work, and it's like it's going to get real cold closer to Christmas and then be like spring again in February."

I opened the automatic doors to the decomposed room and walked in as trace evidence examiner Larry Posner and an Institute student worked on the dead man's clothes.

"I'm always happy to see you guys," I greeted them.

"Well, I've got to admit, you've given us another one of your challenges," said Posner as he used a scalpel to scrape dirt off a shoe onto a sheet of white paper. "You know Carlisle?"

"Is he teaching you anything?" I asked the young man.

"Sometimes," he replied.

"How ya doing, Chuck?" Posner said. "You don't look so good."

"Hanging in there." Chuck kept up his sick routine.

"Sorry about the Richmond P.D.," he said with a sympathetic smile.

Ruffin was visibly shaken.

"Excuse me?" he said.

Posner looked uncomfortable as he replied, "I heard the academy didn't work out. You know, I just wanted to tell you not to be discouraged."

Ruffin's eyes cut to the phone.

"Most people don't know this," Posner went on as he started work on another shoe. "I flunked the first two tests in chemistry one-oh-one at VCU."

"No kidding," Ruffin muttered.

"*Now* you tell me." Carlisle feigned horror and disgust. "And I was told I'd get the best instructors in the world if I came here. I want my money back."

"Got something to show you, Dr. Scarpetta," Posner said, pushing back his face shield.

He set down the scalpel and folded the sheet of paper with a jeweler's fold and moved over to the pair of black jeans Carlisle was working on. They were carefully laid out on the sheet-covered gurney. The waistband had been turned inside out to the hips, and Carlisle was gently collecting hairs with needle-nosed forceps.

"This is the damnedest thing," Posner said, pointing a gloved finger without touching while his trainee carefully folded the jeans down another inch, revealing more hairs.

"We've already collected dozens," Posner was telling me. "You know, we began folding down the jeans and found the expected pubic hair in the crotch, but then there's this blond stuff. And each inch we go, there's more of it. It doesn't make sense."

"It doesn't seem to," I agreed.

"Maybe some sort of animal like a Persian cat?" Carlisle suggested.

Ruffin opened a cupboard and took out the plastic bottle of formalin that contained the tattoo.

"If it was sleeping on top of the jeans while they were inside out, for example?" Carlisle went on. "You know, a lot of times when my jeans are a pain to get off, they end up inside out and tossed on a chair. And my dog loves to sleep on top of my clothes."

"I don't guess hanging things up or putting them in drawers ever occurs to you," Posner remarked.

"Is that part of my homework?"

"I'll go find a bag to put this in," Ruffin said, holding up the jar. "In case it leaks or something."

"Good idea," I said. Then I asked Posner, "How quickly can you take a look at all this?"

"For you, I'll ask the lethal question," he said. "How quickly do you need it?"

I sighed.

"Okay, okay."

"We've got Interpol trying to track down who this guy is. I feel under as much pressure as everybody else, Larry," I said.

"You don't need to explain. I know when you say *jump*, there's always a good reason. I guess I put my foot in my mouth," he added. "What's with that kid? He acted like he didn't know he wasn't accepted at the police academy. Hell, it's all over the building."

"First of all, I didn't know he didn't get in," I said. "And second, I don't know why it's all over the building."

Even as I said it, Marino came to mind. He said he was going to fix Ruffin, and maybe he just did by somehow finding out the news and gleefully spreading it.

"Supposedly Bray's the one who gave him the boot," Posner went on.

Moments later, Ruffin returned with a plastic bag in hand. We left the decomposed room and washed up in our respective locker rooms. I took my time. I made him wait in the hall, knowing his anxiety was heating up with every second that went by. When I finally emerged, we walked together in silence, and he stopped twice to take a nervous drink of water.

"I hope I'm not getting a fever," he said.

I stopped and looked at him, and he involuntarily jerked away when I placed the back of my hand on his cheek.

"I think you're fine," I said.

I accompanied him through the lobby and into the parking lot, and by now he was clearly frightened.

"Is something wrong?" he finally asked, clearing his throat and putting on sunglasses.

"Why would you ask me that?" I innocently said.

"You walking me out here and everything."

"I'm heading to my car."

"I'm sorry I said to you what I did about problems here and the Internet stuff and everything," he said. "I knew it was better to keep it to myself, that you would get mad at me."

"Why would you think I'm mad at you?" I asked as I unlocked my car.

He seemed at a loss for words. I opened the trunk and set the plastic bag inside it.

"You got a nick on the paint there. Probably from a kicked-up rock, but it's starting to rust . . ."

"Chuck, I want you to hear what I'm saying," I calmly told him. "*I know.*"

"What? I don't understand what you mean." He tripped over words.

"You understand completely."

I got into the front seat and turned on the engine.

"Get in, Chuck," I said. "You don't need to stand out in the cold. Especially since you're not feeling well."

He hesitated and exuded fear like an odor as he walked around to the passenger's side.

"Sorry you weren't able to make it to Buckhead's. We had an interesting conversation with Deputy Chief Bray," I said as he shut his door.

His mouth fell open.

"It's a relief to me to have so many questions answered at last," I went on. "E-mail, the Internet, rumors about my career, leaks."

I waited to see what he would say to this and was startled

when he blurted out, "That's why I suddenly didn't make it into the academy, isn't it? You see her last night and this morning I get the news. You bad-mouthed me, told her not to hire me, then spread it everywhere to embarrass me."

"Your name never came up once. And I most certainly haven't spread anything about you anywhere."

"Bullshit." His angry voice trembled as if he might cry. "I've wanted to be a cop all my life, and now you ruined it!"

"No, Chuck, you ruined it."

"Call the chief and say something. You can, you can," he begged like a distraught child. "Please."

"Why were you meeting Bray last night?"

"Because she told me to. I don't know what she wanted. She just sent me a page and told me to be in the parking lot at Buckhead's at five-thirty."

"And of course, in her mind you never showed up. I expect that may have something to do with why you got bad news this morning. What do you think?"

"I guess," he mumbled.

"How are you feeling? Still sick? If not, I've got to head out to Petersburg, and I think you should ride with me so we can finish this conversation."

"Well, I . . ."

"Well what, Chuck?"

"I want to finish the conversation, too," he said.

"Start with how you know Deputy Chief Bray. I find it rather extraordinary that you should have what seems to be a personal relationship with the most powerful person in the police department."

"Imagine how I felt when it all started," he innocently said. "See, Detective Anderson called me a couple months ago, said she was new and wanted to ask me questions about the M.E.'s office, about our procedures, and could I meet her at the River City Diner for lunch. That was when I got on the road to hell, and I know I should've said something to you about her call. I should've told you what I was doing. But you were teaching classes most of the day and I didn't want to bother you, and Dr. Fielding was in court. So I told Anderson I'd be glad to help her out."

"Well, it's pretty obvious she didn't learn anything."

"She was setting me up," he said, "and when I walked into the River City Diner, I couldn't believe it. She was sitting in a booth with Deputy Chief Bray, and she told me she wanted to know all about the way our office runs, too."

"Who did?"

"Bray did."

"I see. Big surprise," I said.

"I guess I was really flattered but nervous, too, because I didn't understand what was going on. I mean, next thing, she's telling me to walk back to police headquarters with her and Anderson."

"Why didn't you tell me all this at the time?" I said as we drove toward Fifth Street to pick up I-95 South.

"I don't know . . ." His voice trailed off.

"I think you do."

"I was scared."

"Might it have anything to do with your ambition of becoming a police officer?"

"Well, let's face it," he said. "What better connection could I have? And somehow she knew I was interested and when we got to her office, she closed the door and sat me across from her desk."

"Was Anderson there?"

"Just Bray and me. She said that with my experience

202

I might think about becoming a crime-scene technician. I felt like I'd won the lottery."

I was working hard at keeping my distance from cement barriers and aggressive drivers while Ruffin continued his choirboy act.

"I have to admit I was in a dream after that and lost interest in my job, and I'm sorry for that," he said. "But it wasn't until two weeks later that Bray e-mailed me . . ."

"Where did she get your e-mail address?"

"Uh, she asked for it. So she e-mailed me and said she wanted me to drop by her house at five-thirty, that she had something very confidential to discuss with me.

"And I'm telling you, Dr. Scarpetta, I didn't want to go. I knew something bad was going to come out of it."

"Such as?"

"I halfway wondered if maybe she was going to hit on me or something."

"Did she? What happened when you got to her house?" I asked.

"Gosh, this is really hard to say."

"Say it."

"She got me a beer and moved her chair real close to the couch where I was sitting. She asked me all kinds of questions about myself like she was really interested in me as a person. And . . ."

A loaded-down logging truck pulled in front of me and I sped around it.

"I hate those things," I said.

"Me, too," Chuck said, and his shoe-licking tone was making me sick.

"And what? You were telling me?" I said.

He took a deep breath. He got very interested in the

trucks bearing down on us and the men working with mounds of asphalt on the roadside. It seemed as if this stretch of I-95 near Petersburg had been under construction since the Civil War.

"She wasn't in a uniform, if you get what I mean," he resumed with overblown sincerity. "She, well, she had on a business suit, but I don't think she was wearing a bra, or at least the blouse . . . you could sort of see through it."

"Did she ever try to seduce you, make any overture at all beyond how she was dressed?" I asked.

"No, ma'am, but it was like maybe she was hoping I would. And now I know why. She wouldn't go for it, but she'd hold it over me. Just one more way to control me. So when she got me my second beer, she got down to what she wanted. She said it was important I know the truth about you."

"Which is?"

"She said you're unstable. Everybody knew you'd *lost your grip*, those were her exact words, that you were almost bankrupt because you're a compulsive shopper . . ."

"Compulsive shopper?"

"She said something about your house and car."

"Why would she know anything about my house?" I asked, realizing that Ruffin knew about both, among many other things.

"I don't know," he said. "I guess the worse thing, though, was what she said about your work. That you'd been screwing up cases and the detectives were beginning to complain except for Marino. He was covering up for you, which was why she was going to have to do something about him eventually."

"And she certainly did," I said without a trace of emotion.

"Gee, do I have to go on?" he said. "I don't want to say all these things to you!"

"Chuck, would you like a chance to start over and undo some of the damage you've done?" I set him up.

"God, if only I could," he said, as if he really meant it.

"Then tell me the truth. Tell me everything. Let's get you back on the right track so you can have a happy life," I encouraged him.

I knew the little bastard would turn on anyone if it was in his best interest.

"She said one of the reasons she'd been hired was the chief, the mayor and city council wanted to get rid of you but didn't know how," Ruffin went on as if the words caused him pain. "That they couldn't because you don't work for the city, the governor basically had to do it. She explained to me it's like when a new city manager is hired because people want to get rid of a bad police chief. It was amazing. She was so convincing, I was sucked in. Then, and I'll never forget it, she got up from her chair and sat next to me. She looked into my eyes.

"She said, 'Chuck, your boss is going to ruin your life, do you understand? She's going to take down everyone around her, especially you.' I asked her *why me?* And she said, 'Because you're a nothing to her. People like her may act nice, but deep down they think they're God and have contempt for minions.' She asked me if I knew what a minion was, and I said I didn't. She told me it was a *servant.* Well, that got me mad."

"I guess so," I said. "I've never treated you or anyone like a servant, Chuck."

"I know. I know!"

I believed some of his account was true. Most of it was self-serving and slanted, I was sure.

"So I started doing things for her. Little things at first," he went on. "And every time I did one bad thing, it got easier to do the next. It's like I got harder and harder inside and talked myself into believing everything I was doing was justified, even right. Maybe so I could sleep at night. Then the things she wanted got big, like the e-mail, only she got Anderson to give me those assignments. Bray's too slippery to get caught."

"What things, for example?" I said.

"Dropping the bullet down the sink. That was bad enough."

"Yes, it was," I said, holding in my contempt for him.

"Which is one of the reasons I knew something really big must be on her mind when she sent me the page about meeting her at Buckhead's last night," he went on. "She said not to say a word to anyone and not answer her back unless there was a problem. Just to show up. Period.

"I was scared to death of her by then," he said, and that part I certainly believed. "She had me, you know. I was dirty and she had me. I was so scared of what she might ask me to do next."

"And what might that have been?"

He hesitated. A transfer truck swerved in front of me and I tapped my brakes. Bulldozers were moving dirt on the embankment, and dust was everywhere.

"Screw up the Container Man case. I knew that was coming. She was going to get me to tamper with something to get you into so much trouble that it was over for you. And what better case than one with Interpol and everything? With all the interest?"

"And have you done something to compromise that case, Chuck?" I said.

"No, ma'am."

"Have you tampered with any case?"

"Other than the bullet, no, ma'am."

"You realize of course you would be committing a felony if you altered or destroyed evidence? Do you realize Bray's heading you toward prison and probably even setting you up for it so she can get you out of the way after she's finished with me?"

"Deep down, I don't think she'd do that to me," he said.

He was nothing to her. He was a flunky who didn't have sense enough to avoid a trap when he found one because his ego and ambition got in the way.

"You're sure about that," I said. "Sure Bray wouldn't make you the fall guy."

He wavered.

"Are you the one who's been stealing things in the office?" I hit the matter head-on and asked.

"I have all of it. She wanted me to do . . . to do anything I could to make you look like you couldn't run the office. It's all at my house in a box. Eventually I was going to leave it in the building somewhere so someone would find it and return the stuff to everyone."

"Why would you let her have this much power over you?" I asked. "So much that you would lie and steal and premeditate tampering with evidence?"

"Oh, please don't let me get arrested, go to prison," he said in a panicky voice that would win him no acting awards. "I have a wife. A baby on the way. I'll commit suicide, I promise I will. I know lots of ways to do it."

"Don't even think such a thing," I said. "Don't ever say that again."

"I will. I'm ruined, and it's all my fault. Nobody else's."

"You're not ruined unless you choose to be."

"It doesn't matter anymore," he muttered, and I was beginning to fear he might be serious.

He was constantly licking his lips, and his words were sticky because his mouth was so dry.

"My wife wouldn't care. And the baby doesn't need to grow up with a father in prison."

"Don't you dare send your body to me," I told him angrily. "Don't you dare have me walk in and find you on one of my tables."

He turned to me, shocked.

"Grow up," I said. "You don't just shoot your brains out when things turn to shit, do you hear me? Do you know what suicide is?"

He stared wide-eyed at me.

"It's getting in the last pissed-off word. It's a big *so there*," I said.

22

The Pit Stop was just past Kate's Beauty Salon and a small house with a sign out front advertising a psychic. I parked next to a beat-up black pickup truck tattooed with multiple bumper stickers that gave me broad hints about Mr. Pit.

The door to his business instantly opened and I was greeted by a man whose exposed skin, every inch of it, including his neck and head, was tattooed. His body piercing made me cringe.

He was older than I had expected, probably in his fifties, a wiry man with a long gray ponytail and a beard. He had a face that looked as if it had been beaten up a few times, and he dressed in a black leather vest over a T-shirt. His wallet was chained to his jeans.

"You must be Pit," I said as I opened the trunk to get out the plastic bag.

"Come on in," he replied in a relaxed way, as if nothing in the world was off kilter or worth worrying about.

He walked in ahead of Ruffin and me and called out, "Taxi, sit, girl." Then he assured us, "Don't worry about her. She's gentler than baby shampoo."

209

I knew I wasn't going to like what was inside his shop.

"I didn't know you were bringing anybody with you," Pit commented, and I noticed his tongue sported a pointed silver post. "What's your name?"

"Chuck."

"He's one of my assistants," I explained. "If you have a place to sit, he'll wait."

Taxi was a pit bull, a brown and black square block of muscle on four legs.

"Oh, yeah," Pit was pointing out a corner of the room where there was a TV and a sitting area. "We gotta have a place for the customers to wait for their appointments. Chuck, you just help yourself. Let me know if you need change for the Coke machine."

"Thanks," he said, subdued.

I didn't like the way Taxi stared at me. I would never trust a pit bull no matter how gentle its owner said it was. To me, the mixture of bulldog and terrier had created the Frankenstein's monster of breeding, and I had seen my share of torn-up people, especially children.

"Okay, Taxi, tummy rub," Pit said in a cooing voice.

Taxi rolled over, legs in the air, and her master squatted and began rubbing her stomach.

"You know'—he looked up at Chuck and me—"these dogs aren't bad unless the owners want 'em to be. They're just big babies. Aren't you, Taxi? I named her 'Taxi' because some taxi driver came in here a year back and wanted a tattoo. Said he'd trade me a pit bull puppy for a Grim Reaper with his ex-wife's name under it. So that's what I did, didn't I, girl? Kind of a joke that she's a Pit and I am, too. We ain't related."

Pit's shop was a world I didn't know and couldn't have

imagined, and I'd visited some very strange places in my career. Walls were covered with flash, every example edge-to-edge. There were thousands of Indians, winged horses, dragons, fish, frogs and cultist symbols that meant nothing to me. Pit's *Trust No One* and *Been There, Fucked That* opinions were everywhere. Plastic skulls grimaced from shelves and tables, and tattoo magazines were placed about for brave hearts to flip through while they waited for the needle.

Oddly, what I would have found so offensive just an hour ago suddenly took on the authority and truth of a creed. People like Pit and probably much of his clientele were outlaws who bucked anything that took away the right of people to be who and what they are. Out of place in all of this was the dead man whose flesh I was carrying in a jar. There was nothing countercultural or defiant about someone dressed in Armani clothes and crocodile shoes.

"How did you get into this?" I asked Pit.

Chuck began browsing sheet-flash as if he were wandering through an art museum. I set the bag on the countertop by the cash register.

"Graffiti," Pit replied. "I bring a lot of that into my style, sort of like Grime at Primal Urge out in San Fran, not that I'm saying I'm anywhere near as good as him. But if you combine bright, more graffiti-like images with the bolder lines of the old school, that's me."

He tapped his finger on a framed photograph of a nude woman smiling slyly, arms provocatively crossed over her breasts. She had a sunset behind a lighthouse on her belly.

"Now that lady there," he said, "she comes in here with her boyfriend and says he's giving her a tattoo for her birthday. She starts out with this little itty-bitty butterfly on her hip, scared to death. After that she comes back every week for another one."

"Why?" I asked.

"It's addicting."

"Most people get more than one?"

"Most who get just one want to tuck it somewhere, usually out of sight. Like a heart on a butt or a boob. In other words, that one tattoo has special meaning. Or maybe the person got it when they were drunk—that happens, too, but not in my shop. I won't touch you if you smell like booze."

"If someone had one tattoo on his back and nowhere else on his body, as best I can tell? Important? Maybe something more than bravado or being drunk?" I asked.

"I'd say so. The back's a place people see, unless you never take your shirt off. So yeah, I'd say it probably meant something."

He looked at the bag on the countertop.

"So the tattoo in there came from the guy's back," he said.

"Two round yellow dots, each one about the circumference of a nailhead."

Pit stood still and pondered this, his face screwed up as if he were in pain.

"They got pupils, like eyes would?" he asked.

"No," I said, glancing at Chuck to see if he was in range of our conversation.

He was sitting on a couch, flipping through a magazine.

"Gosh," Pit said. "That's a hard one. No pupils. Can't think of anything without pupils if it's an animal or bird of some kind. Sounds to me you aren't talking flash. More likely it's custom."

He swept both hands over his shop, conducting his own orchestra of outrageous design.

"Now all that's sheets of flash," he said, "as opposed to a tattoo artist's original work, like Grime. I'm saying, you can look at some tattoos and recognize a particular style. No different than Van Gogh or Picasso. For example, I could spot a Jack Rudy or Tin Tin anywhere, most beautiful gray work you'll ever see."

Pit led me across the shop into what looked like a typical examining room in a doctor's office. It was equipped with an autoclave, ultrasonic cleaner, surgical soap, Biowrap, A & D ointment, tongue depressors and packs of sterile needles in big glass jars. The actual tattooing machine looked like something an electrologist would use, and there was a cart with squirt bottles of bright paints and caps for mixing. Central to all this was a gynecological chair. I supposed stirrups made it easier to work on legs and other parts of the body I didn't want to think about.

Pit spread a towel on a countertop, and we pulled on surgical gloves. He switched on a surgical lamp, pulling it close as I unscrewed the lid from the jar, my nose instantly assaulted by formalin's acrid bite. I dipped into the pink chemical and pulled out the block of skin. It was rubbery, the tissue permanently preserved, and Pit took it from me without pause and held it up in the light. He turned it this way and that and looked at it through a magnifying glass.

"Oh, yeah," he said. "I see those little suckers. Yup, there's claws holding on a branch. If you kinda lift the image out of the background, you can see the tail feathers."

"A bird?"

"It's a bird all right," he said. "Maybe an owl. You know, it's the eyes that jump out at you, and I think they were bigger than this at one time. The shading gives it away. Right here."

I leaned closer, his gloved finger moving over the skin in brush-strokes.

"See it?"

"No."

"It's very faint. Eyes have dark circles, like a bandit, sort of, kind of uneven, not very skillfully drawn. Someone tried to make them a whole lot smaller, and there's stripes radiating out from the edges of the bird. You wouldn't notice it unless you've worked with this sort of thing before, because all of it's so dark, you know, in such bad shape.

"But if you really scrutinize, you can see it's darker and heavier around the eyes, for lack of anything to call them. Yup. The more I look at it, I think it's an owl, and the yellow dots are a messy attempt to cover them up by turning them into owl eyes. Or something like owl eyes."

I was beginning to see the stripes, the feathers in the dark shading he was describing, and the way the bright yellow eyes were lined with dark ink as if someone had wanted to make them smaller.

"Someone gets something with yellow dots, doesn't want it anymore and has something else put on top of it," Pit said. "Since the top layer of skin's gone, most of the new tattoo—the owl—came off. I guess the needles didn't go in as deep on that one. But they went in real deep with the yellow dots. A lot deeper than necessary, which tells me two different artists are involved."

He studied the block of skin some more.

"You can never really cover up an old tattoo," he resumed. "But if you know what you're doing, you can work over and around it so the eye is taken away from it. That's the trick. I guess you could almost call it an optical illusion."

"Is there any way we can figure out what the yellow eyes might originally have been part of?" I asked him.

Pit looked disappointed and sighed.

"It's just a damn shame it's in such bad shape," he muttered, placing the skin on the towel and blinking several times. "Man, those fumes will get you. How do you work around that all the time?"

"Very, very carefully," I said. "Would you mind if I use your phone?"

"Help yourself."

I stepped behind the counter, keeping an uneasy eye on Taxi as she sat up in her bed. She stared at me as if daring me to make one move she didn't like.

"It's okay," I told her in a soothing voice. "Pit? Is it all right if I page someone and give him this number?"

"It ain't a secret. Help yourself."

"You're a good girl." I encouraged Taxi to be one as I stepped around the counter to use the phone.

Her small, dull eyes reminded me of a shark's, her head thick and triangular like a snake's. She looked like something primitive that had evolved no further since the beginning of time, and I thought of what was written on the box inside the container.

"Could it be a wolf?" I said to Pit. "Even a werewolf?"

Pit sighed again, the hard work of payday weekend shadowing his eyes.

"Well, wolves are real popular. You know, pack instinct, lone wolf," he told me. "Hard to cover up one of those with a bird, an owl or whatever."

"Yeah." Marino's voice came over the line.

"Hell, it could be so many things." Pit kept on talking loudly. "Coyote, dog, cat. Whatever's got a furry coat and yellow eyes with no pupils. Had to be small to cover it up with an owl, though. Real small."

"Who the hell is that talking about a furry coat?" Marino rudely asked.

I told him where I was and why, Pit rambling on all the while, pointing out all sorts of furry flash on a wall.

"Great." Marino got mad right away. "Why don't you get one while you're there."

"Maybe another time."

"I can't believe you would go to a tattoo parlor alone. You got an idea the kind of people who go in a place like that? Drug dealers, assholes out on parole, motorcycle gangs."

"It's all right."

"Oh, no it ain't all right!" Marino erupted.

He was upset about something that went beyond my visiting a tattoo parlor.

"What's wrong, Marino?"

"Not a damn thing unless you consider being suspended without pay something wrong."

"There's no justification for that," I angrily said, although I'd been afraid it was inevitable.

"Bray thinks so. I guess I ruined her dinner last night. She says if I do one more thing, I'm fired. The good news is I'm having fun thinking what the *one more thing* is I might decide to do."

"Hey! Let me show you something," Pit called out to me from across the room.

"We'll do something about this," I promised Marino.

"Yeah."

Taxi's eyes followed me as I hung up and picked my way around her. I scanned the flash on the wall and only felt worse. I wanted the tattoo to be a wolf, a werewolf, a small one, when in fact it could be something else entirely and probably was. I couldn't tolerate it when a question remained unanswered, when science and rational thinking went as far as they could go and quit.

I couldn't remember ever feeling this discouraged and unsettled. The walls seemed to move in on me and sheets of flash jumped out like demons. Daggers through hearts and skulls, gravestones, skeletons, evil animals and ghastly ghouls played "Ring Around the Rosie' with me.

"Why do people want to wear death?" I raised my voice and Taxi raised her head. "Isn't living with it enough? Why would someone want to spend the rest of his life looking at death on his arm?"

Pit shrugged and didn't seem bothered in the least that I was questioning his art.

"See," he said, "when you think about it, Doc, there's nothing to fear but fear. So people want death tattoos so they won't be afraid of death. It's kind of like people who are terrified by snakes and then touch one in the zoo. In a way, you wear death every day, too," he said to me. "Don't you think you might fear it more if you didn't look at it every day?"

I didn't know how to answer that.

"See, you got a piece of a dead person's skin in that jar and you're not afraid of it," he went on. "But someone else walking in here and seeing that would probably scream or puke. Now, I'm no psychologist"—he vigorously chewed gum—"but there's something real important behind what someone chooses to have permanently drawn on his body. So you take this dead guy? That owl says something about him. What went on inside him. Most of all, what he was scared of, which may have more to do with whatever's under that owl."

"It would seem that quite a lot of your clients are afraid of voluptuous naked women," I commented.

Pit chewed his gum as if it were trying to get away, and he pondered what I'd said for a moment.

"Hadn't thought about that one," he said, "but it fits. Most of these guys with nudies all over them are really scared of women. Scared of the emotional part."

Chuck had turned on the TV and was watching Rosie O'Donnell, the volume low. I had seen thousands of tattoos on bodies, but I had never thought of them as a symbol of fear. Pit tapped the lid of the jar of formalin.

"This guy was afraid of something," he said. "Looks like he might have had a good reason to be."

218

23

I'd been home only long enough to hang up my coat and drop my briefcase by the door when the telephone rang. It was twenty minutes past eight, and my first thought was Lucy. The only update I'd gotten was that Jo would be transferred to MCV sometime this weekend.

I was frightened and becoming resentful. No matter what policies, protocols or judgment dictated, Lucy could contact me. She could let me know she and Jo were all right. She could tell me where she was.

I quickly grabbed the phone and was both surprised and uneasy when former Deputy Chief Al Carson's voice came over the line. I knew he would not contact me, especially at home, unless it was very important, the news very bad.

"I'm not supposed to be doing this but someone has to," he said right off. "There's been a homicide at the Quik Cary. That convenience store off Cary, near Libbie. You know which one I mean? Kind of a neighborhood market?"

He was talking rapidly and nervously. He sounded scared.

"Yes," I said. "It's close to my house."

I picked up a clipboard and began writing notes on a call sheet.

"An apparent robbery. Somebody came in, cleaned out the drawer and shot the clerk. A female."

I thought of the videotape I had looked at yesterday.

"When did this happen?" I asked.

"We think she got shot not more than an hour ago. I'm calling you myself because your office doesn't know yet."

I paused, not quite sure what he meant. In fact, what he'd just said couldn't possibly be right.

"I called Marino, too," he went on. "I guess there's nothing more they can do to me anymore."

"What do you mean my office *doesn't know yet*?" I asked.

"Police aren't supposed to be calling the M.E. anymore until we finish with the scene. Until the crime techs do, and they're just now getting there. So it could be hours . . ."

"Where the hell is this coming from?" I asked, although I knew.

"Dr. Scarpetta, I was pretty much forced to resign, but I would have anyway," Carson told me. "There are changes I can't live with. You know my guys have always gotten along really well with your office. But Bray's put in all these new people—what she did to Marino, that was enough to make me quit right there. But what matters right now is this makes two convenience store killings in a month. I don't want anything messed up. If it's the same guy, he's gonna do it again."

I called Fielding at home and told him what was going on.

"You want me to . . . ?" he started to say.

"No," I cut him off. "I'm going right now. We're getting goddamn screwed, Jack."

I drove fast. Bruce Springsteen was singing "Santa Claus

Is Coming to Town," and I thought of Bray. I had never really hated anyone before. Hate was poison. I had always resisted it. To hate was to lose, and it was all I could do right now to resist the heat of its flames.

The news came on, the homicide the lead story, covered live at the scene.

". . . in what is the second convenience store murder in three weeks. Deputy Chief Bray, what can you tell us?"

"Details are sketchy at this time," her voice sounded inside my car. "We do know that several hours earlier, an unknown suspect entered the Quik Cary here and robbed it and shot the clerk."

My car phone rang.

"Where are you?" Marino said.

"Getting close to Libbie."

"I'm going to pull into the Cary Town parking lot. I need to tell you what's going on because nobody's gonna tell you the time of day when you get there."

"We'll see about that."

Minutes later, I turned into the small shopping center and parked in front of Schwarzchild Jewelers, where Marino was sitting in his truck. Then he was inside my car, wearing jeans and boots, and a scuffed leather coat with a broken zipper and fleece lining as bald as his head. He had splashed on a lot of cologne, meaning he had been drinking beer. He tossed a cigarette butt and red ashes sailed through the night.

"Everything's under control," he sardonically said. "Anderson's at the scene."

"And Bray."

"She's holding a goddamn press conference outside the convenience store," Marino said with disgust. "Let's go."

I drove back out to Cary Street.

"Start with this, Doc," he began. "The asshole shoots her at the counter, in the head. Then it's looking like he puts out the closed sign, locks the door and drags her to the back, into the storeroom, and beats the holy shit out of her."

"He shot her and then beat her up?"

"Yeah."

"How were the police notified?" I asked.

"At seven-sixteen the burglar alarm went off," he replied. "The back door's armed even when the joint's open for business. Cops get there and find the front door locked, closed sign out, like I said. They go around back, find that door wide open. They go in, she's on the floor, blood everywhere. Tentatively identified as Kim Luong, thirty-year-old Asian female."

Bray continued to dominate the news.

"You said something earlier about a witness," a reporter was asking her.

"Only that a citizen reported seeing a male in dark clothing in the area around the time we believe the homicide took place," Bray replied. "He was ducking into an alleyway right down the block there. The person who reported this did not get a good look. We're hoping if someone else did, he'll call us. No detail is too small. It takes all of us to protect our community."

"What's she doing? Running for office?" Marino said.

"Is there a safe somewhere inside the store?" I asked him.

"In the back where her body was found. It hadn't been opened. So I've been told."

"Video camera?" I asked.

"Nope. Maybe he learned after whacking Gant and is

222

hitting joints that aren't doing the Candid Camera number on him."

"Maybe."

He and I both knew he was making assumptions, pushing hard because he wasn't about to let go of his job.

"Carson tell you all this?" I asked.

"It ain't the cops who've suspended me," he answered. "And already I know you're thinking the M.O.'s a little different. But it ain't a science, Doc. You know that."

Benton used to toss that line at us with that wry smile of his. He was a profiler, an expert in modus operandi and patterns and predicting. But each crime had its own special choreography because every victim was different. Circumstances and moods were different, even the weather was different, and the killer often modified his routine. Benton used to complain about Hollywood renditions of what behavioral scientists could do. He wasn't clairvoyant, and violent people weren't driven by software.

"Maybe she pissed him off or something," Marino went on. "Maybe he'd just had a bad conversation with his mother, who the hell knows?"

"What's going to happen when people like Al Carson don't call you anymore?"

"It's my damn case," he said as if he hadn't heard me. "Gant was my case, and this one is too, any way you look at it. Even if it's not the same killer, who's gonna figure that out before I do, since I'm the one who knows everything there is about it?"

"You can't always barge in with both barrels going," I said. "That's not going to work with Bray. You've got to find a way to make it worth her while to tolerate you, and you better figure that out in the next five minutes."

He was silent as I turned onto Libbie Avenue.

"You're smart, Marino," I added. "Use your head. This isn't about turf or egos. This is about a woman who's dead."

"Shit," he said. "What the fuck's wrong with people?"

The Quik Cary was a small market that had neither a plate-glass front nor gas pumps. It wasn't brightly lit up or located in a spot that attracted customers either coming off or getting on heavily traveled roads. Except during the holidays, it stayed open only until six.

The parking lot throbbed red and blue, and in the midst of rumbling engines, cops and an awaiting rescue crew, Bray gloried in an aura of television lights that floated around her like a flotilla of small suns. She was dressed in a long red wool cape, heels, and diamond earrings that flashed with each turn of her beautiful head. By all appearances she had just rushed out of a black-tie party.

It was beginning to sleet as I lifted my crime case out of the trunk. Bray spotted me before the media did, and then her eyes found Marino and anger touched her face.

". . . will not release that until her family has been notified," she was saying to the press.

"Watch this," Marino said under his breath.

He walked with a sense of urgency toward the store and did something I'd never seen him do before. He left himself wide open for a media ambush. He even went so far as to get on his portable radio as he tensely cast about, sending out every signal imaginable that he was in charge and knew many secrets.

"You in there, two-oh-two?" his voice carried to me as I locked up my car.

"Ten-four," a voice came back.

"In front, comin' in," Marino mumbled.

"Meet ya."

At least ten reporters and cameramen instantly surrounded him. It was amazing how fast they moved.

"Captain Marino?"

"Captain Marino!"

"How much money was stolen?"

Marino didn't shoo them off. Bray's eyes dragged across his face like claws as all attention shifted to him, this man whose neck her foot was on.

"Did they keep less than sixty dollars in the drawer like other convenience stores do?"

"Do you think convenience stores should have security guards this time of year?"

Marino, unshaven and full of beer, looked into the cameras and said, "If it was my store, I sure as hell would."

I locked my car. Bray was walking toward me.

"So you attribute these two robbery-homicides to the Christmas season?" another reporter said to Marino.

"I attribute them to some squirrel who's cold-blooded and got no conscience. He'll do it again," Marino answered. "And we've got to stop him and that's what we're trying to do."

Bray confronted me as I made my way around police cars. She had her cape pulled tightly around her, and she was as cold and stinging as the weather.

"Why do you let him do this?" she asked me.

I stopped in my tracks and looked her in the eye, my frosted breath puffing like a coal train about to run her over.

"*Let* is not a word I use with Marino," I said. "I suspect you're finding that out the hard way."

A reporter for a local gossip magazine raised his voice above the others and said, "Captain Marino! Talk on the street is you're not a detective anymore. What are you doing here?"

"Deputy Chief Bray has me on special assignment," Marino grimly replied into microphones. "I'll be heading up this investigation."

"He's finished," Bray said to me.

"He won't go quietly. You'll never hear so much noise in your life," I promised her as I walked off.

24

Marino met me at the store's front door. When we stepped inside, the first person we saw was Anderson. She stood in front of the counter, wrapping the empty cash drawer in brown paper as crime-scene technician Al Eggleston dusted the cash register for prints. Anderson looked surprised and unhappy when she saw us.

"What are you doing here?" she confronted Marino.

"Came in to buy a six-pack. How you doin', Eggleston?"

"Same-o, same-o, Pete."

"We're not ready for you yet," Anderson said to me.

I ignored her and wondered how much damage she'd already done to the scene. Thank God, Eggleston was doing the important work. I immediately noticed the overturned chair behind the counter.

"Was the chair like that when the police got here?" I asked Eggleston.

"Far as I know."

Anderson abruptly went out of the store, probably to find Bray.

"Uh-oh," Marino said. "Tattletale."

227

"You ain't kidding."

On the wall behind the counter were arcs of blood from an arterial hemorrhage.

"Glad you're here, Pete, but you're poking a snake with a stick."

The sweeping trail led around the counter and through the aisle farthest from the store's front door.

"Marino, come here," I said.

"Hey, Eggleston, see if you can find the guy's DNA somewhere. Put it in a little bottle and maybe we can grow his clone in the lab," Marino said as he walked over to me. "Then we'll know who the hell he is."

"You're a rocket scientist, Pete."

I pointed out the arcs of blood made by the rise and fall of the systolic rhythm of Kim Luong's heart as she had bled to death through her carotid. The blood was low to the floor and stretched over some twenty feet of shelves stocked with paper towels, toilet paper and other household needs.

"Jesus Christ," Marino said as the significance hit him. "He's dragging her while she's spurting blood everywhere?"

"Yes."

"How long would she have survived, bleeding like that?"

"Minutes," I said. "Ten at the most."

She had left no other bloody wake except the faint fringed and narrow parallel impressions made by her hair and fingers as they dragged through her blood. I envisioned him pulling her feet first, her arms opening like wings filled with air, her hair trailing like feathers.

"He had her by the ankles," I said. "She has long hair."

Anderson had stepped back inside and was watching us, and I hated it when I had to guard every word I said around the police. But it happened. Over the years, I had worked

228

with cops who were terrible leaks and I had no choice but to treat them like the enemy.

"She sure as hell didn't die right away," Marino added.

"A hole in your carotid isn't immediately disabling," I told him. "You can have your throat cut and still call nine-one-one. She shouldn't have been immediately immobilized, but clearly she was."

The systolic sweeps got lower and fainter the further down the aisle we went, and I noted that small blood spatters were dry while larger amounts of blood were congealing. We followed streaks and smears past coolers full of beer, then through the doorway leading into the storeroom where crime-scene technician Gary Ham was on his knees while another officer took photographs, their backs to me, blocking my view.

When I stepped around them, I was stunned. Kim Luong's blue jeans and panties had been pulled down to her knees, a chemical thermometer inserted into her rectum. Ham looked up at me and he froze like someone caught stealing. We had worked together for years.

"What the hell do you think you're doing?" I said to him in a hard tone he had never heard from me.

"Getting her temp, Doc," Ham said.

"Did you swab her before inserting the thermometer? In the event she was sodomized?" I demanded in the same angry voice as Marino made his way around me and stared at the body.

Ham hesitated. "No, ma'am, I didn't."

"Way to fucking go," Marino said to him.

Ham was in his late thirties, a tall, nice-looking man with dark hair and big brown eyes and long lashes. It wasn't uncommon for a little experience to begin seducing someone like him into believing he could do the forensic scientist's and medical examiner's work. But Ham had always stayed in bounds. He had always been respectful.

"And just how do I interpret the presence of any injury, now that you've introduced a hard object into one of her orifices?" I said to him.

He swallowed hard.

"If I find a contusion inside her rectum, can I swear in court that the thermometer didn't do it? And unless you can somehow vouch for the sterility of your equipment, any DNA recovered will be in question, too," I said.

Ham's face was red.

"Do you have any idea how many artifacts you've just introduced to this crime scene, Officer Ham?" I asked him.

"I've been very careful."

"Please move out of the way. Now."

I opened my case and angrily pulled on gloves, stretching my fingers and snapping latex all in one motion. I handed Marino a flashlight and studied my surroundings before I did another thing. The storeroom was dimly lit; hundreds of six-packs of sodas and beer as far as twenty feet away were spattered with blood. Inches from the body were Tampax and paper towels, the bottom of the cartons soggy with blood. So far, there was no sign the killer had been interested in anything back here except his victim.

I squatted and studied the body, taking in every shade and texture of flesh and blood, every stroke of the killer's hellish art. I did not touch anything at first.

"God, he really beat the hell out of her, didn't he," said the cop who was taking photographs.

It was as if a wild animal had dragged her dying body off to its lair and mauled it. Her sweater and bra had been ripped open, her shoes and socks removed and tossed nearby. She was a fleshy woman with matronly hips and breasts, and the only way I had a clue about what she had looked like was the driver's license I was shown. Kim Luong had been pretty with a shy smile and shiny long black hair.

"Were her pants on when she was found?" I asked Ham.

"Yes, ma'am."

"What about shoes and socks?"

"They were off. Exactly like you see them. We didn't touch them."

I didn't have to pick up her shoes and socks to see they were very bloody.

"Why would he take off her shoes and socks but not her pants?" one of the cops asked.

"Yeah. Why would someone do something weird like that?"

I took a look. There was dried blood on the bottom of her feet, too.

"I'll have to get her under a better light when we get her to the morgue," I said.

The gunshot wound in the front of her neck was plain to see. It was an entrance wound, and I turned her head just enough to see the exit in the back, angled to the left. It was this bullet that had hit her carotid artery.

"Did you recover a bullet?" I asked Ham.

"Dug one out of the wall behind the counter," he said, barely able to look at me. "No shell so far, if there is one."

There wouldn't be if she was shot with a revolver. Pistols ejected their cartridge cases, which was about the only helpful thing they did when they were used for violence.

"Where in the wall?" I asked.

"If you're facing the counter, it would be to the left of

where the chair would have been if she was sitting at the cash register."

"The exit wound is also off to the left," I said. "If they were face to face when she was shot, you may be looking for a left-handed shooter."

Kim Luong's face was severely lacerated and crushed, the skin split and torn from blows that had been made by some sort of tool or tools that had a pattern of round and linear wounds. It appeared she also had been beaten with his fists. When I palpated for fractures, bits of bone crunched beneath my fingertips. Her teeth were broken and pushed in.

"Hold it here," I directed Marino.

He moved the flashlight as I directed and I gently turned her head to the right and to the left, palpating her scalp through her hair and checking the back and sides of her neck. She was covered with more knuckle bruises, and more of the round and linear injuries, and also striated abrasions here and there.

"Except for pulling down her pants to get her body temp," I said to Ham, because I had to be sure, "she was just like this?"

"Other than her jeans being zipped up and buttoned, yes, ma'am," he replied. "Her sweater and bra were just exactly like that." He pointed. "Ripped right down the middle."

"With his bare hands." Marino squatted beside me. "Damn, he's strong. Doc, she would have pretty much been dead by the time he got her back here, right?"

"Not quite. She still has tissue response to her injuries. Some bruising."

"But for all practical purposes, he's beating the shit out of a dead body," Marino said. "I mean, she sure as hell wasn't sitting up and arguing with him. She wasn't struggling.

You can look around and see that. Nothing knocked over or shoved around. No bloody footprints going all over the place."

"He knew her," Anderson's voice was behind me. "It had to be someone she knew. Otherwise he probably would have just shot her and taken the money and run."

Marino was still down beside me, elbows resting on his big knees, flashlight dangling from one hand. He looked up at Anderson as if she had the intelligence of a banana.

"I didn't know you was a profiler, too," he said. "You take some classes or something?"

"Marino, if you can shine it right there," I said. "It's hard to see."

The light illuminated a blood pattern on the body that I hadn't noticed at first because I was too preoccupied with injuries. Virtually every inch of exposed flesh was smeared with bloody swirls and strokes, as if she had been finger-painted. The blood was drying and beginning to crack. And there were hairs, the same long, pale hairs stuck to her blood.

I pointed this out to Marino. He bent closer.

"Quiet," I warned him as I felt his reaction and knew what I was showing him.

"Here comes the boss," Eggleston announced as he stepped carefully through the doorway.

The room was crowded and airless. It looked as if a thrashing storm had rained blood upon it.

"We're going to string all this," Ham said to me.

"Recovered a cartridge case," Eggleston happily passed on to Marino.

"If you want a break, Marino, I'll hold the flashlight for her." Ham was trying to make up for his unpardonable sin.

"I think it's fairly obvious she was lying right here, immobile, when he beat her," I said, because I didn't think stringing was necessary in this case.

"Stringing will tell us for sure," he promised.

It was an old French technique in which one end of a string was taped at a bloodstain, and the other at the geometrically computed origin of the blood. This was done multiple times, resulting in a three-dimensional string model that showed how many blows were struck and where the victim was when they were.

"There's too many people in here," I loudly said.

Sweat was rolling down Marino's face. I could feel his body heat and smell his breath as he worked close to me.

"Get this to Interpol right away," I told him in a voice no one else could hear.

"No kidding."

"Speer three-eighty. Ever heard of it?" Eggleston said to Marino.

"Yeah. High-performance shit. Gold Dot," Marino replied. "That don't fit, at all."

I got out my chemical thermometer and set it on top of a box of paper plates to get the ambient temperature.

"I can already tell you what it is, Doc," Ham said. "-Seventy-five-point-nine back here. It's warm."

Marino was moving the flashlight as my hands and eyes moved over the body.

"Normal people don't get Speer ammo," he was saying. "You're talking ten, eleven bucks for a box of twenty. Not to mention, your gun can't be a piece of shit or the damn thing will blow apart in your hand."

"The gun probably came off the street, then." Anderson was suddenly next to me. "Drugs."

"Case solved," Marino replied. "Gee, thanks, Anderson. Hey, guys, we can all go home."

I could smell the sweet, cloying odor of Kim Luong's blood as it coagulated, the serum separating from the hemoglobin, cells breaking down. I withdrew the chemical thermometer Ham had inserted inside her. Her core temperature was 88.6 degrees. I looked up. There were three people in this room, not including Marino and me. My anger and frustration continued to build.

"We found her pocketbook and coat," Anderson went on. "Sixteen dollars in her billfold, so it doesn't look like he went in there. And oh, there was a paper bag nearby with a plastic container and fork. Looks like she brought dinner with her and warmed it up in the microwave."

"How do you know she warmed it up?" Marino asked.

Anderson was caught.

"Putting two and two together don't always make twenty-two," he added.

Livor mortis was in its early stages. Her jaw was set, and the small muscles of her neck and hands were, too.

"She's too stiff for only being dead a couple hours," I said.

"What causes it anyway?" Eggleston asked.

"Me, too. I've always wondered that."

"I had one in Bon Air one time . . ."

"What were you doing in Bon Air?" asked the officer taking photographs.

"It's a long story. But this guy has a heart attack during sex. The girlfriend just thinks he's gone to sleep, right? Wakes up the next morning and he's deader than dirt. She doesn't want it to look like he died in bed so she tries to put him in a chair. He was leaning against it like an ironing board."

"We're serious, Doc. What causes it?" Ham asked.

"I've always been curious about that, too." Diane Bray's voice came from the doorway.

She was standing there, her eyes fastened to me like steel rivets.

"When you die, your body quits making adenosine triphosphate. That's why you get stiff," I said, not giving her a glance. "Marino, can you hold her like this so I can get a picture?"

He moved closer to me, and his big gloved hands slid under her left side as I got my camera. I took a photograph of an injury below her left armpit, on the fleshy side of her left breast, as I calculated body temperature versus ambient temperature, and how advanced both livor mortis and rigor mortis were. I could hear footsteps and murmurs and someone coughing. I was sweating behind my surgical mask.

"I need some room," I said.

Nobody moved.

I looked up at Bray and stopped what I was doing.

"I need room," I sharply said to her. "Get these people out of here."

She jerked her head at everyone but me. Cops dropped surgical gloves in a red biological hazard bag as they went out the door.

"You too," Bray ordered Anderson.

Marino acted as if Bray didn't exist. Bray never took her eyes off me.

"I don't ever want to walk in on a scene like this again," I said to her as I worked. "Your officers, your techs, nobody—and I mean *nobody*—touches the body or disturbs it in any way before I get there or one of my medical examiners does."

I looked up at her.

"Are we clear on that?" I said.

She seemed to give what I was saying thoughtful consideration. I loaded film in my thirty-five-millimeter camera. My eyes were getting tired because the light was bad, and I took the flashlight from Marino. I shined it obliquely on the area near the left breast, and then on another area on the right shoulder. Bray stepped in closer, brushing against me to see what I was looking at, and it was odd and startling to smell her perfume mingling with the odor of decomposing blood.

"The crime scene belongs to us, Kay," she said. "I understand you haven't had to work things that way in the past—probably not the entire time you've been here or maybe anywhere. That's what I was talking about when I mentioned . . ."

"That's a bunch of bullshit!" Marino hurled rude words in her face.

"Captain, you stay out of this," Bray fired back at him.

"You're the one who needs to stay out of it," he raised his voice.

"Deputy Chief Bray," I said, "the law of Virginia states that the medical examiner shall take charge of the body. The body is my jurisdiction."

I finished my photographs and met her cold, pale eyes.

"The body is not to be touched, altered or in any way interfered with. Am I clear?" I said again.

I pulled off my gloves and angrily threw them into the red bag.

"You have just cut this lady's heart out evidentially, Deputy Chief Bray."

I closed my scene case and latched it.

"You and the prosecutor are gonna get along real good

on this one," Marino added furiously as he pulled off his gloves, too. "This kind of case is what's called a free lunch."

He poked a thick finger at the dead woman as if it were Bray who had slaughtered her.

"You just let him get away with it!" he yelled at her. "You and your little power games and big tits! Who'd you fuck to get where you are?"

Bray's face went livid.

"Marino!" I grabbed his arm.

"Let me tell you something."

Marino was out of control, yanking his arm away from me, breathing hard like a wounded bear.

"This lady's beat-up face ain't about politics and sound bites, you goddamn-motherfucking-bitch! How'd you like it if it was your sister? Oh hell! What am I saying?" Marino threw his talc-dusted hands up in the air. "You wouldn't know the first fucking thing about caring about anybody!"

"Marino, get the squad in here now," I said.

"Marino's not calling anyone." Bray's tone had the effect of a metal box slamming shut.

"What are you gonna do, fire me?" Marino continued to defy her. "Well, go right ahead. And I'll tell all the reporters from here to fucking Iceland why."

"Firing's too good for you," Bray said. "Better you continue to suffer out of service and without pay. Dear me, this could go on a very, very long time."

She was gone in a flash of red, like a vengeful queen on her way to order armies to march in on us.

"Oh, no!" Marino called after her at the top of his voice. "You got it all wrong, babe. Guess I forgot to tell you *I fucking quit!*"

He got on his radio and raised Ham to tell him that the

squad needed to get in here as my mind streaked through formulas that weren't computing.

"Guess I showed her, huh, Doc?" Marino said, but I wasn't listening.

The burglar alarm had gone off at seven-sixteen and now it was barely nine-thirty. Time of death was elusive and full of deceit if one wasn't careful to account for all of the variables, but Kim Luong's body temperature, livor mortis, rigor mortis and the condition of her spilled blood weren't consistent with her being dead only two hours.

"I feel like this room is shrink-wrapping me, Doc."

"She's been dead at least four or five hours," I said.

He wiped his sweaty face on his sleeve, eyes almost glassy. He couldn't stay still and kept nervously patting the pack of cigarettes in his jeans pocket.

"Since one or two in the afternoon? You're kidding me. What's he doing all that time?"

His eyes kept going to the doorway, waiting to see who would fill it next.

"I think he was doing a lot of things to it," I said.

"I guess I just fucked myself pretty good," Marino said.

Shuffling feet and the clacking of a stretcher sounded from inside the store. Voices were muffled.

"I don't think she heard your last diplomatic comment," I answered him. "Might be smart if you leave it that way."

"You think he might have hung out as long as he did because he didn't want to walk out in broad daylight with blood all over his clothes?"

"I don't think that was the only reason," I said as two paramedics in jumpsuits turned the stretcher sideways to get it through the door.

"There's a lot of blood in here," I told them. "Go around that way."

"Geez," one of them said.

I took the folded disposable sheets off the stretcher and Marino helped me spread one of them open on the floor.

"You guys lift her a few inches and we're going to scoot this sheet right under her," I instructed. "Good. That's fine."

She was on her back. Gory eyes stared out of shattered orbits. Plasticized paper rustled as I covered her with the other sheet. We lifted her up and zipped her inside a dark red pouch.

"It's getting icy out there," one of the paramedics let us know.

Marino's eyes darted around the store and then out the door into the parking lot where red and blue lights still strobed, but the attention had significantly waned. Reporters had dashed back to their newsrooms and stations, and only the crime-scene technicians and a uniformed officer remained.

"Yeah, right," Marino muttered. "I'm suspended but you see any other detective here to work this thing? I ought to just let everything go to hell."

We walked back to my car as an old blue Volkswagen Beetle turned into the parking lot. The engine cut so abruptly the clutch popped, and the driver's door flew open and a teenaged girl with pale skin and short dark hair almost fell out, she was in such a hurry. She ran toward the pouched body as the paramedics loaded it into the ambulance. She raced toward them as if she might tackle them.

"Hey!" Marino yelled, going after her.

She reached the back of the ambulance as the tailgate slammed shut. Marino grabbed her.

240

"Let me see her!" she screamed. "Oh, please let go of me! Let me see her!"

"Can't do that, ma'am," Marino's voice carried.

The paramedics swung open their doors and jumped in.

"Let me see her!"

"It's gonna be all right."

"No! No! Oh, please, God!" Grief tumbled out of her like a waterfall.

Marino had her from behind, holding tight. The diesel engine rumbled awake and I couldn't hear what else he said to her, but he let go of her as the ambulance drove away. She dropped to her knees. She clamped her hands on both sides of her head and stared up at the icy, overcast night, shrieking and wailing and crying out the slain woman's name.

"KIM! KIM! KIM!"

25

Marino decided to stay with Eggleston and Ham, also known as the Breakfast Boys, while they connected the dots with string at a scene where it wasn't necessary. I went home. Trees and grass were glazed with ice, and I thought all I needed now was a power outage, which was exactly what I got.

When I turned into my neighborhood, every house was dark, and Rita, working security, looked as if she were holding a seance in the guardhouse.

"Don't tell me," I said to her.

Candle flames wavered behind glass as she stepped out, pulling her uniform jacket tightly around her.

"Been out since about nine-thirty," she told me, shaking her head. "That's all we ever get in this city is ice."

My neighborhood was in a blackout as if a war were going on, and the sky was too overcast to see even a smudge of the moon. I could barely find my driveway and almost fell going up my front stone steps because of the ice. I clung to the railing and somehow managed to find the right key to unlock the door. My burglar alarm was still armed because it was on a backup battery, but that wouldn't last longer than twelve hours, and outages due to ice had been known to go on for days.

I punched in my code, then reset the alarm. I needed a shower. There was no way in hell I was going out to my garage to toss my scene clothes in the wash, and the thought of running naked through my pitch-dark house and jumping into a dark shower filled me with horror. Silence was absolute except for the quiet smacking of sleet.

I found every candle I could and began strategically placing them around the house. I located flashlights. I built a fire, and the inside of my house was pockets of darkness with shadows pushed back by several small logs with thin fingers of flame. At least the phone was still working, but of course the answering machine was dead.

It was impossible for me to sit still. In my bedroom I finally stripped and washed myself with a cloth. I put on a robe and slippers as I tried to think what I could do to occupy my time, because I was not one to allow empty space in my mind. I fantasized there was a message from Lucy but I couldn't access it right now. I wrote letters and ended up crumpling them and tossing them into the fire. I watched the paper brown around the edges, ignite and turn black. Sleet smacked, and it began to get colder inside.

The temperature in my house slowly dropped, hours slipping deeper into the still morning. I tried to sleep and couldn't get warm. My mind wouldn't get still. My thoughts bounced from Lucy to Benton to the awful scene where I'd just been. I saw a hemorrhaging woman dragged across the floor, and small owl eyes staring out of rotting flesh. I shifted positions continually. Lucy did not call.

Fear picked at my loose threads when I looked out the window into my dark backyard. My breath fogged the glass, and the click-click of sleet turned into knitting needles when I dozed, to my mother knitting in Miami when my father was dying, knitting endless scarves for the poor in some cold place. Not a single car went by. I called Rita at the guard booth. She didn't answer.

My eyes blurred as I tried to drift off again at 3:00 A.M. Tree branches cracked like guns going off, and in the distance a train lumbered along the river. Its forlorn horn seemed to set the pitch for a percussion of screeching, clanking and rumbling that made me more uneasy. I lay in the dark, a comforter wrapped around me, and when daylight bruised the horizon, the power came back on. Marino called minutes later.

"What time you want me to pick you up?" he asked, his voice hoarse from sleep.

"Pick me up for what?" I blearily walked into the kitchen to make coffee.

"Work."

I didn't have a clue what he was talking about.

"You looked out the window, Doc?" he asked. "No way you're going anywhere in that Nazi-mobile of yours."

"I've told you not to say that. It's not funny."

I went to the window and opened the blinds. The world was rock candy and glass coating every shrub and tree. Grass was a thick, stiff carpet. Icicles bared long teeth from the eves, and I knew my car wasn't going anywhere anytime soon.

"Oh," I said. "I guess I need a ride."

Marino's big truck with its big chains churned up Richmond's roads for almost an hour before we reached my office. There wasn't another car in the lot. We carefully made our way into the building, our feet almost going out from

244

under us several times because the pavement was glazed and we were the first to challenge it. I draped my coat over my chair in my office and both of us headed to the locker rooms to change.

The rescue squad had used a transportable autopsy table so we didn't have to lift the body off a gurney. We unzipped the pouch in the vast silence of this empty theater of death and opened the bloody sheets. Under the scrutiny of overhead diffused light, her wounds looked even more terrible. I pulled a fluorescent magnifying lamp closer, adjusting its arm and peering through the lens.

Her magnified skin was a desert of dried, cracked blood and canyons of gashes and gaping wounds. I collected hairs, dozens of them, those pale blond, baby-fine hairs. Most were six or seven or eight inches long. They adhered to her belly, shoulders and breasts. I didn't find any on her face, and I placed the hairs inside a paper envelope to keep them dry.

Hours were thieves slipping past, stealing the morning, and no matter how hard I tried to find an explanation for the ripped tightly knit sweater and underwire bra, there wasn't another one except the truth. The killer had done it with his bare hands.

"I've never seen anything quite like that," I said. "You're talking about incredible strength."

"Maybe he's on cocaine or angel dust or something," Marino said. "That might explain what he did to her, too. It might also account for the Gold Dot ammo, you know, if he's doing drug deals on the street."

"I think that's the ammo Lucy said something about," I seemed to recall.

"Hot shit on the street," Marino said. "Big with dopers."

"If he was wacked out on drugs," I pointed out as I placed

245

fibers in another envelope, "then it strikes me as rather improbable his thinking would be so organized. He put out the *closed* sign, locked the door, didn't go out the back armed door until he was ready. And maybe washed up."

"No evidence he did," Marino let me know. "Nothing in the drains or sink or toilet. No bloody paper towels. No nothing. Not even on the door he opened on his way out of the store-room, so what I'm thinking is he used something—maybe part of his clothing, a paper towel, who knows—to open the door with so he didn't get blood or prints on the knob."

"That's not exactly disorganized. Not the actions of someone under the influence of drugs."

"I'd rather think he was on drugs," Marino said ominously. "The alternative's a really bad one, I mean if he's the Incredible Hulk or something. I wish . . ."

He stopped himself and I knew he was about to say he wished Benton were here to offer his experienced opinion. Yet it was so easy to depend on someone else when not all theories required an expert. Every scene and every wound resonated the emotion of the crime, and this homicide was frenzied and it was sexual and it was rage. That became only more apparent when I found large irregular areas of con-tusion. When I looked at them through a lens I saw small, curvilinear marks.

"Bite marks," I said.

Marino came over to look.

"What's left of them. Beaten with blunt force," I added.

I moved the light around, looking for more and found two on the side of her right palm and one on the bottom of her left foot and two on the bottom of the right.

"Jesus," Marino muttered in an unnerved tone I rarely heard.

He moved from the wounded hands to the feet, staring. "What the hell are we dealing with, Doc?" he asked.

All of the bite marks were contused so badly I could make out the abrasions of teeth but nothing more. The indentations needed for casting had been eradicated. Nothing was going to assist us. There was too little left to ever make a match.

I swabbed for saliva and began taking one-by-one photographs as I tried to imagine what biting palms and soles might mean to whoever had killed her. Did he know her, after all? Were her hands and feet symbolic to him, a reminder of who she was, just as her face had been?

"So he ain't totally ignorant about evidence," Marino said.

"It appears he knows bite marks can identify someone," I replied as I used a spray hose to wash off the body.

"Brrrrr," Marino shivered. "That always makes me cold."

"She doesn't feel it."

"I hope like hell she didn't feel any of what's happened to her."

"I think by the time he started in, she was already dead or close to dead, thank you, Lord," I said.

Her autopsy revealed something else to add to the horror. The bullet that had entered Kim Luong's neck and hit her carotid had also bruised her spinal cord between the fifth and sixth cervical disks, instantly paralyzing her. She could breathe and talk but not move as he dragged her down the aisle, her blood sweeping shelves, her useless arms spread wide, limp, unable to clutch the wound in her neck. In my mind I saw the terror in her eyes. I heard her whimper as she wondered what he was going to do to her next, as she watched herself die.

"Goddamn bastard!" I said.

"I'm sorry as fucking hell they switched to lethal injection," Marino said in a hard, hateful voice. "Assholes like this ought to fry. They ought to choke on cyanide gas till their fucking eyes pop out. Instead, we send them off to a nice little nap."

I swiftly ran the scalpel from the clavicles to the sternum and down to the pelvis in the usual incision shaped like a Y. Marino was quiet for a moment.

"You think you could stick that needle in his arm, Doc? You think you could turn on the gas or strap him in the chair and hit the switch?"

I didn't reply.

"I think about that a lot," he went on.

"I wouldn't think about it too much," I said.

"I know you could do it." He wouldn't let it rest. "And you know what else, I think you'd like it but just won't admit it, not even to yourself. Sometimes I really want to kill someone."

I glanced up at him, blood speckling my face shield and saturating the long sleeves of my gown.

"Now you're really worrying me," I said, and I meant it.

"See, I think a lot of people feel that way and just won't admit it."

Her heart and lungs were within normal limits.

"I think most people *don't* feel that way."

Marino was getting more belligerent, as if his rage over what had been done to Kim Luong made him feel as powerless as she had been.

"I think Lucy feels that way," he said.

I glanced up at him, refusing to believe it.

"I think she just waits for an opportunity. And if she don't get that out of her system, she's gonna end up waiting tables."

"Be quiet, Marino."

"Truth hurts, don't it? Least I admit it. Take the asshole who did this. Me? I'd like to handcuff him to a chair, shackle his ankles and put the barrel of my pistol in his mouth and ask him if he had an orthodontist because he was about to need one."

Her spleen, kidneys, liver were within normal limits.

"Then I'd stick it against his eye, tell him to take a look and let me know if I needed to clean the inside of the barrel."

Inside her stomach were what appeared to be remnants of chicken, rice and vegetables, and I thought of the container and fork that had been found in a paper bag near her pocketbook and coat.

"Hell, maybe I'd just back up like I'm on the fucking firing range and use him as a target, see how much he liked . . ."

"Stop it!" I said.

He shut up.

"Goddamn it, Marino. What's gotten into you?" I asked, scalpel in one hand, forceps in the other.

He was quiet for a while, our silence heavy as I worked and kept him busy with various tasks.

Then he said, "The woman who ran up to the ambulance last night is a friend of Kim's, works as a waitress at Shoney's, was taking night classes at VCU. They lived together. So the friend gets home from class. She's got no idea what's happened and her phone rings, and this dumb-ass reporter says, 'What was your reaction when you heard?'"

He paused. I looked up at him as he stared at the opened-up body, the chest cavity empty and gleaming red, pale ribs gracefully bowed out from the perfectly straight spine. I plugged in the Stryker saw.

"According to the friend, there's no indication she might have known anybody who struck her as weird. Nobody coming into the store and bothering her, giving her the creeps. There was a false alarm earlier in the week, Tuesday, same back door, it happens a lot. People forget it's armed," he went on, his eyes distant. "It's like he just suddenly flew out of hell."

I began sawing through the skull with all its comminuted fractures and areas punched out by violent blows of a tool or tools I couldn't identify. A hot bony dust drifted through the air.

26

By early afternoon, roads had thawed enough so that other diligent, hopelessly behind forensic scientists could come to work. I decided to make my rounds because I was frantic.

My first stop was the Forensic Biology Section, a ten-thousand-square-foot area where only an authorized few had access to electronic cards for the locks. People didn't drop by to chat. They traversed the corridor and glanced at intense scientists in white behind glass but rarely got any closer than that.

I pressed an intercom button to see if Jamie Kuhn was in. "Let me find him," a voice called back.

The instant he opened the door, Kuhn held out a clean, long white lab coat, gloves and mask. Contamination was the enemy of DNA, especially in an era when every pipette, microtome, glove, refrigerator and even pen used for labeling might be questioned in court. The degree of laboratory precautions had become just about as stringent as the sterile procedures found in the operating room.

"I hate to do this to you, Jamie," I said.

"You always say that," he said. "Come on in."

There were three sets of doors to pass through, and fresh lab coats hung in each airlocked space to make sure you exchanged the one you'd just put on for yet another one. Tacky paper on the floors was for the bottom of your shoes. The process was repeated twice more to make sure no one carried contaminants from one area into another.

The examiners' work area was an open, bright room of black counterspace and computers, water baths, containment units and laminar flow hoods. Individual stations were neatly arranged with mineral oil, autopipettes, polypropylene tubes and tube racks. Reagents, or the substances used to cause reactions, were made in big batches from molecular biology-grade chemicals. They were given unique identification numbers and stored in small aliquots away from chemicals kept for general use.

Contamination was managed primarily through serialization, heat denaturation, enzymatic digestion, screening, repeated analysis, ultraviolet irradiation, iodinizing irradiation, use of controls and samples taken from a healthy volunteer. If all else failed, the examiner just quit on certain samples. Maybe he tried again in a few months. Maybe he didn't.

Polymerase chain reaction, or PCR, had made it possible to get DNA results in days instead of weeks. Now with short tandem repeat typing, STR, it was theoretically possible that Kuhn could get results in a day. That was, if there was cellular tissue for testing, and in the case of the pale hair from the unidentified man found in the container, there was not.

"That's a damn shame," I said. "Because it looks like I've found more of it. This time adhering to the body of the woman murdered last night at the Quik Cary."

"Wait a minute. Am I hearing this right? The hair from the container guy's clothing matches hair on her?"

"Looks like it. You can see my urgency."

"Your urgency's about to get more urgent," he said. "Because the hair's not cat hair, dog hair. It's not animal hair. It's human."

"It can't be," I said.

"It absolutely is."

Kuhn was a wiry young man who didn't get excited by much. I couldn't remember the last time I'd seen his eyes light up.

"Fine, unpigmented, rudimentary," he went on. "Baby hair. I figured maybe the guy has a baby at home. But now, two cases? Maybe the same hair on the murdered lady?"

"Baby hair isn't six or seven inches long," I told him. "That's what I collected from her body."

"Maybe it grows longer in Belgium," he dryly said.

"Let's talk about the unidentified man in the container first. What would baby hair be doing all over him?" I asked. "Even if he does have a baby back home? And even if it were possible for baby hair to be that long?"

"Not all of them are that long. Some are extremely short. Like stubble when you shave."

"Any of the hair forcibly removed?" I asked.

"I'm not seeing any roots with follicular tissues still adhering—mostly the bulbous-shaped roots you associate with hair naturally falling out. Shedding, in other words. Which is why I can't do DNA."

"But some of it's been cut or shaved?" I thought out loud, drawing a blank.

"Right. Some's been cut, some hasn't. Like those weird

253

styles. You've seen them—short on top and long and wispy on the sides."

"Not on a baby I haven't," I answered.

"What if he had triplets, quintuplets, sextuplets because his wife had been on a fertility drug?" Kuhn suggested. "The hair would be the same but if it's coming from different kids that might explain the different lengths. The DNA would be the same, too, saying you had anything to test."

In identical twins, triplets, sextuplets, the DNA was identical, only the fingerprints were different.

"Dr. Scarpetta," Kuhn said, "all I can tell you is the hairs are alike visually, their morphology the same, in other words."

"Well, these hairs on this lady are alike visually, too."

"Any short ones, as if they were cut?"

"No," I replied.

"Sorry I don't have more to tell you," he said.

"Believe me, Jamie, you've just told me quite a lot," I said. "I just don't know what any of it means."

"You figure it out," he tried to lighten up, "we'll write a paper on it."

I tried the trace evidence lab next and didn't even bother saying hello to Larry Posner. He was peering into a microscope that probably was more sharply focused than he was when he looked up at me.

"Larry," I said. "Everything's going to hell."

"Always has been."

"What about our unidentified guy? Anything?" I asked. "Because let me tell you, I'm really groping."

"I'm relieved. I thought you dropped by to ask me about your lady downstairs," he replied. "And I was going to have to break the news that I'm not Mercury with winged feet."

"There may be a link between the two cases. Same weird hair found on the bodies. Human hair, Larry."

He thought about this for a long moment.

"I don't get it," he said finally. "And I hate to tell you, but I don't have anything quite so dramatic to report to you."

"Anything you can tell me at all?" I asked.

"Start with the soil samples from the container. PLM picked up the usual," he began, referring to the polarized light microscopy. "Quartz, sand, diatomite, flint and elements like iron and aluminum. Lots of trash. Glass, paint chips, vegetable debris, rodent hairs. You can only begin to imagine all the crap inside a cargo container like that.

"And diatoms all over the place, but what's a little offbeat is what I found when I examined the ones swept up from the container's floor, and the ones from the surface of the body and exterior of the clothes. They're a mixture of salt-water and freshwater diatoms."

"Makes sense if the ship started out in the Scheldt River in Antwerp and then spent most of the voyage at sea," I remarked.

"But the inside of the clothing? That's exclusively fresh-water. Don't get that unless he washed his clothes, shoes, socks, even underwear in a river, lake, whatever. And I wouldn't expect you to launder Armani and crocodile shoes in a river or lake, or swim in clothes like that, either.

"So it's like he's got freshwater diatoms against his skin, which is weird. And the mixture of salt and fresh on the outside, which you'd expect under the circumstances. You know, walking around on the dock, saltwater diatoms in the air, getting on his clothes, but not on the inside of them."

"What about the vertebral bone?" I then asked.

"Freshwater diatoms. Consistent with freshwater drowning, maybe the river in Antwerp. And the hair on the guy's head— all freshwater diatoms. No saltwater ones mixed in."

Posner widened his eyes and rubbed them, as if they were very tired.

"This is really twisting my brain like a dishrag. Diatoms that don't add up, weirdo baby hair and the vertebral bone. Like an Oreo. One side chocolate, the other vanilla, with chocolate and vanilla icing in the middle and a scoop of vanilla on top."

"Spare me the analogies, Larry. I'm confused enough."

"So how do you explain it?"

"I can only offer a scenario."

"Fire away."

"He might have only freshwater diatoms in his hair if his head were immersed in fresh water," I said. "If he were put head-first inside a barrel with fresh water in the bottom, for example. You do that to somebody, they can't get out, just like toddlers who fall head-first into buckets of water— those five-gallon plastic kind detergent comes in. Waist-high and very stable. Impossible to topple it over. Or he could have been drowned in a normal-size bucket of fresh water if someone held him down."

"I'm going to have nightmares," Posner said.

"Don't stay here until the roads start freezing again," I said.

Marino gave me a ride home, and I took the jar of formalin with me because I would not give up hope that the flesh inside it had something else to say. I would keep it on my desk in my study and now and then put on gloves and study it in sidelight like an archaeologist trying to read crude symbols worn away on stone.

"You coming in?" I asked Marino.

"You know, my damn pager keeps going off and I can't figure out who it is," he said, shoving his truck in gear.

He held it up and squinted.

"Maybe if you turned on the overhead light," I suggested.

"Probably some snitch too stoned to dial right," he replied. "I'll eat something if you're offering. Then I gotta go."

As we stepped inside my house, his pager vibrated again. He grabbed it off his belt in exasperation, tilting it until he could read the display.

"Screwed up again! What's five-three-one? Anything you know that's got those numbers in it?" he asked, exasperated.

"Rose's home number does," I said.

27

Rose had grieved when her husband died, and I thought she would fall apart when she'd had to put down one of her greyhounds. Yet somehow she'd always worn her dignity the same way she dressed, properly and with discretion. But when she learned on the news that morning that Kim Luong had been murdered, Rose got hysterical.

"If only, if only . . . ," she went on and on, crying in the wing chair near the fire in her small apartment.

"Rose, you got to quit saying that," Marino said.

She had known Kim Luong because Rose often shopped at the Quik Cary. Rose had gone there last night, probably at the same time the killer was still inside beating and biting and smearing blood. Thank God the store had been closed and locked.

I carried two mugs of ginseng tea into her living room while Marino drank coffee. Rose was shaking all over, face swollen from crying and gray hair hanging over the collar of her bathrobe. She looked like a neglected old woman in a nursing home.

"I didn't have the TV on. I was reading. So I didn't

know about it until I heard it on the news this morning."
She kept telling us the same story in different ways. "I
had no idea, was sitting up in bed reading and worrying
about all the problems in the office. Mainly Chuck. I think
that boy's as twisted as they come and I've been working
to show it."

I set down her tea.

"Rose," Marino said. "We can talk about Chuck another
time. We need you to tell us exactly what happened last—"

"But you've got to listen to me first!" she exclaimed.
"And Captain Marino, you've got to make Dr. Scarpetta
listen! That boy hates her! He hates all three of us. I'm
trying to tell you, you must do anything to get rid of him
before it's too late."

"I'm going to take care of it as soon as . . ." I started to
say.

But she was shaking her head.

"He's pure evil. I believe he's been following me, or at
least someone involved with him," she claimed. "Maybe even
that car you saw in my parking lot and the one following
you. How do you know it wasn't him who rented it under
a phony name so he didn't have to use his car and be recognized right away? How do you know it's not whoever he
might be involved with?"

"Whoa, whoa, whoa," Marino interrupted her, holding
up his hand. "Why would he follow anybody?"

"Drugs," she answered as if she knew it for a fact. "This
past Monday we had an overdose case come in, and it just
so happened I decided to come in an hour and a half early
because I was going to take a long lunch break to get my
hair done."

I didn't believe that Rose just happened to come in early.

I had asked her to help me find out what Ruffin was up to, and of course, she had made that her mission.

"You were out that day," she said to me. "And you had misplaced your appointment book and we looked everywhere with no luck. So by Monday I was obsessed with finding it because I knew how much you need it. I thought I'd check the morgue again.

"And I went in there before I'd even taken my coat off," she went on, "and here's Chuck at six-forty-five in the morning sitting at a desk with the pill counter and dozens of bottles lined up. Well, he looked as if I'd just caught him with his pants down. I asked him why he was getting started so early, and he said it was going to be a busy day and he was trying to get a head start."

"Was his car in the parking lot?" Marino asked.

"He parks in the deck," I explained. "His car wouldn't be visible from our building."

"The drugs were from Dr. Fielding's case," Rose resumed, "and out of curiosity I looked at the report. Well, the woman had about every drug known to man. Tranquilizers, antidepressants, narcotics. A total of some thirteen hundred pills, if you can believe that."

"Unfortunately, I can," I said.

Overdoses and suicides typically came to us with months, even years, of prescription drugs. Codeine, Percocet, morphine, methadone, PDC, Valium and fentanyl patches to name a few. It was an unbearably tedious task to count them to see how many were supposed to have been in the bottle and how many were left.

"So he's stealing pills instead of washing them down the sink," Marino said.

"I can't prove it," Rose replied. "But Monday wasn't

god-awful busy like it usually is. The overdose was the only case. Chuck avoided me as much as he could after that, and every time drugs came in with cases, I wondered if they'd gone in his pocket instead of down the drain."

"We can hook up a VCR where he's not going to see it. You've already got cameras down there. If he's doing it, we'll get him," Marino promised.

"That on top of everything else," I said. "The press about that would be awful. It might even go out on the wire, especially if an investigative reporter started digging and found out about my alleged refusal to take calls from families, and the chat room, and even the subterfuge of running into Bray in a parking lot."

Paranoia pushed against my chest and I took a deep breath. Marino was watching me.

"You're not thinking Bray's got something to do with this," Marino said, skeptically.

"Only in the sense that she helped put Chuck on the road he's on. He himself told me the more bad things he did, the easier it got."

"Well, I think Chuckie-boy's on his own when it comes to stealing prescription drugs. It's too easy for slime like him to resist. Like the cops who can't resist pocketing wads of cash at drug busts and shit like that. Hell, drugs like Lortabs, Lorcet, not to mention Percocet, can go for two to five bucks a pop on the street. What I'm curious about is where he's unloading the stuff."

"Maybe you can find out from his wife if he's out a lot at night," Rose suggested.

"Honey," Marino replied, "bad people do stuff like this in broad daylight."

Rose looked dejected and somewhat embarrassed, as if

261

afraid that her being so upset had sent her spinning threads of truth into a tapestry of conviction. Marino got up to pour more coffee.

"You're thinking he's following you because you're suspicious of his drug dealing?" he asked Rose.

"Oh, I guess it sounds so far-fetched when I hear myself say it."

"Might be someone involved with Chuck, if we want to keep going down this path. And I don't think we should dismiss anything right now," Marino added. "If Rose knows, then you do," he said to me. "Chuck sure as hell knows that."

"If this is tied in with drugs, then what's the motive if Chuck's involved in our being followed? To hurt us? To intimidate us?" I asked.

"This much I can guarantee," Marino replied from the kitchen. "He's mixed up with people who are way out of his league. And we're not talking small amounts of money. Think how many pills come in with some of these bodies. Cops have to turn in every bottle they find. Think of all the leftover pain medication or who-knows-what in your average person's medicine cabinet."

He came back into the living room and sat down, blowing into the cup as if that really would cool his coffee in a hurry.

"Add that to the shitload of other stuff they're actively taking or supposed to be taking and what do you get?" he went on. "That the only reason Chuckie-boy needs his job in the morgue is to steal drugs. Hell, he doesn't need the pay, and that may have something to do with why he's been doing such a shitty job over the last few months."

"He could be taking in thousands of dollars a week," I said.

"Doc, you got any reason to think he might be hooked

up with your other offices, getting somebody to do the same thing? They get him the pills, he gives them a small cut."

"I have no idea."

"You got four district offices. You steal drugs from all of them, you're getting into really big bucks now," Marino said. "Hell, the little shit may even be involved in organized crime, just one more drone bringing stuff to the hive. Problem is, this ain't shopping at Wal-Mart. He thinks it's so easy making deals with some guy in a suit, some foxy woman. This person moves the merchandise along to the next person in the chain. Maybe it's eventually traded for guns that end up in New York."

Or Miami, I thought.

"Thank God you alerted us, Rose," I said. "The last thing I want is anything flowing out of the office and ending up in the hands of people who will hurt others or even kill them."

"Not to mention, Chuck's days are probably going to be numbered, too," Marino said. "People like him usually don't live too long."

He got up and moved to the end of the couch, closer to Rose.

"Now, Rose," he gently said. "What's making you think what you've just told us has anything to do with Kim Luong's murder?"

She took a deep breath and turned off the lamp next to her as if it was bothering her eyes. Her hands were shaking so badly that when she reached for her mug, she spilled some of her tea. She dabbed the wet spot on her lap with a tissue.

"On my way home from the office last night, I decided to pick up shortbreads and a few other things," she began, her voice getting shaky again.

"Do you know exactly what time this was?" Marino asked.

"Not to the minute. Around ten of six as best I can say."

"Let me be sure I've got this straight," Marino said, taking notes. "You stopped at the Quik Cary at about six o'clock P.M. Was it closed?"

"Yes. Which irritated me a little because it's not supposed to close until six. I thought ugly thoughts, and now I feel so bad about that, too. Here she is dead in there and I'm mad at her because I couldn't get cookies . . . !" she sobbed.

"Did you see any cars in the lot?" Marino asked. "Any person or persons?"

"Not a one," she barely said.

"Think hard, Rose. Was there anything that struck you at all?"

"Oh, yes," she said. "And this is what I've been trying to get at. I could see from Libbie that the market was closed because the lights were out, so I pulled into the lot to turn around, and I saw the *closed* sign on the door. I got back on Libbie and hadn't gone any farther than the ABC store when this car was suddenly behind me with its high beams on."

"Were you headed home?" I asked.

"Yes. And I really didn't think anything until I turned on Grove and he did, too, staying on my bumper with those darn lights about to blind me. Cars going the other way were flicking their lights up and down to tell him his high beams were on, in case he didn't know. But he clearly intended for them to be on. By now I was getting frightened."

"Any idea what kind of car? Could you see anything?" Marino asked.

"I was practically blinded, and then I was so confused. Immediately I thought of the car in my parking lot on Tuesday night when you came by," she said to me. "And then your telling me you'd been followed. And I started thinking about Chuck and drugs and the sort of horrible people who get involved in that."

"So you're driving along Grove," Marino got her back on track.

"Of course, I drove right on past my apartment building, trying to figure out where to go to get away with him. And I don't know how I thought of it, but I suddenly cut over to the left and did a U-turn. Then I drove to where Grove ends at Three Chopt and took a left, him still behind me. The next right was the Country Club of Virginia, and I turned in there and drove straight to the entrance where the valets were. Needless to say, whoever it was vanished."

"That was damn smart of you," Marino said. "Damn smart. But why didn't you call the police?"

"It wouldn't have done any good. They wouldn't have believed me and I couldn't have described a thing, anyway."

"Well, you should have called me, at least," Marino said.

"I know."

"After this where did you go?" I asked.

"Here."

"Rose, you're scaring me," I said. "What if he was waiting for you somewhere?"

"I couldn't stay out all night, and I went a different route home."

"Any idea what time it was when he vanished?" Marino asked.

"Somewhere between six and six-fifteen. Oh, dear Lord, I just can't believe when I pulled up to that store she was in there. And what if he was? If only I'd known. I can't stop thinking there must have been something I should have noticed. Maybe even when I was in there Tuesday night."

"Rose, you couldn't have known a damn thing unless you're a gypsy with a crystal ball," Marino told her.

She took a deep, shaky breath and pulled her robe more tightly around her.

"I can't seem to get warm," she said. "Kim was such a nice girl."

She stopped again, her face contorted by grief. Tears filled her eyes and spilled.

"She was never rude to anyone and worked so hard. How could anybody do something like that! She wanted to be a nurse! She wanted to spend her life helping people! I remember worrying about her being alone in there so late at night, oh, God help me. It even crossed my mind when I was there on Tuesday but I didn't say anything!"

Her voice tumbled as if it were falling down a steep flight of stairs. I came over and knelt beside her, pulling her close.

"It's like when Sassy wasn't feeling well . . . so lethargic and I just thought she had eaten something she shouldn't have . . ."

"It's okay, Rose. Everything's going to be okay," I said.

"And it turned out she'd somehow gotten hold of a piece of glass . . . My little baby was bleeding inside . . . And I didn't do anything."

"You didn't know. We can't know everything." I felt a spasm of grief, too.

"If only I'd taken her to the vet sooner . . . I'll never, ever forgive myself for that. Poor little girl a prisoner in a little cage and muzzle and some monster hit her with something and broke her nose . . . at that *goddamn dog track*! And then I let her suffer and die!"

She wept as if outraged over every loss and act of cruelty

the world had ever suffered. I held her clenched fists in both of my hands.

"Rose, now you listen to me," I said. "You saved Sassy from hell just as you've saved others. There's nothing you could have done for Sassy any more than there was anything you could have done when you stopped to get your short-breads. Kim was dead. She had been dead for hours."

"What about him?" she cried. "What if he had still been inside that store and had come out just as I had pulled in? I'd be dead, too, wouldn't I? Shot and dumped somewhere like garbage. Or maybe he would have done awful things to me, too."

She closed her eyes, exhausted, tears sneaking down her face. She went limp all over as the violent storm passed. Marino leaned forward on the couch and touched her knee.

"You got to help us out," he said. "We need to know why you think your being followed and the murder might be connected."

"Why don't you come home with me?" I said.

Her eyes cleared as she began to regain her composure.

"That car pulling out after me right there where she was murdered? Why didn't he start following me long before that?" she said. "And an hour, an hour and a half, before the alarm went off. Don't you find that an amazing coincidence?"

"Sure I do," Marino said. "But there've been a lot of amazing coincidences in my career."

"I feel foolish," Rose said, looking down at her hands.

"All of us are tired," I said. "I've got plenty of room . . ."

"We're gonna nail Chuckie-boy for drugs," Marino said to her. "Not a damn thing foolish about that."

"I'm going to stay here and go on to bed," Rose said.

I continued to sort through what she'd told us as we went down the stairs and into the parking lot.

"Look," Marino said, unlocking his car. "You've been around Chuck a whole lot more than I have. You know him a lot better, which is too bad for you."

"And you're going to ask me if he's the one in the rental car following us," I said as he backed out and turned on Randy Travis. "The answer's no. He's a sneak. He's a liar and a thief, but he's a coward, Marino. It takes a lot of arrogance to boldly tailgate someone with your high beams on. Whoever's doing it is very sure of himself. He has no fear of being caught because he thinks he's too smart for that."

"Sort of the definition of a psychopath," he said. "And now I feel worse. Shit. I don't want to think that guy who just did Luong is the one following you and Rose."

Roads had frozen over again and Richmond drivers, lacking sense, were sliding and spinning all over the place. Marino had his portable police radio on and was monitoring accidents.

"When are you going to turn that thing in?" I asked.

"When they come and try to take it from me," he replied. "I ain't turning in shit."

"That's the spirit."

"The hard thing about every case we've ever worked," he said, "is there's never just one thing going on. Cops try to connect so much crap that by the time we solve the case, we could have written the victim's biography. Half the time we find a connection, it's not one that matters. Like the husband who gets mad at his wife. She goes out the door, pissed, and ends up abducted from a mall parking lot, raped and murdered. Her husband pissing her off didn't make it happen. Maybe she was going shopping anyway."

He turned into my driveway and put the truck in park. I gave him a long look.

"Marino, what are you going to do about money?"

"I'll be all right."

I knew it wasn't true.

"You could help me out as a field investigator for a while," I said. "Until this suspension nonsense ends."

He was silent. As long as Bray was there, it would never end. Suspending him without pay was her way of forcing Marino to resign. If he did that, he was out of the way like Al Carson.

"I can hire you two ways," I went on. "A case-by-case basis and you'll get fifty dollars per—"

He snorted. "Fifty dollars my ass!"

"Or I can hire you part-time and eventually I'll have to advertise the position and you'll have to apply for it like everybody else."

"Don't make me sick."

"How much are you earning now?"

"About sixty-two plus benefits," he replied.

"The best I could do is make you a P-fourteen at senior level. Thirty hours a week. No benefits. Thirty-five a year."

"Now that's a good one. One of the funniest things I've heard in a while."

"I can also take you on as an instructor and coordinator in death investigation at the Institute. That's another thirty-five. So that's seventy. No benefits. Actually, you'll probably make out better."

He thought about it for a moment, sucking smoke.

"I don't need your help right now," he said rudely. "And hanging around medical examiners and dead bodies ain't part of my life's plan."

I climbed out of his truck.

"Good night," I said.

He angrily roared away and I knew it wasn't me he was really so angry with. He was frustrated and furious. His self-respect and vulnerability were naked in front of me and he didn't want me to see it. All the same, what he'd said hurt.

I threw my coat over a chair in the foyer and pulled off leather gloves. I put Beethoven's "Eroica' symphony on the CD player and my discordant nerves began to restore their rhythm like the strings that played. I ate an omelet and settled in bed with a book I was too tired to read.

I fell asleep with the light on and was shocked awake by the hammering of my burglar alarm. I got my Glock out of a drawer and fought the impulse to disarm the system. I couldn't stand the awful clangor. But I didn't know what had set it off. The phone rang several minutes later.

"This is ADT . . ."

"Yes, yes," I said loudly. "I don't know why it's gone off."

"We're showing zone five," the man said. "The kitchen back door."

"I have no idea."

"Then you'd like us to dispatch the police."

"I guess you'd better," I said as the air raid in my house went on.

28

I supposed a strong gust of wind might have set off the alarm, and minutes later I silenced it so I could hear the police arrive. I sat on my bed, waiting. I didn't go through the dreaded routine of securing every inch of my house, of walking into rooms and showers and dark spaces of fear.

I listened to silence and became acutely aware of the sounds of it. I heard the wind, the faint clicking of numbers rolling on the digital clock, heat blowing, my own breathing. A car turned into my driveway and I hurried to the front door as one of the officers sharply rapped with a baton or blackjack instead of ringing the bell.

"Police," a woman's no-nonsense voice announced.

I let them in. There were two officers, a young woman and an older man. The woman's nameplate identified her as J. F. Butler, and there was something about her that had an effect on me.

"The zone's the one for the kitchen door that leads outside," I told them. "I very much appreciate your coming so quickly."

"What's your name?" her partner, R. I. McElwayne, asked me.

271

He was acting as if he didn't know who I was, as if I were just a middle-aged lady in a bathrobe who happened to live in a nice house in a neighborhood that rarely needed the police.

"Kay Scarpetta."

His tight demeanor loosened a bit, and he said, "I didn't know if you really existed. Heard about you a lot, but I never been to the morgue, not once in eighteen years, for which I'm grateful."

"That's because back then you didn't have to go to demo posts and learn all these scientific things," Butler picked on him.

McElwayne tried not to smile as his eyes roamed curiously around my house.

"You're welcome to come watch a demo post anytime you want," I said to him.

Butler's attention was everywhere, her body on alert. She hadn't been dulled yet by the weight of her career, unlike her partner, whose main interest at this moment was my house and who I was. He had probably pulled a thousand cars and answered just as many false alarms by now, all for little pay and even less appreciation.

"We'd like to look around," Butler said to me, locking the front door. "Starting with down here."

"Please. Look anywhere you want."

"If you'll just stay right here," she said, heading toward the kitchen, and then it hit me hard, emotions catching me completely off guard.

She reminded me of Lucy. It was the eyes, the straight bridge of the nose, and the way she gestured. Lucy couldn't move her lips without moving her hands, as if she were conducting a conversation instead of having one. I stood in the foyer and could hear their feet on hardwood, their muffled voices, the shutting of doors. They took their time, and I imagined it was Butler who was making sure they didn't ignore a single space big enough to hide a human being.

They came down the stairs and went out into the icy night, the beams of their strong flashlights sweeping over windows, streaking across blinds. This went on another fifteen minutes, and when they knocked on the door to come back inside, they led me into the kitchen, McElwayne blowing on his cold, red hands. Butler had something important on her mind.

"Are you aware there's a bent place in the jamb of the kitchen door?" she asked.

"No," I said, startled.

She unlocked the door near the table by the window, where I usually ate when I was with friends or alone. Raw, freezing air rushed in as I moved close to her to see what she was talking about. She shone her light on a small indented impression in the strike plate and edge of the wooden frame where it appeared someone had tried to pry open the door.

"It could have been there for a while and you haven't noticed," she said. "We didn't check when your alarm went off on Tuesday because it was the zone for the garage door."

"*My* alarm went off on Tuesday?" I said in amazement. "I don't know anything about that."

"I'm going out to the car," McElwayne said to his partner as he walked out of the kitchen, still rubbing his hands. "Be right back."

"I was working day shift," she explained to me. "It appears your housekeeper accidentally set it off."

I couldn't understand why Marie would have set off the alarm in the garage, unless she'd gone out that way for some reason and had ignored the warning beep for too long.

"She was pretty shook up," Butler went on. "Apparently couldn't remember the code until we were already here."

"What time was this?" I asked.

"Around eleven hundred hours."

Marino wouldn't have heard the call come over the radio because at eleven o'clock he was in the morgue with me. I thought of the alarm not being set when I got home that night, of the soiled towels and dirt on the rug. I wondered why Marie hadn't left a note for me saying what had happened.

"We had no reason to check this door," Butler said. "So I can't say whether the pry mark was here on Tuesday or not."

"Even if it wasn't," I said, "obviously someone tried to get in at some point."

"Unit three-twenty," Butler said. "Ten-five to a precinct B and E detective."

"Unit seven-ninety-two," came the response.

"Can you respond, reference B and E attempt?" she said, giving out my address.

"Ten-four. Take me about fifteen minutes."

Butler set her radio upright on the kitchen table and studied the lock a little more. Cold gusting air blew a stack of napkins on the floor and sent pages of a newspaper fluttering.

"He's coming out of Meadow and Cary," she told me, as if it were something I ought to know. "That's where the precinct is."

She shut the door.

"They're not part of the detective division anymore," she went on, watching for my reaction. "So they got moved, are part of uniform operations now. I guess this was about a month ago," she added as I began to suspect where the conversation was headed.

274

"I guess B and E detectives are under Deputy Chief Bray now," I said.

She hesitated, then replied with an ironic smile, "Isn't everybody?"

"Would you like a cup of coffee?" I asked.

"That would be nice. I don't want to put you out."

I got a bag of coffee from the freezer. Butler sat down and started filling out an offense report while I got out mugs and cream and sugar, and dispatchers and cops jumped in and out in ten-codes on the air. The doorbell rang and I let the B&E detective in. I didn't know him. It seemed I didn't know anyone anymore since Bray had taken people away from jobs they had learned so well.

"This the door right here?" the detective was asking Butler.

"Yeah. Hey, Johnny, you got a pen that works better than this?"

A headache began boxing with my brain.

"You got one that works at all?"

I couldn't believe what was going on.

"What's your D.O.B.?" McElwayne was asking me.

"Not too many people have alarm systems in their garage," Butler said. "In my opinion, the contacts are weaker than they're going to be in a regular door. Lightweight metal, a really big surface area. You get a strong gusting wind . . ."

"I've never had a strong wind set off the alarm in my garage," I said.

"But if you're a burglar and figure a house has a burglar alarm," Butler continued to reason, "you might not assume the garage door's on it. And maybe there's something in there worth stealing."

"In broad daylight?" I asked.

The detective was dusting the doorjamb while more cold air blew in.

"Okay, let's see, Doc." McElwayne took over filling out the report. "Got your home address. Need the one downtown, and your home and business telephone numbers."

"I really don't want my unlisted phone number in a press basket," I said, trying to restrain my building resentment of this intrusion, well intended or not.

"Dr. Scarpetta, you got any prints on file?" the detective asked, brush poised, black magnetic powder dirtying the door.

"Yes. For exclusionary purposes."

"Thought you might. I think all M.E.s ought to in case they touch something they're not supposed to," he said, not intending to insult me but doing it anyway.

"Do you understand what I'm saying?" I tried to get McElwayne to look up at me and listen. "I don't want this in the paper. I don't want every news reporter and God knows who else calling me at home and knowing my exact address and my Social Security number and D.O.B., race, sex, where I was born, height, weight, eye color, next of kin."

"Anything happened lately we should know about?" McElwayne continued questioning me as Butler handed the detective lifting tape.

"A car followed me Wednesday night," I reluctantly replied.

I felt all eyes on me.

"It seems my secretary was followed, too. Last night."

McElwayne was writing all of this down, too. The doorbell sounded again, and I saw Marino in the video display of the Aiphone on the wall by the refrigerator.

"And I'd better not read about that in the paper," I warned as I walked out of the kitchen.

"No, ma'am, it will be in the supplementary report. That doesn't go in the press basket," Butler's voice followed me.

"Goddamn it, do something," I said to Marino as I opened the door. "Someone tries to break into my goddamn house and now my privacy's going to be broken into next."

Marino was vigorously chewing gum and looked like I was the one who had committed a crime.

"It'd be nice if you'd let me know when someone tries to break into your house. I shouldn't have to hear about it on the fucking scanner," he said, his angry strides carrying him toward the sound of voices.

I'd had enough and retreated to my study to call Marie. A young child answered the phone, then Marie got on.

"I just found out about the alarm going off while you were here on Tuesday," I said to her.

"I'm very sorry, Mrs.. Scarpetta," she said in a pleading voice. "I didn't know what to do. I didn't do anything to set it off. I was vacuuming and then it happened. I couldn't remember the code because I was so scared."

"I understand, Marie," I said. "It scares me, too. It just went off again tonight, so I know exactly what you mean. But I need you to tell me these things when they happen."

"The police didn't believe me. I was sure of it. I told them I didn't go into the garage, and I could tell . . ."

"It's all right," I said again.

"I was afraid you would be angry with me because the police . . . that maybe you wouldn't want me working for you anymore . . . I should have told you. I will always. I promise."

"You don't need to be afraid. The police aren't going to

hurt you in this country, Marie. It's not the same thing as where you're from. And I want you to be very careful when you're at my house. Keep the alarm on and make sure it's on when you leave. Did you notice anyone or maybe a car that caught your attention for some reason?"

"I remember it was raining hard and very cold. I didn't see anyone."

"You let me know if you do," I said.

278

29

Somehow the supplemental part of the attempted burglary offense report made it into the press basket in time for the six o'clock news on Saturday night. Reporters began calling both Rose and me at home with question after question about our being followed.

I had no doubt Bray was behind that little slip. It was a nice little bit of amusement for her on an otherwise cold, dreary weekend. Of course she didn't give a damn that my sixty-four-year-old secretary lived alone in a community that did not have a guard gate.

Late Sunday afternoon I sat in my great room, a fire burning, as I worked on a long overdue journal article that I had no heart for. The wretched weather continued and my concentration drifted. By now, Jo should have been admitted to MCV and Lucy should be in D.C., I supposed. I didn't know for sure. But of one thing I was certain. Lucy was angry, and whenever she was angry, she cut herself off from me. It could go on for months, even a year.

I had managed to avoid calling my mother or my sister

Dorothy, which might have seemed pretty cold of me, but I didn't need one more watt of stress. I finally relented early Sunday evening. Apparently Dorothy wasn't home. I tried my mother next.

"No, Dorothy's not here," my mother said. "She's in Richmond, and maybe you would know that if you ever bothered to call your sister and your mother. Lucy's in a shooting, and you can't be bothered . . ."

"Dorothy's in Richmond?" I said in disbelief.

"What do you expect? She's her mother."

"So Lucy's in Richmond, too?" The thought sliced through me like a scalpel.

"That's why her mother's going there. Of course Lucy's in Richmond."

I didn't know why I should have been surprised. Dorothy was a narcissistic upstager. Whenever there was drama, she had to be the center of it. If that meant suddenly assuming the role of mother to a child she cared nothing about, Dorothy would.

"She left yesterday and didn't want to bother to ask about staying in your house, since you don't seem to care about your family," my mother said.

"Dorothy never wants to stay in my house."

My sister was quite fond of hotel bars. At my house, there was no possibility of meeting men, at least not any I was willing to share with her.

"Where is she staying?" I asked. "And is Lucy staying with her?"

"No one will tell me, all this secrecy business, and here I am, her grandmother . . ."

I couldn't stand it anymore.

"Mother, I've got to go," I said.

I practically hung up on her and called the orthopedic department chair, Dr. Graham Worth, at home.

"Graham, you've got to help me out," I told him.

"Don't tell me a patient in my unit died," he wryly said.

"Graham, you know I wouldn't ask for your help unless it was something very important."

Levity gave way to silence.

"You've got a patient under an alias. She's ATF, was shot in Miami. You know who I mean."

He didn't answer me.

"My niece, Lucy, was involved in the same shooting," I went on.

"I know about the shooting," he replied. "Certainly it's been in the news."

"I'm the one who asked Jo Sanders's ATF supervisor to transfer her to MCV. I promised to personally look after her, Graham."

"Listen, Kay," he said. "I've been instructed that under no circumstances am I allowed to let anyone but immediate family in to see her."

"No one else?" I said in disbelief. "Not even my niece?"

He paused, then said, "It pains me to tell you this, but *especially* not her."

"Why? That's ridiculous!"

"It's not my call."

I couldn't imagine Lucy's reaction if she was being barred from seeing her lover.

"She's got a shattered, comminuted fracture of the left femur," he was explaining. "I've had to put in a plate. She's in traction and on morphine, Kay. She fades in and out. Only her parents are seeing her. I'm not even sure she really understands where she is or what happened to her."

"What about the head injury?" I asked.

"Just a grazing wound that opened the flesh."

"Has Lucy been there at all? Maybe waiting outside the room? Her mother might be with her."

"She was there earlier. Alone," Dr. Worth replied. "Sometime this morning. I doubt she's still there."

"At least give me a chance to talk to Jo's parents."

He wouldn't answer me.

"Graham?"

Silence.

"For God's sake. They're comrades. They're best friends."

Silence.

"Are you still there?"

"Yes."

"Damn it, Graham, they love each other. Jo might not even know if Lucy's alive."

"Jo is very well aware your niece is fine. Jo doesn't want to see her," he said.

I got off the phone and stared at it. Somewhere in this goddamn city my sister was checked into a hotel, and she knew where Lucy was. I went through the Yellow Pages, starting with the Omni, the Jefferson, the obvious hotels. I soon found that Dorothy had checked into the Berkeley in the historic area of the city known as Shockhoe Slip.

She didn't answer the phone in her room. There were only so many places in Richmond where she could carouse on a Sunday, and I hurried out of the house and got into my car. The skyline was shrouded in clouds, and I valet-parked my car in front of the Berkeley. I knew right away when I walked inside that Dorothy would not be here. The small, elegant hotel had an intimate, dark bar with high-backed leather chairs and a quiet clientele. The bartender wore a white jacket and was very attentive when I went up to him.

"I'm looking for my sister and wonder if she's been in here," I said. I described her and he shook his head.

I walked back outside and crossed the cobblestone street to the Tobacco Company, an old tobacco warehouse that had been turned into a restaurant with an exposed glass and brass elevator constantly gliding up and down through an atrium of lush plants and exotic flowers. Just inside the front door was a piano bar with a dance floor, and I spotted Dorothy sitting at a table crowded with five men. I walked up to them, clearly on a mission.

People at nearby tables stopped talking, all eyes on me as if I were a gunslinger who had just pushed her way through a saloon's swinging doors.

"Excuse me," I politely said to the man on Dorothy's left. "Do you mind if I sit here for a moment?"

He did mind, but he surrendered his chair and wandered off to the bar. Dorothy's other companions shifted about uncomfortably.

"I've come to get you," I said to Dorothy, who clearly had been drinking for a while.

"Well, look who's here!" she exclaimed, and she raised her stinger in a toast. "My big sister. Let me introduce you," she said to her companions.

"Be quiet and listen to me," I said in a low voice.

"My legendary big sister."

Dorothy always got mean when she drank. She didn't slur her words or bump into things, but she could sexually tease men into misery and use her tongue like a nettle. I was ashamed of her demeanor and the way she dressed, which sometimes seemed an intended parody of me.

This night she wore the handsome dark blue suit of a professional, but beneath the jacket her tight pink sweater offered her companions more than a hint of nipples. Dorothy had always been obsessed with her small breasts. To have men staring at them somehow reassured her.

"Dorothy," I said, leaning closer to her ear, almost overwhelmed by Chanel Coco, "you need to come with me. We have to talk."

"Do you know who she is?" she went on as I cringed. "The chief medical examiner of this fine Commonwealth. Can you believe it? I have a big sister who's a coroner."

"Wow, that's got to be really interesting," one of the men said.

"What can I get you to drink?" said another.

"So what do you think is the truth about the Ramsey case? Think the parents did it?"

"I'd like somebody to prove those were really Amelia Earhart's bones they found."

"Where's the waitress?"

I put my hand on Dorothy's arm and we got up from the table. One thing was true about my sister: she had too much pride to cause a scene that didn't make her look clever and appealing. I escorted her out into a dispirited night of darkened windows and fog.

"I'm not going home with you," she announced, now that there was no one to hear. "And let go of my fucking arm."

She pulled in the direction of her hotel while I tugged her toward my car.

"You're coming with me and we're going to figure out what to do about Lucy."

"I saw her earlier at the hospital," she said.

I put her in the passenger's side.

"She didn't mention anything about you," my ever-sensitive sister said.

I got in and locked the doors.

"Jo's parents are very sweet," she added as we drove off. "I was very taken aback that they didn't know the truth about Lucy and Jo's relationship."

"What did you do? Tell them, Dorothy?"

"Not in so many words, but I suppose I implied certain things because I just assumed they knew. You know, it seems so odd to see a skyline like this when you're used to Miami."

I wanted to slap her.

"Anyway, after talking with the Sanderses for a while, I came to realize they're the Jerry Falwell type and weren't about to condone a lesbian relationship."

"I wish you wouldn't use that word."

"Well, that's what they are. Descended from the Amazon types on the island of Lesbos in the Aegean Sea, off the coast of Turkey. Turkish women have so much hair. You ever noticed?"

"You ever heard of Sappho?"

"Of course I've heard of him," Dorothy said.

"*She* was a Lesbian because she lived on Lesbos. *She* was one of the greatest lyric poets in antiquity."

"Ha. Nothing poetic about some of these body-pierced, stocky hockey players I see. And of course, the Sanderses didn't come right out and say they thought Lucy and Jo were lesbians. Their reasoning was Jo had been horribly traumatized, and to see Lucy would bring it all back. It was too soon. They were quite emphatic in a very nice way, and when Lucy showed up, they were very kind and sympathetic when they told her."

I passed through the toll plaza.

"Unfortunately, you know how Lucy is. She challenged them. She said she didn't believe them, and got pretty loud and rude. I explained to the Sanderses that she was just very upset after all she'd been through. They were very patient and said they'd pray for her, and next thing I knew a nurse told Lucy she had to leave.

"She stormed out," my sister said. She looked over at me to add, "Of course, mad at you or not, she'll come looking for you, just like she always does."

"How could you do that to her?" I asked. "How could you get between her and Jo? What kind of person are you?"

Dorothy was taken aback. I could feel her bristle.

"You've always been so jealous of me because you're not her mother," she answered.

I turned off on the Meadow Street exit instead of keeping on toward home.

"Why don't we just settle this once and for all," Dorothy and her stingers said. "You're nothing but a machine, a computer, one of those high-tech instruments you love so much. And one has to ask what's wrong with a person who chooses to spend all her time with dead people. Refrigerated, stinky, rotting dead people, most of them low-lifes to begin with."

I got on the Downtown Expressway again, heading back downtown.

"Versus me. I believe in relationships. I spend my time in creative pursuits, in reflection and relationships, and I believe our bodies are our temples and we should take care of them and be proud of them. Look at you." She paused for effect. "You smoke, you drink, you don't even belong to a gym, I bet. Don't ask me why you're not fat and flabby, unless it's cutting through all those ribs and running around crime scenes or being on your feet all day in a goddamn morgue. But let's get to what the worst thing is."

She leaned close to me, her vodka breath an unpleasant vapor.

"Fasten your shoulder harness, Dorothy," I quietly said.

"What you've done to my daughter. My only child. You never had a child because you've always been too busy. So you took mine," she blasted me with her boozy breath. "I should have never, never, ever let her visit you. Where was my brain when I let her stay summers with you?"

She dramatically clutched her head in both hands.

"You filled her with all this guns and ammo and crime-solving shit! You turned her into a fucking little computer nerd by the time she was ten, when little girls should be going to birthday parties and riding ponies and making friends!"

I let her rail on, paying attention to the road.

"You exposed her to a big, ugly redneck cop, and let's face it. He's really your only close relationship with a man. I hope like hell you don't sleep with a pig like that. And I have to tell you, as sorry as I am about what happened to Benton, he was weak. Not enough sap in that tree, oh no. No yolk in that egg.

"Huh. You were the *man* in that relationship, *Miss doctor-lawyer-chief*. I've told you before and I'll tell you again, you're nothing but a man with big tits. You fool everybody because you look *so elegant* in your Ralph Lauren and ritzy-titzy car. You think you're so fucking sexy with those big tits, always making me feel something's wrong with me and making fun of me when I ordered Mark Eden and all those other contraptions. And remember what Mother said?

"She gave me a photograph of a man's hairy hand and said, 'That's what makes a woman's breasts get big.'"

287

"You're drunk," I said.

"We were teenagers and you made fun of me!"

"I never made fun of you."

"You made me feel stupid and ugly. And you had this blond hair and a chest and all the boys talked about you. Especially since you were smart, too. Oh, you've always thought you're so fucking smart because I couldn't do anything but English."

"Stop it, Dorothy."

"I hate you."

"No, you don't, Dorothy."

"But you don't fool me. Oh, no."

She shook her head side to side, wagging her finger in my face.

"Oh, no. You can't fool me. I've always suspected the truth about you."

I was parked in front of the Berkeley Hotel, and she didn't even notice. She was screaming, tears streaming down her face.

"You're a closet diesel dyke," she said hatefully. "*And you turned my daughter into one!* And now she almost gets killed and she thinks I'm lower than a sewer!"

"Why don't you go inside your hotel and get some sleep," I said to her.

She wiped her eyes and looked out the window, surprised to see her hotel, as if it were a spaceship that had silently landed.

"I'm not dumping you out on the roadside, Dorothy. But right now I think it's best we're not together."

She sniffled, her rage fading like fireworks in the night.

"I'll get you to your room," I said.

She shook her head, her hands motionless in her lap, tears sliding down her miserable face.

"She didn't want to see me," she said in a voice as quiet as a breath. "The minute I came off the elevator in that hospital, she looked as if someone had just spat on her food."

A group of people were walking out of the Tobacco Company. I recognized the men who had been at Dorothy's table. They were walking unsteadily and laughing too loudly.

"She's always wanted to be just like you, Kay. Do you have any idea how that feels?" she cried. "I'm a somebody, too. Why can't she want to be like me?"

She suddenly moved over and hugged me. She cried into my neck, sobbing, shaking. I wanted to love her. But I didn't. I never had.

"I want her to adore me, too!" she exclaimed, carried away by emotion and alcohol and her own addiction to drama. "I want her to admire me, too! I want her to brag about me like she does you! I want her to think I'm brilliant and strong, that everyone turns around and looks at me when I walk into a room. I want her to think and say all those things she thinks and says about you! I want her to ask *my* advice and want to grow up to be just like me."

I put the car in gear and drove up to the entrance of the hotel.

"Dorothy," I said, "you're the most selfish person I've ever known."

30

It was almost nine o'clock by the time I got home, and I worried that I should have brought Dorothy with me instead of leaving her at the hotel. I wouldn't have been the least bit surprised if she had gone right back across the street to the bar. Maybe there were a few lonely men left she could amuse.

I checked my telephone messages, annoyed by hang-ups. There were seven of them, and caller-ID read *unavailable* each time. Reporters didn't like to leave messages, even at my office, because it gave me the option of not calling them back. I heard a car door shut in the driveway and almost wondered if it were Dorothy, but when I checked, a yellow taxi was driving away as Lucy rang the bell.

She was carrying one small suitcase and a tote bag and dropped them in the foyer, shoving the door shut without hugging me. Her left cheek was one dark purple bruise, and several smaller ones were beginning to turn yellow at the edges. I had seen enough injuries like that to know she had been punched.

"I hate her," she started in, glaring at me as if I were to blame. "Who told her to come here? Was it you?"

"You know I would never do something like that," I said. "Come on. Let's talk. We have so much talking to do. My God, I was beginning to think I was never going to see you again."

I sat her in front of the fire and tossed in another log. Lucy looked awful. She had dark circles under her eyes, her jeans and sweater were hanging off her, her reddish-brown hair was falling over her face. She propped a foot up on my coffee table. Velcro ripped as she took off her ankle holster and gun.

"You got anything to drink in this house?" she asked. "Some bourbon or something? There was no damn heat in the back of the taxi and the window wouldn't close. I'm frozen. Look at my hands."

She held them out. The nails were blue. I took both of them in mine and held them tight. I moved closer to her on the couch and put my arms around her. She felt so thin.

"What happened to all that muscle?" I tried to be funny.

"I haven't had much food . . . ." She stared into the fire.

"They don't have food in Miami?"

She wouldn't smile.

"Why did Mother have to come? Why can't she just leave me alone? All my life she doesn't do a goddamn fucking thing except subject me to all her men, men, men," she said. "Parade herself around with all these dicks fawning over her while I had nobody. Hell, they had nobody, either, and didn't even know it."

"You've always had me."

She shoved her hair out of her eyes and didn't seem to hear me.

"You know what she did at the hospital."

"How did she know where to find you?" I had to have that question answered first, and Lucy knew why I asked it.

"Because she's my birth mother," she said with singsong sarcasm. "So she's listed on various forms whether I like it or not, and of course she knows who Jo is. So Mom tracks down Jo's parents here in Richmond and finds out everything because she's so manipulative and people always think she's wonderful. The Sanderses tell her where Jo's room is and Mother shows up at the hospital this morning and I didn't even know she was here until I was sitting there in the waiting area and she walked in like the prima donna she is."

She clenched and unclenched her fists as if her fingers were stiff.

"Then guess what?" she went on. "Mom puts on this big sympathetic act with the Sanderses. Is bringing them coffee, sandwiches, giving them all her little pearls of philosophy. And they're talking and talking, and I'm just sitting there like I don't exist, and then Mom comes over and pats my hand and says, *Jo isn't having any visitors today.*

"I ask her who the hell she is, telling me that. She says the Sanderses wanted her to tell me because they didn't want to hurt my feelings. So I finally just fucking leave. Mom may still be there for all I know."

"She's not," I said.

Lucy got up and stabbed a log with the poker. Sparks swarmed as if in protest.

"She's gone too far. This time she's done it," my niece said.

"Let's don't talk about her. I want to talk about you. Tell me what happened in Miami."

She sat on the rug, leaning against the couch, staring into the fire. I got up and went to the bar and poured her a Booker's bourbon.

"Aunt Kay, I've got to see her."

I handed Lucy the drink and sat back down. I massaged

her shoulders and she began to loosen up, her voice getting drowsy.

"She's in there and doesn't know I'm waiting for her. Maybe she thinks I can't be bothered."

"Why in the world would she think that, Lucy?"

She didn't answer me, but seemed drawn into smoke and flames. She sipped her drink.

"When we were driving there in my hot little V-twelve Benz," she said in a distant voice, "Jo had this bad feeling and she told me she did. I said it was normal to have a *bad feeling* when you're about to do a takedown. I even kidded her about it."

She paused, just staring at flames as if she were seeing something else.

"We get to the door of the apartment that these One-Sixty-Five assholes are using as their clubhouse," she resumed, "and Jo goes first. There're six of them in there instead of three. Right away we know we're had and I know what they're going to do. One of them grabs Jo and sticks a gun to her head to make her tell them where the Fisher Island place is we'd set up for the hit."

She took a deep breath and was silent, as if she couldn't go on. She sipped the bourbon.

"God, what is this stuff? The vapors alone are knocking me out."

"A hundred and twenty proof. Usually I'm not a pusher, but it wouldn't be such a bad thing for you to be knocked out right now. Stay here with me for a while," I said.

"ATF and DEA did everything right," she told me.

"These things happen, Lucy."

"I had to think so fast. The only thing I knew to do was act like I didn't care if they blew her brains out or not.

Here they are holding a gun to her head and I start acting pissed off at her, which wasn't at all what they were expecting."

She took another swallow of bourbon. It was hitting her hard.

"I walked up to this Moroccan asshole with the gun and get right in his face and tell him to go ahead and waste her, that she's a stupid bitch and I'm sick of her always getting in my way. But if he does her now, all he's going to do is fuck himself and everybody else."

She stared into the fire, eyes wide and unblinking, as if watching it again in her mind.

"I say, *You think I didn't expect you would use us and then do this? You think I'm stupid? Well, guess what? I forgot to tell you Mr. Tortora is expecting our company*—and I look at my watch—*in exactly one hour and sixteen minutes. I thought it would be nice to entertain him before you motherfuckers showed up and blew his guts out and took all his guns and money and fucking cocaine. What happens if we don't show up? You think he won't get nervous?*"

I couldn't take my eyes off Lucy. Images flew at me from all directions. I imagined her playing out this dangerous act, and I saw her in battle dress when she was at fire scenes and flying a helicopter and programming computers. I envisioned her as the irritating, irrepressible child I had virtually raised. Marino was right. Lucy thought she had so much to prove. Her first impulse had always been to fight.

"I didn't think they really believed me," she said. "So I turn to Jo. I'll never forget the look in her eyes, the pistol barrel right against her temple. Her eyes." She paused. "They're so calm as she looks in mine because . . ."

Her voice shook.

"Because she wants me to know she loves me . . ." Lucy

choked on sobs. "She loves me! She wants me to know because she believes . . ." Her voice went up and stopped. "She believes we're going to die. And that's when I start yelling at her. I call her a stupid fucking bitch and slap her face so hard my hand goes numb.

"And she just looks at me as if I'm all there is, blood trickling out of her nose and the sides of her mouth, a red river down her face, dripping off her chin. She didn't even cry. She's out of the story, lost her role, her training, everything she damn well knows what to do. I grab her. I shove her hard to the ground and get on top of her, swearing and slapping and yelling."

She wiped her eyes and stared straight ahead.

"And what's so awful, Aunt Kay, is part of it's real. I'm so angry with her for quitting on me, for just giving up. She was going to just give up and die, goddamn it!"

"Like Benton did," I quietly said.

Lucy wiped her face on her shirt. She didn't seem to hear what I'd said.

"I'm so fucking tired of people giving up and leaving me," she said in a shattered voice. "When I need them and they fucking give up!"

"Benton didn't give up, Lucy."

"I just keep swearing at Jo, screaming and hitting her and telling her I'm going to kill her as I straddle her, shaking her by her hair. It wakes her up, maybe even pisses her off, too, and she starts fighting back. Calls me a Cuban cunt and spits blood in my face, punches me, and by this time the guys are laughing and whistling and grabbing their crotches . . ."

She took another long breath and shut her eyes, barely able to sit up. She leaned against my legs, firelight playing on her strong, beautiful face.

"She starts really struggling. My knees are so tight against her sides I'm surprised I didn't break her ribs, and while we're going at each other like that, I tear open her shirt, and this really gets the guys going and they don't see me grab my gun out of my ankle holster. I start firing. I just fire. Fire. Fire. Fire. Fire . . ." Her voice trailed off.

I bent over and put my arms around her.

"You know? I'm wearing those wide-legged street jeans to hide my Sig. They say I fired eleven rounds. I don't even remember dropping the empty magazine, putting in a full one. Racking it back. Agents are everywhere and somehow I'm dragging Jo out the door. And she's bleeding heavily from her head."

Lucy's lower lip trembled as she tried to go on, her voice far away. She wasn't here. She was there, living it again.

"Fire. Fire. Fire. Her blood on my hands."

Her voice rose to God.

"I hit her and hit her. I can still feel the sting of her cheek against the palm of my hand."

She looked at her hand as if it should be put to death.

"I felt it. How soft her skin was. And she bled. I made her bleed. The skin I had touched and loved. I drew blood from it. Then the guns, the guns, the guns, and smoke and ringing in my ears and it's a blaze when it happens like that. It's over and never started. I knew she was dead."

She bowed her head and wept quietly, and I stroked her hair.

"You saved her life. And you saved yours," I finally said. "Jo knows what you did and why you did it, Lucy. She should love you all the more."

"I'm in trouble this time, Aunt Kay," she said.

"You're a hero. That's what you are."

"No. You don't understand. It doesn't matter if it was a good shooting. It doesn't matter if ATF gives me a medal."

She sat up and got to her feet. She stared down at me with defeat in her eyes and another emotion I didn't recognize. Maybe it was grief. She'd never shown grief when Benton was murdered. All I'd ever seen was rage.

"The bullet they took out of her leg? It's a Hornady Custom Jacketed hollowpoint. Ninety grains. What I had in my gun."

I didn't know what to say.

"I'm the one who shot her, Aunt Kay."

"Even if you did . . ."

"What if she never walks again . . . ? What if she's finished in law enforcement because of me?"

"She won't be jumping out of helicopters anytime soon," I said. "But she's going to be fine."

"What if I permanently damaged her face with my fucking fist?"

"Lucy, listen to me," I said. "You saved her life. If you killed two people to do that, then so be it. You had no choice. It's not that you wanted to."

"The hell I didn't," she said. "I wish I'd killed all of them."

"You don't mean that."

"Maybe I'll just be a mercenary soldier," she bitterly said. "Got any murderers, rapists, car jackers, pedophiles, drug dealers you need to get rid of? Just call one-eight-hundred-L-U-C-Y."

"You can't bring Benton back through killing."

Still, it was as if she didn't hear me.

"He wouldn't want you to feel this way," I said.

The telephone rang.

"He didn't abandon you, Lucy. Don't be angry with him because he died."

The phone rang a third time, and she couldn't restrain herself. She grabbed it, unable to hide the hope and fear in her eyes. I couldn't bring myself to tell her what Dr. Worth had told me. Now was not the time.

"Sure, hold on," she said, and disappointment and more hurt touched her face as she handed me the phone.

"Yes," I reluctantly answered.

"Is this Dr. Kay Scarpetta?" an unfamiliar male voice asked.

"Who is this?"

"It's important I verify who you are." The accent was American.

"If you're another reporter . . ."

"I'm going to give you a phone number."

"I'm going to give you a promise," I said. "Tell me who you are, or I'm hanging up."

"Let me give you this number," and he began reciting it before I could refuse.

I recognized the country code for France.

"It's three o'clock in the morning in France," I said, as if he didn't know.

"It doesn't matter what time it is. We have been getting information from you and running it through our computer system."

"Not from me."

"No, not in the sense that you typed it into the computer, Dr. Scarpetta."

His voice was baritone and smooth, like fine polished wood.

"I'm at the secretariat in Lyon," he informed me. "Call the number I gave you and at least get our after-hours voice mail."

"How much sense does that . . . ?"

"Please."

I hung up and tried, and a recording of a woman with a

298

heavy French accent said "Bonjour, hello," and gave the office hours in both languages. I entered the extension he had given me, and the man's voice came back over the line.

"*Bonjour, hello?* And that's supposed to identify who you are?" I said. "You could be a restaurant for all I know."

"Please fax me a sheet of your letterhead. When I see that I'll fill you in."

He gave me the number. I put him on hold and went back to my study. I faxed a sheet of my stationery to him while Lucy remained in front of the fire, elbow on her knee, chin in her hand, listless.

"My name's Jay Talley, the ATF liaison at Interpol," he said when I got back with him. "We need you to come here right away. You and Captain Marino."

"I don't understand," I said. "You should have my reports. I have nothing more to add to them at this time."

"We wouldn't ask you if it wasn't important."

"Marino doesn't have a passport," I said.

"He went to the Bahamas three years ago."

I had forgotten that Marino had taken one of his many bad choices in women on a three-day cruise. Their relationship didn't last much longer than that.

"I don't care how important this is," I said. "There's no way I'm getting on a plane and flying to France when I don't know what—"

"Hold on a second," he cut in, politely but with authority. "Senator Lord? Sir, are you there?"

"I'm here."

"Frank?" I said in amazement. "Where are you? Are you in France?"

I wondered how long he had been conferenced in and listening.

"Now listen, Kay. This is important," Senator Lord told me in a voice that reminded me of who he was. "Go, and go right away. We need your help."

"We?"

Then Talley spoke. "You and Marino need to be at the Millionaire private terminal at four-thirty. That's A.M. your time. Less than six hours from now."

"I can't leave right now . . ." I started to say as Lucy filled my doorway.

"Don't be late. Your New York connection leaves at eight-thirty," he told me.

I thought Senator Lord had hung up, but suddenly his voice was there.

"Thank you, Agent Talley," he said. "I'll talk to her now."

I could hear Talley get off the line.

"I want to know how you're doing, Kay," my friend the senator said.

"I've got no idea."

"I care," he said. "I won't let anything happen to you. Just trust me. Now tell me how you're feeling."

"Other than being summoned to France and about to be fired and . . ." I started to add what had happened to Lucy, but she was standing right there.

"Everything's going to be fine," Senator Lord said.

"Whatever *everything* is," I replied.

"Trust me."

I always had.

"You're going to be asked to do things that you're going to resist. Things that will scare you."

"I don't scare easily, Frank," I said.

31

Marino picked me up at quarter of four. It was a heartless hour of the morning that reminded me of sleepless rotations in hospitals, of early days in my career when I was the one who got the calls for cases nobody else wanted.

"Now you know what it feels like to be on midnight shift," Marino commented as we cut through icy roads.

"I know all about it anyway," I replied.

"Yeah, but the difference is, you don't have to. You could send someone else to scenes and stay home. You're the chief."

"I'm always leaving Lucy when she needs me, Marino."

"I'm telling you, Doc, she understands. She's probably gonna be heading up to D.C. anyway to deal with all this review board shit."

I hadn't told him about Dorothy's visit. It would have served no purpose other than to set him off.

"You're on the faculty at MCV. I mean, you're a real doctor."

"Thank you."

"Can't you just go talk to the administrator or something?" he said, punching in the cigarette lighter. "Couldn't you pull some strings so Lucy could go in there?"

"As long as Jo isn't capable of making decisions, her family has complete control over who visits and who doesn't."

"Fucking religious wackos. Bible-banging Hitlers."

"There was a time when you were pretty narrow-minded, too, Marino," I reminded him. "Seems to me you used to talk about queers and fags. I don't even want to repeat some of the words I've heard you use."

"Yeah. Well, I never meant any of it."

At the Millionaire jet center the temperature was in the low twenties and hard, icy wind grabbed and shoved me as I collected luggage out of the back of the truck. We were met by two pilots who didn't say much as they opened a gate to lead us across the tarmac, where a Learjet was hooked up to a power cart. A thick manila envelope with my name on it was in one of the seats, and when we took off into the clear, cold night, I turned off cabin lights and slept until we landed in Teterboro, New Jersey.

A dark blue Explorer glided our way as we climbed down the metal steps. It was snowing small flakes that stung my face.

"Cop." Marino gave the nod as the Explorer stopped close to the plane.

"How do you know?"

"I always know," he said.

The driver was in jeans and a leather coat and looked as if he'd seen life from every angle and was happy to pick us up. He packed our baggage in the trunk. Marino climbed in front and off they sailed into one comment and story after another because the driver was NYPD and Marino used to be. I floated in and out of their conversation as I dozed.

". . . Adams in the detective division, he called around

eleven. I guess Interpol got him first. I didn't know he had anything to do with them."

"Oh yeah?" Marino's voice was muted and soporific like bourbon on the rocks. "Some tear-ass I bet . . ."

"Naw. He's okay . . ."

I slept and drifted, city lights touching my eyelids as I began to feel that empty ache again.

". . . got so shit-faced one night I woke up the next morning and didn't know where my car or creds were. That was my wake-up call . . ."

The only other time I had flown supersonic had been with Benton. I remembered his body against me, the intense heat of my breasts touching him as we sat in those small gray leather seats and drank French wine, staring at jars of caviar we had no intention of eating.

I remembered exchanging hurtful words that turned into desperate lovemaking in London, in a flat near the American Embassy. Maybe Dorothy was right. Maybe sometimes I was too much in my mind and not as open as I wanted to be. But she was wrong about Benton. He had never been weak, and we had never been tepid in bed.

"Dr. Scarpetta?"

A voice grabbed my attention.

"We're here," our driver said, eyeing me in the rearview mirror.

I rubbed my face with my hands and stifled a yawn. Winds were stronger here, the temperature lower. At the Air France ticket counter I checked us in because I didn't trust Marino with tickets or passports or even finding the right gate without being an ass. Flight 2 left in about an hour and a half, and the instant I sat down in the Concorde lounge, I felt exhausted again, my eyes burning. Marino was in awe.

"Look at that, will you?" he whispered too loudly. "They got a full bar. That guy over there's drinking a beer and it's seven o'clock in the morning."

Marino took that as his wake-up call.

"Want anything?" he asked. "How 'bout a newspaper?"

"Right now I don't give a damn what's going on in the world." I wished he would leave me alone.

When he returned, he was carrying two plates piled high with Danish, cheese and crackers. He had a can of Heineken under an arm.

"Guess what," he said, setting his breakfast snack on the coffee table next to him. "It's almost three o'clock in the afternoon, French time."

He popped open the beer.

"They got people mixing champagne and orange juice, you ever heard of that? And I'm pretty sure there's somebody famous sitting over there. She's got sunglasses on and everybody's staring."

I didn't care.

"The guy she's with looks famous, too, sort of like Mel Brooks."

"Does the woman in sunglasses look like Anne Bancroft?" I muttered.

"Yeah!"

"Then it's Mel Brooks."

Other passengers, dressed far more expensively than we were, glanced our way. A man rattled *Le Monde* and sipped espresso.

"Saw her in *The Graduate*. You remember that?" Marino went on.

I was awake now and wished I could hide somewhere.

"That was my fantasy. Shit. Like that schoolteacher giving

304

you *tutoring* after hours. The one who made you cross your legs."

"You can see the Concorde through the window over there," I pointed.

"I can't believe I didn't bring a camera."

He swallowed another mouthful of beer.

"Maybe you should go find one," I suggested.

"You think they'd have those little disposable cameras around here?"

"Only French ones."

He hesitated for a moment, then gave me a dirty look.

"I'll be back," he said.

Of course, he left his ticket and passport in the pocket of the coat draped over his chair, and when the announcement came that we were about to board, I got an urgent text message on my pager that no one would let him back inside the lounge. He was waiting at the desk, face flushed with anger, a security guard beside him.

"Sorry," I said, handing one of the attendants Marino's passport and ticket.

"Let's not begin the trip this way," I said to him under my breath as we walked back through the lounge, following other passengers to the plane.

"I told them I'd go get it. Bunch of French sons of bitches. If people would speak English like they're supposed to, this kinda shit wouldn't happen."

Our seats were together, but fortunately, the plane wasn't full, so I moved across the aisle from him. He seemed to take this personally until I gave him half of my chicken with lime sauce, my sponge roll with vanilla mousse, and my chocolates. I had no idea how many beers he drank, but he was up and down a lot, making his way along the narrow

305

aisle while we flew twice the speed of sound. We arrived at Charles de Gaulle airport at 6:20 P.M.

A dark blue Mercedes was waiting for us outside the terminal, and Marino tried to strike up a conversation with the driver, who would neither let him sit in the front seat nor pay any attention to him. Marino sullenly smoked out his window, cold air washing in as he watched abject apartments scarred with graffiti and miles of switchyards draw us into a lit-up skyline of a modern city. The great corporate gods of Hertz, Honda, Technics and Toshiba glittered in the night from their Mount Olympian heights.

"Hell, this may as well be Chicago," Marino complained. "I feel really weird."

"Jet lag."

"I been to the West Coast before and didn't feel like this."

"This is worse jet lag," I said.

"I think it's got something to do with going that fast," he went on. "Think about it. You're looking out this little porthole like you're in a spaceship, right? You can't even see the damn horizon. No clouds that high, air's too thin to breathe, probably a hundred degrees below zero. No birds, no normal planes, no nothing."

A police officer in a blue and white Citroën with red stripes was pulling a speeder near the Banque de France. Along the Boulevard des Capucines shops turned into designer boutiques for the very rich, and I was reminded that I had failed to find out the exchange rate.

"That's why I'm hungry again," Marino continued his scientific explanation. "Your metabolism's got to pick up when you're going that fast. Think how many calories that is. I didn't feel nothing once I got through customs, did you? Not drunk or stuffed or nothing."

306

Not much decorating had been done for Christmas, not even in the heart of the city. Parisians had strung modest lights and swags of evergreen outside their bistros and shops, and so far I had seen not a single Santa except the tall inflatable one in the airport that was flapping his arms as if he were doing calisthenics. The season was celebrated a bit more, with poinsettias and a Christmas tree, in the marble lobby of the Grand Hôtel, where our itinerary let us know we were staying.

"Holy shit," Marino said, looking around at columns and at a huge chandelier. "What do you think a room in this joint costs?"

The musical trilling of telephones was nonstop, the line at the reception desk depressingly long. Baggage was parked everywhere, and I realized with growing despondency that a tour group was checking in.

"You know what, Doc?" Marino said. "I won't even be able to afford a beer in this place."

"If you ever make it to the bar," I replied. "It looks like we may be here all night."

Just as I said that, someone touched my arm, and I found a man in a dark suit standing next to me, smiling.

"Madame Scarpetta, Monsieur Marino?" He motioned us out of line. "I'm so sorry, I just now saw you. My name is Ivan. You're already checked in. Please, I will show you to your rooms."

I couldn't place his accent, but it certainly wasn't French. He led us through the lobby to mirror-polished brass elevators, where he pushed the button for the third floor.

"Where are you from?" I asked.

"All over, but I have been in Paris many years."

We followed him down a long hallway to rooms that were

next to each other, but not connected. I was startled and unnerved to find our baggage was already inside them.

"If you need anything, call for me specifically," Ivan said. "It's probably best you eat in the café here. There's a table for you, or of course, there's room service."

He briskly walked away before I could tip him. Marino and I both stood in our doorways staring inside our rooms.

"This is weirding me out," he said. "I don't like secret squirrel shit like this. How the hell do we know who he is? I bet he don't even work for this hotel."

"Marino, let's not have this conversation in the hall," I said quietly. I thought if I did not have even a few moments away from him I might become violent.

"So, when you want to eat?"

"How about I call your room," I said.

"Well, I'm really hungry."

"Why don't you go on to the café, Marino?" I suggested, praying he would. "I'll get something later."

"No, I think we better stick together, Doc," he replied.

I walked inside my room and shut the door, astonished to discover my suitcase unpacked, my clothes neatly folded and already in drawers. Slacks, shirts and a suit were hanging in the closet, toiletries lined up on the counter in the bathroom. Instantly, my phone rang. I had no doubt who it was.

"What?" I said.

"They got into my shit and put everything away!" Marino blared like a radio turned up too high. "Now, I've about had it. I don't like nobody digging in my bags. Who the hell they think they are over here? This some French custom or something? You check into a ritzy hotel and they go through your luggage?"

"No, it's not a French custom," I said.

"So it must be some Interpol custom," he retorted.

"I'll call you later."

A fruit basket and bottle of wine centered a table, and I sliced a blood orange and poured a glass of merlot. I pulled back heavy drapes and stared out the window at people in evening dress getting into fine cars. Gilt sculptures on the old opera house across the street flaunted their golden, naked beauty before the gods, and chimney pots were dark stubble on miles of roofs. I felt anxious and lonely and intruded upon.

I took a long bath and thought about abandoning Marino for the rest of the night, but decency overruled. He had never been to Europe before, certainly not to Paris, and more to the point, I was afraid of leaving him alone. I dialed his extension and asked if he wanted to have a light dinner sent up. He picked pizza, despite my warning that Paris wasn't known for it, and he raided my minibar for beer. I ordered oysters on the half shell and nothing more, and turned the lights very low because I'd seen enough for one day.

"There's something I've been thinking about," he said after the food had arrived. "I don't like to bring it up, Doc, but I'm getting a really oddball feeling, odd as hell. I mean, well'—he took a bite of pizza—"I'm just wondering if you're feeling it, too. If the same thing might be floating in your head, sort of out of nowhere like a UFO."

I put down my fork. The lights of the city sparkled beyond my windows and even in the dim lighting I could see his fear. I responded in kind.

"I haven't a clue as to what you're talking about," I said, reaching for my wine.

"Okay, I just think we need to consider something for a minute."

I didn't want to listen.

"Well, first you get this letter delivered by a United States senator who just happens to be the chairman of the Judiciary Committee, meaning he's got about as much power with federal law enforcement as any other person I can think of. Meaning he's going to know all kinds of shit going on with Secret Service, ATF, FBI, you name it."

An alarm began to sound inside me.

"You gotta admit it's interesting timing that Senator Lord delivers this letter to you from Benton and now all of a sudden we're over here going to Interpol . . ."

"Let's don't do this." I cut him off as my stomach tightened and my heart began to pound.

"You gotta hear me out, Doc," he replied. "In the letter Benton's saying for you to stop grieving, that everything's all right and he knows what you're doing right this minute . . ."

"Stop it," I raised my voice and threw my napkin on the table as emotions began crashing in on all sides.

"We got to face it." Marino was getting emotional, too. "How do you know . . . I mean, what if the letter really wasn't written several years ago? What if it was written now . . . ?"

"No! How dare you!" I exclaimed as tears filled my eyes. I pushed back my chair and got up.

"Leave," I told him. "I won't be subjected to your goddamn UFO theories. What do you want? To make me live through this hell all over again? So I can hope something when I've worked so hard to accept the truth? Get out of my room."

Marino pushed back his chair, and it fell over as he jumped to his feet. He snatched his pack of cigarettes off the table.

"What if he's fucking still alive?" He raised his voice, too. "How do you know for a fact he didn't have to disappear for a while because of some big thing going on that involves ATF, FBI, Interpol, shit, maybe NASA, for all we know?"

I grabbed my wine, my hands shaking so badly I could barely hold it without spilling, my entire existence ripped open again. Marino was stalking the room and gesturing wildly with his cigarette.

"You don't know it for a fact," he said again. "All you saw was burned-up bone in a stinking black fire hole. And a Breitling watch like his. So fucking what!"

"You son of a bitch!" I said. "You goddamn son of a bitch! After all I've been through, and then you have to—"

"You're not the only one who's been through it. You know, just because you slept with him doesn't mean you fucking owned him."

I took quick steps toward him and caught myself before I slapped him hard across the face.

"Oh, God," I muttered as I stared into his shocked eyes. "Oh, God."

I thought of Lucy striking Jo, and I walked away from him. He turned to the window and smoked. The room was overcast with misery and shame, and I leaned my head against the wall and shut my eyes. I'd never come even close to violence with anyone in my life, not anyone like this, not someone I knew and cared about.

"Nietzsche was right," I muttered in a defeated way. "Be careful who you choose for an enemy because that's who you become most like."

"I'm sorry," Marino barely said.

"Like my first husband, like my idiot sister, like every out-of-control cruel, selfish person I've ever known. Here I am. Like them."

"No, you ain't."

My forehead was pressed against the wall, as if I were praying, and I was grateful we were in shadows, my back to him, so he could not see my anguish.

"I didn't mean what I said, Doc. I swear I didn't. I don't even know why I said it."

"It's all right."

"All I'm trying to do is look at everything because there's pieces that aren't fitting right."

He walked over to an ashtray and stabbed out his cigarette. "I don't know why we're here," he said.

"We're not here to do this," I said.

"Well, I don't know why they couldn't have exchanged info with us through the computer, over the phone, like they always do. Do you?"

"No," I whispered as I took a deep breath.

"So it started sneaking into my thoughts that maybe Benton . . . What if there was something going on and he had to be a protected witness for a while. Change his identity and all that. We didn't always know what he was into. Not even you always knew, because he couldn't always tell you, and he would never want to hurt us by telling us something we shouldn't know. Especially not hurt you or make you worry about him all the time."

I did not answer him.

"I'm not trying to stir anything up. I'm just saying it's something we should think about," he lamely added.

"No, it isn't," I replied, clearing my throat and aching all over. "It's not something we should think about. He was identified, Marino, by every possible means. Carrie Grethen didn't just conveniently kill him so he could disappear for a while. Don't you see how impossible this is? He's dead, Marino. He's dead."

"Did you go to his autopsy? Did you see his autopsy report?" He wouldn't let it go.

Benton's remains had gone to the Philadelphia medical examiner's office. I had never asked to review his case.

"No, you didn't go to his autopsy, and if you had, I would have thought you were the most fucked-up person I've ever met," Marino said. "So you didn't see nothing. You only know what you've been told. I don't mean to keep hammering you with that, but it's the truth. And if anyone wanted to cover up that those remains weren't his, how would you know if you never took a look?"

"Pour me some Scotch," I said.

32

I turned toward Marino, my back against the wall as if I didn't have the strength to stand on my own two feet.

"Man, you see how much whiskey costs over here?" Marino commented as he closed the door to the minibar.

"I don't care."

"Interpol's probably paying, anyway," he decided.

"And I need a cigarette," I added.

He lit a Marlboro for me and the first hit punched my lungs. He presented me with a tumbler of straight single malt on the rocks in one hand, a Beck's beer in the other.

"What I'm trying to say," Marino resumed, "is if Interpol can do all this secret shit with electronic tickets and ritzy hotels and Concordes, and no one ever meets a soul who's ever talked to whoever these people are, then what makes you think they couldn't have faked everything else?"

"They couldn't have faked his being murdered by a psychopath," I replied.

"Yes, they could have. Maybe that was the perfect timing." He blew out smoke and gulped down beer. "Point is, Doc, I think anything can be faked, if you think about it."

"DNA identified . . ."

I couldn't finish the statement. It brought images before me I had suppressed for so long.

"You can't say the reports were true."

"Enough!"

But the beer had crumbled what walls he had, and he would not stop his increasingly fantastic theories and deductions and wishful thoughts. His voice went on and on and began to sound far away and unreal. A shiver crept over me. A splinter of light glinted in that dark, devastated part of me. I desperately wanted to believe that what he was suggesting was true.

When 5:00 A.M. came around, I was still dressed and asleep on the couch. I had a hammering headache. My mouth tasted like stale cigarettes and my breath was alcohol. I showered and stared for a long time at the phone by my bed. The anticipation of what I had decided to do electrified me with panic. I was so confused.

In Philadelphia, it was almost midnight, and I left a message for Dr. Vance Harston, the chief medical examiner. I gave him the number to the fax machine in my room and left the *do not disturb* sign on the door. Marino met me in the hall, and I said nothing to him but an inaudible good morning.

Downstairs, dishes clattered as the buffet was set up and a man cleaned glass doors with a brush and a cloth. There was no coffee this early, and the only other guest awake was a woman with a mink coat draped over a chair. In front of the hotel, another Mercedes taxi awaited us.

Our driver this day was sullen and in a hurry. I rubbed my temples as motorcycles sped past in lanes of their imagination, weaving between cars and roaring through many narrow tunnels. I was depressed by reminders of the car crash that killed Princess Diana.

I remembered waking up and hearing about it on the news, and my first thought was we tended to disbelieve that mundane, random deaths can happen to our gods. There is no glory or nobility in being killed by a drunk driver. Death is the great equalizer. It doesn't give a damn who you are.

The sky was dusky blue. Sidewalks were wet from washing and green garbage cans had been set out along the streets. We bumped over cobblestones at the Place de la Concorde and drove along the Seine, which we could not see most of the time because of a wall. A digital clock outside the Gare de Lyon let us know it was seven-twenty, and inside feet shuffled and people hurried into Relais Hachette to buy papers.

I waited behind a woman with a poodle at the ticket counter, and a sharp-featured, well-dressed man with silver hair jolted me. He looked like Benton from a distance. I could not help but scan the crowd as if I might find him, my heart throbbing as if it couldn't survive much more of this.

"Coffee," I told Marino.

We sat at a counter inside L'Embarcadère and were served espresso in tiny brown cups.

"What the hell is this?" Marino grumbled. "I just wanted regular coffee. How 'bout handing me some sugar," he said to the woman behind the counter.

She dropped several packs on the counter.

"I think he'd rather have a café crème," I told her.

She nodded. He drank four of them and ate two ham baguettes and smoked three cigarettes in less than twenty minutes.

"You know," I said to him as we boarded a *train à grande vitesse*, or TGV, "I really don't want you to kill yourself."

"Hey, not to worry," he replied, taking a seat across from me. "If I tried to clean up my act, the stress would do me in."

Our car was barely a third full, and those passengers seemed interested only in their newspapers. The silence prompted Marino and me to speak in very low voices, and the bullet train made no sound as it suddenly lurched forward. We glided out of the station, then blue sky and trees were flying by. I felt flushed and very thirsty. I tried to sleep, sunlight flashing over my shut eyes.

I came to when an Englishwoman two rows back began talking on a portable phone. An old man across the aisle was working a crossword puzzle, his mechanical pencil clicking. Air buffeted our car as another train sped by, and near Lyon, the sky turned milky and it began to snow.

Marino's mood was getting increasingly curdled as he stared out the window, and he was rude when we disembarked in the Lyon Part-Dieu. He had nothing to say during our taxi ride, and I got angrier with him as I replayed the words he had recklessly thrown at me last night.

We neared the old part of the city where the Rhône and Saône rivers joined, and apartments and ancient walls built into the hillside reminded me of Rome. I felt awful. My soul was bruised. I felt as alone as I'd ever felt in my life, as if I didn't exist, as if I were part of another person's bad dream.

"I don't hope nothing," Marino finally spoke apropos of nothing. "I might say *what if*, but I don't hope. There's no point. My wife left me a long time ago and I've still never found anybody that fits. Now I'm suspended and thinking about working for you. I did that? You wouldn't respect me anymore."

"Of course I would."

"Bullshit. Working for someone changes everything and you know it."

He looked dejected and exhausted, his face and slumped posture showing the strain of the life he'd lived. He'd spilled coffee on his rumpled denim shirt, and his khakis were ridiculously baggy. I'd noticed that the bigger he got, the larger the size of the pants he bought, as if he fooled himself or anyone else.

"You know, Marino, it's not very nice to imply that working for me would be the worst thing that ever happened to you."

"Maybe it wouldn't be the worst thing. But pretty close," he said.

33

Interpol's headquarters stood alone on the Parc de la Tête d'Or. It was a fortress of reflective pools and glass and did not look like what it was. I was certain the subtle signs of what went on inside were missed by virtually all who drove past. The name of the plantain tree-lined street where it was located wasn't posted, so if you didn't know where you were going, you quite likely would never get there. There was no sign out front announcing *Interpol.* In fact, there were no signs anywhere.

Satellite dishes, antennas, concrete barricades and cameras were very hard to see, and the razor wire-topped green metal fence was well disguised by landscaping. The secretariat for the only international police organization in the world silently emanated enlightenment and peace, appropriately allowing those who worked inside to look out and no one to look in. On this overcast, cold morning, a small Christmas tree on the roof ironically tipped its hat to the holidays.

I saw no one when I pressed the intercom button on the front gate to say we had arrived. Then a voice asked us to identify ourselves and when we did, a lock clicked free.

Marino and I followed a sidewalk to an outbuilding, where another lock released, and we were met by a guard in suit and tie who looked strong enough to snatch up Marino and hurl him back to Paris. Another guard sat behind bullet-proof glass and slid out a drawer to exchange our passports for visitor badges.

A belt carried our personal effects through an X-ray machine, and the guard who had greeted us gave us instructions with gestures rather than words to step, one at a time, inside what looked like a floor-to-ceiling transparent pneumatic tube. I complied, halfway expecting to be sucked up somewhere, and a curved Plexiglas door shut. Another one released me on the other side, every molecule of me scanned.

"What the hell is this? *Star Trek?*" Marino said to me after he'd been scanned, too. "How you know something like that can't give you cancer? Or if you're a man, give you other problems."

"Be quiet," I said.

It seemed we waited a very long time before a man appeared on a breezeway connecting the secure area to the main building, and he was not at all what I expected. He walked with the easy spring of a youthful athlete, and an expensive charcoal flannel suit draped elegantly over what was clearly a sculpted body. He wore a crisp white shirt and a rich Hermès tie in maroon, green and blue, and when he firmly shook our hands I noticed a gold watch, too.

"Jay Talley. Sorry to make you wait," he said.

His hazel eyes were so penetrating I felt violated by them, his dark good looks so striking I instantly knew his type, because men that beautiful are all alike. I could tell Marino had no use for him, either.

"We spoke on the phone," he said to me, as if I didn't remember.

"And I haven't slept since," I said, unable to take my eyes off him, no matter how hard I tried.

"Please. If you'll come with me."

Marino gave me a look and wiggled his fingers behind Talley's back, the way he did when he decided on the spot that someone was gay. Talley's shoulders were broad. He had no waist. His profile had the perfect slope of a Roman god, and his lips were full and his jaw was flared.

I concentrated on being puzzled by his age. Usually, overseas posts were much coveted and were awarded to agents with seniority and rank, yet Talley looked barely thirty. He led us into a marble atrium four stories high that was centered by a brilliant mosaic of the world and washed in light. Even the elevators were glass.

After a series of electronic locks and buzzers and combinations and cameras that cared about our every move, we got off on the third floor. I felt as if I were inside cut crystal. Talley seemed to blaze. I felt dazed and resentful because it hadn't been my idea to come here, and I didn't feel in charge.

"So what's up there?" Marino, the model of politeness, pointed.

"The fourth floor," Talley impassively said.

"Well, the button don't have a number and it looks like you have to key yourself up," Marino went on, staring at the elevator ceiling. "I was just wondering if that's where you keep all your computers."

"The secretary general lives up there," Talley matter-of-factly stated, as if there were nothing unusual about this.

"No shit?"

"For security reasons. He and his family live in the

building," Talley said as we passed normal-looking offices with normal-looking people inside them. "We're meeting him now."

"Good. Maybe he won't mind telling us what the hell we're doing here," Marino replied.

Talley opened another door, this one made of rich, dark wood, and we were politely greeted by a man with a British accent who identified himself as the director of communication. He took orders for coffee and let Secretary-General George Mirot know we had arrived. Minutes later he showed us into Mirot's private office, where we found an imposing gray-haired man seated behind a black leather desk amid walls of antique guns and medals and gifts from other countries. Mirot got up and shook our hands.

"Let's be comfortable," he said.

He showed us to a sitting area before a window overlooking the Rhône while Talley collected a thick accordion file from a table.

"I know this has been quite an ordeal and I'm sure you must be exhausted," he said in precise English. "I can't thank you enough for coming. Especially on such short notice."

His inscrutable face and military bearing revealed nothing, and his presence seemed to make everything around him smaller. He settled into a wing chair and crossed his legs. Marino and I chose the couch and Talley sat across from me, setting the file on the rug.

"Agent Talley," Mirot said, "I'll let you start. You'll excuse me if I get right to the point?" He directed this at us. "We have very little time."

"First, I want to explain why ATF's involved in your unidentified case," Talley said to Marino and me. "You're familiar with HIDTA. Because of your niece Lucy, perhaps?"

"This has nothing to do with her," I assumed uneasily.

"As you probably know, HIDTA has violent crimes-fugitive task forces," he said instead of answering my question. "FBI, DEA, local law enforcement, and of course ATF, combining resources in high priority, especially difficult cases."

He pulled up a chair and sat across from me.

"About a year ago," he went on, "we formed a squad to work murders in Paris we believed are being committed by the same individual."

"I'm not aware of any serial murders in Paris," I said.

"In France, we control the media better than you do," the secretary general commented. "You must understand, the murders have been in the news, Dr. Scarpetta, but in very little detail, no sensationalizing. Parisians know there's a murderer out there, and women have been warned not to open their doors to strangers, and so on. But that's all. We believe it serves no good purpose to reveal the gore, the shattered bones, torn clothes, bite marks, sexual deviations."

"Where did the name Loup-Garou come from?" I asked.

"From him," Talley said as his eyes almost touched my body and flew off like a bird.

"From the killer?" I asked. "You mean, he calls himself a werewolf?"

"Yes."

"How the hell can you know something like that?" Marino elbowed his way in, and I knew by his body language that he was about to cause trouble.

Talley hesitated and glanced at Mirot.

"What's the son of a bitch been doing?" Marino continued. "Leaving his nickname on little notes at the scenes? Maybe he pins them to the bodies like in the movies, huh? That's what

323

I hate about big organizations getting involved in crap like this.

"The best people to work crimes is the schmucks like me out there walking around getting our boots muddy. Once you get these big-shot task forces and computer systems involved, the whole thing gets off in the ozone. It gets too *smart*, when what started the whole ball rolling ain't smart in the college sense of the word . . ."

"That's where you're quite mistaken," Mirot cut him off. "Loup-Garou is very smart. He had his self-serving reasons to let us know his name in a letter."

"A letter to who?" Marino wanted to know.

"To me," Talley said.

"When was this?" I asked.

"About a year ago. After his fourth murder."

He untied the file and pulled out a letter protected by plastic. He handed it to me, his fingers brushing against mine. The letter was in French. I recognized the handwriting as the same strange boxlike style I'd found on the carton inside the container. The stationery was engraved with a woman's name, the paper smeared with blood.

"It says," Talley translated, *"For the sins of one shall they all die. The werewolf.* The stationery belonged to the victim and it's her blood. But what mystified me at the time was how he knew I was involved in the investigation. And this all moves us closer to a theory that's the root of why you're here. We have ample reason to believe the killer is from a powerful family, the son of people who know exactly what he's doing and have made certain he doesn't get caught. Not necessarily because they give a damn about him, but because they must do whatever's necessary to protect themselves."

"Including shipping him off in a container?" I asked. "Dead

and unidentified, thousands of miles from Paris because they've had enough?"

Mirot studied me, leather creaking as he shifted his position in his chair and stroked a silver pen.

"Probably not," Talley said to me. "At first, yes. That's what we thought, because every indicator pointed to the dead man in Richmond as this killer: Loup-Garou written on the carton, the physical description as best you could tell, considering the state the body was in. The expensive way he was dressed. But when you supplied us with further information about the tattoo with, quote, *yellow eyes that might have been altered in an attempt to make them smaller . . .*"

"Whoa, whoa, whoa," Marino cut in. "You saying this Garou guy's got a tattoo with yellow eyes?"

"No," Talley replied. "We're saying his brother did."

"*Did?*" I asked.

"We'll get to that, and maybe you'll begin to pick up on why what happened to your niece is tangentially connected with all this," Talley said, filling me with torment again. "Are you familiar with an international criminal cartel we've come to call the One-Sixty-Fivers?"

"Oh, God," I said.

"Named such because they seem to be very fond of one-sixty-five-grain Speer Gold Dot ammo," Talley explained. "They smuggle the stuff. They use it exclusively in their own guns and we can generally tell their hits because Gold Dot's going to be the bullet recovered."

I thought of the Gold Dot cartridge case recovered from the Quik Cary.

"When you sent us information about Kim Luong's murder—and thank God you did—pieces began to fit together," Talley said.

Then Mirot spoke. "All members of this cartel are tattooed with two bright yellow dots."

He drew them on a legal pad. They were the size of dimes.

"A symbol of membership in a powerful, violent club, and a reminder that once in, you're in for life, because tattoos don't come off. The only way out of the One-Sixty-Fiver cartel is death."

"Unless you are able to make the gold dots smaller and turn them into eyes. A small owl's eyes—so simple and so quick. Then escape to some place where nobody will think to look for you."

"Like a niche port in the unlikely city of Richmond, Virginia," Talley added.

Mirot nodded. "Exactly."

"What for?" Marino asked. "Why suddenly does this guy freak out and run? What's he done?"

"He's crossed the cartel," Talley replied. "He'd betrayed his family, in other words. We believe this dead man in your morgue," he said to me, "is Thomas Chandonne. His father is the godfather, for lack of a better term, of the One-Sixty-Fivers. Thomas made the small mistake of deciding to make his own dope and do his own gun trafficking and cheat the family."

"Mind you," Mirot said, "the Chandonne family has lived on the Île Saint-Louis since the seventeenth century, one of the oldest, wealthiest parts of Paris. The people there call themselves Louisiens, and are very proud, very elitist. Many don't consider the island part of Paris, even though it's in the middle of the Seine in the heart of the city.

"Balzac, Voltaire, Baudelaire, Cézanne," he said. "Just a few of its better-known residents. And it is where the Chandonne family has been hiding behind their noblesse facade, their visible philanthropy and high place in politics while they run one of the biggest, bloodiest organized crime cartels in the world."

"We've never been able to get enough on them to nail them," Talley said. "With your help, we might have a chance."

"How?" I asked, although I wanted nothing to do with a murderous family like that.

"Verification, to start with. We need to prove the body is Thomas. I have no doubt. But there are those little legal nuisances we law enforcers have to put up with." He smiled at me.

"DNA, fingerprints, films? Do we have anything for comparison?" I asked, knowing full well what the answer would be.

"Professional criminals make it a point to avoid such things," Mirot remarked.

"We've found nothing," Talley replied. "And that's where Loup-Garou comes into the picture. His DNA could identify his brother's."

"So we're supposed to put an ad in the paper and ask the Loup to drop by and give a blood sample?" Marino was getting surlier as the morning went on.

"Here's what we think might have happened," Talley said, ignoring him. "On this past November twenty-fourth, just two days before the *Sirius* set sail for Richmond, the man who calls himself Loup-Garou made what we believe was his last murder attempt in Paris. Notice I say *attempt*. The woman escaped.

"This was around eight-thirty in the evening," Talley began his account of the events. "There was a knock on her door. When she answered it, she found a man standing on her porch. He was polite and articulate; he seemed very refined; and she thought she remembered an elegant long dark coat, maybe leather, and a dark scarf tucked into the collar. He said he'd just been in a minor car accident and could he please use her phone to call the police. He was very convincing. She was about to let him in when her husband called out something from another room and the man suddenly fled."

"She get a good look at him?" Marino asked.

"The coat, the scarf, maybe a hat. She's fairly certain he had his hands in his pockets and was kind of hunched against the cold," Talley said. "She couldn't see his face because it was dark. Overall, it was her impression he was a polite, pleasant gentleman."

Talley paused.

"More coffee? Water?" he asked everyone while he looked at me. I noticed his right ear was pierced. I hadn't seen the tiny diamond until it caught the light as he bent over to fill my glass.

"Two days after the murder attempt, on November twenty-sixth, the *Sirius* was to sail out of Antwerp, as was another vessel called the *Exodus*, a Moroccan ship that regularly brings phosphate to Europe," Talley resumed as he returned to his chair.

"But Thomas Chandonne had a sweet little diversion going, and the *Exodus* ended up in Miami with all sorts of guns, explosives—you name it—hidden inside bags of phosphate. We've known what he was doing, and maybe you're beginning to see the HIDTA connection? The takedown your niece was involved in? It was just one of many spinoffs of Thomas's activities."

"Obviously, his family caught on," Marino said.

"We believe he got away with it for a long time by using strange routes, altering books, you name it," Talley replied.

"On the street, you call it spanking. In legal business, you call it embezzling. In the Chandonne family, you call it suicide. And we don't know exactly what happened, but something did, because we expected him to be on the *Exodus* and he wasn't.

"And why not?" Talley posed it almost as if it were a rhetorical question. "Because he knew he was had. He altered his tattoo. He chose a small port where no one was likely to look for a stowaway." Talley looked at me. "Richmond was a good choice. There are very few niche ports left in the United States, and Richmond has a steady stream of vessels going back and forth to Antwerp."

"So Thomas, using an alias . . ." I started to say.

"One of many," Mirot inserted.

"He'd already signed on as crew for the *Sirius.* Point was, he was supposed to end up in the safe haven of Richmond while the *Exodus* went on its way to Miami to make a run without him," Talley said.

"And where does the werewolf come into all this?" Marino wanted to know.

"We can only speculate," Mirot answered. "Loup-Garou's getting increasingly out of control, his last murder attempt has gone haywire. Now maybe he's been seen. Maybe his family's had enough, plans to get rid of him and he knows it. Maybe he somehow knows his brother plans to leave the country on the *Sirius.* Maybe he was stalking Thomas, too, knew about the altered tattoo, and so on. He drowns Thomas, locks the body inside the container and tries to make it appear this dead person is him, this Loup-Garou."

"Swapped clothes with him?" Talley directed this at me.

"If he planned to take Thomas's place on a ship, he's not going to show up in Armani," I surmised.

329

"What was found in the pockets?" Talley seemed to lean into me even when he was sitting up straight.

"Transferred," I said. "The lighter, the money, all of it. Stuffed inside the pockets of the designer jeans his dead brother—if it is his brother—was wearing when his body turned up at the Richmond port."

"Pocket contents swapped, but no form of identification turned up."

"Yes," I said. "And we don't know that all of this change of clothing happened after Thomas was dead. That's rather cumbersome. Better to force your victim to undress."

"Yes." Mirot nodded. "I was coming around to that. Exchange clothes that way before killing the person. Both people undress."

I thought of the inside-out underwear, the grit on the naked knees and buttocks. The scuffs on the back of the shoes might have been caused later when Thomas was drowned, his body dragged into the corner of the container.

"How many crewmen was the *Sirius* supposed to have?" I asked.

It was Marino who answered. "There was seven on the list. All of them was questioned, but not by me since I don't speak the language. Some guy in customs had the honors."

"The crewmen all knew each other?" I asked.

"No," Talley replied. "Which isn't unusual when you consider that these ships only earn money when they're moving. Two weeks out to sea, two weeks back, nonstop, there's going to be rotating crew. Not to mention, you're talking about the kind of guys who never stay with anything very long, so you could have a crew of seven and only two of them might have sailed together before."

"Same seven men on board when the ship sailed back to Antwerp?" I asked.

"According to Joe Shaw," Marino replied, "none of them ever left the Richmond port. Ate and slept on their ship, unloaded and was gone."

"Ah," Talley said. "But that's not quite the case. One of them supposedly had a family emergency. The shipping agent took him to the Richmond airport but never actually saw him get on the plane. The name on his seaman's book was Pascal Léger. This Monsieur Léger doesn't seem to exist and quite possibly was Thomas's alias, the one he was using when he was killed, the alias Loup-Garou may have taken after he drowned him."

"I'm having trouble envisioning this deranged serial killer as Thomas Chandonne's brother," I said. "What makes you so certain?"

"The cover-up tattoo, as we've said," Talley replied. "Your most recent information about the details of Kim Luong's murder. The beating, biting, the way she was undressed, all the rest of it. A very, very unique and horrific M.O. When Thomas was a boy, Dr. Scarpetta, he used to tell his classmates he had an older brother who was an *espèce de sale gorille*. A stupid, ugly monkey who had to live at home."

"This killer isn't stupid," I said.

"Not hardly," Mirot agreed.

"We can't find any record of this brother. Not his name, nothing," Talley said. "But we believe he exists."

"You'll understand all of this better when we go through the cases," Mirot added.

"I'd like to review them now," I said.

34

Jay Talley picked up the accordion folder and withdrew numerous thick files. He set them on the coffee table in front of me.

"We've translated them into English," he said. "All the autopsies were done at the Institut Médico-Légal in Paris."

I began to go through them. Each victim had been beaten beyond recognition, and autopsy photographs and reports showed bruising imprints and stellate lacerations where the skin had split when a blow was struck with some type of weapon that I didn't believe was the same type as the one used on Kim Luong.

"The punched-out areas of her skull," I commented as I turned pages, "a hammer, something like that. I presume no weapon was found?"

"No," Talley said.

All facial structures were broken. There were subdural hematomas, bleeding over the brain and into the chest cavity. The victims' ages ranged from twenty-one to fifty-two. Each had multiple bite marks.

"Massive comminuted fractures of the left parietal bone,

depressed fractures that drove the inner table of the skull into underlying brain," I scanned out loud, flipping through one autopsy protocol after another. "Bilateral subdural hematomata. Disruption of cerebral tissue beneath with accompanying subarachnoid hemorrhaging . . . eggshell-like fractures . . . fracture of the right frontal bone extending down the midline into the right parietal bone . . . Clotting suggests survival time of at least six minutes from the time the injury was inflicted . . ."

I looked up and said to them, "Rage. Overkill. Frenzied overkill."

"Sexual?" Talley held my eyes.

"Ain't everything?" Marino asked.

Each victim was half-naked, her clothing ripped open or torn off from the waist up. All were barefoot.

"Strange," I said. "It doesn't appear he had any interest in their buttocks, their genitals."

"It seems he has a breast fetish," Mirot blandly commented.

"Certainly a symbol of mother," I replied. "And if it's true he was kept at home throughout his childhood, there must be some interesting pathology there."

"What about robbery?" Marino asked.

"Not sure in all cases. But definitely in some. Money, that's it. Nothing that could be traced, like jewelry he might pawn," Talley answered.

Marino patted his cigarettes the way he did when he was desperate to smoke.

"Be my guest," Mirot invited him.

"Possible he's killed elsewhere? Other places besides Richmond, saying he murdered Kim Luong?" I asked.

"He did her, all right," Marino said. "Never seen another M.O. like that one."

"We don't know how many times he's killed," Talley said. "Or where."

Mirot said, "If there's a connection to be made, our software can make the match as quickly as in two minutes. But there will always be cases we may not be aware of. We have one hundred and seventy-seven member countries, Dr. Scarpetta. Some utilize us more than others."

"It's just an opinion," Talley said, "but I suspect this guy isn't a world traveler. Especially if he's got some disability that's made it necessary for him to stay at home, and I'm guessing he was probably still living at home when he started his killings."

"Are the murders getting closer together? Does he wait as long between them?" Marino asked.

"The last two we know of were in October, then there was the recent attempt, meaning he struck three times within a five-week period," Tally said. "Just reinforcing our suspicions this guy's out of control, it's gotten too hot for him, and he's fled."

"Maybe he hoped he could start over and stop killing," Mirot said.

"Don't happen like that," Marino said.

"There's no mention of any evidence being turned into any labs," I said as I began to feel the chill of the dark place where this was headed. "I don't understand. Wasn't anything tested for in these cases? Swabs for body fluids? Hairs, fibers, a torn fingernail? Anything?"

Mirot glanced at his watch.

"Not even fingerprints?" I said, incredulous.

Mirot got out of his chair.

"Agent Talley, will you please take our guests to our cafeteria for lunch?" he said. "I'm afraid I can't join you."

Mirot walked us to the door of his formidable office.

"I must thank you again for coming," he said to Marino and me. "I realize your work is just beginning, but hopefully in a direction that will soon lay this terrible matter to rest. Or at least strike a blow that will bring it to its knees."

His secretary pushed a button on the phone.

"Undersecretary Arvin, are you there?" she said to whoever was on hold. "I can conference you now?"

Mirot nodded at her. He returned to his office and softly shut the door.

"You didn't call us all the way over here just to review these cases," I said to Talley as he led us through a confusion of hallways.

"Let me show you something," he said.

He directed us around a corner, where we were confronted by a ghastly portrait gallery of dead faces.

"*Corpse to Be Identified*," Talley said. "Black notices."

The posters were in grainy black and white and included fingerprints and other identifying characteristics. All of the information was written in English, French, Spanish and Arabic, and it was obvious that most of the nameless individuals had not died peacefully.

"Recognize yours?" Talley pointed at the most recent addition.

Fortunately, my unidentified case's grotesque face did not stare out at us, but instead the notice displayed an unexciting dental chart and fingerprints and a narrative.

"Other than the posters, Interpol is a paperless organization," Talley explained.

He walked us to an elevator.

"Paper files are electronically scanned into our mainframe, kept for a limited period of time, then destroyed."

He pushed a button for the first floor.

"Better hope the Y-two-K bug don't get you," Marino said.

Talley smiled.

Outside the cafeteria, suits of armor and a rampant brass eagle guarded all who patronized it. Tables were crowded with several hundred men and women in business dress, all police who had come here from around the world to combat various organized criminal activities ranging from stolen credit cards and forgery in the U.S. to bank numbers involving cocaine trafficking in Africa. Talley and I selected roasted chicken and salad. Marino went after the barbecued ribs.

We settled into a corner.

"The secretary general usually doesn't get directly involved like this," Talley let us know. "Just so you get an idea of the importance."

"I guess we're supposed to feel honored," Marino said.

Talley cut off a bite of chicken and kept the fork in the same hand, European style.

"I don't want us to be blinded by how much we want this unidentified body to be Thomas Chandonne," Talley went on.

"Yeah, sure would be embarrassing if you took the black notice out of your fancy computer and then guess what? Turns out the son of a bitch ain't dead and Loup-Garou's just some local fruit loop who keeps on killing. No relationship between the two," Marino said. "Maybe Interpol loses some of its membership fees, huh?"

"Captain Marino, this is not about membership fees," Talley said with a dead-on stare. "I know you've worked many, many difficult cases in your career. You know how all-consuming they can be. We need to free up our people to

336

work other crimes. We need to bring down the people shielding this dirtbag. We need to destroy the hell out of all of them."

He pushed away his tray without finishing his food. He slid a pack of cigarettes out of the inner pocket of his suit jacket.

"That's one thing nice about Europe," he smiled. "Bad for your health but not antisocial."

"Well, let me ask you this," Marino kept going. "If it's not about membership fees, then who pays for all this shit? Learjets, Concordes, ritzy hotels, not to mention Mercedes cabs?"

"Many of the taxis over here are Mercedes."

"We prefer beat-up Chevies and Fords back home," Marino said sarcastically. "You know, buy American."

"Interpol isn't in the habit of supplying Learjets and luxury hotels," Talley said.

"Then who did?"

"I guess you can ask Senator Lord all about that," Talley replied. "But let me remind you of something. Organized crime is all about money, and most of this money comes from honest people, honest businesses and corporations who want to run these cartels out of business as badly as we do."

Marino's jaw muscles were flexing.

"I can only suggest that for a Fortune Five Hundred company to buy a couple of Concorde tickets isn't much to ask if millions of dollars of electronic equipment or even guns and explosives are being diverted."

"Then some Microsoft-company-type paid for all this?" Marino asked.

Talley's patience was being tried. He didn't answer him.

"I'm asking you. I want to know who paid for my ticket. I want to know who the hell went through my suitcase. Some Interpol agent?" Marino persisted.

"Interpol doesn't have agents. It has liaisons from various law enforcement agencies. ATF, FBI, the postal service, police departments and so on."

"Yeah, right. Just like the CIA doesn't snuff people."

"For God's sake, Marino," I said.

"I want to know who fucking went through my suitcase," Marino said as his face turned a deeper red. "That pisses me off more than anything has in a hell of a long time."

"I can see that," Talley replied. "Maybe you should complain to the Paris police. But my guess is, if they had anything to do with it, it was for your own good. In the event you might have brought a gun over here, for example?"

Marino didn't say anything. He picked through what was left of his ribs.

"You didn't," I said to him in disbelief.

"If someone isn't familiar with international travel, well, innocent mistakes can be made," Talley added. "Especially American police who are used to carrying guns everywhere and perhaps don't understand what serious trouble they could get into over here."

Still, Marino was silent.

"I suspect the only motivation was to prevent any inconveniences for either of you," Talley added, tapping an ash.

"All right, all right," Marino grumbled.

"Dr. Scarpetta," Talley then said, "are you familiar with our magistrate system over here?"

"Enough to know that I'm glad we don't have one in Virginia."

"The magistrate's appointed for life. The forensic pathologist is appointed by the magistrate, and it's the magistrate who decides what evidence is submitted to the labs and even what the manner of death is," Talley explained.

"Like our coroner system at its worst," I said. "Whenever politics and votes are involved—"

"Power," Talley cut in. "Corruption. Politics and criminal investigation should never be in the same room."

"But they are. All the time, Agent Talley. Maybe even here, in your organization," I said.

"Interpol?" He seemed to find this very amusing. "There's really no motivation for Interpol to do the wrong thing, as sanctimonious as that might sound. We don't take credit. We don't want publicity, cars, guns or uniforms; we don't fight over jurisdictions. We have a surprisingly small budget for what we do. To most people we don't even exist."

"You say this *we* shit like you're one of them," Marino commented. "I'm confused. One minute you're ATF, the next minute you're a secret squirrel."

Talley raised an eyebrow and blew out smoke. "*Secret squirrel?*" he asked.

"How'd you end up over here anyway?" Marino wouldn't relent.

"My father's French, my mother American. I spent most of my childhood in Paris, then my family moved to Los Angeles."

"Then what?"

"Law school, didn't like it, ended up with ATF."

"For how long?" Marino continued his interrogation.

"I've been an agent about five years."

"Yeah? And how much of that's been over here?" Marino was getting more belligerent with each question.

"Two years."

"That's kinda cushy. Three years on the street, then you end up over here drinking wine and hanging out in this big glass castle with all these hot-shit people."

"I've been extremely fortunate." Talley's graciousness carried a sting. "You're absolutely right. I suppose it helps somewhat that I speak four languages and have traveled extensively. I also got into computers and international studies at Harvard."

"I'm hitting the john." Marino abruptly got up.

"It's the Harvard part that really got him," I said to Talley as Marino stalked off.

"I didn't mean to piss him off," he said.

"Of course you did."

"Oh. Such a bad impression you have of me so quickly."

"He's usually not quite this bad," I went on. "There's a new deputy chief who's thrown him back in uniform, suspended him and tried everything short of a bullet to destroy him."

"What's his name?" Talley asked.

"It's a *her*," I answered. "Sometimes the *hers* are worse than *hims*, it's been my experience. More threatened, more insecure. Women tend to do each other in when we should be helping each other along."

"You don't seem to be like that." He studied me.

"Sabotage takes too much time."

He wasn't sure how to take that.

"You'll find I'm very direct, Agent Talley, because I have nothing to hide. I'm focused and I mean business. I'll fight you or I won't. I'll confront you or I won't, and I'll do it strategically but mercifully because I have no interest in watching anybody suffer. Unlike Diane Bray. She poisons people and sits back and watches, enjoying the show as the person slowly and in agony wastes away."

"Diane Bray. Well, well," Talley said, "toxic waste in tight clothes."

"You know her?" I asked, surprised.

"She finally left D.C. so she could ruin some other police

department. I was at headquarters briefly before getting assigned here. She was always trying to coordinate what her cops were doing with what the rest of us were doing. You know, FBI, Secret Service, us. Not that there's anything wrong with people working together, but that wasn't her agenda. She just wanted to get in thick with the power brokers, and damn if she didn't."

"I don't want to waste energy talking about her," I said. "She's taken far too much of my energy already."

"Would you like dessert?"

"Why has no evidence been tested in the Paris cases?" I got back to that.

"How about coffee?"

"What I'd like is an answer, Agent Talley."

"Jay."

"Why am I here?"

He hesitated, glancing toward the door as if worried that someone he didn't want to see might walk in. I decided he was thinking about Marino.

"If the killer is this Chandonne wacko, as we very much suspect, then his family would prefer that his nasty habit of slashing, beating and biting women isn't made public. In fact'—he paused, his eyes digging into mine—"it would seem his family hasn't wanted it known that he was ever on this planet. Their dirty little secret."

"Then how do you know he exists?"

"His mother gave birth to two sons. There's no record of one dying."

"Sounds like there's no record of anything," I said.

"Not on paper. There are other ways of finding out things. Police have spent hundreds of hours interviewing people, especially those on Île Saint-Louis. In addition to what

341

Thomas's former classmates allege, it has also become rather much a legend that there is a man who's sometimes seen walking along the shore of the island at night or in the early morning, when it's dark."

"Does this mysterious character swim or just walk around?" I asked. I was thinking of the freshwater diatoms inside the dead man's clothes.

Talley gave me a surprised look.

"It's funny you should say that. Yes. There have been reports of a white male swimming nude in the Seine off the shore of Île Saint-Louis. Even in very cold weather. Always when it's dark."

"And you believe these rumors?" I asked.

"It's not my job to believe or not believe."

"What's that supposed to mean?"

"Our role here is to facilitate and get all the troops thinking and working together, no matter where they are or who they are. We're the only organization in the world able to do that. I'm not here to play detective."

He paused for a long moment, his eyes reaching into mine to find places I was afraid to share with him.

"I don't pretend to be a profiler, Kay," he said.

He knew about Benton. Of course he would.

"I don't have those skills, and I certainly don't have the experience," he added. "So I won't even begin to paint some sort of portrait of the guy who's doing this. I have no feeling for what he looks like, walks like, talks like—except I know he speaks French and maybe other languages as well.

"One of his victims was Italian," he went on. "She spoke no English. One has to wonder if he may have spoken Italian to her to get inside her door."

Talley leaned back in his chair and reached for his water.

"This guy's had ample opportunity to be self-educated," Talley said. "He may dress well, because certainly Thomas is reputed to have quite a penchant for fast cars, designer clothes, jewelry. Maybe the pitiful brother hidden in the basement got Thomas's hand-me-downs."

"The jeans the unidentified man was wearing were a little big in the waist," I recalled.

"Thomas's weight fluctuated, supposedly. He worked very hard to be slender, was very vain about the way he looked. So who knows?" Talley said, shrugging. "But one thing's certain, if his alleged brother's as weird as people are saying, I doubt he goes shopping."

"Do you really think this person comes home after one of his slaughters and his parents wash his bloody clothes and protect him?"

"He's being protected by someone," Talley reiterated. "That's why these cases in Paris have stopped at the morgue door. We don't know what went on in there beyond what we've shown you."

"The magistrate?"

"Someone with a lot of influence. That could be any number of people."

"How did you get hold of the autopsy reports?"

"The normal route," he replied. "We requested the records from the Paris police. And what you see is what we got. No evidence going to the labs, Kay. No suspects. No trials. Nothing, except that the family has probably gotten a bit tired of shielding their psychopathic son. He's not only an embarrassment, he's a potential liability."

"How will proving Loup-Garou is the psychopathic son of the Chandonnes help you take down this One-Sixty-Five cartel?"

"For one thing, we hope Loup-Garou will talk. He gets nailed for a string of murders, especially the one in Virginia . . . Well, we will have leverage. Not to mention'—he smiled—"we I.D. Monsieur Chandonne's sons, we get probable cause to search their lovely three-hundred-year-old Île Saint-Louis home and offices and bills of lading and on and on and on."

"Assuming we catch Loup-Garou," I said.

"We have to."

His eyes met mine and held them for a long, tense moment.

"Kay, we need you to prove the killer's Thomas's brother."

He held the pack of cigarettes out to me. I didn't touch it.

"You may be our only hope," he added. "It's the best chance we've had so far."

"Marino and I could be in serious danger if we get anywhere near this," I said.

"Police can't go inside the Paris morgue and start asking questions," he said. "Not even undercover cops. And it goes without saying that no one here at Interpol can."

"Why not? Why can't Paris police go in there?"

"Because the medical examiner who did the cases won't talk to them. She trusts no one, and I can't say I blame her. But it seems she trusts you."

I was silent.

"You should be motivated by what happened to Lucy and Jo."

"That's not fair."

"It's fair, Kay. That's how bad these people are. They tried to blow your niece's brains out. Then they tried to blow her up. It's not an abstraction to you, now is it?"

"Violence is never an abstraction to me." Cold sweat was sliding down my sides.

"But it's different when it's someone you love," Talley said. "Right?"

"Don't tell me how I feel."

"Abstraction or not, you feel the cruel, cold jaws of it when it crushes someone you love." Talley wouldn't let it go. "Don't let these assholes crush anyone else. You have a debt to pay. Lucy was spared."

"I should be home with her," I said.

"Your being here will help her more. It will help Jo more."

"I don't need you to tell me what's best for my niece or her friend. Or for me, for that matter."

"To us, Lucy is one of our finest agents. To us, she's not your niece."

"I suppose I should feel good about that."

"You certainly should."

His attention drifted down my neck. I felt his eyes like a breeze that stirred nothing but me, and then he stared at my hands.

"God, they're strong," he said, and he reached for one. "The body that turned up in the container. Kim Luong. They are your cases, Kay'—he studied my fingers, my palm. "You know all the details. You know the questions to ask, what to look for. It makes sense for you to drop by to see her."

"Her?" I pulled my hand away and wondered who was watching.

"Madame Stvan. Ruth Stvan. The director of legal medicine and chief medical examiner of France. You two have met."

"Of course I know who she is, but we've never met."

"In Geneva in 1988. She's Swiss. When you met she wasn't married. Her maiden name is Dürenmatt."

He searched my face to see if I remembered. I didn't.

"You were on a panel together. Sudden Infant Death Syndrome. SIDS."

"And how could you possibly know that?"

"It's in your vita," he said, amused.

"Well, there's certainly no mention of her in my vita," I defensively replied.

His eyes wouldn't let go of me. I couldn't stop looking at him, and it was hard to think.

"Will you go see her?" he asked. "It wouldn't seem unusual for you to drop by to say hello to an old friend while you're visiting Paris, and she's agreed to talk to you. That's really why you're here."

"Nice of you to let me know now," I said as my indignation rose.

"You may not be able to do anything. Maybe she knows nothing. Maybe there's not a single other detail she can offer to help us with our problem. But we don't believe that. She's a very intelligent, ethical woman who's had to work very hard against a system that's not always on the side of justice. Maybe you can relate to her?"

"Just who the hell do you think you are?" I asked. "You think you can just pick up the phone and summon me here and ask me to just *drop by* the Paris morgue while some criminal cartel isn't looking?"

He said nothing, his gaze never wavering. Sunlight filled the window beside him and turned his eyes the amber of tiger-eye.

"I don't give a damn whether you're Interpol or Scotland Yard or the Queen of England," I said. "You don't get to put me or Dr. Stvan or Marino in jeopardy."

"Marino won't be going to the morgue."

"I'll let you tell him that."

"If he accompanied you, that would raise suspicions, especially since he's such a model of decorum," Talley remarked. "Besides, I don't think Dr. Stvan would like him very much."

"And if there's evidence, then what?"

He didn't answer me, and I knew why.

"You're asking me to tamper with the chain of evidence. You're asking me to steal evidence, aren't you? I don't know what you call it here, but in the United States it's called a felony."

"Impairment or falsification of evidence, according to the new penal code. That's what it's called here. Three hundred thousand francs, three years in prison. Possibly you could get charged with a breach of respect due the dead, I suppose, if one really wants to push the matter, and that's another hundred thousand francs, another year in prison."

I shoved back my chair.

"I must say," I coldly told him, "it's not been often in my profession that a federal agent begs me to break the law."

"I'm not asking. This is between you and Dr. Stvan."

I got up. I didn't listen.

"You may not have gone to law school, but I did," I said. "Maybe you can recite a penal code, but I know what it means."

He didn't move. Blood was pounding in my neck and sunlight was so bright in my face I couldn't see.

"I've been a servant to the law, to the principles of science and medicine, for half my life," I went on. "The only thing you've done for half your life, Agent Talley, is make it through adolescence in that Ivy League world of yours."

"Nothing bad's going to happen to you," Talley calmly replied as if he hadn't listened to an insulting word I'd said.

"Tomorrow morning, Marino and I are flying home."

"Please sit down."

"So you know Diane Bray? Is this her grand finale? To get me thrown into a French prison?" I went on.

"Please sit," he said.

Reluctantly, I did.

"If you do something Dr. Stvan asks and should get caught, we'll intercede," he said. "Just as we did with what I was sure Marino would have packed in his suitcase."

"I'm supposed to believe that?" I asked, incredulous. "French police with their machine guns snatch me in the airport and I say, *It's all right. I'm on a secret mission for Interpol?*"

"All we're doing is getting you and Dr. Stvan together."

"Bullshit. I know exactly what you're doing. And if I get in trouble, you guys will be like every other agency in the goddamn world. You'll say you don't even know me."

"I would never say that."

He held my gaze, and the room was so hot I needed fresh air.

"Kay, we would never say that. Senator Lord would never say that. Please trust me."

"Well, I don't."

"When would you like to return to Paris?"

I had to stop to think. He had me so befuddled and furious.

"You're scheduled on the late afternoon train," he reminded me. "But if you'd like to stay for the night, I know of a wonderful little hotel on the rue du Boeuf. It's called La Tour Rose. You'd love it."

"No, thank you," I said.

He sighed, getting up from the table and collecting both our trays.

"Where's Marino?" It occurred to me that he had been gone for a long time.

"I was beginning to wonder that myself," Talley said as we walked through the cafeteria. "I don't think he likes me very much."

"That's the most brilliant deduction you've made all day," I said.

"I don't think he likes it when another man pays attention to you."

I didn't know how to answer that.

He slid the trays into a rack.

"Will you make the phone call?" Talley was relentless. "Please?"

He stood perfectly still in the middle of the cafeteria and touched my shoulder, almost boyishly, as he asked me again.

"I hope Dr. Stvan still speaks English," I said.

349

35

When I got Dr. Stvan on the phone, she remembered me without hesitation, which reinforced what Talley had told me. She was expecting my call and wanted to see me.

"I teach at the university tomorrow afternoon," she told me in English that sounded as if it had not been practiced in a while. "But you can come by in the morning. I get in at eight."

"Will eight-fifteen give you enough time to get settled?"

"Of course. Is there something I can help you with while you're in Paris?" she asked in a tone that made me suspect others could hear.

"I'm interested in how your medical examiner system works in France." I followed her cue.

"Not very well some of the time," she replied. "We're near the Gare de Lyon, off the Quai de la Rapée. If you drive yourself, you can park in back where the bodies are received. Otherwise, come in to the front."

Talley looked up from telephone messages he was sifting through.

"Thanks," he said when I hung up.

"Where do you suppose Marino has wandered off to?" I asked.

I was getting anxious. I didn't trust Marino on his own. No doubt he was offending someone.

"There are but so many places he can go," Talley replied.

We found him downstairs in the lobby, sitting glumly by a potted palm. It seemed he had wandered through too many doors and had locked himself out of every floor. So he had taken the elevator down and hadn't bothered to ask for assistance from security.

I hadn't seen him this petulant in a while, and he was so surly on our way back to Paris that I finally moved to another seat and turned my back to him. I closed my eyes and dozed. I wandered to the dining car and bought a Pepsi without asking him if he wanted one. I bought my own pack of cigarettes and offered him nothing.

When we walked into the lobby of our hotel, I finally broke down.

"How about I buy you a drink?" I said.

"I gotta go to my room."

"What's wrong with you?"

"Maybe I should ask you that," he retorted.

"Marino, I don't have any idea what you're talking about. Let's relax in the bar for a minute and figure out what to do next about this mess we've gotten ourselves into."

"Only thing I'm doing next is going to my room. And it ain't me who's gotten us into a mess."

I let him step inside the elevator alone and watched his stubborn face disappear behind closing brass doors. I climbed the long, curved flights of carpeted stairs and was reminded how bad smoking was for my health. I unlocked my door and was not prepared for what I saw. Cold fear seized me as I walked over to the fax machine and stared at what the chief medical examiner of Philadelphia,

Dr. Harston, had sent. I sat down on the bed, paralyzed.

The lights of the city were bright, the sign for the Grand Marnier distillery was huge and high, and the Café de la Paix was busy below. I collected the paper off the fax machine, my hands shaking, my nerves jumping as if I had some awful disease. I got three Scotches from the minibar and poured all of them at once. I didn't bother to get ice. I didn't care if I felt like hell the next day because I knew I was going to anyway. There was a cover sheet from Dr. Harston.

Kay, I was wondering when you'd ask. Knew you would when you were ready. Let me know if you have further questions. I'm here for you.

Vance.

Time numbly passed, as if I were catatonic, as I read the medical examiner's report of initial investigation, the description of Benton's body, what was left of it, in situ, in the gutted building where he died. Phrases floated past my eyes like ashes on the air. *Charred body with burn fractures of the wrists* and *hands absent* and *skull shows laminar peeling burn fractures* and *charred down to muscle over the chest and abdomen.*

The entrance of the gunshot wound to his head had left a half-inch hole in the skull that showed internal beveling of the bony fracture. It had entered behind the right ear causing radial fractures and impacting and terminating in the right petrous region.

He had a *slight diastema between the maxillary centrals.* I had always loved that subtle space between his front teeth. It made his smile more endearing because he was so precise in every other way, his teeth otherwise perfect because his perfect, proper New England family had made sure he wore braces.

. . . Suntan pattern of swimming trunks. He had left for Hilton Head without me because I was called to a scene. If only I'd said *no* and gone with him. If only I'd refused to work the first in what would prove to be a series of horrendous crimes that would eventually claim him as the final victim.

None of what I was looking at was manufactured. It couldn't be. Only Benton and I knew about the two-inch linear scar on his left knee. He had cut himself on glass in Black Mountain, North Carolina, where we had first made love. That scar had always seemed a stigma of adulterous love. How odd it was spared because soggy insulation from the roof had fallen on it.

That scar had always seemed a reminder of a sin. And now it seemed to turn his death into a punishment that culminated in my envisioning everything the reports described because I had seen it all before, and those images knocked me to the floor, where I sat crying and mumbling his name.

I did not hear the knocking of the door until it turned to pounding.

"Who is it?" I called out in a husky, ruined voice.

"What's wrong with you?" Marino said loudly through the door.

I weakly got up and almost lost my balance as I let him in.

"I've been knocking for five minutes . . ." he started to say. "Jesus-fucking-Christ. What the hell's the matter?"

I turned my back to him and walked over to the window.

"Doc, what is it? What is it?" He sounded frightened. "Did something happen?"

He came over and put his hands on my shoulders, and it was the first time he'd ever done that in all the years I'd known him.

"Tell me. What are all these body diagrams and shit on the bed. Is Lucy okay?"

"Leave me alone," I said.

"Not until you tell me what's wrong!"

"Go away."

He removed his hands and I felt coolness where they had been. I felt our space. He walked across the room. I heard him pick up the faxes. He was silent.

Then he said, "What the shit are you doing? Trying to make yourself crazy? Why the hell do you want to be looking at something like this?" His voice rose as his pain and panic did. "Why? You've lost your mind!"

I wheeled around and lunged for him. I grabbed the faxes. I shook them in his face. Copies of body diagrams, and toxicology and submitted evidence reports, the death certificate, toe tag, dental charts, what had been in his stomach, all of it drifting and scattering over the rug like dead leaves.

"Because you just *had* to say it," I yelled at him. "You just *had* to open your big, rude mouth and say he wasn't dead! So now we know, right? Read it your goddamn self, Marino."

I sat down on the bed and wiped my eyes and nose with my hands.

"Just read it and don't ever talk to me about it again," I said. "Don't you ever say anything like that again. Don't you say he's alive. Don't you ever do that to me again."

The phone rang. He snatched it up.

"What!" he blurted out. "Oh, yeah?" he added after a pause. "Well, they're right. We *are* making a fucking disturbance, and you send fucking security up, I'll just send 'em right back down 'cause I'm a goddamn-fucking cop and I'm in a goddamn-fucking-shitty mood right now!"

He slammed down the receiver. He sat down on the bed next to me. Tears filled his eyes, too.

354

"Now what do we do, Doc? Now what the hell do we do, huh?"

"He wanted us to have dinner together so we would fight and hate and cry like this," I muttered, tears slipping down my face. "He knew we would turn on each other and blame each other because there was no other way for us to let it out and go on."

"Yeah, I guess he profiled us," Marino said. "I guess he did. Like he somehow knew it would happen, and how we'd act."

"He knew me," I muttered. "Oh, God, did he know me. He knew I would handle it worse than anybody. I don't cry. I don't want to cry! I learned not to when my father was dying, because to cry was to feel, and it was too much to feel. It was as if I could make myself get dry inside like a dry pod that rattles, my feelings tiny, hard . . . rattling. I'm devastated, Marino. I don't think I can get over it. Maybe it would be a good thing if I got fired, too. Or quit."

"That ain't gonna happen," he said.

When I didn't reply, he got up and lit a cigarette. He paced.

"You want some dinner or something?"

"I just need to sleep," I said.

"Maybe getting out of this room would be a good thing."

"No, Marino."

I knocked myself out with Benadryl and felt thick-headed and bleary when I forced myself out of bed the next morning. I looked in the bathroom mirror and saw exhausted, puffy eyes. I splashed cold water on my face and dressed and got a cab at seven-thirty, this time without any help from Interpol.

The Institut Médico-Légal, a three-story building of red brick and pitted limestone, was in the east section of the city. The Voie Expressway cut it off from the Seine, which this morning was the color of honey. The taxi driver dropped me off in front, where I walked through a small, lovely park with primroses, pansies, daisies and wild flowers, and old plantain trees. A young couple necking on a bench and an old man walking his dog seemed oblivious to the distinct stench of death seeping through the Institut's barred windows and black iron front door.

Ruth Stvan was well known for the unusual system she ran. Visitors were received by hostesses, so when the bereft came through the door, they were immediately intercepted by someone kind who helped them find their way, and one of these hostesses reached out to me. She led me along a tile corridor where investigators waited in blue chairs, and I understood enough of what they were saying to gather that someone had jumped out of a window the night before.

I followed my silent guide past a small chapel with stained glass where a couple was crying over a young boy inside an open white casket. Handling the dead here was different from what we did. In America, there simply wasn't time or funding for hostesses, chapels and hand-holding in a society in which shootings came in every day and no one lobbied for the dead.

Dr. Stvan was working on a case in the Salle d'Autopsie, designated as such by a sign over automatically opening doors. When I walked in, I was overwhelmed by anxiety again. I shouldn't have come here. I didn't know what I would say. Ruth Stvan was placing a lung in a hanging scale, her green gown splashed with blood, glasses speckled with it. I knew her case was the man who had jumped. His face was smashed, feet split open, shin bones driven up into his thighs.

"Give me one minute, please," Dr. Stvan said to me.

There were two other cases going on, those doctors wearing white. On chalkboards were names and case numbers. A Stryker saw was opening a skull while water ran loudly in sinks. Dr. Stvan was quick and energetic, fair and big-boned and older than me. I remembered that when we were in Geneva she had kept to herself.

Dr. Stvan covered her unfinished case with a sheet and pulled off her gloves. She began untying her gown in back as she walked over to me with sure, strong steps.

"How are you?" she asked.

"I'm not sure," I said.

If she thought this an odd answer, she didn't show it.

"Follow me, please, and we'll talk as I clean up. Then get a coffee."

She took me into a small dressing room and dropped her gown in a clothes bin. Both of us washed our hands with disinfectant soap, and she scrubbed her face, too, and dried it with a rough, blue towel.

"Dr. Stvan," I said, "obviously I'm not here for a friendly chat or to dabble into what your M.E. system is like over here. We both know that."

"Of course," she replied, meeting my eyes. "I'm not friendly enough for a social visit." She smiled a little. "Yes, we met in Geneva, Dr. Scarpetta, but we didn't socialize. It's a shame, really. There were so few women back then."

She talked as we walked along the corridor.

"When you called, I knew what it was about because I'm the one who asked you here," she added.

"It makes me a little nervous to hear you say that," I replied. "As if I'm not nervous enough."

"We're after the same things in life. If you were me, I'd be visiting you, do you see? I would be saying, we can't let this continue. We can't let other women die this way. Now in America, in Richmond. He's a monster, this Loup-Garou."

We stepped inside her office, where there were no

windows, and stacks of files and journals and memos spilled from every surface. She picked up the phone and dialed an extension, and asked someone to bring us coffee.

"Please, make yourself comfortable, if that's possible. I'd move things out of the way but I've no place to put them."

I pulled a chair close to her desk.

"I felt very out of place when we were in Geneva," she said, her mind apparently jumping back to that memory as she shut the door. "And part of the reason is the system here in France. Forensic pathologists are completely isolated here and that's not changed and perhaps never will in my lifetime. We're allowed to talk to no one, which isn't always so bad because I like to work alone."

She lit a cigarette.

"I inventory the injuries and police tell the whole story, if they choose. If a case is sensitive, I talk to the magistrate myself and maybe I get what I need, maybe I don't. Sometimes when I raise the question, no lab is appointed for the tests, do you understand?"

"Then, in a sense," I said, "your only job is to find the cause of death."

She nodded. "For each case I receive a mission from the magistrate to determine the cause of death, and that's all."

"You don't really investigate."

"Not the way you do. Not the way I want to," she replied, blowing smoke out of the side of her mouth. "You see, the problem with French justice is the magistrate is independent. I can report to no one but the magistrate who appointed me, and only the minister of justice can take a case away and give it to another magistrate. So if there's a problem, I don't have the power to do anything about it. The magistrate does what he wants to my report. If I say it's a homicide and he doesn't agree, so be it. It's not my problem. This is law."

"He can change your report?" The idea was outrageous to me.

"Of course. I'm alone against everyone. And I suspect you are, too."

I didn't want to think about how alone I was.

"I'm keenly aware if anyone knew we were talking, it could be very bad, especially for you——" I started to say.

She held up her hand for me to be quiet. The door opened and the same young woman who had escorted me came in with a tray of coffee, cream and sugar. Dr. Stvan thanked her and said something else in French I didn't get. The woman nodded and quietly left, shutting the door behind her.

"I told her to hold all calls," Dr. Stvan informed me. "I need to let you know right away that the magistrate who appointed me is someone I very much respect. But there are pressures above him, if you understand what I mean. Pressures even above the minister of justice. I don't know where all of it comes from, but there was no lab work done in these cases, which is why you were sent."

"Sent? I thought it was you who asked for me."

"How do you take your coffee?" Dr. Stvan asked.

"Who told you I was sent?"

"Certainly, you've been sent in to relieve me of my secrets, and I'll give them up to you gladly. Do you take sugar and cream?"

"Black."

"When the woman was murdered in Richmond, I was told you'd be sent here if I'd talk to you."

"So you didn't request that I come?"

"I would never have asked such a thing, because I would never imagine such a request would be granted."

I thought of the private jet, the Concorde and all the rest of it.

"Could you spare a cigarette?" I said.

"I'm so sorry I didn't ask. I didn't know you smoke."

"I don't. This is just a detour. One that's lasted about a year. Do you know who sent me, Dr. Stvan?"

"Someone with enough influence to get you here almost instantly. Beyond that, I don't know."

I thought of Senator Lord.

"I'm worn down by what Loup-Garou brings to me. Eight women now," she said, staring off, a glazed, pained look in her eyes.

"What can I do, Dr. Stvan?"

"There's no evidence they were raped vaginally," she said. "Or sodomized. I took swabs of the bite marks, very strange bite marks with missing molars, occlusion and tiny teeth widely spaced. I collected hairs and all the rest of it. But let's go back to the first case, when everything got strange.

"As you might expect, the magistrate instructed me to submit all evidence to the lab. Weeks went by, months went by, no results ever came back. From then on, I learned. With subsequent cases believed to be Loup-Garou, I didn't ask to submit anything."

She was silent for a moment, her thoughts elsewhere.

Then she said, "He's a strange one, this Loup-Garou. Biting the palms, the soles of the feet. It must mean something to him. I've never seen anything like it. And now you must contend with him as I have."

She paused, as if what she had to say next was very hard.

"Please be very careful, Dr. Scarpetta. He will come after you as he did me. You see, I'm the one who survived."

I was too stunned to speak.

"My husband is a chef at Le Dome. He is almost never home at night, but as God would have it, he was sick in bed when this creature came to my door several weeks ago. It was raining. He said his car had just been in an accident and needed to call the police. Of course, my first thought was to help. I wanted to make certain he wasn't injured. I was very concerned.

"That was my vulnerability," she went on. "I think physicians have a savior complex, you know? We can take care of problems, no matter what they are, and that's the impulse he counted on, in retrospect, where I was concerned. There was nothing suspicious about him in the least, and he knew I would let him in, and I would have. But Paul heard voices and wanted to know who was there. The man ran off. I never got a good look at him. My house light was out, you see, because he'd unscrewed it, I found out later."

"Did you call the police?"

"Only a detective I trust."

"Why?"

"One has to be careful."

"How did you know it was the killer?"

She sipped her coffee. By now, it was cold, and she added a little to both of ours to warm them up.

"I could *feel* it. I remember smelling a wet animal smell, but I think now I must have imagined it. I could feel the evil, the lust in his eyes. And he wouldn't show himself. I never saw his face, just the glint of his eyes as light spilled out the open door."

"Wet animal smell?" I asked.

"Different from a body odor. A dirty odor, like a dog that needs to be bathed. That's what I remember. But all of it happened so fast, and I can't be sure. Then the next day I received a note from him. Here. Let me show you."

She got up and unlocked a drawer of a metal filing cabinet, where files were squeezed so tightly together she had difficulty pulling one out. It was not labeled, and inside was a torn piece of blood-speckled brown paper protected by a transparent plastic evidence bag.

"*Pas la police. Ça va, ça va. Pas de problème, tout va bien. Le Loup-Garou,*" she read. "It means *No police. It's all right. It's okay. Everything's fine. The werewolf.*"

I stared at the familiar block letters. They were mechanical and almost childish.

"The paper looks like a piece of a torn bag from the market," she said. "I can't prove it's from him, but who else would it be from? I don't know whose blood it is, because again, I can do no tests, and only my husband knows I got this."

"Why you?" I asked. "Why would he come after you?"

"I can only suppose it's because he saw me at the crime scenes. So I know he watches. When he kills, he's out there in the dark somewhere, watching what people like us do. He's very intelligent, cunning. I have no doubt he knows exactly what happens when his bodies come to me."

I tilted the note in lamplight, looking for hidden strokes that might have been pressed into the paper by the force of someone writing on whatever had been on top of it. I saw none.

"When I read the note, the corruption became so plain to me, as if there had been any doubt," Dr. Stvan was saying. "Loup-Garou knew it would do no good to submit his note to the police, to the labs. He was telling me, even warning me, not to bother, and it's very odd, but I feel he was also telling me he won't try again."

"I wouldn't be so quick to assume that," I said.

"As if he needs a friend. The lonely beast needs a friend. I suppose in his fantasies he matters to me because I saw him and didn't die. But who can know a mind like that?"

She got up from her desk and unlocked another drawer in another filing cabinet. She lifted out an ordinary shoe box, peeled off tape and removed the lid. Inside were eight small, ventilated paper boxes and just as many small manila envelopes, each labeled with case numbers and dates.

"It's unfortunate no impressions were made of the bite marks," she said. "But to do that I would have to call in a dentist, and I knew that wouldn't be permitted. But I did swab them, and maybe that will help. Maybe it won't."

"He tried to eradicate the bite marks in Kim Luong's murder," I told her. "We can't cast them. Even photographs would do no good."

"I'm not surprised. He knows there's no one to protect him now. He's—how do you say—on your turf? And I'll tell you, it wouldn't be hard to identify him by his dentition. He has very strange pointed teeth, widely spaced. Like some sort of animal."

I began to get a strange sensation.

"I recovered hair from all of the bodies," she was saying. "Catlike hair. I've wondered if he breeds angora cats, something like that."

I leaned forward in my chair.

"Catlike?" I said. "Did you save it?"

She peeled tape off a flap and retrieved a pair of forceps from a drawer in her desk. She dipped into an envelope, withdrawing several hairs. They were so fine they floated like down as she lowered them to the ink blotter.

"All the same, you see? Nine or ten centimeters long, pale blond. Very fine, baby-fine."

"Dr. Stvan, this isn't cat hair. It's human hair. It was on the clothing of the unidentified man we found in the cargo container. It was on the body of Kim Luong."

Her eyes widened.

"When you submitted evidence in the first case, did you submit some of these hairs?" I asked.

"Yes."

"And you heard nothing back?"

"To my knowledge the labs never analyzed what I sent."

"Oh, I bet they analyzed it, all right," I said. "I bet they know damn well these hairs are human and are too long for baby hair. They know what the bite marks mean and may even have recovered DNA from them."

"Then we should get DNA, too, from the swabs I'm giving you," she said, getting increasingly unsettled.

I didn't care. It no longer mattered.

"Of course, you can't do much with the hairs," she rambled. "Hirsute, no pigmentation. They would simply be consistent with each other, wouldn't they . . . ?"

I wasn't listening. I was thinking of Kaspar Hauser. He spent the first sixteen years of his life in a dungeon because Prince Charles of Baden wanted to make sure Kaspar didn't have any claims to the crown.

". . . no DNA without roots, I suppose . . ." Dr. Stvan went on.

At age sixteen he was found by a gate, a note pinned to him. He was pale like a cave fish, nonverbal like an animal. A freak. He couldn't even write his name without someone's guiding his hand.

"The mechanical, block letters of a beginner," I thought out loud. "Someone shielded, never exposed to others, never schooled except at home. Maybe even self-taught."

Dr. Stvan stopped talking.

"Only a family could shield someone from the time he

was born. Only a very powerful family could circumvent the legal system, allowing this anomaly to keep on killing without being caught. Without embarrassing them, drawing unwanted attention to them."

Dr. Stvan was silent as every word I said torqued what she believed and aroused a new, more pervasive fear.

"The Chandonne family knows exactly what these hairs, the abnormal teeth, all of it means," I said. "And he knows. Of course he does, and he would have to suspect you know, even if the labs tell you nothing, Dr. Stvan. I think he came to your house because you saw his reflection in what he did to the bodies. You saw his shame, or he thought you did."

"Shame . . . ?"

"I don't think the purpose of that note was to assure you he wouldn't try again," I continued. "I think it was mocking you, telling you he could do what he wanted with sovereign immunity. That he would be back and wouldn't fail next time."

"But it would appear he's not here anymore," Dr. Stvan answered me.

"Obviously, something changed his plans."

"And the shame he thinks I saw? I never got a good look at him."

"What he did to his victims is the only look at him we need. The hair isn't coming from his head," I said. "He's shedding it from his body."

36

I had seen only one case of hypertrichosis in my life, when I was a resident physician in Miami and rotating through pediatrics. A Mexican woman gave birth to a girl, and two days later the infant was covered with a fine light-gray hair almost two inches long. Thick tufts protruded from her nostrils and ears, and she was photophobic, her eyes overly sensitive to light.

In most hypertrichotic people, hairiness progressively increases until the only areas spared are mucous membranes and palms and soles, and in some extreme cases, unless the person frequently shaves, the hair on the face and brow can become so long it has to be curled so the person can see. Other symptoms can be anomalies of the teeth, stunted genitalia, more than the normal number of fingers and toes and nipples, and an asymmetrical face.

In earlier centuries, some of these wretched souls were sold to carnivals or royal courts for amusement. Some were thought to be werewolves.

"Wet, dirty hair. Like a wet, dirty animal," Dr. Ruth Stvan supposed. "I wonder if the reason I saw only his eyes when he appeared at my door is because his entire face was covered with hair? And maybe he had his hands in his pockets because they were covered with hair, too?"

"Certainly, he couldn't go out in normal society looking like that," I replied. "Unless he goes out only after dark. Shame, sensitivity to light and now murder. He might limit his activities to darkness, anyway."

"I suppose he could shave," Stvan pondered. "At least those areas people might see. Face, forehead, neck, tops of the hands."

"Some of the hair we found appeared to have been shaved," I said. "If he were on a ship, he had to do something."

"He must undress, at least partially, when he kills," she said. "All this long hair he leaves."

I wondered if his genitalia were stunted, and if this might have something to do with why he undressed his victims only from the waist up. Perhaps to see normal adult female genitalia was to remind him of his own inadequacy as a male. I could only imagine his humiliation, his rage. It was typical for parents to shun a hypertrichotic infant at birth, especially if they were like the powerful, proud Chandonnes on the rich, exclusive Île Saint-Louis.

I imagined this tormented son, this *espèce de sale gorille*, living in a dark space inside his family's centuries-old home and going out only at night. Criminal cartel or not, a wealthy family with a respected name might not want the world to know he was their son.

"There's always the hope record checks can be run in France to see if there have been any babies born with this condition," I said. "That shouldn't be hard to track, since hypertrichosis is so rare. Only one in a billion people, or something like that."

"There will be no records," Stvan matter-of-factly stated.

I believed her. His family would have made certain of that. Close to noon, I left Dr. Stvan with fear in my heart and ill-gotten evidence in my briefcase. I went out through the back of the building, where vans with curtains in the windows waited for their next sad journey. A man and a woman in the drab clothing of sparrows waited on a black bench against the old brick wall. He held his hat in his hand, staring down at the ground. She looked up at me, her face pinched by grief.

I walked very fast on cobblestones along the Seine as terrible images came to me. I imagined his hideous face flashing out of the dark when a woman opened her door to him. I imagined him wandering like a nocturnal beast, selecting and stalking until he struck and savaged again and again. His revenge in life was to make his victims look at him. His power was their terror.

I stopped and scanned. Cars were relentless and fast. I felt dazed as traffic roared and kicked grit in my face, and I had no idea how I was going to get a taxi. There was no place for one to pull over. Side streets I passed were empty of traffic and I saw no hope of a taxi along any of them, either.

I began to get a panic attack. I fled back up stone steps, back into the park, and sat on a bench, catching my breath while the scent of death continued to drift through flowers and trees. I closed my eyes and turned my face up to the winter sun, waiting for my heart to run a little slower while beads of cold sweat slid under my clothes. My hands and feet were numb, my aluminum briefcase hard between my knees.

"You look like you could use a friend." Jay Talley's voice suddenly sounded above me.

I jumped and gasped.

"I'm sorry," he softly said as he sat next to me. "I didn't mean to startle you."

"What are you doing here?" I asked as thoughts madly clashed, muddy and bloody and slamming into one another like foot soldiers on a battlefield.

"Didn't I tell you we'd look after you?"

He unbuttoned his tobacco-colored cashmere overcoat and slipped out a pack of cigarettes from an inside pocket. He lit one for each of us.

"You also said it was too dangerous for any of you to show up here," I said accusatorially. "So I go in and do my dirty work, and here you are, sitting in the damn park right at the Institut's damn front door."

I angrily blew out smoke and got to my feet. I grabbed my briefcase.

"Just what kind of game are you playing with me?" I asked him.

He dipped into another pocket and pulled out a cellular phone.

"I thought you might need a ride," he said. "I'm not playing a game. Let's go."

He pressed numbers on his phone and said something in French to whoever was at the other end.

"Now what? Is the Man from U.N.C.L.E. coming to pick us up?" I bitterly said.

"I just called a taxi. I believe the Man from U.N.C.L.E. retired a few years ago."

We walked out to one of the quiet side streets, and minutes later a taxi pulled over. We climbed in and Talley stared at the briefcase in my lap.

"Yes," I answered his unspoken question.

369

When we reached my hotel, I took him up to my room, because there was no other place we could talk without the risk of being overheard. I tried Marino, and he didn't answer.

"I need to get back to Virginia," I said.

"That's easy enough to arrange," he said. "Whenever you want."

He hung the *do not disturb* sign outside the door and fastened the burglar chain.

"First thing in the morning."

We settled in the sitting area by the window, a small table between us.

"I take it Madame Stvan opened up to you," he said. "That was the harder nut to crack, if you must know. By now the poor woman's so paranoid—and for good reason— we didn't think she'd tell the truth to anyone. I'm glad my instincts were right."

"*Your* instincts?" I asked.

"Yes." His eyes stayed on mine. "I knew if anyone could get through to her, it would be you. Your reputation precedes you and she can't have anything but the utmost respect for you. But it helps just a little that I have personal insight about you, too." He paused. "Because of Lucy."

"You know my niece?" I didn't believe him.

"We were in various training programs at the same time in Glynco," he replied, referring to the national academy in Glynco, Georgia, where ATF, Customs, Secret Service, Border Patrol and some sixty other law enforcement agencies did their basic training. "I used to feel kind of sorry for her, in a way. Her presence always managed to generate a lot of talk about you, as if she didn't have any talents on her own."

"I can't do a tenth of what she can," I said.

"Most people can't."

370

"What does any of this have to do with her?" I wanted to know.

"I think she has to be Icarus and fly too close to the sun because of you. I hope she doesn't push that myth too far and fall from the sky."

The comment shot fear through me. I had no idea what Lucy was doing right now. Talley was right about what he said, too. My niece always had to do everything bigger, better, faster and riskier than I did, as if competing against me would finally win the love she didn't believe she deserved.

"Hair transferred from the killer to his victims in the Paris cases is definitely not the hair of the unidentified man in my cooler," I said, and I explained the rest to him.

"But this weird hair was on his clothes?" Talley tried to understand.

"On the *inside* of them. Just think of this as a hypothetical. Let's say the clothing was worn by the killer and his body is covered with this dense, long baby-fine hair. So it transfers to the inside of his clothing, which he takes off and makes his victim put on before he drowns him."

"The victim being the guy in the container. Thomas." Talley paused. "This hair's all over Loup-Garou's body? Then he obviously doesn't shave it."

"It wouldn't be easy shaving your entire body on a regular basis. Most likely, he shaves only those areas people might see."

"And there's no effective treatment. No drug or anything."

"Lasers are being used with some success. But he may not know that. Or more likely, his family wasn't going to permit him to show up at a clinic, especially after he started killing."

"Why do you think he exchanged clothes with the man you found in the container? With Thomas."

"Maybe if you're going to escape on a ship, you wouldn't want to be in designer clothes, assuming your theory about the hand-me-downs is true. It could also be spite, contempt. Getting in the last word. We could speculate all day long, but there's never a formula, only the damage left behind."

"Can I get you anything?" he asked.

"An answer," I said. "Why didn't you tell me Dr. Stvan was the one who survived? You and the secretary-general sat there telling me this story when you knew all along it was she you were talking about."

Talley was silent.

"You were afraid it would scare me off, weren't you?" I said. "The Loup-Garou sees her and tries to kill her, so maybe he would see me and try to kill me, too?"

"Various people involved were doubtful you would go see her if you knew the whole story."

"Well, then these various people don't know me very well," I said. "In fact, I would be more likely to go if I knew something like that. The hell with how well you think you know me and can predict this and that after having met Lucy one or two times."

"Kay, it was because of Dr. Stvan's insistence. She wanted to tell you herself for a very good reason. She'd never divulged all of the details to anyone, not even the detective who is her friend. He was only able to supply us with a rough sketch."

"Why?"

"Again, the people protecting the killer. If they somehow found out and thought she might have gotten a good look at him, she was afraid they might do something to her. Or to her husband or two children. She believed you wouldn't betray her by talking to anyone who might place her in a vulnerable position. But in terms of how much she told you, she said she wanted to make that decision when she was with you."

"In case she didn't trust me after all."

"I knew she would."

"I see. So mission accomplished."

"Why are you so angry with me?" he asked.

"Because you're so presumptuous."

"I don't mean to be," he said. "I just want us to stop this werewolf-freak before he kills and mutilates anybody else. I want to know what makes him tick."

"Fear and avoidance," I said. "Suffering and rage because he was punished for something that wasn't his fault. He anguished alone. Imagine being intelligent enough to comprehend all that."

"He would hate his mother most," Talley said. "He might even blame her."

Sunlight polished his hair like ebony and caught his eyes at the edge, flecking them with gold. I saw his feelings before he could rush them back into hiding. I got up and looked out the window because I did not want to look at him.

"He would hate women he sees," Talley said. "Women he could never have. Women who would scream in horror if they saw him, saw his body."

"Most of all, he would hate himself," I said.

"I know I would."

"You paid for this trip, didn't you, Jay?"

He got up and leaned against the window frame.

"Not some big corporation after this One-Sixty-Fiver cartel," I went on.

I looked at him.

"You got Dr. Stvan and me together. You facilitated everything. You set all of it up and paid for it," I said as I became more convinced and my incredulity grew. "You could do that because you're very rich. Because your family's very rich. That's why you went into law enforcement, isn't it. To get away from being rich. And then you act rich, look rich, anyway."

For an instant, he was caught.

"You don't like it when you're not the one doing the interrogating, do you?" I said.

"It's true I didn't want to be like my father. Princeton, crewing, marrying into the proper family, kids all proper, everything proper."

We were side by side now, looking down at the street as if something interesting was going on in the world outside our window.

"I don't think you've bucked your father," I said. "I think you fool yourself by being contraire. And certainly getting a badge and carrying a gun and piercing your ear is contraire if you went to Harvard and are a millionaire."

"Why are you saying all this to me?"

He turned to look at me, and we were so close I could smell his cologne and feel his breath.

"Because I don't want to wake up tomorrow and realize I'm part of some contraire script you've spun in your mind. I don't want to believe I've just broken the law and every oath I've ever sworn to because you just happen to be a spoiled rich boy whose idea of being contraire is to encourage someone like me to do something so contraire it could ruin my career. What's left of my career. And maybe land me in some fucking French prison."

"I'd come visit you."

"This isn't funny."

"I'm not spoiled, Kay."

I thought of the *do not disturb* sign, the chained door. I touched his neck and traced the angle of his strong jaw, lingering on the corner of his mouth. I had not felt a man's beard against my skin in more than a year. I reached up with both hands and pushed my fingers through his thick hair. It was warm from the sun, and his eyes were in mine, waiting to see what I might do with him.

I pulled him to me. I kissed and touched him aggressively, running my hands up and down his hard, perfect body as he fought with my clothes.

"God, you're so beautiful," he said into my mouth. "Christ, you've been driving me insane . . . !" He tore off a button and bent hooks. "Sitting there in front of the fucking secretary general and I'm trying not to stare at your breasts."

He gathered them into his hands. I wanted it raw and without limits. I wanted the violence in me to make love to his violence, because I didn't want to be reminded of Benton, who had known how to slowly smooth me like a stone and skip me through erotic waters.

I pulled Talley into the bedroom, and he was no match for me because I had experience and skills he knew nothing of. I controlled him. I dominated. I helped myself to him until we were exhausted and slippery with sweat. Benton wasn't in that room. But had he somehow seen what I just did, he would have understood.

The afternoon moved on and we drank wine and watched shadows change on the ceiling as the sun got weary of the day. When the phone rang, I didn't answer it. When Marino thumped on the door and called out to me, I pretended no one was home. When the phone rang again, I shook my head.

"Marino, Marino," I said.

"Your bodyguard."

"He didn't do a very good job this time," I said as Talley fit as much of me into his mouth as he could. "I suppose I'll have to fire him."

"I wish you would."

"Tell me I haven't committed yet another felony this day. And that your name, Agent Talley, has nothing to do with keeping score."

"Okay. My name has nothing to do with keeping score. But I don't know about the felony part."

It seemed that Marino gave up on me, and as it got dark, Talley and I took a shower together. He washed my hair and made a joke about the age difference between us. He said it was another example of his being contraire. I said we should go to dinner.

"What about the Café Runtz?" he asked.

"What about it?"

"What the French would call *chaleureux, ancien et familial*— warm, old, familiar. The Opéra-Comique is next door, so there are photographs of opera singers all over the walls."

I thought of Marino. I needed to let him know I was not lost somewhere in Paris.

"It's a nice walk," Talley was saying. "Maybe only fifteen minutes. Twenty at the most."

"I need to find Marino first," I said. "He's probably in the bar."

"Would you like me to look for him and send him up?"

"I'm sure he would be most appreciative," I said facetiously.

Marino found me before Talley found him. I was still drying my hair when Marino showed up at my door, and the look on his face told me he knew why he had not been able to reach me.

"Where the hell you been?" he asked as he walked in.

"The Institut Médico-Légal."

"All day?"

"No, not all day," I said.

Marino looked at the bed. Talley and I had made it, but it didn't look quite the way the housekeepers had left it this morning.

"I'm going out to . . ." I started to say.

"With him," Marino raised his voice. "I goddamn knew this would happen. I can't believe you fell for it. Je-sus Christ. I thought you was above . . ."

"Marino, this is none of your business," I wearily said.

He blocked the door, hands on his hips like a stern nanny. He looked so ridiculous, I had to laugh.

"What's the matter with you?" he exclaimed. "One minute you're looking at Benton's autopsy report and the next you're screwing around with some playboy, snotty, stuck-on-himself kid! You couldn't even wait twenty-four hours, Doc! How could you do that to Benton?"

"Marino, for God's sake keep your voice down. There's been quite enough yelling in this room."

"How could you?" He looked at me with disgust, as if I were a whore. "You just get his letter and have me and Lucy over and then last night you're sitting here crying. And what? None of it happened? You just start all over like nothing happened? With some womanizing *punk*?"

"Please leave my room." I'd had enough.

"Oh, no." He began to pace, wagging his finger at me. "Oh, no. I ain't going nowhere. You want to fuck around with pretty boy, you can just do it in front of me. 'Cause guess why? I'm not gonna let it happen. Someone's got to do the right thing here, and looks like it's gonna be me."

He paced and paced, getting more livid with each word. "It's not about your letting or not letting something happen." My fury was gathering. "Who the hell do you think you are, Marino? Stay out of my life."

"Well, poor Benton. A damn good thing he's dead, huh? Shows how much you loved him, all right."

He stopped pacing and jabbed his finger at my face.

"And I thought you was different! What was you doing when Benton wasn't looking? That's what I want to know! And all this time I'm feeling sorry for you!"

"Get out of my room now." My self-control snapped. "You goddamn jealous son of a bitch! How dare you even allude to my relationship with Benton. What do you know? Nothing, Marino. He's dead, Marino. He's been dead for over a year, Marino. And I'm not dead and you're not dead."

"Well, right now I wish you was."

"You sound like Lucy when she was ten."

He stalked out and slammed the door so hard paintings shifted on the wall and the chandelier shook. I picked up the phone and called the front desk.

"Is there a Jay Talley in the lobby?" I asked. "Tall, dark, young. Wearing a beige leather jacket, jeans?"

"Yes, I see him, madame."

Seconds later Talley was on the phone.

"Marino just stormed out of here," I said. "Don't let him see you, Jay. He's crazy."

"Actually, he's just getting off the elevator now. And you're right. He looks a little crazy. Gotta go."

I ran out of my room. I ran as fast as I could through the corridor and down the winding, carpeted steps, ignoring the odd stares I got from well-dressed, civilized people who walked at a leisurely pace and didn't get into fistfights in

378

the Grand Hôtel in Paris. I slowed down when I reached the lobby, lungs burning and out of breath, and to my horror watched Marino taking swings at Talley while two bellmen and a valet tried to intervene. A man at the registration desk frantically dialed the phone, probably calling the police.

"Marino, no!" I said loudly and with authority as I hurried over to him. "Marino, *no!*" I grabbed his arm.

He was glassy-eyed and sweating profusely, and thank God he had no gun because I was afraid he might have used it just then. I kept hold of his arm while Talley talked in French and gestured, assuring everyone there was no problem and not to call the police. I led Marino by the hand through the lobby like a mother about to discipline a very bad little boy. I escorted him past valets and expensive cars and out onto the sidewalk, where I stopped.

"Do you have any idea what you're doing?" I asked him.

He wiped his face on the back of his hand. He was breathing so hard he was wheezing. It occurred to me he might have a heart attack.

"Marino." I shook his arm. "Listen to me. What you just did in there is unconscionable. Talley has done nothing to you. I've done nothing to you."

"Maybe I'm sticking up for Benton 'cause he ain't here to do it himself," Marino said in a flat, worn-out voice.

"No. You were throwing punches at Carrie Grethen, at Joyce. It's them you want to beat up, maim, kill."

He took deep, defeated breaths.

"Don't you think I know what you're doing?" I went on in an intense, quiet voice.

People were shadows drifting past us on the sidewalk. Light spilled out of brasseries and cafés that were having busy nights, their small outdoor tables full.

"You have to take it out on someone," I went on. "That's the way it works. And who is there to go after? Carrie and Joyce are dead."

"At least you and Lucy got to kill the motherfuckers. Shoot their goddamn asses out of the air." Marino began to sob.

"Come on," I said.

I took his arm in mine and we started walking.

"I had nothing to do with killing them," I said. "Not that I would have hesitated, Marino. But Lucy pulled the trigger. And you know what? She doesn't feel the better for it. She still hates and simmers and beats and shoots her way through life. She'll have her day of reckoning, too. And this is yours. Let it go."

"Why did'ya have to go and do that with him?" he asked in a small, pained voice as he wiped his eyes on his sleeve. "How come, Doc? Why him?"

"There's no one good enough for me, is that it?" I said.

He had to think about that.

"And there's no one good enough for you. No one as good as Doris. When she divorced you, that was hard, wasn't it? And I've never thought any woman you've been with since is even close to what she was. But we have to try, Marino. We have to live."

"Yeah, and they all dumped me, too. Those women who ain't good enough for me."

"They dumped you because they're bowling-alley bimbos."

He smiled in the dark.

37

The streets of Paris were waking up and getting lively as Talley and I walked to the Café Runtz. The air was cool and felt good on my face, but I was anxious and full of doubt again. I wished I'd never come to France. When we crossed the Place de l'Opéra and he reached for my hand, I wished I had never met Jay Talley.

His fingers were warm and strong and slender, and I never expected that such a gentle form of affection would jolt and revulse me when what we'd done in my room hours earlier had not. I felt ashamed of myself.

"I want you to know this matters to me," he said. "I don't have flings, Kay. I'm not into one-night stands. It's important you know that."

"Don't fall in love with me, Jay." I looked up at him.

His silence said everything about how those words made him feel.

"Jay, I'm not saying I don't care."

"You'll really like this café," he said. "It's a secret. You'll see. No one in here speaks anything but French and if you don't speak French, you have to point on the menu or get out your little dictionary, and the owner will be amused by you. Odette is very no-nonsense but very nice."

I was scarcely hearing a word.

"She and I have a détente. If she's pleasant, I patronize her establishment. If I'm pleasant, she lets me patronize her establishment."

"I want you to listen to me," I said, slipping my hand up his arm and leaning against it. "The last thing I ever want to do is hurt anyone. I didn't want to hurt you. And I already have."

"How could I feel hurt? This afternoon was incredible."

"Yes, it was," I said. "But . . ."

He stopped on the sidewalk and looked into my eyes as people flowed around us and light from shops unevenly shoved back the night. I was raw and alive where he had touched me.

"I didn't ask you to love me," he said.

"That's not something you should have to ask."

We started walking again.

"I know it's not something you freely offer, Kay," he said. "Love is your *loup-garou*. The monster you fear. And I can see why. It's tracked you down and hurt you all your life."

"Don't try to psychoanalyze me. Don't try to change me, Jay."

People bumped us as they jostled past.

Several teenagers with body piercing and dyed hair bumped into us and laughed. A small crowd was staring and pointing at an almost life-size yellow biplane attached to the side of the Grand Marnier building advertising a Breitling watch show. Roasting chestnuts smelled burnt.

"I've not touched anyone since Benton died," I said. "That's where you are in my food chain, Jay."

"I wasn't trying to be cruel . . ."

"I'll fly home in the morning."

"I wish you wouldn't."

"I have a mission, remember?" I said.

Anger slipped out of hiding, and when Talley tried to hold my hand again, I slipped my fingers away from him.

"Or should I say I'll *sneak* home in the morning," I said. "With a briefcase of illegal evidence that's also, by the way, a biological hazard. I'll follow my orders, trooper that I am, and get DNA from the swabs if possible. Compare it to the unidentified body's DNA. Eventually determine that he and the killer are brothers. Meanwhile, maybe the cops will luck out and find a werewolf wandering the streets and he'll tell you guys everything about the Chandonne cartel. And maybe only two or three other women will be savaged before all this happens."

"Please don't be so bitter," Jay said.

"Bitter? I shouldn't be bitter?"

We turned off the Boulevard des Italiens onto the Rue Favard.

"I shouldn't be bitter when I was *sent* here to solve problems—when I've been a pawn in some scheme I knew nothing about?"

"I'm sorry you look at it that way," he said.

"We're bad for each other," I said.

Café Runtz was small and quiet, with green checked cloths and green glassware. Red lamps glowed and the chandelier was red. Odette was making a drink at the bar when we walked in. Her way of greeting Talley was to throw her hands up in despair and chastise him.

"She's accusing me of staying away two months and then not calling before I come in," he translated for me.

He leaned over the bar and kissed her on both cheeks to make amends. Regardless of how crowded the café was, she managed to fit us into a choice corner table because Talley had that effect on people. He was used to getting what he wanted. He picked out a Santenay red burgundy since he remembered I'd told him how much I liked burgundies, although I didn't recall when I'd said that or if I really had. By now I wasn't sure what he already knew and what he'd gotten directly from me.

"Let's see," he said, scanning the menu. "I highly recommend the Alsacienne specialities. But to start? The *salade de gruyère*—shaved gruyère that looks like pasta on lettuce and tomato. It's filling, though."

"Maybe that's all I'll get, then," I said, with no appetite.

He reached inside his jacket pocket and pulled out a small cigar and clipper.

"Helps me cut back on cigarettes," he explained. "Would you like one?"

"Everybody in France smokes too much. It's time I quit again," I said.

"They're very good." He snipped off the tip. "Dipped in sugar. This one's vanilla, but I also have cinnamon and sambuca." He fired a match. "But I like the vanilla the best." He puffed. "You really should taste this."

He offered it to me.

"No, thank you," I said.

"I order them from a wholesaler in Miami," he went on, flourishing his cigar and throwing his head back to blow out smoke. "Cojimars. Not to be confused with Cohibas, which are wonderful, but illegal if they're Cuban versus those made in the Dominican Republic. Illegal in the U.S., at any rate. And I know that because I'm ATF.

Yes, ma'am, I know my alcohol, tobacco and firearms."

He had already finished his first glass of wine.

"The three Rs. Running, Running and Running. Ever heard that? They teach it in the school of hard knocks."

He refilled his glass and topped off mine.

"If I came back to the States, would you see me again? For the sake of argument, what would happen if I transferred . . . let's say, back to Washington?"

"I didn't mean to do this to you," I said.

Tears touched his eyes and he quickly looked away.

"I never meant to. It's my fault," I softly said.

"Fault?" he said. "*Fault?* I didn't realize there was *fault* involved, as in something to be blamed. As in a mistake."

He leaned into the table and smiled smugly, as if he were a detective who'd just tripped me with a trick question.

"Fault. Hmmm," he pondered, blowing smoke.

"Jay, you're so young," I said. "Someday you'll understand—"

"I can't help my age." He interrupted me in a voice that caused glances.

"And you live in France, for God's sake."

"There are worse places to live."

"You can dance around words all you want, Jay," I said. "But reality always has its way with people."

"You're sorry, aren't you?" He leaned back. "I know so much about you, and then I go and do something as stupid as that."

"I never said it was stupid."

"It's because you aren't ready."

I was getting upset, too.

"You can't possibly know if I'm ready or not ready," I told him as the waiter appeared to take our order and then discreetly moved on. "You spend far too much time in my mind and maybe not enough in your own."

"Okay. Don't worry. I won't ever try to anticipate your feelings or thoughts again."

"Ah. Petulance," I replied. "At last you're acting your age."

His eyes flashed. I sipped my wine. He'd already finished another glass.

"I deserve respect, too," he said. "I'm not a child. What was this afternoon, Kay? Social work? Charity? Sex education? Foster care?"

"Maybe we shouldn't talk about this here," I suggested.

"Or maybe you just used me," he went on.

"I'm too old for you. Please lower your voice."

"*Old* is my mother, my aunt. The deaf widow who lives next door to me is old."

I realized I had no idea where Talley lived. I didn't even have his home telephone number.

"*Old* is the way *you* act when you're overbearing and condescending and a chicken," he said, raising his glass to me.

"A *chicken*? I've been called a lot of things, but never a chicken."

"You're an emotional chicken." He drank as if trying to put out a fire. "That's why you were with him. He was safe. I don't care how much you say you loved him. He was safe."

"Don't talk about something you know nothing about," I warned him as I began to tremble.

"Because you're afraid. You've been afraid ever since your father died, ever since you felt different from everyone because you *are* different from everyone and that's the price people like us pay. We're special. We're alone and we rarely think it's because we're special. We just think there's something wrong with us."

I placed my napkin on top of the table and pushed back my chair.

"That's the problem with you intelligence-gathering assholes," I said in a low, calm voice. "You appropriate the secrets, the treasures and tragedies and ecstasies of someone as if they are your own. At least I have a life. At least I don't live voyeuristically through people I don't know. At least I'm not some kind of spy."

"I'm not a spy," he said. "It was my job to find out as much as I could about you."

"And you did your job extraordinarily well," I said, stung. "Especially this afternoon."

"Please don't leave," he quietly said as he reached across the table for my hand.

I pulled away from him. I walked out of the restaurant as other diners stared. Someone laughed and made a comment I didn't need to translate to understand. It was obvious that the handsome young man and his older lady friend were having a lovers' spat. Or maybe he was her gigolo.

It was almost nine-thirty and I walked with determination toward the hotel while everyone else in the city, it seemed, continued to venture out. A woman police officer wearing white gloves whistled traffic through as I waited with a great crowd to cross the Boulevard des Capucines. The air was bright with voices and cold light from the moon. The aromas of crepes and beignets and chestnuts roasting in small grills made me heartsick and dizzy.

I hurried like a fugitive evading apprehension, and yet I lingered at street corners because I wanted to be caught. Talley did not come after me. When I reached my hotel, breathless and upset, I couldn't bear the thought of seeing Marino or returning to my room.

I got a taxi because I had one more thing to do. I would do it alone and at night because I felt reckless and desperate.

"Yes?" the driver said, turning around to look at me. "Madame?"

I felt pieces of me had been rearranged and I didn't know where to put them because I couldn't remember where they'd been before.

"Do you speak English?" I asked.

"Yes."

"Do you know much about the city? Could you tell me about what I'm seeing?"

"Seeing? You mean now?"

"Seeing as we drive," I said.

"Am I tour guide?" He thought I was very funny. "No, but I live here. Where would you like to go?"

"Do you know where the morgue is? On the Seine near the Gare de Lyon?"

"You want to go there?" He turned around again and frowned at me as he waited to insert himself in traffic.

"I *will* want to go there. But first I want to go to the Île Saint-Louis," I said, scanning, looking for Talley as hope got dark like the street.

"What?" My driver laughed as if I were the premier crazy. "You want to go to the morgue and Île Saint-Louis? What connection is that? Someone rich die?"

I was getting annoyed with him.

"Please," I said. "Let's go."

"Okay, sure. If that's what you want."

Tires over cobblestone sounded like kettle drums, and lamplight flashing off the Seine looked like schools of silver fish. I rubbed fog off my window and opened it enough so I could see better as we crossed the Pont Louis-Philippe and entered the island. I instantly recognized the seventeenth-century homes that once had been the private hotels of the noblesse. I had been here before with Benton.

We had walked these narrow cobblestone streets and browsed the historic plaques on some of the walls that told who once had lived here. We had stopped in outdoor cafés, and across the way bought ice cream at Berthillon. I told my driver to circle the island.

It was solid with gorgeous homes of limestone pitted by the years, and balconies were black wrought iron. Windows were lit up, and through them were glimpses of exposed beams, bookcases and fine paintings, but I saw no one. It was as if the elitist people who lived here were invisible to the rest of us.

"Have you ever heard of the Chandonne family?" I asked my driver.

"But of course," he said. "Would you like to see where they live?"

"Please," I said with great misgivings.

He drove to the Quai d'Orléans, past the residence where Pompidou died on the second floor, the blinds still drawn, and onto the Quai de Béthune toward the eastern tip of the island. I dug in my satchel and got out a bottle of Advil.

The taxi stopped. I sensed my driver didn't care to get any closer to the Chandonne home.

"Turn the corner there," he pointed, "and walk to Quai d'Anjou. You will see doors carved with chamois. That is the Chandonne crest, I guess you would call it. Even the drain-pipes are chamois. It is really something. You can't miss it.

And stay away from the bridge over there on the right bank," he said. "Underneath it, that is where the homeless and homosexuals are. It is dangerous."

The *hôtel particulier* where the Chandonne family had lived for hundreds of years was a four-story town house with multiple dormer windows, chimneys and an Oeil de Boeuf, or beef's eye, which was a round window at the roof. The front doors were dark wood ornately carved with chamois, and fleet-footed goats held on tooth and tail to form gilded drainpipes.

The hair pricked up on my flesh. I tucked myself in shadows and stared across the street at the lair that had spawned this monster who called himself the Loup-Garou. Through windows, chandeliers sparkled and bookcases were crowded with hundreds of books. I was startled when a woman suddenly appeared in the glass. She was enormously fat. She wore a dark red robe with deep sleeves, the material rich like satin or silk. I stared, transfixed.

Her face was impatient, her lips moving fast as she talked to someone, and almost instantly a maid appeared with a small silver tray bearing a liqueur glass. Madame Chandonne, if that's who the woman was, sipped her drink. She lit a cigarette with a silver lighter and walked out of view.

I walked fast to the tip of the island, less than a block away, and from a small park there I could barely make out the silhouette of the morgue. I guessed it was but several miles upriver, on the other side of the Pont Sully. I scanned the Seine and fantasized that the killer was the son of the obese woman I just saw, that for years he had bathed nude here without her knowing, moonlight shining on his long, pale hair.

I imagined him emerging from his noble home and wandering to this park after dark to dip into what he hoped would heal him. How many years had he waded in that frigid, dirty water? I wondered if he ranged about the right bank, where he watched people who were as estranged from society as he was. Maybe he even mingled with them.

Stairs led down from the street to the quai, and the river was so high it lapped over cobblestones in murky ruffles that smelled faintly of sewage. The Seine was swollen from unrelenting rain, the current very strong, and an occasional duck flowed past even though ducks weren't supposed to swim at night. Iron gas lamps glowed and dashed flakes of gold in patterns over the water.

I took the cap off the bottle of Advil and poured the pills on the ground. I carefully ventured down slick stone stairs to the quai. Water lapped around my feet as I swished the plastic bottle clean and filled it with frigid water. I snapped the cap back on and returned to the taxi, glancing back several times at the Chandonne home, halfway expecting cartel criminals to suddenly spring out after me.

"Take me to the morgue, please," I said to my driver.

It was dark, and razor wire not noticeable during the day reflected light from cars speeding past.

"Pull into the back parking lot," I said.

He turned off the Quai de la Rapée into the small area behind the building where vans had been parked and the sad couple had waited on a bench earlier in the day. I got out.

"Stay right here," I said to my driver. "I'm just going to walk around for a minute."

His face was wan, and when I got a better look at him, I realized he was very wrinkled and missing several teeth.

He looked uneasy, his eyes darting about as if maybe he was thinking about speeding away.

"It's all right," I said to him as I got a notebook out of my satchel.

"Oh, you're a journalist," he said with relief. "You're here working on a story."

"Yes, a story."

He grinned, hanging halfway out his open window.

"You had me worried, madame! I thought maybe you were some sort of ghoul!"

"Give me just a minute," I said.

I wandered around, feeling the damp cold of old stone and air blowing off the river as I moved around in the darkness of deep shadows and took interest in every detail, as if I were he. He would have been fascinated by this place. It was the hall of dishonor that displayed his trophies after his kills and reminded him of his sovereign immunity. He could do whatever he wanted, whenever he pleased and leave all the evidence in the world and he wouldn't be touched.

He probably could have walked from his house to the morgue in twenty or thirty minutes, and I envisioned him sitting in the park, staring at the old brick building and imagining what was going on inside, what work he had created for Dr. Stvan. I wondered if the odor of death excited him.

A faint breeze stirred acacia trees and touched my skin as I replayed what Dr. Stvan had said about the man who had come to her door. He had come to murder her and had failed. He returned to this very spot and left her a note the next day.

Pas la police . . .

Perhaps we were trying to make his modus operandi far too complicated.

Pas de problème . . . Le Loup-Garou.

Perhaps it was as simple as a raging, murderous lust he could not control. Once the monster in him was aroused by someone, there was no escape. I was certain if he were still in France, Dr. Stvan would be dead. Perhaps when he fled to Richmond, he thought he could control himself for a while. And maybe he did for three days. Or maybe he had been watching Kim Luong the entire time, fantasizing until he couldn't resist the evil impulse any longer.

I hurried back to my taxi and the windows were so fogged up I could not see through them as I pulled open the back door. Inside, the heater was blasting, my driver half asleep. He sat up with a start and swore.

38

Concorde flight 2 left Charles de Gaulle airport at eleven and arrived in New York at 8:45 A.M., Eastern Standard time, which was before we'd left, in a sense. I walked into my house mid-afternoon terribly out of sorts, my body confused about time, my emotions screaming. The weather was getting bad, with predictions of freezing rain and sleet again, and I had errands to run. Marino went home. He had that big truck, after all.

Ukrops grocery store was mobbed because whenever sleet or snow was predicted, Richmonders lost their minds. They envisioned starving to death or having nothing to drink, and by the time I got to the bread section, there wasn't a single loaf left. There was no turkey or ham in the deli. I bought whatever I could, because I expected Lucy to stay with me for a while.

I headed home a little past six and didn't have the energy to negotiate a peace settlement with my garage. So I parked my car out front. Wispy white clouds over the moon looked exactly like a skull, then shifted and were formless, rushing on as the wind blew harder, trees shivering and whispering.

I felt achy and woozy as if I might be getting sick, and I got increasingly worried when once again Lucy didn't call or come home.

I assumed she was at MCV, but when I contacted the Orthopedic Unit, I was told she hadn't been there since yesterday morning. I began to get frantic. I paced the great room and thought hard. It was almost ten o'clock when I got back in my car and drove toward downtown, tension stringing me so tight I thought I might snap.

I knew it was possible Lucy had gone on to D.C., but I couldn't imagine her doing that without at least leaving me a note. Whenever she disappeared without a word, it never meant anything good. I turned off on the Ninth Street exit and drove through downtown's vacant streets and wandered through several levels of the hospital's parking deck before I found a space. I grabbed a lab coat off the backseat of my car.

The orthopedic unit was in the new hospital, on the second floor, and when I got to the room I slipped my lab coat on and opened the door. A couple I assumed was Jo's parents were inside, sitting by the bed, and I walked over to them. Jo's head was bandaged, her leg in traction, but she was awake and her eyes immediately fixed on me.

"Mr. and Mrs. Sanders?" I said. "I'm Dr. Scarpetta."

If my name meant anything to them, they didn't acknowledge it, but Mr. Sanders politely stood and shook my hand.

"Nice to meet you," he said.

He wasn't at all what I'd envisioned. I supposed after Jo's description of her parents' rigid attitudes, I expected stern faces and eyes that judged everything they saw. But Mr. and Mrs. Sanders were overweight and frumpy, not formidable-looking in the least. They were very polite, even shy, as I asked them about their daughter. Jo continued to stare at me, a look in her eyes that called out to me to help.

"Would you mind if I speak to the patient in private for a moment?" I asked them.

"That would be fine," Mrs. Sanders said.

"Now, Jo, you do what the doctor says," Mr. Sanders told his daughter in a dispirited way.

They went out and the instant I shut the door, Jo's eyes filled with tears. I bent over and kissed her cheek.

"You've had all of us worried sick," I said.

"How's Lucy?" she whispered as sobs began to shake her and tears flowed.

I placed tissues in a hand that was tethered by IV tubes.

"I don't know. I don't know where she is, Jo. Your parents told her you didn't want to see her and . . ."

Jo started shaking her head.

"I knew they'd do that," she said in a dark, depressed tone. "I knew they would. They told me she didn't want to see me. She was too upset, because of what happened. I didn't believe them. I know she would never do something like that. But they ran her off and now she's gone. And maybe she believes what they said."

"She feels what happened to you is her fault," I said. "It's very possible the bullet in your leg came from her gun."

"Please bring her to me. Please."

"Do you have any idea where she might be?" I asked. "Is there any place she might go when she's upset like this? Maybe back to Miami?"

"I'm sure she wouldn't go there."

I sat down in a chair by the bed and blew out a long, exhausted breath.

"A hotel maybe?" I asked. "A friend?"

"Maybe New York," Jo said. "There's a bar in Greenwich Village. Rubyfruit."

"You think she went to New York?" I asked, dismayed.

"The owner's name is Ann, a former cop," her voice shook. "Oh, I don't know. I don't know. She scares me when she runs away. She doesn't think right when she gets like that."

"I know. And with all that's gone on, she can't be thinking right anyway. Jo, you should be getting out of here in another day or so if you behave," I said with a smile. "Where do you want to go?"

"I don't want to go home. You'll find her, won't you?"

"Would you like to stay with me?" I asked.

"My parents aren't bad people," she muttered as morphine dripped. "They don't understand. They think . . . Why is it wrong . . . ?"

"It's not," I said. "Love is never wrong."

I left the room as she drifted.

Her parents were outside the door. Both looked exhausted and sad.

"How is she?" Mr. Sanders asked.

"Not too well," I said.

Mrs. Sanders began to cry.

"You have a right to believe the way you do," I said. "But preventing Lucy and Jo from seeing each other is the last thing your daughter needs right now. She doesn't need more fear and depression. She doesn't need to lose her will to live, Mr. and Mrs. Sanders."

Neither of them replied.

"I'm Lucy's aunt," I said.

"She's about back in this world anyway, I guess," Mr. Sanders said. "Can't keep anybody from her. We were just trying to do what's best."

"Jo knows that," I replied. "She loves you."

They didn't say good-bye but watched me as I got on the elevator. I called Rubyfruit the minute I got home and asked for Ann over the loud noise of voices and a band.

"She's not in great shape," Ann said to me, and I knew what that meant.

"Will you take care of her?" I asked.

"I already am," she said. "Hold on. Let me get her."

"I saw Jo," I said when Lucy got on the phone.

"Oh," was all she said, and it was obvious from one word that she was drunk.

"Lucy!"

"I don't want to talk right now," she said.

"Jo loves you," I said. "Come home."

"Then what do I do?"

"We bring her to my house from the hospital and you take care of her," I said. "That's what you do."

I barely slept. At 2:00 A.M. I finally got up and went into the kitchen to fix a cup of herbal tea. It was still raining hard, water running off the roof and splashing on the patio, and I couldn't seem to get warm. I thought about the swabs and hair and photographs of bite marks locked inside my briefcase, and it almost seemed the killer was inside my house.

I could feel his presence, as if those parts of him emanated evil. I thought about the awful irony. Interpol summoned me to France and after all was said and done, the only legal evidence I had was an Advil bottle filled with water and silt from the Seine.

When it got to be 3:00 A.M., I sat up in bed writing draft after draft of a letter to Talley. Nothing sounded right. I was frightened by how much I missed him and what I had done to him. Now he was striking back and it was exactly what I deserved.

I crumpled another sheet of stationery and looked at the phone. I calculated what time it was in Lyon and imagined him at his desk in one of his fine suits. I thought of him on the phone and in meetings or maybe escorting someone else around and not giving me a thought. I thought of his hard, smooth body and I wondered where he had learned to be such a lover.

I went on to work. When it was almost two in the afternoon in France, I decided to call Interpol.

". . . Bonjour, hello . . ."

"Jay Talley, please," I said.

I was transferred.

"HIDTA," a man answered.

I paused, confused. "Is this Jay Talley's extension?"

"Who is this?"

I told him.

"He's not here," the man said.

Fear shot through me. I didn't believe him.

"And to whom am I speaking?" I inquired.

"Agent Wilson. I'm the FBI liaison. We didn't meet the other day. Jay's out."

"Do you know when he'll be back?"

"I'm not really sure."

"I see," I said. "Is it possible for me to reach him? Or can you ask him to call me?"

I knew I sounded nervous.

"I really don't know where he is," he replied. "But if he checks in, I'll let him know you called. Is there something I can help you with?"

"No," I said.

I hung up and felt panicky. I was certain Talley didn't want any contact with me and had instructed people that if I called, he wasn't there.

"Oh, God, oh, God," I whispered as I walked past Rose's desk. "What have I done?"

"Are you talking to me?" She looked up from her keyboard, peering at me over her glasses. "Did you lose something again?"

"Yes," I said.

At half past eight, I walked into the staff meeting and took my usual place at the head of the table.

"What have we got?" I asked.

"Black female, thirty-two years old, from Albemarle County," Chong began. "Ran off the road and flipped her car. Apparently she just veered off the road and lost control. She has a fracture of the right leg, a basilar skull fracture, and the M.E. for Albemarle County, Dr. Richards, wants us to do a post." He looked up at me. "I'm just wondering why? Her cause and manner seem pretty clear."

"Because the code says we supply services to the local M.E.," I replied. "They ask, we do it. We can take an hour to post her now, or we can take ten hours later on to sort it out if there's a problem."

"Next is an eighty-year-old white female last seen yesterday morning around nine A.M. Her boyfriend found her last night at six-thirty . . ."

I had to work very hard not to tune in and out.

". . . no known drug abuse or foul play," Chong droned on. "Nitroglycerin present at scene."

Talley made love as if he were starving. I couldn't believe I was having erotic thoughts in the middle of a staff meeting.

"She needs a look-see for injury, and toxicology," Fielding was saying. "Needs a view."

400

"Anybody know what I'm teaching at the Institute next week?" toxicologist Tim Cooper asked.

"Toxicology, probably."

"Really." Cooper sighed. "I need a secretary."

"I've got three court appearances today," Assistant Chief Riley was saying. "Which is impossible since they're all over the place."

The door opened and Rose stuck her head inside and motioned to me to come out into the hall.

"Larry Posner's got to leave in a little while," she said. "And he's wondering if you could stop by his lab right now?"

"On my way," I said.

When I walked in, he was making a permanent slide, using a pipette to touch a drop of Cargille melt mount on the edge of a cover slip while other slides warmed up on a hot plate.

"I don't know if it adds up to much," he said right off. "Take a look in the scope. Diatoms from your un-I.D.'d guy. Keep in mind the only thing an individual diatom will tell you, with rare exception, is if it's saltwater, brackish or fresh."

I peered into the lens at little organisms that looked as if they were made of clear glass, in all sorts of shapes that brought to mind boats, chains and zigzags and slivered moons and tiger stripes and crosses and even stacks of poker chips. There were pieces and parts that reminded me of confetti and grains of sand and other particles of different colors that probably were minerals.

Posner removed the slide from the stage and replaced it with another.

"The sample you brought back from the Seine," he said. "Cymbella, Melosira, Navicula, Fragilaria. On and on. Common

401

as dust. All freshwater, so at least that's good, but they really tell us nothing in and of themselves."

I leaned back in the chair and looked at him.

"You ordered me here to tell me that?" I said, disappointed.

"Well, I'm no Robert McLaughlin," he dryly said, referring to the world-renowned diatomist who had trained him.

He leaned over the microscope and adjusted the magnification to 1000X and began moving slides around.

"And no, I didn't ask you to drop by for nothing," he went on. "Where we lucked out is in the frequency of occurrence of each species in the flora."

Flora was a botanical listing of plants by species, or in this case, diatoms by species.

"Fifty-one percent occurrence of Melosira, fifteen percent occurrence of Fragilaria. I won't bore you with all of it, but the samples are very consistent with each other. So much so, actually, I would almost call them identical, which I find rather miraculous, since the flora where you dipped in your Advil bottle might be totally different a hundred feet away."

It chilled me to think of Île Saint-Louis's shore, of the stories of the nude man swimming after dark so close to the Chandonne house. I imagined him dressing without showering or drying off, and transferring diatoms to the inside of his clothes.

"If he swims in the Seine and these diatoms are all over his clothes," I said, "he isn't washing off before he dresses. What about Kim Luong's body?"

"Definitely not the same flora as the Seine," Posner said. "But I did take a sample of water from the James River, close to where you live, as a matter of fact. Again, nearly the same frequency distribution."

"Flora on her body and flora in the James, consistent with each other?" I had to make sure.

"One question I do have is whether diatoms from the James are going to be everywhere around here," Posner said.

"Well, let's see," I said.

I got Q-tips and swabbed my forearm, my hair and the bottoms of my shoes, and Posner made more slides. There wasn't a single diatom.

"In tap water maybe?" I asked.

Posner shook his head.

"So they shouldn't be all over a person, I wouldn't think, unless that person has been in the river, lake, ocean . . ."

I paused as an odd thought came to me.

"The Dead Sea, the Jordan River," I said.

"What?" Posner asked, baffled.

"The spring at Lourdes," I said, getting more excited. "The Sacred River Ganges, all believed to be places of miracles where the blind, the lame and the paralyzed could enter the water to be healed."

"He's swimming in the James this time of year?" Posner said. "The guy must be nuts."

"There's no cure for hypertrichosis," I said.

"What the hell's that?"

"A horrible, extremely rare disorder, hair all over your body when you're born. A baby-fine hair that can get up to six, seven, nine inches long. Among other anomalies."

"Ehhh!"

"Maybe he bathed nude in the Seine hoping he might be miraculously healed. Maybe now he's doing the same thing in the James," I said.

"Jesus!" Posner said. "Now that's a creepy thought."

When I returned to my office, Marino was sitting in a chair by my desk.

"You look like you been up all night," he said to me, slurping coffee.

"Lucy ran off to New York. I talked to Jo and her parents."

"Lucy did what?"

"She's on her way back. It's all right."

"Well, she'd better mind her ps and qs. This ain't a good time for her to be acting squirrelly."

"Marino," I quickly said, "it's possible the killer bathes in rivers with some notion it might cure his disorder. I'm wondering if he's staying someplace near the James."

He thought about this for a minute, an odd expression spreading over his face. Running footsteps sounded in the hall.

"Let's hope there ain't some old estate along there where the owner ain't been heard from for a while," Marino said. "I have a bad feeling."

Then Fielding was in my office yelling at Marino.

"What the hell's wrong with you!"

Veins and arteries were bulging in Fielding's neck, his face bright red. I'd never heard him raise his voice to anyone.

"You let the fucking press find out before we can even get to the goddamn scene!" he accused.

"Hey," Marino said. "Calm down. Let the fucking press know what?"

"Diane Bray's been murdered," Fielding said. "It's all over the news. They've got a suspect in custody. Detective Anderson."

404

39

It was very overcast and rain had begun to fall when we reached Windsor Farms, and it seemed bizarre to be driving the office's black Suburban past Georgian brick and Tudor homes on gracious acres beneath old trees.

I'd never known my neighbors to worry much about crime. It seemed that old family money and genteel streets with English names had created a fortress of false security. I had no doubt that was about to change.

Diane Bray's address was at the outer limits of the neighborhood, where the Downtown Expressway ran loudly and continuously on the other side of a brick wall. When I turned onto her narrow street, I was dismayed. Reporters were everywhere. Their cars and television trucks blocked traffic and outnumbered police vehicles three to one in front of a white Cape Cod with a gambrel roof that looked like it belonged in New England.

"This is as close as I can get," I said to Marino.

"We'll see about that," he replied, jerking up his door handle.

He got out in heavy rain and stalked over to a radio van

405

that was halfway on the lawn in front of Bray's house. The driver rolled down his window and was foolish enough to poke his microphone Marino's way.

"Move!" Marino said with violence in his voice.

"Captain Marino, can you verify . . . ?"

"Move your fucking van, now!"

Tires spun, clawing up grass and mud as the driver of the van pulled out. He stopped in the center of the street and Marino kicked the back tire.

"*Move!*" he ordered.

The van driver rolled away, windshield wipers flying. He parked on someone's lawn two houses away. Rain whipped my face and strong gusts of wind pushed me like a hand as I got my scene case out of the back of the Suburban.

"I hope your latest act of graciousness doesn't make it on the air," I said when I reached Marino.

"Who the hell's working this thing?"

"I hope you are," I said, walking fast with head bent.

Marino grabbed my arm. A dark blue Ford Contour was parked in Bray's driveway. A patrol car was parked behind it, an officer in front, another in back with Anderson. She looked angry and hysterical, shaking her head and talking fast in words I couldn't hear.

"Dr. Scarpetta?" A television reporter headed toward me, the cameraman on his heels.

"Recognize our rental car?" Marino quietly said to me, water running down his face as he stared at the dark blue Ford with the familiar number RGG-7112 on the license plate.

"Dr. Scarpetta?"

"No comment."

Anderson didn't look at us as we walked past.

"Can you tell . . . ?" Reporters were relentless.

"No," I said, hurrying up the front steps.

"Captain Marino, I understand the police were led here by a tip."

Rain smacked and engines rumbled. We ducked under the yellow crime-scene tape stretching from railing to railing. The door suddenly swung open and an officer named Butterfield let us in.

"Glad as hell to see you," he said to both of us. "Thought you were on vacation," he added to Marino.

"Yeah. I got vacated, you're right."

We put on gloves, and Butterfield shut the door behind us. His face was tight, his attention going everywhere.

"Tell me about it," Marino said, eyes sweeping the foyer and zooming into the living room beyond.

"Got a nine-one-one call made from a phone booth not too far from here. We get here, and this is what we find. Someone beat the holy hell out of her," Butterfield said.

"What else?" Marino asked.

"Sexual assault. Looks like robbery, too. Billfold on the floor, no money in it, everything in her purse dumped out. Watch where you step," he added as if we didn't know better.

"Damn, she had big bucks, no kidding," Marino marveled, looking around at the very expensive furnishings of Bray's very expensive home.

"You ain't seen nothing yet," Butterfield replied.

What struck me first was the collection of clocks in the living room. There were wall clocks and hanging shelf clocks in rosewood, walnut and mahogany, and calendar and steeple clocks, and novelty clocks, all of them antique and perfectly synchronized. They tick-tocked loudly and would have driven me mad were I to live amidst their monotous reminder of time.

She was fond of English antiques that were grand and unfriendly. A scroll-end sofa and a revolving bookcase with dummy leather book dividers faced the TV. Placed here and there with no thought of company in mind, it seemed, were stiff armchairs with ornate upholstery and a satinwood pole-screen. A massive ebonized sideboard overpowered the room. The heavy gold damask draperies were drawn, and cobwebs laced box-pleated valances. I saw no art, not a single sculpture or painting, and with every detail I took in, Bray's personality became colder and more overbearing. I liked her less. That was hard to acknowledge about someone who had just been beaten to death.

"Where did she get her money?" I asked.

"Got no idea," Marino answered.

"All of us been wondering that ever since she came here," Butterfield said. "You ever seen her car?"

"No," I replied.

"Huh," Marino retorted. "She takes a brand-new Crown Vic home with her every night."

"A damn Jaguar, fire-engine red. In the garage. Looks like a ninety-eight or ninety-nine. Can't even guess what that cost." The detective shook his head.

"About two years of your working ass," Marino commented. "Tell me."

They talked on about Bray's tastes and wealth as if her battered dead body didn't exist. I saw no evidence that an encounter had occurred in the living room, or that anyone even used it much or bothered to clean it thoroughly.

The kitchen was off the living room to the right, and I glanced inside it, again checking for blood or any other sign of violence and finding none. The kitchen did not feel lived in, either. Countertops and the stove were spotless. I saw no food, only a bag of Starbucks coffee and a small wine rack holding three bottles of merlot.

Marino came up from behind and edged past me through the doorway. He opened the refrigerator with gloved hands.

"Doesn't look like she was into cooking," he said, scanning sparsely stocked shelves.

I surveyed a quart of two-percent milk, tangerines, margarine, a box of Grape-Nuts and condiments. The freezer held no more promise.

"It's like she was never home, or ate out all the time," he said, stepping on a pedal to pop up the trash-can lid.

He reached inside and pulled out pieces of a torn-up Domino's pizza box, a wine bottle and three St. Pauli Girl beer bottles. He pieced together fragments of the receipt.

"One medium pepperoni, extra cheese," he mumbled. "Ordered last night at five-fifty-three."

He dug around some more and found crumpled napkins, three slices of the pizza and at least half a dozen cigarette butts.

"Now we're cookin'," he said. "Bray didn't smoke. Looks like she had company last night."

"When did the nine-one-nine call come in?"

"Nine-oh-four. About an hour and a half ago. And it don't look to me like she was up making coffee, reading the paper or anything else this morning."

"I'm pretty sure she was already dead by this morning," Butterfield offered.

We moved on, following a carpeted hallway to the master bedroom in the back of the house. When we reached the open doorway, both of us stopped. Violence seemed to absorb all light and air. Its silence was complete, its stains and destruction everywhere.

"Holy shit," Marino said under his breath.

Whitewashed walls, floor, ceiling, overstuffed chairs, chaise longue were spattered so completely with blood it almost seemed part of a decorator's plan. But these droplets, smears and streaks weren't dye or paint; they were fragments from a terrible explosion caused by a psychopathic human bomb. Dried speckles and drips sullied antique mirrors, and the floor was thick with coagulated puddles and splashes. The king-size bed was soaked with blood and oddly stripped of its linens.

Diane Bray had been beaten so severely I couldn't have told her race. She was on her back, green satin blouse and black underwire bra on the floor. I picked them up. They had been ripped from her body. Every inch of skin was dried wipes and smears and swirls reminding me of fingerpainting again, her face a mush of splintered bone and battered tissue. On her left wrist was a smashed gold watch. On her right ring finger, a gold band was beaten into the bone.

For a long time we stared. She was naked from the waist up. Her black corduroy pants and belt didn't seem to have been touched. The soles of her feet and her palms were chewed up, and this time Loup-Garou hadn't bothered eradicating his bite marks. They were circles of widely spaced, narrow teeth that didn't look human. He had bitten and sucked and beaten, and Bray's complete degradation, her mutilation, especially of her face, instantly screamed rage. It cried out that she might have known her killer, just as Loup-Garou's other victims had.

Only, he didn't know them. Before he showed up at the door, he and his victims had never met except in his hellish fantasies.

"What's wrong with Anderson?" Marino was asking Butterfield.

"She heard about it and freaked."

"That's kinda interesting. That mean we don't got a detective here?"

"Marino, let me see your flashlight, please," I said.

I shone the light all around. Blood was spattered on the headboard and a bedside lamp, caused when the impact of blows or slashes projected small droplets away from the weapon. There were low-velocity stains as well, blood that had dripped to the carpet. I got down and probed the bloody hardwood floor next to the bed, and I found more pale long hairs. They were on Bray's body, too.

"The word we got was to secure the scene and wait for a supervisor," one of the cops was saying.

"What supervisor?" Marino asked.

I shone light obliquely on bloody footprints close to the bed. They had a distinctive tread and I looked up at the officers in the room.

"Uh, I think the chief himself. I think he wants to assess the situation before anything's done," Butterfield was talking to Marino.

"Well, that's tough shit," Marino said. "And he shows up, he can stand out in the rain."

"How many people have been inside this room?" I asked.

"I don't know," one of the officers answered.

"If you don't know, then it's too many," I replied. "Did either of you touch the body? How close did you get to it?"

"I didn't touch her."

"No, ma'am."

"Whose footprints are these?" I pointed them out. "I need to know, because if they aren't yours, then the killer hung around long enough for the blood to dry."

Marino looked at the officers' feet. Both men were wearing

black crosstrainers. Marino squatted and looked at the faint tread pattern on the hardwood floor.

"Could it be Vibram?" he sarcastically said.

"I need to get started," I said, getting swabs and a chemical thermometer out of my case.

"We got too damn many people in here!" Marino announced. "Cooper, Jenkins, go find something useful to do."

He jerked his thumb at the open doorway. They stared at him. One of them started to say something.

"Swallow it, Cooper," Marino told him. "And give me the camera. And maybe you followed orders by securing the scene, but you weren't told to work the damn scene. What? Couldn't resist seeing your deputy chief like this? That the deal? How many other assholes been in here gawking?"

"Wait a minute . . ." Jenkins protested.

Marino snatched the Nikon out of his hands.

"Give me your radio," Marino snapped.

Jenkins reluctantly detached it from his duty belt and handed that over to him, too.

"Go," Marino said.

"Captain, I can't leave without my radio."

"I just gave you permission."

No one dared remind Marino that he had been suspended. Jenkins and Cooper left in a hurry.

"Sons of bitches," Marino declared in their wake.

I turned Bray's body on its side. Rigor mortis was complete, suggesting she had been dead at least six hours. I pulled down her pants and swabbed her rectum for seminal fluid before inserting the thermometer.

"I need a detective and some crime-scene techs," Marino was saying on the air.

"Unit nine, what's the address?"

412

"The one in progress," Marino cryptically replied.

"Ten-four, unit nine," said the dispatcher, a woman.

"Minny," Marino said to me.

I waited for an explanation.

"We go way back. She's my radio room snitch," he said.

I withdrew the thermometer and held it up.

"Eighty-eight-point-one," I said. "The body usually cools about one and a half degrees an hour for the first eight hours. But she's going to cool a little quicker because she's partially unclothed. It's what? Maybe seventy degrees in here?"

"I don't know. I'm burning up," he said. "For sure she was murdered last night, that much we know."

"Her stomach contents may tell us more," I said. "Do we have any idea how the killer got in?"

"I'm gonna check out the doors and windows after we finish up in here."

"Long linear lacerations," I said, touching her wounds and looking for any trace evidence that might not make it to the morgue. "Like a tire iron. Then there are these punched-out areas, too. Everywhere."

"Could be the end of the tire iron," Marino said, looking on.

"But what made this?" I asked.

In several places on the mattress, blood had been transferred from some object that left a striped pattern reminiscent of a plowed field. The stripes were approximately an inch and a half long with maybe an eighth of an inch of space between them, the total surface area of each transfer about the size of my palm.

"Make sure we check the drains for blood," I said as voices sounded down the hall.

"Hope that's the breakfast boys," Marino said, referring to Ham and Eggleston.

413

They showed up carrying large Pelican cases.

"You got any idea what the hell's going on?" Marino asked them.

The two crime-scene technicians stared.

"Mother of God," Ham finally said.

"Does anyone have any idea what happened here?" Eggleston asked, his eyes fixed on what was left of Bray on the bed.

"You know about as much as we do," Marino replied. "Why weren't you called earlier?"

"I'm surprised *you* found out," Ham said. "No one told us until now."

"I got my sources," Marino said.

"Who tipped the media?" I asked.

"I guess they got their sources, too," said Eggleston.

He and Ham began opening the cases and setting up lights. Marino's unit number blared from his purloined radio, startling both of us.

"Shit," he mumbled. "Nine," he said over the air.

Ham and Eggleston put on gray binocular magnifiers, or "Luke Skywalkers," as the cops called them.

"Unit nine, ten-five three-fourteen," the radio came back.

"Three-fourteen, you out there?" Marino said.

"Need you to step outside," a voice returned.

"That's a ten-ten," Marino said, refusing.

The techs began taking measurements in millimeters with additional magnifiers that looked rather much like jeweler's lenses. The binocular headsets alone could magnify only three-and-a-half, and some blood spatters were too small for that.

"There's someone who needs to see you. Now," the radio went on.

"Man, there's castoff all over the place." Eggleston was referring to blood thrown off during the backswing of a weapon, creating uniform trails or lines on whatever surface it impacted.

"Can't do it," Marino answered the radio.

Three-fourteen didn't respond, and I unhappily suspected what this was all about, and I was right. In minutes, more footsteps sounded in the hall, and then Chief Rodney Harris was standing in the doorway, his face stone.

"Captain Marino," Harris said.

"Yes, sir, Chief." Marino studied an area of floor near the bathroom.

Ham and Eggleston in their black fatigues, latex gloves and binocular headsets only added to the cold horror of the scene as they worked with angles and axes and points of convergence to reconstruct, through geometry, where in space each blow was struck.

"Chief," they both said.

Harris stared at the bed, jaw muscles bunching. He was short and homely, with thinning red hair and an ongoing battle with his weight. Maybe these misfortunes had shaped him. I didn't know. But Harris had always been a tyrant. He was aggressive and made it obvious he didn't like women who strayed from their proper place, which was why I'd never understood his hiring Bray, unless it was simply that he thought she'd make him look good.

"With all due respect, Chief," Marino said, "don't step one damn inch closer."

"I want to know, did you bring the media, Captain?" Harris said in a tone that would have frightened most people I knew. "Are you responsible for that, too? Or did you just directly counter my orders?"

"I guess it's the latter, Chief. I had nothing to do with the media. They was already here when the doc and I pulled up."

Harris looked at me as if he'd just now noticed I was in the room. Ham and Eggleston climbed up on their stepladders, hiding behind their task.

"What happened to her?" Harris asked me, and his voice faltered a little. "Christ."

He closed his eyes and shook his head.

"Beaten to death with some sort of instrument, maybe a tool. We don't know," I said.

"I mean, is there anything . . . ?" he started to say, and his iron facade was rapidly slipping away. "Well . . ." He cleared his throat, his eyes pinned to Bray's body. "Why would someone do this? Who? Anything?"

"That's what we're working on, Chief," Marino said. "Don't have a single damn answer right now, but maybe you can answer a few questions for me."

The crime-scene techs had begun painstakingly taping bright pink surveyor's string above droplets of blood spattered on the white ceiling. Harris looked ill.

"You know anything about her personal life?" Marino asked.

"No," Harris said. "In fact, I didn't know she had one."

"She had someone over last night. They ate pizza, maybe drank a little. Appears her guest smoked," Marino said.

"I never heard her say anything about going out with someone." Harris tore his attention away from the bed. "We weren't really what I'd call friendly with each other."

Ham stopped what he was doing, the string he held connected only to air. Eggleston peered up through his Optivisor at blood droplets on the ceiling. He moved a measuring magnifier over them and wrote down millimeters.

"What about neighbors?" Harris then asked. "Did anyone hear anything, see anything?"

"Sorry, but we ain't had time to canvas the neighborhood yet, especially since nobody called any detectives or techs until I finally did," Marino said.

Harris abruptly walked off. I looked at Marino and he avoided my eyes. I was certain he had just lost what was left of his job.

"How're we doing here?" he asked Ham.

"Already running out of shit to hang this on." Ham taped one end of string over a blood droplet the size and shape of a comma. "Okay, so where do I tape the other end? How about you move that floor lamp over here. Thanks. Set it right there. Perfect," Ham said, taping the string to the lamp's finial.

"You ought to quit your day job, Captain, and come work with us."

"You would hate it," Eggleston promised.

"You got that right. Nothing I hate more than wasting my time," Marino said.

Stringing wasn't a waste of time, but it was a nightmare of tedium unless one was fond of protractors and trigonometry and had an anal-retentive mind. The point was that each droplet of blood has its individual trajectory from the impact site, or wound, to a target surface such as a wall, and depending on velocity, distance traveled and angles, droplets have many shapes that tell a gory story.

Although these days computers could come up with the same results, the scene work required just as much time, and all of us who had testified in court had learned that jurors would rather see brightly colored string in a tangible, three-dimensional model than hatch lines on a chart.

But calculating the exact position of a victim when each blow was struck was superfluous unless inches mattered, and they didn't matter here. I didn't need measurements to tell me this was a homicide versus a suicide or that the killer had been enraged and frenzied and all over the place.

"We need to get her downtown," I said to Marino. "Let's get the squad up here."

"I just can't figure how he got in," Ham said. "She's a cop. You'd think she'd know better than to open the door to a stranger."

"Assuming he was a stranger."

"Hell, he's the same damn maniac who killed the girl in the Quik Cary. Gotta be."

"Dr. Scarpetta?" Harris's voice came from the hall.

I turned around with a start. I'd thought he was gone.

"Where's her gun? Has anybody found it?" Marino asked.

"Not so far."

"Could I see you for a minute, please?" Harris asked me.

Marino threw Harris a dirty look and stepped into the bathroom, calling out a little too loudly, "You guys know to check the drains and pipes, right?"

"We'll get there, boss."

I joined Harris in the hall and he moved us away from the door where no one could hear what he had to say. Richmond's police chief had surrendered to tragedy. Anger had turned to fear, and that, I suspected, was what he didn't want his troops to see. His suit jacket was draped over an arm, his shirt collar open and tie loose. He was having a hard time breathing.

"Are you all right?" I asked.

"Asthma."

"You have your inhaler?"

"Just used it."

"Take it easy, Chief Harris," I calmly said, because asthma could get dangerous fast and stress made everything worse.

"Look," he said, "there've been rumors. That she was involved in certain activities in D.C. I didn't know anything about it when I hired her. Where she gets her money," he added, as if Diane Bray weren't dead. "And I know Anderson follows her around like a puppy."

"Maybe followed her when Bray didn't know it, as well," I said.

"We've got her in a patrol car," he said, as if this were news to me.

"As a rule, it's not my place to voice opinions about who's guilty of murder," I replied, "but I don't think Anderson committed this one."

He got out his inhaler again and took two puffs.

"Chief Harris, we've got a sadistic killer out there who murdered Kim Luong. The M.O. here is the same. It's too unique to be someone else. There aren't enough details known for it to be a copycat—many details are known only by Marino and me."

He struggled to breathe.

"Do you understand what I'm saying?" I asked. "Do you want others to die like this? Because it will happen again. And soon. This guy's losing control at a lightning rate. Maybe because he left his safe haven in Paris and now he's like a hunted wild animal with no place to run? And he's enraged, desperate. Maybe he feels challenged and he's taunting us," I added as I wondered what Benton would have said. "Who knows what goes on inside a mind like that."

Harris cleared his throat.

"What do you want me to do?" he asked.

"A press release, and I mean now. We know he speaks French. He may have a congenital disorder that results in excessive hairiness. He may have long pale hair on his body.

419

He may shave his entire face, neck and head, and have deformed dentition, widely spaced, small, pointed teeth. His face is probably going to look odd, too."

"Jesus Christ."

"Marino needs to handle this," I told him, as if it were my right to do so.

"What did you say? We're supposed to tell the public we're looking for some man with hair all over his body and pointed teeth? You want to start a panic like this city's never seen?" He couldn't catch his breath.

"Calm down. Please."

I put my fingers on his neck to check his pulse. It was running away with his life. I walked him into the living room and made him sit down. I brought him a glass of water and massaged his shoulders, talking quietly to him, gently coaxing him to be still, until he was soothed and breathing again.

"You don't need the pressure of this," I said. "Marino should be working these cases, not riding around in a uniform all night. God help you if he's not working these homicides. God help all of us."

Harris nodded. He got up and moved in slow steps back to the doorway of that terrible scene. Marino was rooting around in the walk-in closet by now.

"Captain Marino," Harris said.

Marino stopped what he was doing and gave his chief a defiant look.

"You're in charge," Harris said to him. "Let me know if there's anything you need."

Marino's gloved hands went through a section of skirts.

"I want to talk to Anderson," he said.

420

40

Rene Anderson's face was as hard and glazed as the glass she stared through when attendants carried Diane Bray's pouched body past on a stretcher and loaded it into a van. It was still raining.

Dogged reporters and photographers poised like swimmers on blocks, all of them staring at Marino and me as we approached the patrol car. Marino opened Anderson's passenger's door and poked his head inside.

"We need to have a little chat," he said to her.

Her frightened eyes jumped from him to me.

"Come on," Marino said.

"I've got nothing to say to her," she said, glancing at me.

"I guess the doc must think you do," Marino said. "Come on. Get out. Don't make me have to help you."

"I don't want them taking pictures!" she exclaimed, and it was too late.

Cameras were already on her like a storm of hurled spears.

"Just put your coat over your head to cover your face like you see on TV," Marino said with a trace of sarcasm.

I walked over to the removal van to have a word with the two attendants as they shut the tailgate doors.

"When you get there," I said as cold raindrops fell and my hair began to drip, "I want the body escorted into the cooler with security present. I want you to contact Dr. Fielding and make sure he supervises."

"Yes, ma'am."

"And we don't talk about this to anyone."

"Never do."

"But especially not this one. Not one word," I said.

"We sure wouldn't."

They climbed inside the van and backed out as I walked to the house and paid no attention to questions and cameras and flashes going off. Marino and Anderson sat in the living room, and Diane Bray's clocks said it was eleven-thirty now. Anderson's jeans were wet, and her shoes were caked with mud and grass, as if she'd fallen down at some point. She was cold and trembling.

"You know we can get DNA off a beer bottle, right?" Marino was saying to her. "We can get it off a cigarette butt, right? Hell, we can get it off a damn pizza crust."

Anderson was slumped on the couch and didn't seem to have much fight left in her.

"It's got nothing to do with . . ." she started to reply.

"Salem menthol butts in the kitchen trash," he continued his interrogation. "Believe that's what you smoke? And yeah. It does have to do with it, Anderson. Because I believe you was here last night not long before Bray was murdered. And I also believe she didn't struggle, maybe even knew the person who beat the shit out of her back in the bedroom."

Marino didn't believe for a nanosecond that Anderson had murdered Bray.

"What happened?" he asked. "She tease you until you couldn't take it no more?"

I thought of the sexy satin blouse and lacy lingerie Bray had been wearing.

"She eat a little pizza with you and tell you to go on home like you was nothing to her? She dis you for the last time last night?" Marino asked.

Anderson silently stared down at her motionless hands. She kept licking her lips, trying not to cry.

"I mean, it would be understandable. All of us can only take so much, isn't that right, Doc? Like when someone's fucking around with your career, just as an example. But we'll get to that part a little later."

He leaned forward in his antique chair, big hands on his big knees until Anderson's bloodshot eyes lifted and met his.

"You got any idea how much trouble you're in?" he said to her.

Her hand shook as she pushed back her hair.

"I was here early last night." She spoke in a flat, depressed voice. "I dropped by and we ordered pizza."

"This a habit of yours?" Marino asked. "To drop by? Were you invited?"

"I would come over here. Sometimes I dropped by," she said.

"*Sometimes* you dropped by unannounced. That's what you're saying."

She nodded, wetting her lips again.

"Did you do that last night?"

Anderson had to think. I could see yet one more lie condensing like a cloud in her eyes. Marino leaned back in his chair.

"Damn, this is uncomfortable." He rolled his shoulders. "Like sitting in a tomb. I think it might be a good idea to tell the truth, don't you? 'Cause guess what? I'm going to find out one way or other, and you lie to me, I'll bust your chops so bad you'll eat cockroaches in prison. Don't think we don't know about you and that goddamn rental car sitting out there."

"There's nothing unusual about a detective having a rental car." She fumbled and knew it.

"Sure as hell is if it's following people everywhere," he retorted, and now it was my time to speak.

"You parked it in front of my secretary's apartment," I said. "Or at least somebody in that car did. I've been followed. Rose was followed."

Anderson didn't speak.

"I don't suppose your e-mail address would happen to be M-A-Y-F-L-R." I spelled it out for her.

She blew on her hands to warm them.

"That's right. I forgot," Marino said. "You was born in May. The tenth, in Bristol, Tennessee. I can tell you your Social Security number, address, too, if you want."

"I know all about Chuck," I said to her.

Now she was getting very nervous and scared.

"Fact is," Marino stepped in, "we got ol' Chuckie-boy on tape stealing prescription drugs from the morgue. You know that?"

She took a deep breath. We really didn't have that on tape yet.

"A lot of money. Enough for him and you and even Bray to have pretty good lives."

"He stole them, not me," Anderson spoke up. "And it wasn't my idea."

424

"You used to work in vice," Marino replied. "You know where to unload shit like that. I just bet you were the mastermind of the whole fucking thing because as much as I don't like Chuck, he wasn't a drug dealer before you appeared on the scene."

"You were following Rose, following me, to intimidate us," I said.

"My jurisdiction is the city," she said. "I cruise all over the place. Doesn't mean I have some motive in mind if I'm behind you."

Marino got up and made a rude noise to voice his disgust.

"Come on," he said to her. "Why don't we just go on back to Bray's bedroom. Since you're such a good detective, maybe you can look at the blood and brains everywhere and tell me what you think happened. Since you weren't following no one and the drug dealing wasn't your fault, may as well get back to work and help me out here, *Detective* Anderson."

Her face got pale. Terror leapt through her eyes like scattering deer.

"What?" Marino sat next to her on the couch. "You got a problem with that? That mean you don't want to go to the morgue and watch the autopsy, either? Not eager to do your job?"

He shrugged and got up again, pacing, shaking his head.

"I tell you, it's not for weak stomachs, that's for sure. Her face looks like hamburger . . ."

"Stop it!"

"And her breasts are chewed up so bad . . ."

Anderson's eyes filled with tears and she covered her face in her hands.

"Like somebody wasn't getting their desires satisfied and

just exploded in this sexual rage. A real lust-hate thing. And doing that to someone's face is usually pretty personal."

"*Stop it!*" Anderson screamed.

Marino got quiet, staring at her in a studious way as if she were a math problem written on a chalkboard.

"Detective Anderson," I said. "What was Deputy Chief Bray wearing when you came over last night?"

"A light green blouse. Sort of satiny," her voice trembled and caught. "Black corduroys."

"Shoes and socks?"

"Ankle boots. Black. And black socks."

"Jewelry?"

"A ring and a watch."

"What about underwear, a bra?"

She looked at me and her nose was running and she talked as if she had a cold.

"It's important I know these things," I said.

"It's true about Chuck," she said instead. "But it wasn't my idea. It was hers."

"Bray's?" I followed where she was going.

"She took me out of vice and put me in homicide. She wanted you a million miles out of the way," she said to Marino. "She's been making money off of pills and I don't know what all else for a long time, and she took a lot of pills, too, and she wanted you gone."

She returned her attention to me and wiped her nose on the back of her hand. I dug in my satchel and handed her tissues.

"She wanted you gone, too," she said.

"That's been rather obvious," I replied, and it didn't seem possible that this person we were talking about was the mauled remains I had examined moments earlier just rooms away in the back of this house.

"I know she had on a bra," Anderson then said. "She used to always wear things. Open neck or top buttons undone. And she would lean over so you could see down her shirt. She did it all the time, even at work, because she liked the reaction she got."

"What reaction?" Marino asked.

"Well, people definitely reacted. And skirts with slits that looked normal unless you were sitting in her office with her and she'd cross her legs in certain ways . . . I told her she shouldn't dress like that."

"What reaction?" Marino asked again.

"I told her all the time she shouldn't dress that way."

"Takes a lot of nerve for a lowly detective to tell a deputy chief how to dress."

"I didn't think officers should see her like that, look at her like that."

"Made you a little jealous, maybe?"

She didn't answer.

"And I bet she knew it made you jealous, made you really squirm, just fucking miserable and mad, right? Bray got off on it. She's the type who would. Wind you up and then take your battery out so what you want don't go nowhere."

"She had on a black bra," Anderson said to me. "It had lace around the top. I don't know what else she had on."

"She used the hell out of you, didn't she?" Marino said. "Made you her drug mule, gofer, little Cinderella on the hearth. What else she ask you to do?"

Anger was beginning to warm up Anderson.

"She make you take her car to be washed? That was the rumor. She made you look like a sucking-up, moonstruck ass-kisser nobody took seriously. Sad thing is, maybe you wouldn't be such a shitty detective if she'd left you alone.

You never even had a chance to find out, not with her keeping you on a leash the way she did. Let me tell you something. Bray was no more going to sleep with you than the man in the moon. People like her don't sleep with anybody. They're like snakes. They don't need nobody else to keep them warm."

"I hate her," Anderson said. "She treated me like dirt."

"Then why'd you keep coming here?" Marino asked.

Anderson fixed on me as if she hadn't heard Marino. "She'd sit right in that chair where you are. And she'd make me get her a drink and rub her shoulders and wait on her hand and foot. Sometimes she wanted me to give her massages."

"Did you?" Marino asked.

"She'd have on nothing but a robe and lie on that bed."

"Same one she was murdered on? Did she take her robe off when you massaged her?"

Anderson's eyes were blazing as they turned on him.

"She always kept herself covered just enough! I took her clothes to the dry cleaner and filled her fucking Jaguar with gas and . . . She was so mean to me!"

Anderson sounded like a child angry with her mother.

"She sure was," Marino said. "She was mean to a lot of people."

"But I didn't kill her, *good God!* I never touched her except when she wanted me to, like I already told you!"

"What happened last night?" Marino asked. "You stop by because you just *had* to see her?"

"She was expecting me. To drop off some pills, some money. She liked Valium, Ativan, BuSpar. Things that made her relax."

"How much money?"

"Twenty-five hundred dollars. Cash."

"Well, it ain't here now," Marino said.

"It was on the table. The table in the kitchen. I don't know. We ordered pizza. We drank a little and talked. She was in a bad mood."

"Over what?"

"She heard you'd gone to France," she said to both of us. "To Interpol."

"I wonder how she found that out?"

"Probably your office. Maybe Chuck found out. Who knows? She always got what she wanted, found out what she wanted. She thought she was the one who should have gone over there. To Interpol, I mean. That's all she would talk about. And she started blaming me for all the screwups. Like the restaurant parking lot, the e-mail, the way things happened at the Quik Cary scene. Just everything."

The clocks all chimed and gonged. It was noon.

"What time did you leave?" I asked when the concert stopped.

"Maybe nine."

"Did she ever shop at the Quik Cary?"

"She may have dropped in there before," she replied. "But as you could probably tell from looking around her kitchen, she wasn't much into cooking or eating at home."

"And you probably brought in food all the time," Marino added.

"She never offered to pay me back. I don't make much money."

"What about that nice little allowance from prescription drugs? I'm confused," Marino said. "You saying you didn't get a fair cut?"

"Chuck and I got ten percent each. I'd bring her the rest once a week, depending on what drugs came in. Into the morgue or maybe if I got some from a scene. I never stayed long when I came over here. She was always in a hurry. Suddenly, she had things to do. I have car payments. That's what my ten percent's gone to. Not like her. She doesn't know what it's like to worry about a car payment."

"You ever fight with her?" Marino asked.

"Sometimes. We'd argue."

"Did you argue last night?"

"I guess so."

"Over what?"

"I didn't like her mood. Same thing."

"Then?"

"I left. Like I said. She had things to do. She always decided when a discussion or argument was over."

"You driving the rental car last night?" Marino wanted to know.

"Yes."

I imagined the killer watching her leave. He was there, somewhere in the dark. Both of them had been at the port when the *Sirius* had come in, when the killer arrived in Richmond using the alias of a seaman named Pascal. He probably saw her. He probably saw Bray. He would have been interested in all of those who had come to investigate his crime, including Marino and me.

"Detective Anderson," I said. "Did you sometimes come back here after you'd left, to try to talk to Bray some more?"

"Yes," she confessed. "It wasn't fair for her to just push me out like that."

"You came back often?"

"When I was upset."

"What would you do, ring the bell? How did you let her know you were here?"

"What?"

"It seems the police always knock, at least when they come to my house," I said. "They don't ring the bell."

"'Cause half the rattraps we go to don't have doorbells that work," Marino remarked.

"I knocked," she said.

"And how would you do it?" I asked as Marino lit a cigarette and let me talk.

"Well . . ."

"Twice, three times? Hard, soft?" I kept going.

"Three times. Loud."

"And she would always let you in?"

"Sometimes she wouldn't. Sometimes she'd just open the door and tell me to go home."

"Did she ask who was there, anything? Or did she just open the door."

"If she knew it was me," she said, "she just opened it."

"If she *thought* it was you, you mean," Marino said.

Anderson picked her way along our train of thought and then she stopped. She could go no further. She couldn't bear it.

"But you didn't come back last night, did you?" I said.

Her silence was her answer. She hadn't come back. She hadn't knocked three times, hard. The killer had, and Bray opened the door without pause. She probably was already saying something, resuming the argument when suddenly the monster was pushing his way into her house.

"I didn't do anything to her, I swear," Anderson said. "It's not my fault," she said again and again because it wasn't her nature to assume responsibility about anything.

"Just a damn good thing you didn't come back last night," Marino told her. "Assuming you're telling the truth."

"I am. I swear to God!"

"If you'd showed up, you might have been next."

"I had nothing to do with it!"

"Well, in a way you did. She wouldn't have opened the door . . ."

"That's not fair!" Anderson said, and she was right. Whatever she had with Bray, it wasn't the fault of either of them that the killer had been stalking and waiting.

"So you go home," Marino said. "You try to call her later? See if you could patch things up?"

"Yes. She didn't answer her phone."

"This was how long after you left?"

"Maybe twenty minutes. I called several more times, just thinking she didn't want to talk to me. Then I started getting worried when I tried several times after midnight and kept getting her machine."

"You leave messages?"

"Well, a lot of times I didn't." She paused, swallowing hard. "And this morning I came to check on her, around six-thirty. I knocked and there was no answer. The door was unlocked and I went in."

She started trembling again, her eyes wide with horror.

"And I went back there . . ." Her voice went up and stopped. "And I ran. I was so scared."

"Scared?"

"Of whoever . . . I could almost feel him, this horrible presence in that room, and I didn't know if he was still somewhere . . . I had my gun in my hand and ran and drove away as fast as I could and stopped at a pay phone and called nine-one-one."

"Well, I'll give you this much credit," Marino said in a tired voice. "At least you identified yourself and didn't try none of this anonymous-call shit."

"What if he comes after me now?" she asked, and she looked so small and ruined. "I've been in the Quik Cary before. I stop in there sometimes. I used to talk to Kim Luong."

"Nice of you to tell us now," Marino said, and I realized how Kim Luong might be linked to all this.

If the killer had been watching Anderson, she may have unwittingly led him to the Quik Cary, to his first Richmond victim. Or maybe Rose had. Maybe he'd been watching when Rose and I had walked to the parking lot at my office, or even when I stopped by her apartment.

"We can lock you up if that'd make you feel safer," Marino was saying, and he meant it.

"What am I going to do?" she cried. "I live alone . . . I'm scared, I'm scared."

"Conspiracy to distribute and actual distribution of schedule-two drugs," Marino thought out loud. "Plus possession without a prescription. All felonies. Let's see. Since you and Chuckie-boy are both gainfully employed and have led such clean lives, bond won't be set high. Probably twenty-five hundred bucks, which you can probably cover with your drug allowance. So that's nice."

I dug in my satchel and got out my portable phone and called Fielding.

"Her body just got here," he told me. "Do you want me to start on her?"

"No," I said. "Do you know where Chuck is?"

"He didn't come in."

"I just bet he didn't," I said. "And if he does, sit him in your office and don't let him go anywhere."

41

At not quite 2:00 P.M. I pulled into the enclosed bay and parked out of the weather as two funeral home attendants loaded a pouched body into an old-model black hearse with blinds over the windows in back.

"Good afternoon," I said.

"Yes, ma'am. How are you?"

"Who you got here?" I asked.

"The construction worker from Petersburg."

They shut the tailgate and peeled off latex gloves.

"One who got hit by that train," they went on, both talking at once. "Can't imagine that. Not the way I want to go. You have a nice day."

I used my card to unlock a side door and entered the well-lit corridor, where the floor was finished in biohazard epoxy and all activity was monitored by closed-circuit television cameras mounted on the walls. Rose was irritably pushing the Diet Coke button on the drink machine when I walked into the break room in search of coffee.

"Damnation," she blurted out. "I thought we'd gotten it fixed." She worked the change return in vain.

"Well, it's doing the same damn thing. Doesn't anybody do anything right anymore?" she complained away. "Do this, do that and still nothing works, just like state employees."

She exhaled a loud, frustrated breath.

"Everything's going to be all right," I said with no conviction. "It's okay, Rose."

"I wish you could get some rest," Rose sighed.

"I wish we all could."

Staff mugs were hung on a peg board next to the coffee machine, and I looked for mine with no success.

"Try your bathroom, on the sink, that's where you usually leave it," Rose said. The reminder of the mundane minutiae of our normal worlds was a welcome relief, no matter how brief it might be.

"Chuck won't be back," I said. "He's going to be arrested, if he hasn't already been."

"The police have already been here. I won't be shedding any tears."

"I'll be in the morgue. You know what I'll be doing, so no phone calls unless it's urgent," I told her.

"Lucy called. She's picking up Jo tonight."

"I wish you'd come stay with me, Rose."

"Thank you. I need to stay put."

"It would make me feel better if you came home with me."

"Dr. Scarpetta, if it's not him, it's always someone, isn't it? Always someone evil out there. I have to live my life. I can't be held hostage by fear and old age."

In the locker room, I changed into a plastic apron and surgical gown. My fingers were clumsy with ties and I kept dropping things. I felt chilled and achy, as if I were coming down with the flu. I was grateful I could suit up in a face shield, mask, cap, booties, layers of gloves, and all that protected me from biological hazards and my emotions. I wanted no one to see me now. It was bad enough that Rose had.

Fielding was photographing Bray's body when I walked into the autopsy room, where my two assistant chiefs and three residents were working on new cases because the day kept bringing in the dead. There was then the noise of running water and steel instruments against steel, muted voices and sounds. The telephones wouldn't stop ringing.

There was no color in this steel place except the hues of death. Contusions and suffusion were purple-blue and livor mortis was pink. Blood was bright against the yellow of fat. Chest cavities were open like tulips and organs were in scales and on cutting boards, the smell of decay strong this day.

Two other cases were juveniles, one Hispanic, one white, both of them etched with crude tattoos and stabbed multiple times. Their faces of hate and anger were relaxed into those of the boys they might have been had life landed them on a different doorstep, perhaps with different genes. A gang had been their family, the street their home. They had died the way they lived.

". . . deep penetration. Four inches over the left lateral back, through twelfth rib and aorta, over a liter of blood in left and right chest cavity," Dan Chong was dictating into the microphone clipped to his scrubs as Amy Forbes worked across the table from him.

"Did he hemoaspirate?"

"Very minimally."

"And an abrasion on the left arm. Maybe from the terminal fall? Did I tell you I'm learning to scuba dive?"

"Huh. Good luck around here. Wait until you do your open water dive in the quarry. That's real fun. Especially in winter."

"God," Fielding said. "Je-sus Christ."

He was spreading open the body bag and bloody sheet inside it. I went to him and felt the shock all over again as we freed her from her wrappings.

"Jesus Christ," Fielding kept saying under his breath.

We lifted her onto the table and she stubbornly resumed the same position she'd had on the bed. We broke the rigor mortis in her arms and legs, relaxing those rigid muscles.

"What the fuck's wrong with people?" Fielding loaded film into a camera.

"Same thing that's always been wrong with them," I said.

We lock-attached her transportable autopsy table to one of the wall-mounted dissecting sinks. For a moment, all work in the room stopped as the other doctors came over to look. They couldn't help themselves.

"Oh, my God," Chong muttered.

Forbes could not speak as she stared in shock.

"Please," I said, searching their faces. "This is not a demo autopsy and Fielding and I will handle it."

I began going over the body with a lens, collecting more of that long, fine hellish hair.

"He doesn't care," I said. "He doesn't care if we know all about him."

"You think he knows you went to Paris?"

"I don't know how," I said. "But I suppose he could be in touch with his family. Hell, they probably know everything."

I envisioned their big house and its chandeliers and myself scooping water out of the Seine in possibly the very spot where the killer waded in to cure his affliction. I thought of Dr. Stvan and hoped she was safe.

"He's got a dusky brain, too." Chong had gotten back to his own work in progress.

"Yeah, so does the other one. Heroin again, maybe. Fourth case in six weeks, all in the city."

"Must be some good stuff going around. Dr. Scarpetta?" Chong called over to me as if this were any other afternoon, and I was working any other case. "Same tattoo, like a home-made rectangle. In the web of the left hand, must of hurt like hell. Same gang?"

"Photograph it," I said.

There were distinctive pattern injuries, especially on Bray's forehead and left cheek, where the crushing force of the blows had lacerated the skin and left striated impact abrasions that I had seen before.

"Possibly the threads of a pipe?" Fielding ventured.

"It doesn't quite fit a pipe," I answered.

The external examination of Bray took two more hours as Fielding and I meticulously measured, drew and photographed every wound. Her facial bones were crushed, the flesh lacerated over bony prominences. Her teeth were broken. Some were knocked out with such force they were halfway down her throat. Her lips, ears and the flesh of her chin were avulsed off the bone, and X rays revealed hundreds of fractures and punched-out areas in bone, especially the bone table of the skull.

I was taking a shower at 7:00 P.M., and the water running off of me was pale red because I had gotten so bloody. I felt weak and lightheaded, because I hadn't eaten since early morning. There was no one left in the office but me. I walked out of the locker room drying my hair with a towel, and Marino suddenly emerged from my office. I almost screamed. I placed a hand on my chest as adrenaline shocked me.

"Don't startle me like that!" I exclaimed.

"Didn't mean to." He looked grim.

"How'd you get in?"

"Night security. We're pals. I didn't want you walking out to your car by yourself. I knew you'd still be here."

I ran my fingers through my damp hair, and he followed me into my office. I draped the towel over my chair and began collecting everything that needed to go home with me. I noticed lab reports Rose had left on my desk. Fingerprints on the bucket found inside the container matched the unidentified dead man's.

"Well, a shitload of good that does," Marino said.

In addition, there was a DNA report with a note from Jamie Kuhn. He had used short tandem repeats, or STR, and already had results.

". . . found a profile . . . very similar with very slight differences," I scanned out loud without much heart for it. ". . . consistent with the depositor of the biological sample . . . close relative . . ."

I looked up at Marino.

"So, long story short, the unidentified man's and the killer's DNA are consistent with these two individuals being related to each other. Period."

"*Consistent*," Marino said in disgust. "I hate all this scientific *consistent* shit! The two assholes are brothers."

I had no doubt of that.

"We need blood samples from the parents to prove it," I said.

"Let's just call 'em up and see if we can drop by," Marino cynically replied. "The lovely Chandonne sons. Hooray."

I threw the report on top of my desk.

"Hooray is right," I said.

"Who gives a shit."

"I sure would like to know what tool he used," I said.

"I've spent all afternoon calling these big hoity-toity mansions on the river." Marino had changed his lane of thought. "The good news is everyone seems to be present and accounted for. The bad news is we still got no idea where he's hanging out. And it's twenty-five degrees out there. No way he's just walking around or sleeping under a tree."

"What about hotels?"

"Nobody hairy with a French accent or ugly teeth. Nobody even close. And no-tell motels ain't too chatty with cops."

He was walking along the hallway with me, and he seemed in no hurry to leave, as if he had something else on his mind.

"What's wrong?" I asked. "Besides everything?"

"Lucy was supposed to be in D.C. yesterday, Doc, to go before the review board. They've flown in four Waco guys to counsel her, the whole nine yards. And she insists on staying here until Jo's okay."

We walked out into the parking lot.

"Everybody understands that," he went on as my anxieties grew. "But that ain't the way it works when the director of ATF is rolling up his sleeves in this and she's a no-show."

"Marino, I'm sure she's let them know what's . . ." I started to defend her.

"Oh yeah. She's been on the phone and promised she'll be there in a few days."

"They can't wait a few days for her to get there?" I asked as I unlocked my car.

"The whole fuckup down there was videotaped," he said as I slid into a cold leather seat. "And they've been going through it over and over again."

I started the engine as the night suddenly seemed darker and colder and emptier.

"There's a lot of questions." He dug his hands in the pocket of his coat.

"About whether the shooting was justified? Isn't saving Jo's life, her own life, justification enough?"

"I think it's her attitude, mainly, Doc. She's so, well, you know. So ready to charge in and fight all the time. It comes across in everything she does, which is why she's so damn good. But it can also be one hell of a problem if it gets out of hand."

"You want to get inside the car so you don't freeze?"

"I'm going to follow you home, then I got things to do. Lucy's going to be there, right?"

"Yes."

"Otherwise I ain't leaving you alone, not with that asshole still on the loose out there."

"What do I do about her?" I quietly asked.

I no longer knew. I felt my niece was beyond my reach. Sometimes I wasn't even sure she loved me anymore.

"This is all about Benton, you know," Marino said. "Sure, she's pissed at life in general and goes off on a regular basis. Maybe you should show her his autopsy report, make her face it, get it the hell out of her system before she does herself in."

"I will never do that," I said as old pain rushed back, but not as intensely.

"Jesus, it's cold. And getting closer to a full moon, which is exactly what I don't want to see right now."

"All a full moon means is that if he tries again, it will be easier to see him," I said.

"Want me to follow you?"

"I'll be fine."

"Well, you call me if for some reason Lucy ain't there. No way you're staying alone."

I felt like Rose as I drove toward home. I knew exactly what

441

she meant about being held hostage by fear, by old age, by grief, by anything or anyone. I had almost reached my neighborhood when I decided to turn around and cut over to West Broad Street, where I occasionally went to Pleasants Hardware on the twenty-two-hundred block. It was an old neighborhood store that had expanded over the years and tended to carry more than just the standard tools and garden supplies.

When I shopped here, I never arrived earlier than seven o'clock in the evening, when most men came in after work and cruised the aisles like boys coveting toys. There were many cars, trucks and vans in the parking lot, and I was in a hurry as I walked past close-out lawn furniture and discontinued power tools. Just inside the door, spring flower bulbs were on special, and clearance-sale gallon cans of blue and white paint were stacked in a pyramid.

I wasn't sure what class of tool I was looking for, although I suspected the weapon that had killed Bray was something like a pickaxe or a hammer. So I kept an open mind and went up and down aisles, scanning shelves of nails, nuts, fasteners, screw hooks, hinges, hasps and latches. I wandered through thousands of feet of neatly coiled rope and cord, and weatherizers and caulk and just about everything one needed for plumbing. I saw nothing that mattered, not in the large section of bars and claws and hammers, either.

Pipes didn't quite work, because the threads weren't thick or widely spaced enough to have left the strange striped pattern we found on Bray's mattress. Tire tools didn't even come close. I was getting very discouraged by the time I reached the masonry section of the store, and I saw the tool hanging on a distant peg board and I felt flushed, my heart jumping.

It looked like a black iron pickaxe with a coiled handle that brought to mind a thick large spring. I went over and picked one up. It was heavy. One end was pointed, the other like a chisel. The tag on it said it was a chipping hammer and cost six dollars and ninety-five cents.

The young man who rang it up had no idea what a chipping hammer was, and didn't know the store carried such a thing.

"Is there anyone here who would know?" I asked.

He got on an intercom and asked for an assistant manager named Julie to come to his register. She got there right away and seemed far too proper and well dressed to know about tools.

"It can be used in welding to knock off slag," she let me know. "But much more commonly it's used in masonry. Brick, stone, whatever. It's a multipurpose tool, as you can probably tell by looking at it. And the orange dot on the tag means it's ten percent off."

"So you might find these at any site where masonry is involved? It must be a rather obscure tool," I said.

"Unless you're into masonry, or maybe welding, you'd have no reason to know about it."

I bought a chipping hammer for ten percent off and drove home. Lucy was not there when I pulled into the driveway, and I hoped she had gone to MCV to pick up Jo and bring her back to my house. A flat bank of clouds was moving in seemingly out of nowhere, and it was beginning to feel like it might snow. I backed my car into the garage and went inside my house, heading straight for the kitchen. I thawed a package of chicken breasts in the microwave oven.

I poured barbecue sauce over the chipping hammer, especially on the coiled handle, and dropped it and rolled it on a white pillow case. The striping was unmistakable. I pounded chicken breasts with both ends of that ominous black iron tool and recognized the punched-out shapes right away. I called Marino. He wasn't home. I paged him. He didn't get back to me for fifteen minutes. By then my nerves were shorting out.

"Sorry," he said. "The battery went dead in my phone, had to find a pay phone."

"Where are you?"

"Driving around. We got the state police fixed-wing plane circling the river, probing everything with a searchlight. Maybe the bastard's eyes glow in the dark like a dog. You seen the sky? Goddamn, they're suddenly saying we might get six inches of snow. It's already started."

"Marino, Bray was killed with a chipping hammer," I said.

"What the hell is that?"

"Used in masonry. You aware of any construction along the river that might involve stone, brick or something like that? On the off chance he got the tool from there because he's staying there?"

"Where did you find a chipping hammer? I thought you was going home? I hate it when you do shit like this."

"I *am* home," I impatiently said. "And maybe he is, too, right this minute. Maybe it's some place putting in pavers or a wall."

Marino paused.

"I wonder if you use something like that on a slate roof," he said. "There's this big old house behind gates, way back from Windsor Farms, right on the river. They're putting on a new slate roof."

"Is anybody living there?"

"I didn't think anything about it, since construction guys are crawling around it all day long. Nobody's in it. It's for sale," he said.

"He could be inside during the day and come out after

dark when the crew is gone," I replied. "Maybe the alarm isn't on for fear the construction noise would set it off."

"I'm on my way."

"Marino, please don't go there alone."

"ATF's got people all over the place," he said.

I built a fire and when I went out for more wood, it was snowing hard, the moon a faint face behind low clouds. I cradled split logs in one arm and tightly gripped my Glock in my hand as I kept my eye on every shadow and tuned my ear to every sound. The night seemed to bristle with fear. I hurried inside my house and reset the alarm.

I sat in the great room, flames lashing the sooty throat of the chimney, and I worked on sketches. I tried to reconstruct how the killer might have gotten Bray back to the bedroom without inflicting a single blow. Despite her years in administration, she was a trained police officer. How did he incapacitate her seemingly so easily without apparent injury or a struggle? My television was on, and every half hour or so the local networks had news breaks.

The so-called Loup-Garou couldn't have been pleased about what was being said, assuming he had access to a radio or television.

". . . been described as stocky, maybe six feet tall, maybe bald. According to the chief medical examiner, Dr. Scarpetta, he may have a rare disease that causes excess hairiness and a deformed face and teeth . . ."

Thanks a lot, Harris, I thought. He had to pin all that on me.

". . . are urged to exercise extreme care. Don't answer the door until you're sure who it is."

Harris was right about one thing, though. People were going to panic. My phone rang at almost ten.

"Hey," Lucy said, and she sounded more cheerful than I'd heard her in a while.

"Are you still at MCV?" I asked.

"Closing up things here. You see the snow out there? It's coming down like a bitch. We should be home in about an hour."

"Drive carefully. Call me when you pull up so I can help get Jo inside."

I put two more logs on the fire, and no matter how secure my fortress was, I started to feel scared. I tried to distract myself by watching an old Jimmy Stewart movie on HBO while I paid bills. I thought of Talley and got depressed again, and I was angry with him. No matter my ambivalence, he hadn't really given me a chance. I had tried to get in touch with him, and he hadn't bothered to call back.

When the phone rang again, I jumped and a stack of bills fell off my lap.

"Yes?" I said.

"The son of a bitch's been staying there, all right," Marino exclaimed. "But he ain't there now. Trash, food wrappers, crap all over the place. And hairs in the damn bed. The sheets stink like a dirty, wet dog."

Electricity crackled up my veins.

"HIDTA's got a squad out somewhere, and I've got cops all over the place. He takes one dip in the river and we got his ass."

"Lucy's bringing Jo home, Marino," I said. "She's out there, too."

"You're by yourself?" he blurted out.

"Inside, locked up, alarm on, pistol on the table."

"Well, you stay right where you are, you hear me!"

"Don't worry."

"One good thing is, it's snowing really hard. About three inches already, and you know how snow lights up everything. Ain't a good time for him to be out wandering around."

I hung up and skipped from channel to channel, but nothing interested me. I got up and wandered into my office to check my e-mail but didn't feel like answering any of it. I picked up the jar of formalin and held it up to the light, looking at those small yellow eyes that were really gold dots reduced in size, and I thought about how off-base I'd been about so much. I anguished over every slow step and every wrong turn I'd taken. Now two more women were dead.

I set the jar of formalin on the coffee table in the great room. At eleven I turned to NBC to watch the news. Of course, it was all about this evil man, this Loup-Garou. As I changed to another channel, I was shocked by my burglar alarm. The remote control fell to the floor as I jumped up and fled to the back of the house. My heart was coming out of my chest. I locked my bedroom door and grabbed my Glock, waiting for the phone to ring. Minutes later it did.

"Zone six, the garage door," I was told. "Do you want the police?"

"Yes! I want them now!" I said.

I sat on my bed and let the alarm beat my eardrums as it hammered and hammered. I kept an eye on the Aiphone monitor, and then remembered it would not work if the police didn't ring the bell. And, as I knew so well, they never did. I had no choice but to turn the alarm off and reset it and sit and wait in silence, straining so hard to hear every sound that I imagined I could hear the snow falling.

Barely ten minutes later, there was a sharp rapping on my front door and I hurried down the hallway as a voice on the porch loudly called out "Police."

447

With great relief I placed my pistol on the dining-room table and said, "Who is it?"

I wanted to be sure.

"Police, ma'am. We're responding to your alarm."

I opened the door and the same two officers from several nights before knocked snow off their boots and came in.

"You've not been having a good time of it lately, have you?" Officer Butler said as she pulled off her gloves, her eyes moving around. "You might say we've taken a personal interest in you."

"Garage door this time," McElwayne, her partner, said. "Okay, let's take a look."

I followed them through the mud room and into the garage, and instantly knew this was no false alarm. The garage door had been pried up about six inches, and when we got down to look through the opening, we saw footprints in the snow leading to the door and then away from it. There were no apparent tool marks except for scrapes on the rubber strip at the bottom of the door. The footprints were lightly dusted with snow. They had been left recently, and that was consistent with when the alarm had gone off.

McElwayne got on the radio and requested a B&E detective, who showed up twenty minutes later and took photographs of the door and footprints and dusted for fingerprints. But once again, there really was nothing more the police could do other than follow the trail of footprints. It led along the edge of my yard and out to the street, where the snow was chopped up by tires.

"All we can do is step up patrol around here," Butler told me as they left. "We'll keep an eye on your house as best we can, and if anything else happens, call nine-one-one right away. Even if it's just a noise that bothers you, okay?"

I paged Marino. By now it was midnight.

"What's going on?" he asked.

I told him.

"I'm coming over right now."

"Listen, I'm all right," I said. "Rattled, but all right. I'd rather you stay out there looking for him instead of coming here to baby-sit me."

He seemed unsure. I knew what he was thinking.

"It doesn't seem his style is to break in anyway," I added.

Marino hesitated, then he said, "There's something you ought to know. I didn't know if I should tell you. Talley's here."

I was stunned.

"He's the head of the squad HIDTA sent in."

"How long has he been here?" I tried to sound curious and nothing more.

"Couple days."

"Tell him hello," I said as if Talley meant very little to me anymore.

Marino wasn't fooled.

"Sorry he turned out to be such an asshole," he said.

The minute I hung up, I contacted the orthopedic unit at MCV and the nurse on duty didn't know who I was and wouldn't release any information about anything. I wanted to talk to Senator Lord. I wanted to talk to Dr. Zimmer, to Lucy, to a friend, to someone who cared, and at that moment I missed Benton so acutely I thought I couldn't go on. I thought of being buried in the wreckage of my life. I thought of dying.

I tried to revive the fire, but it was stubborn because the wood I'd carried in was damp. I stared at the pack of cigarettes on the coffee table but didn't have the energy to light one up. I sat on the couch and buried my face in my hands until the spasms of grief subsided. When a sharp rapping sounded on the door again, my nerves ached but I was just so tired.

"Police," a male voice said from outside as he rapped again with something hard like a nightstick or blackjack.

"I didn't call the police," I said through the door.

"Ma'am, we've gotten a call about a suspicious person on your property," he said. "Are you all right?"

"Yes, yes," I said as I turned off the alarm and opened the door to let him in.

My porch light was out, and it had never occurred to me he might be able to speak without a French accent, and I smelled that dirty, wet doglike smell as he pushed his way in and shut the door with a back-kick. I choked on the scream in my throat as he smiled his hideous smile and reached out a hairy hand to touch my cheek, as if his feelings for me were tender.

Half of his face was lower than the other and covered with a fine blond stubble, and uneven, crazed eyes burned with rage and lust and mockery from hell. He tore off his long black coat to net it over my head and I ran and this all happened in a matter of seconds.

Panic hurled me into the great room and he was on my heels making guttural sounds that didn't sound human. I was too terrified to think. I was reduced to the childish impulse of wanting to throw something at him and the first thing I saw was the jar of formalin that held part of the flesh of the brother he had murdered.

I snatched it off the coffee table and jumped on the couch and over the back of it and fumbled with the lid, and he had out his tool now, that hammer with the coiled handle, and as he raised it and grabbed for me I dashed a quart of formalin in his face.

He shrieked and grabbed his eyes and throat as the chemical burned and made it difficult for him to breathe. He squeezed shut his eyes, shrieking and grabbing at his doused shirt to rip it off, gasping and burning like fire as I ran. I grabbed my gun off the dining-room table and hit the panic alarm as I fled out the front door into the snow. On the steps my feet went out from under me and my left arm shot down like a brace to stop my fall. When I tried to get up, I knew I'd broken my elbow, and I was shocked to see him staggering after me.

He clutched the railing as he blindly made his way down, still screaming, and I was sitting at the bottom of the steps, panicking, pushing myself back as if I were crewing. His upper body was dense with long pale hair that hung from his arms and swirled over his spine. He fell to his knees, scooping up handfuls of snow and rubbing it into his face and neck again and again as he fought for breath.

He was within reach of me and I imagined him springing up any moment like a monster that wasn't human. I raised my pistol but couldn't pull back the slide. I tried and tried, but my fractured elbow and torn tendons wouldn't let me bend my arm.

I couldn't get up. I kept slipping. He heard my noise and crawled closer as I scooted back and slipped and then tried to roll. He gasped and then lay facedown in the snow, the way children make angels, as he tried to lessen the pain of his severe chemical burns. He dug up snow like a dog, piling it over his head and holding handfuls against his neck. He reached out a matted arm to me. I couldn't understand his French, but I believed he was begging me to help him.

He was crying. Shirtless, he was shivering from the cold. His nails were filthy and ragged, and he wore the boots and pants of a laborer, perhaps someone who worked on a ship. He writhed and screamed, and I almost felt sorry for him. But I wouldn't get close to him.

Tissue was hemorrhaging into my fractured joint. My arm was swelling and throbbing, and I didn't hear the car drive up. Then Lucy was running through the snow, almost losing her balance several times as she racked back the slide in the forty-caliber Glock she loved so much, and she fell to her knees close to him, assuming a combat position. She pointed the stainless steel barrel at his head.

"Lucy, don't!" I said, trying to pull myself up to my knees. She was breathing hard, her finger on the trigger.

"You goddamn son of a bitch," she said. "You fucking piece of shit," she said as he continued to moan and wipe his eyes with snow.

"Lucy, no!" I yelled as she gripped the pistol more tightly in both hands, steadying it.

"I'm going to put you out of your misery, you fucking son of a bitch!"

I crawled toward her as feet and voices sounded and car doors shut.

"Lucy!" I said. "No! *For God's sake no!*"

It was as if she didn't hear me or anyone. She was in some hateful, angry world of her own. She swallowed hard as he writhed and held his hands over his eyes.

"Stop moving!" she yelled at him.

"Lucy," I moved closer and closer, "put the gun down."

But he couldn't stop moving, and she was frozen in her position, and then she wavered just a bit.

"Lucy, you don't want to do this," I said. "Please. Put the gun down."

She wouldn't. She didn't answer me or look my way. I

became aware of feet all around me, of people in dark battle dress, of rifles and pistols all held in safe positions.

"Lucy, put the gun down," I heard Marino say.

She didn't move. The pistol was shaking in her hands. This wretched man called Loup-Garou struggled for air and moaned. He was inches from her feet and I was inches from her.

"Lucy, look at me," I said. "Look at me!"

She glanced in my direction and a tear slid down her cheek.

"There's been enough killing," I said. "Please. No more. This is a *bad* shooting, Lucy. This isn't self-defense. Jo's in the car waiting for you. Don't do this. Don't do this, please. We love you."

She swallowed hard. I carefully reached out my hand.

"Give me the gun," I said. "Please. I love you. Give me the gun."

She lowered it and tossed it into the snow, where the steel shone like silver. She stayed where she was, her head bent, and then Marino was with her, saying things I couldn't focus on as my elbow throbbed like drums. Someone lifted me with sure hands.

"Come on," Talley gently said to me.

He pulled me close and I looked up at him. It seemed so out of place to see him in ATF fatigues. I wasn't sure he was there. It was a dream or a nightmare. None of this could happen. There was no such thing as a werewolf and Lucy wouldn't shoot anyone and Benton wasn't dead and I was about to faint and Talley held me up.

"We need to get you to a hospital, Kay. Bet you could name a few around here," Jay Talley said.

"We need to get Jo out of the car. She must be cold. She can't move," I muttered.

My lips were numb. I could barely speak.

"She'll be fine. Everything will be taken care of."

My feet were wood as he helped me down the walk. He moved as if snow and ice had no effect on him.

"I'm sorry for how I acted," he said.

"I did it first," I could barely push out words.

"I could get an ambulance, but I'd like to take you myself," he said.

"Yes, yes," I said. "I'd like that."